ACKNOWLEDGMENTS

I would like to thank John M. Collins, author of "U.S.–Soviet Military Balance Concepts and Capabilities 1960–1980," probably the best book on net assessment ever written and J. B. Kelly, author of "Arabia The Gulf & The West," a timely and useful guide to the states of the Persian Gulf, particularly the mind-sets of the Arab tribal mentality. Both books saved me much research time.

Doris Ober has my special thanks for her very unique contribution to the completion of this novel in its present published form. She is a gifted and creative writer whose contribution went far beyond anything an editor or collaborator might have done to make this novel what it is. Her role really approaches that of co-author, and I would be the first to say that without her contribution, the novel would be no more than a raw manuscript with a story and structure. Any mistakes in technical matters or liberties taken with international law are my responsibility, not hers.

THE
ALASKA
DECEPTION

A Novel by
William M. Brinton

MERCURY
HOUSE™

Mercury House Incorporated
San Francisco

With several obvious exceptions, this is a work of
fiction. Names, characters, places and incidents
are either the product of the author's imagination
or are used fictitiously. Any resemblance to actual
events, locales or persons, living or dead, with the
several obvious exceptions, is entirely coin-
cidental.

Published by Mercury House℠
300 Montgomery Street, San Francisco,
California, 94104

Mercury House℠ and Colophon are registered trademarks of
Mercury House Incorporated
Designed by Adrien Day
Manufactured in the United States of America

Library of Congress Cataloging in Publication Data
Brinton, William M. date
The Alaska Deception

84-060271
ISBN 0-916515-00-1

This book is dedicated to
Ruby P. Johnson, whose skills, patience, ideas and tolerance
represent a contribution beyond mere compensation.

CHAPTER ONE

Moscow, December 3

Moscow is an old city, old as Methuselah, old as the hills, older than the wall that has enclosed its heart, the Kremlin, for 500 years. Inside the ancient walls ornate towers reach like stalagmites into this crackling third December day. At ten o'clock in the morning the shadow of the northernmost tower sweeps in slow motion across the flat roof where the Council of Ministers meet.

The Minister's conference room does not accommodate all of its hundred-plus members. It is tacitly understood that this is the exclusive territory of the Politburo, the elite of the Council of Ministers. The room is long and narrow; tall arched windows run the length of both walls from the ornate double-doored entrance to a raised platform at the end. Four chandeliers, heavy with cut crystal, proceed down the middle of the room, each hung high in the vaulted ceiling. Their function is strictly ornamental. The only furniture is a long U-shaped table of heavy, highly polished mahogany, and fifteen chairs.

On this day four men were seated around the table's parabola, waiting. Each man had a crystal glass, an ashtray, a pad of paper and two sharp pencils before him. A pitcher of mineral water sat on a small cloth on the table.

The outer doors to the Council chambers protested the fifth arrival with a familiar groan of hinges and Alexi Kolkin's shadow fell tall and dark in a pale rectangle on the tiled floor. He shrugged his greatcoat into the hands of an attendant, nodded to his body guard, a great ape of a man, who responded by positioning himself solidly to the right of the doors into the conference room, legs apart like two rooted trees.

With varying degrees of enthusiasm, all of the men rose and stood until Kolkin waved them back into their seats. He was a big man, six feet tall, with a florid complexion, dark hair and heavy

1

jowls. His ability to maneuver a consensus in the Politburo before he would commit to any major policy had given him the reputation of standard bearer for Soviet decision making. His most successful technique was to allow opposing positions to wear themselves out in their separate dialectics. Kolkin knew that in these contests there would always be a winner and a loser. His particular talent was for anticipating the winner before the dust settled. In his short career his calls had been mostly accurate. On those occasions when a decision proved to be the wrong one, Kolkin could not be challenged by his Comrades because to accuse him was to accuse every other member of the power elite—and that would be a deadly mistake. He had succeeded to the most powerful position in the Soviet Union after a great deal of this sort of political maneuvering. He had made several powerful enemies in the process.

One of them was a tough sixty-eight years old, with heavy white eyebrows and a scar in the shape of a crescent on his left cheek. This was Boris Argunov. Argunov was favored over Kolkin to succeed the preceding General Secretary, but a split within the Politburo had edged him out.

Details of the war never surfaced in the Western press except for a brief statement from TASS that: "On instruction of the Politburo of the Communist Party Central Committee, Boris Argunov, member of the Politburo and Secretary of the Central Committee nominated Alexi Izmanovich Kolkin for election to the post of General Secretary of the Central Committee of the Communist Party, Soviet Union." The plenary meeting had unanimously elected Kolkin as General Secretary, and on the same day he was also elected President of the Presidium of the United Soviet Socialist Republic Supreme Soviet.

Argunov had been bitterly disappointed by his defeat and publically humiliated by his instructions to nominate Kolkin. However, he still maintained his position as chairman of the Central Committee, the policy making body of the Politburo. In that capacity he held almost as much power as Kolkin. His specialized area within the Central Committee was in the International and Americas Departments, to whom the KGB reported—and often had to answer.

Viktor Sorokin was another survivor, with deepset eyes and a tightly controlled temper. Sorokin was the Chairman of the KGB, sitting to Kolkin's left. He was a small, narrow man, younger at fifty-eight than any other of those present.

Seated next to him was Dimitri Bukov whose birthday it was today, and who was experiencing a variety of feelings, none of which had to do with this morning's meeting. He was sixty-six years old. The figure intrigued him. He had drawn three rows of sixes on the small pad in front of him. Bukov had a hard time believing he was sixty-six; he felt no more than forty-five, maybe forty-six. It was a good time in his life. His wife was still young, fifty-two, and still passionate. And he knew he looked fine, no different than twenty years ago, he thought. Perhaps a little stouter. Certainly stouter. But the face, that hadn't changed much. A smooth face, good lines—it hadn't wrinkled. He thought he was doing quite well. He was careful in his affairs, took his chess game seriously, attended the theatre regularly and enjoyed the drama of his position and his work.

Andrei Gromyko, that wily Minister of Foreign Affairs and the Minister of Defense Vasily Svetlov, a nervous, ambitious man, were also present—Gromyko and Bukov to Sorokin's left, and Svetlov seated between Kolkin and Argunov.

The room was silent as Kolkin reached for the pitcher and poured himself a glass of water. Without preamble, he turned to Sorokin and said, most amiably, "Something about an urgent announcement, Comrade?"

Sorokin was caught slightly off-guard. He had expected the more customary opening statement and then something like, 'Now Comrades, our Director Viktor Sorokin has news of great import.' Sorokin was annoyed at Kolkin's easy going manner. He darted a sharp look at Kolkin to his right, then looked down at the notes in front of him and began in his strident voice.

"That is correct, Comrade—special intelligence from our military attache at the Washington embassy." He paused and looked up. Kolkin still had that pleasant air about him. He would really like to shake that man.

Since it appeared that Sorokin was waiting for a cue, Kolkin went along. "And what might that intelligence be, Comrade?"

Sorokin frowned. "The United States plans to announce a phased reduction in numbers of tactical nuclear weapons in Western Europe on the day after the new president's inauguration." He stopped abruptly, allowing the news to sink in.

Kolkin looked down at his pencils.

"He also plans to announce a separate nuclear weapons initiative on the same day," Sorokin said. He glanced over at Argunov. "I think we can anticipate a proposal which places much greater reliance on conventional weapons. But, of course, there will have to be five or ten times as many conventional weapons as nuclear ones, or each must be five or ten times more powerful as what we have come to know as conventional."

Although his face remained impassive and he was still offended by Kolkin's attitude, the self-congratulatory tone in Sorokin's voice was not lost on Boris Argunov. Sorokin had not brought this information to him before presenting it here. It was a glaring breach of procedure, particularly pointed since it was what Argunov had predicted all along.

Sorokin's eyes darted to each man. Argunov's expression was blank. Sorokin continued. "It would be advantageous, perhaps, to launch a campaign to suggest the dangers of such an act."

A muscle twitched in Argunov's jaw. It was incredible. Sorokin was telling him in front of these men what his job was. In fact, Argunov had inherited a fairly sophisticated propaganda program, one which no longer required circulation of forged documents (although they persisted in third world countries). Clumsy though effective, the old methods had become in a way, déclassé. Instead, Argunov's Department financed seven international press agencies, organized by his predecessor, subscribed to by mass print and electronic services throughout the world. Up until ten or fifteen years ago, Soviet disinformation had been mainly directed toward the elite and semi-literate peoples of the Mideast, Africa and Latin America, only more recently toward Western Europe and the United States. This level of propaganda reached hundreds of thousands, perhaps millions, of people.

Kolkin spoke, turning to the Minister of Defense. "Comrade Svetlov, how long would such a thing take—the removal and replacement of such weapons?"

Vasily Svetlov looked alarmed. "Well, certainly three months, at least. I would think. Of course, I will confirm this to you when I have studied the. . . ."

"Thank you, Comrade," Kolkin interrupted. "Comrade Sorokin, perhaps this information is not accurate?"

There was silence in the room. On the windows, steam was beginning to form around the edges of each separate pane of glass.

Sorokin's chin lifted and he answered defensively, "I will have verification from Athens by the end of the week." He scowled. "But my Washington source is most reliable."

Kolkin looked over at Gromyko who seemed unperturbed. Then he sighed, almost wistfully. "Think of it. Won't NATO consider it a threat to its own defense? This Baker is an ideologist—we all know the type. Of course he considers such an action, but pressure in Western Europe will combine with a great outcry in the highest levels of his own government. To dare to turn so many degrees away from the previous administration. . . ."

He shook his head, "And to antagonize his Pentagon—on the first day of his office? What is the thought behind that? Perhaps the old actor could have pulled it off, but I understand this new president is a schoolteacher." Kolkin chuckled.

Svetlov growled in response, and Gromyko, impassive as usual, glanced at Bukov, sitting silent in his chair. But Argunov was reminded of the last time the United States had perpetrated such a trick in Reagan's Zero Option proposal, and he wasn't laughing. No one wanted to be reminded of the Soviet Union's political setback of late 1983 when the first Pershing IIs and Cruise missiles were deployed in England and West Germany. And if the new president made a unilateral move, like this. Well, he just didn't want to think about the political fall-out.

Sorokin's pallid complexion was turning red. He considered Kolkin's complacent reception of his announcement a personal affront, his joking out of order, and his seeming lack of concern suspicious. In fact, Sorokin was of the mind that Kolkin was becoming dangerously lackadaisical in his treatment of serious matters of state. He would have been even more alarmed had he solicited Marshall Svetlov's views. These, kept to himself out of fear, rested on his growing belief that a nuclear exchange would destroy the national interests his army existed to defend.

"Comrade Argunov," Kolkin said, "What is your opinion?"

Argunov fixed Sorokin with a cold stare. "I think we will wait and see."

There was silence for a moment more. Then Gromyko touched his forefinger to the table, twice, very discreetly. It was a gesture that somehow altered the rhythm in the room. Kolkin cleared his throat, and said to Argunov, "We are interested in *your* report now, Comrade."

Argunov leaned into the table, his head thrust forward. "With your permission, Comrades, I would like an approval of the plan we reviewed at much length yesterday. As you remember, Comrade Kolkin asked for a summary of the *1978 Law on the Procedure for the*

Conclusion, Execution and Denunciation of International Treaties of the USSR. This law superseded the decrees of 1925 and '38. I have prepared copies for you . . . ." Argunov reached down to the right of his chair, pulled a heavy briefcase onto the table, and removed four slim bound folders. As he slid them to his left, he said, "My understanding is that we are in total accord with Article 72. The law says a proposal to denounce an international treaty must first be submitted to this Council. Comrade Gromyko has given us copies of that proposal, and I think we are all agreed . . ." He paused and looked around the room.

Kolkin was staring back impassively; Gromyko appeared undisturbed, hands folded over his stomach, poker-faced as usual; Svetlov was nodding agreeably; Sorokin and Bukov exchanged the briefest of glances. Not one man touched the folder in front of him.

"I think we are all agreed," Argunov repeated, "to pass the proposal, and to proceed with preparations for a public announcement." Again he paused and looked at the men in the room.

Alexi Kolkin was turning one of his pencils in his fingers. "Comrade," he said softly, "legally, in the eyes of the world, this . . ."

"Comrade," Argunov began to recite from the 1978 Law, "legally, 'to further the realization of the purposes and principles of the Union of Soviet Socialist Republics foreign policy which are proclaimed and consolidated by the Union of Soviet Socialist Republics Constitution . . .'" Argunov took a breath, "we can do any damn thing necessary. Besides . . ." he forced himself to smile. Two stainless steel teeth flashed, then disappeared. "This particular treaty was unlawfully approved by the Emperor, and was certainly signed under duress by the Privy Counsellor."

Kolkin nodded. It didn't matter—the treaty denunciation was not the issue, as all the men here knew. They had already made up their minds, and although each man's motive was perhaps a little different, they would vote unanimously to approve the Foreign Minister's proposal, and Argunov's program. It was just the beginning.

CHAPTER TWO

Santa Barbara, California, December 10

Sylvia Baker had confided to her husband that she was tired of smiling. That for the next two weeks she planned to see as few people as possible, and to frown. He had laughed, but he knew it was hard for her.

She was a sensitive girl. After thirty-two years he still thought of her as a girl—the serious, quiet girl who had loved the order of their academic life and who was now sometimes overwhelmed by the lack of privacy, the chaos despite scheduling so complex it required a monster computer and a full staff, the evolution of her husband's career.

For himself, Alan Baker was taking things in stride. Right now he was held in great favor by almost everyone. He had not yet taken office, he was still safe from criticism; his presentation was easy, if slightly guarded.

He was recognized wherever he went, but he knew recognition was nothing compared to the scrutiny he and his wife could expect from now on. Knowing this, when he walked across the carpeted lounge of the Biltmore Hotel and was aware of a hush or a quick huddle, whispers, eyes that followed his long gait or riveted on his face and then the back of his head, he felt little discomfort. In fact, he enjoyed the privilege of walking through a public place alone.

Now as he strode toward the short stairway up to a mezzanine conference room, Alan Baker was aware of a man and a woman who had detached themselves from a corner and were moving purposefully toward him. He recognized the woman. At the foot of the stairs, he was several paces ahead of them, but he stopped and turned, smiling. A skein of fine lines wrinkled at the sides of his eyes.

"You're an ace reporter, Miss DiMarco. How did you find me here?"

7

She laughed. "Just coincidence, Mr. Baker. Joe and I are here on a story about the airport. . . ." She stopped, looked over at her companion and smiled an apology. "I'm sorry, this is Joe Martinez, *L.A. Tribune*—Joe, the President-elect." She said it with a flourish.

Alan Baker shook the young man's hand.

"We were having breakfast and there was a whole table of people who had seen you come in last night." Miss DiMarco's eyes swept the lobby. "Is Mrs. Baker still here?"

Baker chuckled. "No, we snuck her out very early. She said something about some packing. . . ."

"How long are you planning to be in California?" Miss DiMarco said at the same time Joe Martinez asked, "Why are you in California, sir?"

They had become reporters. Notepads materialized. Down to business.

Baker raised a hand, saying, "Whoa—come on, folks. I'm here for a few days, just to relax. No story."

Joe Martinez persisted. "Do you have any comment on these charges, Mr. President?" He offered the *Tribune's* morning edition, pointing at the headline: SALT III TALKS IN UPROAR: *Soviets Accuse U.S. of Concealing Facts on Missile Development.*

Baker glanced at the newspaper, then back at the eager young reporter. "I'm not the President yet, Mr. Martinez, and I won't be until January 20." He smiled at them both. "It's good to have met you—nice seeing you again, Miss DiMarco. . . ." And he turned gracefully and moved up the stairs.

Actually, he was here to spend more than several days at a secluded retreat loaned by a personal friend. Baker hoped he'd be able to relax on this visit, but in fact he had work to do, and had arranged a battery of meetings with members of his cabinet over the next two weeks.

Harry Smyth who had served as Baker's Defense Issues Advisor during the campaign, and who would serve the administration as Secretary of Defense; and George Heath, a trusted colleague and Baker's choice for Secretary of State, were waiting for him in the small conference room when he entered. Smyth was slouched in a corner chair, hidden behind a newspaper from which a billow of smoke raised itself. Heath reminded the press, at any rate, of the late Dean Acheson, silver-haired and moustached, always immaculately dressed, more often than not in a Saville Row pinstripe. He was concluding a phone conversation.

Harry Smyth pushed himself up with a grunt, disposed of his cigarette, folded his paper, looked around him to see if he had everything, saw his jacket tossed over the back of a chair, retrieved it and finally presented himself to Baker with an oddly boyish grin.

Seeing his expression, Baker almost laughed. Instead he approached the big, older man, and put a hand on his shoulder. "It's good to see you, Harry," he said sincerely. Harry had become a close friend over the past year. It had been a month since the election and their last meeting. "How're things at home?"

"Quiet," Smyth replied. "Eerily quiet." He had just 'married off,' as he phrased it, the last of four daughters.

"'Fie on this quiet life. I want to work,'" said Heath.

Baker and Smyth both turned and stared at him.

"Shakespeare," Heath said, a little embarrassed. "Sorry."

A limousine waited for them at a private exit—it took no more than twenty minutes to reach the Spanish-style home that sprawled across a crest with a clear view of the Pacific Ocean. It was a manicured property of twenty-five acres on which a smaller house nestled close to the main structure. The acreage included a tennis court and a large solar heated pool, a small citrus orchard and beautifully maintained grounds.

* * * * *

It was a violently blue California day. Smyth, in slightly baggy pants and slightly wrinkled shirt had gone casual. In fact, Harry Smyth had a slightly rumpled look to him on the most formal occasions. They were sitting comfortably in a spacious living room furnished with a large white sectional sofa and soft square easy chairs upholstered in heavy cambric muslin. To the right of the seating cluster and up a step stood a bow-legged chess table inlaid with marble, with heavy carved marble pieces. George Heath had been delighted. In this company were at least two other players.

Admiral Robert Smilie, Chairman of the Joint Chiefs of Staff, and CIA Director Larry Apple had joined them yesterday. This was the first time the Admiral and Alan Baker had met. Despite Baker's efforts to put him at ease, Smilie appeared even to sit in a state of attention. There was a tensile quality to his trim starched appearance. He had very light blue eyes and finely lined skin that years of sea duty had aged beyond fifty-six years. He had pulled a straight-back chair into the circle, and sat poised on the edge of his seat facing a huge picture window which framed the sky and ocean in one wall. His eyes gained color in the vast blueness outside.

Larry Apple had succeeded to the Directorship of the CIA during the preceding administration. Though more relaxed than the Admiral, Apple walked a tightrope of his own fashioning. He had quizzed Alan Baker on the necessity of his joining this planning session. Apple wanted it clear from the beginning that the Central Intelligence Agency took no political sides, voiced no political opinions or recommendations, and would tolerate no political manipulation.

Understood, Baker had said. Apple's presence at this meeting was only to receive intelligence. His personal opinion was valuable to the administration, but Baker would not compromise him. And with those assurances the young Director listened without comment to Smyth's conclusion on the origins of the nuclear freeze and disarmament movements in this country.

"Reagan did it, sure as I'm sitting here," he said, "with that defense budget in the early '80s. Caught everyone's attention. Scared hell out of them." He reached for a crumpled pack of Camels on the low table in front of the couch, and fished out a last bent cigarette. "I wonder if he's ever been properly thanked."

Someone chuckled and as Smyth touched a flame to his cigarette, Alan Baker rose from his chair and paced a few feet. He had been silent for most of the preceding conversation, perhaps looking for a way to begin. Now, a little stiffly, he said, "I agree with you, Harry. And I think we all agree that no one 'wins' a nuclear war. Now you and I, gentlemen, are in a position to take steps to discourage such a war."

The room was very still and bright with the Pacific. "The last five administrations have used an 'after you' policy with the Soviets on arms control—until the President opened the door for us by deploying fewer Pershing II and Cruise missiles in Europe than NATO had requested in 1978. Delivery was to occur over four years or even longer.

Baker turned toward the window, said thoughtfully, "I've often wondered how we could push the Soviets a little further in the direction of dismantling a lot of those SS-20s."

Another pause, and Baker continued. "Right now we have about 6,000 tactical nuclear weapons in Western Europe. On January 21—the Monday following my inauguration—I want to announce two related policies. First, a phased reduction in the number of those nuclear weapons in place, but conditional on Kolkin's doing the same. We start as soon as we're satisfied they've withdrawn and dismantled a hundred or so of theirs."

Baker looked around. He almost felt he could hear these men listening. "*And,* I want to make it clear from day one of this administration that we've adopted a no first use policy for our tactical and strategic nuclear weapons."

Of course they had discussed it before. They had consulted with members of the previous administration regarding social, economic and tactical ramifications. Baker and Smyth had spent a week last month conferring with Helmut Kohl because of the special nature of their particular nuclear relationship.

Kohl had told them that the Pershing II with conventional warheads was not the whole answer. Some of these with nuclear warheads had already been deployed after a highly charged debate in November 1983. And that had spawned the idea for deployment of a different version of the Pershing II and the Cruise missile. In the future, Kohl had said, 50% of the Pershing IIs and the Cruise missiles could have conventional warheads. The other half would have enhanced radiation warheads. Baker and Smyth had said these were essential for use against "hardened" Warsaw Pact sites, and even these would be removed from West Germany if the Soviet Union dismantled a negotiated number of SS-20s and tactical nuclear weapons.

At the time of the deployment, Kohl suggested, Baker could announce their presence to the Soviet Union and offer to replace the neutron weapons with conventional warheads if Moscow would dismantle all of its theater nuclear weapons, including the SS-20s. "No," Baker had said. "We're not removing anything until Kolkin satisfies us he's dismantling a fixed number—not just moving them back behind the Urals. We will even invite Soviet technicians to inspect the type of warheads on each. We do believe in on-site verification, and we will set a precedent for them to follow."

Sharing a common border with Warsaw Pact forces, and with no nuclear weapons of its own, West Germany would be the first battlefield in any conflict on the central front. Kohl and his military advisors, Baker knew, would have to be satisfied that conventional force levels in place on the front and those available for prompt reinforcement would be adequate for their protection.

Kohl had to be able to tell his military advisors that neutron warheads would be available for defensive purposes against Warsaw Pact command, control and communications centers as well as aircraft, troop and tank concentrations, in the event of an attack.

Baker had agreed in principle and said he would take up the matter with his Cabinet after January 20th, but he wanted to place the no first use policy at the head of his agenda.

Each man in the room had considered and discussed a nuclear weapons policy that might lead to mutual disarmament. Baker's idea was not shocking. But to hear a day of the week affixed to the proposition . . . to hear the proposition become a resolution . . . there was an almost audible gasp throughout the room.

The President-elect looked at them one at a time registering their reactions, searching their faces for dismay or objection. He saw neither. Smilie and Apple were both expressionless. Baker was sure the Admiral hadn't blinked in five minutes, Harry Smyth was puffing complacently on his cigarette.

"Harry, you'll have to determine the mix of replacement weapons—more artillery, more aircraft and deep strike weapons. U.S. troops are in Europe to fight a defensive war, not to launch an attack against Warsaw Pact forces. You're going to have to talk to the West German military people. I don't like these military sales of German planes, tanks and missiles to Saudi Arabia. Raises hell with an already delicate Middle East balance. Tell them, too, we'll even pay a negotiated part of the cost, and German forces can use them at home. It'll be a lot less expensive than what the Pentagon has been paying for the same hardware." Baker nodded slightly. He had the habit of punctuating affirmative statements with a very subtle inclination of the head, as if to remind himself, "Yes, this is true."

He walked over to the wide blue window. His monologue was almost professorial. "Let's look at NATO. For us to modify a nuclear umbrella guarantee will require a major change in the assumptions of its member states. But Great Britain and France both have nuclear weapons, and Harry tells me they have no objections to an American no first use policy. Of course no other NATO member depends on them to use their nuclear weapons except in their own ultimate self-defense."

Smyth was stubbing out his cigarette. Looking up, he said, "NATO is in a much better position to defend itself than it's ever been. West Germany's got over 3,000 Leopard tanks now plus that runway buster bomb we helped pay for, the Stabo. It's a good stand-off missile, and we've given them the Locpod to carry them. It's cheap and nasty with an airlaunched range of about 20 miles. Then the French have their Voisin nuclear missiles."

Baker nodded. "Well, that's my proposal. What do you think?"

Larry Apple looked like he had something on his mind. "Larry?" Baker prodded.

"A detail—I understand your wanting to make this a first gesture of office. And I think it's a powerful psychological move. But the timing—we've got less than two months. I assume you'll ask the incumbent Secretaries of Defense and State to notify the NATO capitals?"

Baker nodded. "I have to. . . ."

"It's just a matter of itinerary, Larry," Heath inserted. "They know the track pretty well by now." He looked around. "They've been around it often enough. And NATO is prepared. It's not as if we never discussed it."

Baker sat down opposite Admiral Smilie. "Admiral, do you have any objections in principle?"

Smilie blinked, then sat up straighter, if that was possible. "No objection, sir. I agree we can't continue trying to get a lowest common denominator concensus on nuclear arms out of NATO. As long as West Germany is satisfied, and England and France will accept it. . . ."

Leaning forward, Heath assured the Admiral, "After two wars, Europe has reason to know the difference between legitimate national defense and weapons of mass destruction."

And Larry Apple pointed out, "Even in our own country a dozen or more states have initiated nuclear freeze policies—this weapons policy and no first use are the next logical steps. We reinforce their efforts at home, they support us overseas."

"I take it then there's no opposition?"

"Not here, Alan." This from George Heath. "We're all behind you, certainly. But we're going to have to anticipate the whole spectrum of reaction—national as well as international—beginning with the administration still in office. For or against, the demonstrations are going to be one hell of a roar."

Admiral Smilie shook his head and smiled for the first time that morning. "Nothing like the noise you're going to hear from Pentagon brass. But that's alright. It's about time they were reminded of just who is Commander in Chief."

Baker smiled, and said with some surprise and a hint of laughter, "And I'll be damned if I'm not looking forward to reminding them."

CHAPTER THREE

Anchorage, Alaska, January 20

There are places in Alaska in winter where the weather can warm as much as thirty degrees in three minutes, from minus twenty degrees to ten above, from ten to thirty minutes later. Stalwart trees webbed and wound in snow shudder at the sudden warmth of a southern wind. Like big birds molting, a whole forest bares itself, spiny limbs accusing the sky, for now it is warm enough to snow again.

But those places are in northern and central Alaska. In Anchorage there is no magic, winter is just cold: two or three feet of snow cover the ground, the temperature worries between ten and twenty degrees, the mountains are white, the air feels too thin. The fishing fleet and the state's only international airport lend Anchorage a certain urban ambiguity. The oil industry keeps it civilized.

On this day in January, the occupancy rate for hotels was down, though daily traffic through Anchorage International was about average. Inside the large terminal, Lufthansa, British Airways, Japan Air Lines, Northwest Orient and Pan Am counters each had a CRT system televising a tape-delay of Alan Baker's inauguration. Commentators followed the day long ceremony, parade included, interrupted by sporadic flight announcements, waves of chatter as a group of arrivals spilled into the marble lobby, the shrill cry of an excited child.

At Japan Air Lines, gate seven, a short heavily muscled man whose bald head was disguised by a black fur hat, stepped off a flight he had booked from Tokyo to San Francisco. There was an hour layover in Anchorage. There was a furtive exchange of diplomatic passport and ticket in a booth in the transit lounge men's room. And when the plane resumed its scheduled flight, another man, short and stocky, in a black fur hat, took the first man's place.

15

Not even the passenger who had been seated next to him on the flight from Tokyo was any the wiser.

As the bald man walked toward the main terminal from the loading gates, he watched airport security running carry-on luggage through their scanners in the opposite direction, heard the familiar beep, and then, "Sorry, sir, would you go through the metal detector again? Please put all coins and metal objects. . . ."

Anchorage is only 800 miles from the Soviet border and airlines here are strict about searching hand-carried luggage. Occasionally there is a quiet body search.

It was ten o'clock in the morning and still dark when the bald man entered the main terminal, and he was surprised at the small knots of travelers who stood unmoving at most airline counters—it was not the usual hubbub of activity. His walk slowed. He could distinguish the excited call of an announcer over the rush of a cheer and fragments of a boisterous march . . . it was "Hail to the Chief."

"Here they are now, the President allowing President-elect Alan Baker to precede him up the steps to the platform . . ."

The bald man moved closer to the Pan American counter. The President was grinning and waving. Baker was smiling, he turned and said something to the President who nodded and clapped a hand on Baker's shoulder. The Vice-President and his successor, James Pell, were already on the platform along with a crowd of dignitaries and guests, members of the old Administration and their families, and two former Presidents and their wives.

As they took their places, the Reverend Harris George of Washington, began his invocation. The camera panned over a crowd of 30,000 packed into the Capitol Plaza. The bald man looked around him at the smaller crowd, quiet in front of the screen.

"Let us bow our heads," the Reverend said, "and give thanks for a new day and a venerable ideal—the American ideal of freedom, of democracy, of progress. Let us thank God for the men who are committed to uphold these ideals in the coming days and for all time in the pursuit of peace."

After the Vice President had taken his oath of office, and the minister had retired to his seat, President-elect Alan Baker took the podium. His opening words had not appeared in advance copies of the speech given the press.

"Thank you, Reverend George, It *is* peace we seek. In its pursuit, I will this afternoon sign an order directing the Secretary of

Defense to withdraw five hundred tactical nuclear weapons from Western Europe—immediately. As soon as the Soviet Union matches this first step, as I believe it will, I will order the withdrawal of another five hundred such weapons. None of these will be replaced by new tactical nuclear weapons."

Baker paused, as if to absorb the moment of unbelieving silence from the spectators shivering in the cold.

"The idea that even a limited nuclear exchange can be 'won' by either of the superpowers is a cruel and dangerous illusion. Those perfectly honorable people who opposed the deployment of the Pershing II missiles should now redirect their energy towards finding nonnuclear ways of defending Western Europe. Then, and only then, will we all feel a little safer in a dangerous world." Another pause, but this time the moment of silence preceded thunderous and prolonged applause.

The bald man was riveted to the screen. Those gathered at the Pam Am counter gaped at what they were hearing. Raising his arms for quiet, the President went on. "As of today, I have signed a letter addressed to Secretary Alexi Kolkin in Moscow, guaranteeing that 50% of our Pershing II and Cruise missiles will in the future be deployed with conventional warheads, and the other 50% deployed with enhanced radiation warheads. These weapons will be targetted for specific hardened sites whose only possible use is offensive such as command, control and communications centers, airbases and tank concentrations. I have invited Secretary Kolkin to send military technicians to verify all of our launch sites and the targetting of these missiles."

Shifting slightly, Baker altered his tone, projecting an impression of confidentiality. "We have, I firmly believe, an obligation to bridge the boundaries between countries and ideologies, and an obligation to respond to the legitimate fear of a nuclear exchange and its frightening consequences. In the Soviet Union, there is a growing feeling at the highest levels that after a nuclear exchange, the living will envy the dead. So I do not look at this move as unilateral disarmament. I fully expect a reciprocal move from Secretary Kolkin. If one is not forthcoming within a reasonable time, my proposal will be given further consideration or even withdrawn."

The camera had framed Baker to fill the screen. The bald man felt the concentration of the people massed in front of him as palpable. He took a step back as Baker closed his stunning remarks with an entreaty: "And with your support and understanding, we shall overcome both fear and destruction."

A wave of applause swept through Capitol Plaza. At the airport, a separate round of applause rose up, and the bald man turned from the screen, smiling to himself, and walked out of the Anchorage terminal.

* * * * *

Four men, including the bald man, were sitting around a metal folding table in a cold bare room. They had arrived at the airport within an hour and a half of one another: the young one, speaking now, had come in during the motorcade up Pennsylvania Avenue; the bald man had seen the invocation; the little man, the nervous one, had watched Baker be sworn in. The man who did not speak, had seen only the end of the ceremony when Baker kissed his wife, pale and solemn-looking beside him. They would all miss the parade, which the new President himself would have been delighted to forgo.

The fifth man, sipping from a pint of bourbon, had been in Alaska for a month. A communications specialist, had had already set up a receiver for transmissions they expected to receive on a pre-set frequency. He had, the month before, established a small but very powerful transmitter near the shore of Tikchik Lake.

These men, each one, had been chosen for a specific skill. The young man had just finished describing the security system at Dillingham fish cannery, and was now tapping a rolled blueprint into a long narrow tube. The bald man's specialty was his resourcefulness. He was also a demolition expert. His reputation and his years of experience in similar operations had made him the bank as well, and now he removed a fat envelope from his breast pocket and passed around a stack of bills to each man.

"We are right on schedule, then. This week Jon will have the plans for the airport. I am picking up the printing equipment on Friday. And we will meet here again on January 30—ten days. Are there any problems, then, before we depart?"

There were no problems.

The bald man rose, and shook hands with each of the men. In pairs, several minutes apart, the members of the Free Alaska Committee disappeared into the darkening day.

CHAPTER FOUR

Washington D.C., March 12

Alexandr Yegorov walked slowly down the steps leading from the public entrance of the State Department. After four years he still felt a sting descending the wide public staircase. In 1981 it had been the Soviet Ambassador's privilege to use the private entryway, but that year Yegorov's predecessor Anatoly Dobrynin, had been told brusquely that he would have to use the front doors just like the British and Italian Ambassadors. The slight was President Reagan's annoyed response to some incident long since forgotten.

These Americans had a very narrow sense of diplomacy. Yegorov turned at the bottom of the stairs, and scowling, looked back up at the big drab State Department building. And no sense of architectural style. He turned his collar up against the inhospitable morning, thinking he would like to see the President's face when he received the news Yegorov had just had the honor to deliver. The little man's scowl became a smirk.

* * * * *

Seven floors up, Peter Jefferson had risen to extend his hand across his large mahogany desk at the conclusion of their meeting. There had been a slight but calculated hesitation on Yegorov's part, before he put out his own pudgy hand to shake. When the door had closed behind him, Jefferson's polite expression vanished. He sank back into his large leather swivel chair and stared down at the Soviet Ambassador's note, then lifted the bridge of his glasses off his nose and rubbed his eyes in a subconscious effort to make the note disappear, or at least rewrite itself.

19

Jefferson sighed and reached for the phone, buzzing his secretary. "Grace, get me Schweman. And could you bring me another cup of coffee?"

He picked up the note, rose from his chair, walked slowly around his desk with it—and found himself at the large window which occupied most of the south wall of his office, looking down just as Yegorov's face turned up flushed with self-importance. It was eerie. And he could no more interpret the Ambassador's expression than the message he had delivered.

Grace Sherwood sat in a small alcove just outside the Under Secretary's door, flipping a well-worn Rolodex to Al Schweman's number. She punched the combination into the phone with the eraser end of her pencil and waited, tapping the pencil lightly against the edge of her desk.

Al Schweman was acting Legal Advisor to the Secretary of State. The new Republican administration had not yet agreed upon a replacement for that post, and Schweman watched their efforts with some amusement. It seemed those members who supported Moral Majority precepts, were at odds with other members of the Senate, insisting on appointments which reflected "ideologically pure" principles, particularly for State and Defense. As far as Schweman could tell, no one really understood what an ideologically pure principle was.

"Schweman here. What can I do for you today?"

Grace smiled. "It's Mr. Jefferson's office, Mr. Schweman. I'll put him on for you."

Grace signalled the Under Secretary to pick up his phone, and then walked quickly down a well-waxed corridor toward the coffee maker which had been awarded its own private room three doors away.

A few moments later, while Schweman ambled down the long glossy hallway toward the elevator bank, Grace knocked lightly on Peter Jefferson's door and walked in.

Advancing over the long stretch of light cocoa-colored carpet, she glanced automatically around the room, noting that the dark-wood book cases which lined two walls of the office appeared neat, and that the several framed diplomas, membership certificates and acknowledgments hung straight next to the window which was washing the room in pale grey light. A long, oak library table stood near the right wall of books. Today, in honor of the Soviet Ambassador's visit, the table was conspicuously uncluttered. Grace set the coffee down on Jefferson's desk and moved around to adjust one of the three tufted chairs in front of him. Leaning casually against the chair, she smiled and said, "Anything else?"

He looked up from the two sheets of paper in front of him. "No, thanks, Grace. And thanks for the coffee."

She smiled wider and nodded. She liked Peter Jefferson. He was comparatively young for the position of Under Secretary for Political Affairs at the State Department, forty-four, and nice looking—tall, a little on the thin side, sort of lanky and athletic looking despite horn-rimmed glasses—and he was smart and very polite. He had been married, she knew, much earlier, but was divorced by the time the Senate had confirmed him just over three months ago.

His confirmation was accomplished with little argument because he was a career professional who had somehow managed to offend no one who really mattered, and he had a fine record from Georgetown University days in the sixties, through service inconspicuous and estimable at various embassies outside the United States—Paris for a year, Moscow for two, and most lately in Rome as First Secretary of the Embassy. He was fluent in all three languages, and his traveling had given him a refined understanding of sociology. What had started as a natural sensitivity to new surroundings became a curiosity about the people, their culture, their environment. And that curiosity had become a fascination in the organization, function, even the psychology of their societies. He was valuable to the State Department for that, and for a certain earnestness about him.

This note bothered Peter Jefferson, and he was relieved when Schweman leaned into his office and walked in, making himself comfortable in one of the chairs in front of the desk.

"So," Schweman said inquisitively, "What tidings does Comrade Yegorov bear?"

"Not glad ones, I'll tell you," Jefferson answered. He shook his head. "I wish you had been here. He looks so much like a penguin, you know. He sort of waddled in, right up to the desk, and pulled out a sealed envelope—sealed, mind you, with wax—and handed it over to me." Jefferson paused, allowing Schweman to get the picture. "So far, he hadn't said a word."

Schweman grinned. "Drama—Yegorov loves drama."

"I break open the seal, and Yegorov yanks the envelope right out of my hands, steps back two paces, and starts reading. The note is in *English,* you understand, even if I couldn't read Russian. And all the time I'm trying to get past the fact that there's this little performing penguin in my office."

Schweman laughed out loud.

Peter Jefferson nodded. "It really was a very strange scene." He paused and lifted the two page letter. "This is notification of our having violated the right of innocent passage in the Bering Strait ten days ago. Specifically . . ." he looked down the first page of the Ministry note, found the place and read, " '. . . the U.S.S. New Jersey, converted for cruise missile capability and fully equipped with surface-to-air missiles; a Trident-class submarine; and five Spruance-class missile destroyers.' "

Jefferson looked up. "Evidently they were en route to the Arctic Ocean on some sort of maneuvers, and the Trident was cruising submerged." He flipped to page two. "It finishes by saying that a submerged warship violates the right of innocent passage, and . . ." again he quoted from the letter, " 'U.S. officials have neither notified the Soviet Union nor sought prior authorization from any coastal state for such infraction. This is to formally advise you of a breach of Article 16 (4) of the 1958 Convention on the Territorial Sea, and unauthorized passage through territorial waters of the Soviet Union.' "

Schweman raised an eyebrow. "Violation of Soviet frontiers, huh?" He shook his head. "The Bering Strait and transit is covered under the freedom of navigation, not innocent passage—so long as our ships don't wander into the three-mile limit. But the Bering Strait is well over six miles wide, and passage through it is from one high sea to another. If Alaska were part of Russia, he might have a point. . . ." Schweman paused and frowned. "Nothing on this has changed since the Edisto and Eastwind incident in 1967, and we issued a bulletin on that one—Bulletin 362, I think—I'll review it when I get back downstairs. But unless I'm overlooking something, territorial waters violation just doesn't wash."

Jefferson made no response, and handed Yegorov's note across the desk. Schweman reached forward and then settled back to read it.

Al Schweman had begun his government career with the General Accounting Office, working in the Procurement System

Acquisition Division, a department which analyzed the quality, cost and performance of American and NATO weapons systems. His expertise was international law, and his had been the job of reviewing the legal aspects of weapons sales to foreign governments. In 1979 he had requested and obtained a transfer to the staff of Legal Advisor to the Secretary of State. In that capacity he was well respected for a knack of almost total recall, an unruffled attitude in the face of crises, and a canny feeling for what was really going on; if anyone could decipher this unlikely "notification," he could, Jefferson thought.

Schweman scanned the two pages, and cleared his throat. "Did Yegorov seem nervous?"

"Same as usual. Sneery. And fat."

Schweman chuckled, then said, "I'm not really sure what this is about. Let me check the record on the draft convention for the U.N.'s Third Conference on the Law of the Sea. It could be one of those cases where the Russians find some language we've agreed to, and then even if the agreement or treaty is never adopted, they argue consensus."

"I'm not sure I'm following you."

"Well, they insist that the latest usage—the later language—constitutes our reinterpretation of an earlier treaty covering the same subject, this 1958 Convention, for instance."

"Wonderful. Do you think you can draft a reply to this note—and for God's sake, watch the language you use." Jefferson smiled fleetingly, then continued. "There's something I don't like about this whole thing. And I've got to get to the Secretary before he hears it on the six o'clock news."

CHAPTER FIVE

Washington, March 12

Sometimes Bob Van Vleck remembered special, sublime days in Boston Commons when he was just a kid and he and his father, and maybe half a dozen other fathers and sons maneuvered model ships and sailboats across a smooth round pond that had been designed just for that sport. When his own son was eight years old, Bob Van Vleck had gone back, taking the boy and a perfect model of a World War I four-stacker destroyer, three feet long, remote controlled, to the same pond. He had been stunned by how small the pond had grown, and how large the crowd of boys and men. Traffic on the pond itself allowed only restricted movement. Collisions on the waterway infected owners on land. There was a lot of noise, and his son had started crying.

Robert Van Vleck had some naval experience outside of the Commons, having served as a naval aviator during the Vietnam war, but Van Vleck was a lawyer, and preferred to think of himself as a gentleman and a scholar. He had graduated from Harvard and Harvard Law, had married well, accepted a job in a prestigious New York law firm, and now at the age of 48, and with a sense of wonder, he found himself the President's appointee to the position of Secretary of the Navy.

Van Vleck had been a successful fundraiser and major contributor to Baker's campaign, but his appointment was recognized more for his having chaired the Defense Expenditure Task Force in 1983. In that capacity he had seen first hand expenditures that indicated to him shocking disregard for economics, and in some cases, reason.

Sometimes, as now, the image of that last disturbing visit to the park would intrude ironically on the Secretary's thoughts. This morning he was reviewing his department's request for more ship-based cruise missiles with multiple conventional warheads and

25

additional precision guided or "smart" weapons. Reason and economics were served in the president's plan to replace nuclear weapons with conventional ones, but Van Vleck had trouble putting down that funny claustrophobic feeling that overcame him when he made his quantitative analyses.

He was interrupted by the low-pitched buzz of the intercom on his desk.

"Yes?"

"Mr. Jefferson on line one, Mr. Van Vleck."

Van Vleck punched extension one on his phone and said, "How are you, Mr. Jefferson?"

"Fine, thank you, Mr. Secretary. I wonder if I can see you this afternoon—I received a communique from the Soviet Ambassador this morning regarding a submerged Trident in the Bering Strait. I'd like to go over it with you, if you've got some time."

Van Vleck glanced over at his appointment calendar. "I've got a 1:30 appointment that shouldn't take long. How does 2:00 sound— too soon?"

"No, that's fine. I'll see you in a half hour."

The Secretry made a note on his calendar, then rang his secretary, asking her to prepare him a rundown on current activity in the Bering Strait. As they spoke, Van Vleck's 1:30 appointment arrived in the reception room outside his office, and a moment later the door swung open to admit the Director of the National Security Agency, and his deputy.

Yesterday, late afternoon, after Jerry Newman had called to make this appointment, Bob Van Vleck had had to pull a copy of the Agency Directory to find out that the NSA was an organization whose responsibility was the establishment and operation of signals intelligence. Never having met Mr. Newman or his deputy, the Secretary of the Navy had formed an image of what such men would look like. They were pale-skinned, myopic, overweight, short, balding, and they wore earphones. No such person was advancing toward him now, however, as he stood behind his desk.

Admiral Jerry Newman had allowed his deputy to precede him, not so much for reasons of etiquette as for the effect Peggy Montague had on the older, usually conservative Pentagon personnel with whom he was often required to consult. Once he had asked her if she was aware of the stir she created, and she looked at him with a funny smile and said, "Oh, yes, I'm aware of it. I don't always consider it flattery, though. Sometimes, in fact, it can make me really miserable, or embarrassed, or even afraid."

On this occasion, Peggy Montague, a tall, willowy blonde, was expressing none of those symptoms. She looked self-possessed and confident as she stretched her arm across the Secretary's desk to shake hands. She was dressed conservatively in a tailored coffee-colored suit and an ivory silk blouse. Simple gold button earrings glittered when she turned her head.

It wasn't that she was a woman in a predominantly male society, or that she was such a fine looking woman—although that was the initial startling quality that one responded to. But there is a pleasant surprise in certain incongruities, an appreciation when, for instance, the author of *The Application of Very High Pulsed Power Techniques to Laser Beam Penetration of Atmospheric and Ionized Layers of Earth* turns out to be a beautiful soft-spoken woman with blue-green eyes.

Peggy had earned two doctoral degrees, in quantum and high energy physics, and electronic engineering. Her work in physics had been awarded a government grant, and when her thesis was completed it was immediately classified. In March, she had worked for the NSA for five years, and was thirty-six years old.

"How do you do, Mr. Secretary. I'm Peggy Montague. This is our director, Admiral Newman." Grinning, Jerry Newman, who much more approached the Secretary's impression of a signal intelligence man, without earphones, stepped over to the desk and shook Van Vleck's hand.

"Good to meet you," Van Vleck said, not realizing he was only speaking to Peggy.

Jerry Newman cleared his throat, and the Secretry of the Navy quickly recovered his manners, asking them to sit. Then with the candor for which he was noted, he confessed, "You know, I'm afraid I'm not familiar with the kind of work you folks do over at NSA. Signals intelligence—what is it?"

Newman smiled. "Put very simply, it's the monitoring of signals—mostly radio signals—whenever and wherever we have reason to believe there might be a contribution to the intelligence community. Our focus is on signals issuing from foreign territory. We have a department of cryptanalysis for decoding transmissions.

A lot of it is propaganda; we watch for particular subjects, timing, place of origin of the signal, target areas, that sort of thing. In some areas, we intercept and tape military radio traffic."

Van Vleck nodded. "And how does that involve the Navy?"

"In this case, I hope you can tell me," Newman answered. "Last year, in late September, we began receiving burst transmissions originating from the Soviet Union. . . ."

Van Vleck held up a hand. "You'll have to excuse my ignorance. Could you explain a 'burst' transmission?"

Newman glanced at Peggy, who replied, "Typically, they're brief coded messages lasting no more than a minute, usually less. They contain up to 300 letter groups. So far we've not been able to decode these particular bursts, so we're assuming the senders are using one-time codes."

Jerry Newman took over. "Now, in addition to these burst transmissions, we've begun recording heavier than normal radio traffic between ships at sea and Soviet bases. *Much* heavier than normal. These signals started appearing weekly or bi-weekly in December. . . ."

"The traffic itself isn't any more than usual, you understand," inserted Peggy Montague. "Just the communication."

Van Vleck nodded.

"In the course of our regular monitoring, we've noted what appears to be some sort of propaganda campaign being broadcast from Radio Moscow, in the Eskimo language. There's been some suggestion in these transmissions of collusion between Japan and the United States. They indicate that the United States is allowing Japanese fishermen to pick up more than their quota of salmon. It may not sound very significant, but a great many Alaskan Indians make their living by fishing, either directly or indirectly. It's distinctly provocative.

"Then, ten days ago, we picked up another burst transmission which we believe originated on the Alaska side of the Bering Strait. . . ."

"The Bering Strait? That's strange—I just got a call about a complaint from the Soviets regarding a submerged ship in the Bering Strait."

"One of ours?" Newman asked with some surprise.

"Yes."

Newman raised an eyebrow and looked at Peggy. "How do you suppose they spotted a submerged ship?" he said.

Peggy said nothing for a moment, and then turned toward the Secretary. "Until now, we've assumed we knew Russian tracking equipment pretty well. A couple of years ago, we designed an airborne surveillance system for the Department of Defense. One of its features was a system employing ultra violet and infra red scanning with a video display unit to read the difference in water temperature so that we can follow the thermal track of a submarine, even if it is submerged. We thought we were the only ones who had it, though." She smiled a little ruefully.

"Peggy is too modest," Newman said, patting her hand. "Actually, it was *her* design. Don't feel bad, Peg. There may be someone on the other side of the world as smart as you. Or maybe we have a leak."

"Let's hope it's someone smart," said Bob Van Vleck. "Have you decoded this transmission from the Bering Strait?"

"Not yet," Newman answered.

"Who else have you spoken to about it?"

"The National Security Council. They asked me to fill you in."

"Well, it sounds like something's going on over there. I've got an appointment with Mr. Jefferson from the State Department," Van Vleck looked at his watch; "he should be here any moment. I'll share this with him and see if we can come up with something that makes sense. If you can get back to me with a translation of this last transmission as soon as you've got it, it might help. And I'll keep you informed of anything new from this end."

Jerry Newman stood and shook Van Vleck's hand. As Peggy rose, the Secretary walked around his desk to say goodbye and walk them to the door. "Thank you for coming by—and for the instruction," Van Vleck said.

"Our pleasure, Mr. Secretary," said Jerry Newman.

"Good to meet you, Mr. Secretary," said Peggy Montague.

* * * * *

Peter Jefferson was just entering the reception room when Peggy Montague and Jerry Newman left the Secretary's office. Peggy stopped abruptly in her tracks, and Newman was forced to stop short behind her to avoid a collision. Peter Jefferson also stood stock still.

Hastily, Peggy turned. "I'm sorry, Jerry," she said with a slight flush. She turned back to face Peter Jefferson and said, "I didn't make the connection when the Secretary said he was expecting a 'Mr. Jefferson.' Jerry, this is Peter Jefferson. Peter, this is Admiral Newman of the National Security Agency."

Peter stepped forward to accept Jerry's handshake. Then he said to Peggy, "It's—I'm so glad to see you. What are you—are you working here?"

Peggy felt herself flushing. "I work over at the National Security Agency, with Jerry."

"Can I call you? It's been . . . I'd like to talk to you," Peter said, trying to keep his voice low. Both Jerry Newman and Van Vleck's secretary were apparently very interested in this exchange.

"I'd like that."

"Good. Well—I'll—I'll call you."

Peggy nodded.

Still nobody moved. Finally, Jerry Newman cleared his throat, and touching Peggy lightly on the arm, ushered her to the outer door. "Nice to meet you Mr. Jefferson," he said over his shoulder.

Peter Jefferson nodded at the door as it swung closed behind him. Then he glanced over at Van Vleck's secretary who was staring at him. Jefferson felt almost out of breath, and more than a little ridiculous. "Do you think you could tell the Secretary I'm here?" he said, with a little too much bite.

"Oh, yes sir; I'm sorry, sir, of course." With a flurry of movement, the secretary swung around in her chair and buzzed Robert Van Vleck.

"Mr. Jefferson is here. And I have a file on the Bering Strait for you. . . . Yes sir." She looked up and said, "Please go right in," motioning to the door and rising to follow him with the file. As she stepped around the desk the phone rang and she answered while Jefferson walked into Van Vleck's office.

He was just sitting down when the secretary entered, placed the file on Van Vleck's desk, and said, "The Secretary of State is on line one for Mr. Jefferson."

"Thanks, Margaret," Van Vleck said as the girl left the room and he handed the phone across the desk.

Jefferson picked up the receiver and told George Heath's secretary he was on the line. He listened without comment for several moments when Heath got on. Finally Jefferson said, "Unbelievable!

Why—well, never mind. . . . I've got Yegorov's note over at my office; I'll pick it up and be over to you in half an hour. . . . Yes, I'll tell him."

Jefferson hung up the phone, and looked over at Bob Van Vleck who was staring back with undisguised curiosity.

"Moscow has abrogated the Alaska Purchase Treaty. They're claiming that the Soviet frontier now extends to the present border of Alaska with Canada." Jefferson shook his head with wonder. "I've got to get over to the Secretary's office, Mr. Van Vleck. I'll get you a full report."

When Jefferson had left, the Secretary of the Navy sank back in his chair and clasped his hands behind his head. He thought, under the circumstances, it would probably be all right to table these cruise missile requests for another day.

* * * * *

As Peggy and Jerry Newman walked into the gusty grey afternoon she was quiet and he was not quite sure what to say.

"What did you think of Van Vleck?" he tendered.

"He seemed nice."

They approached Washington Boulevard in silence. Afternoon traffic was heavy. Pedestrians hunched into their winter wear like soft turtles. It was just beginning to snow.

Standing on the corner waiting for the light to change, Jerry said gently, "You know, if you ever need to talk about—about anything. . . ."

Peggy turned and took his hand. "Thank you, Jerry. To be honest, I wouldn't have an idea of what to say." She gave a light laugh, and then said, "There's the light—let's go!" And still holding hands, they dashed across the street.

* * * * *

When Peter Jefferson left the Secretary's office he was not thinking about Peggy Montague. He was remembering Alexandr

Yegorov's upturned face, the smug knowing leer from the steps of the State Department building. It wasn't until he had turned his low white car toward Washington and the snow began to fall, that she returned to him. In the measured whisper of his windshield wipers he spoke her name aloud.

CHAPTER SIX
Moscow, March 12

Bob Detwiler and his wife stared down at the plates that had been set in front of them and then looked across at one another. Louise waited until the waiter had left, then said quietly, "What do you suppose it *is?*"

He grinned, poking his fork through a congealing gravy that lacquered some form of meat. "They're selling it as veal. Here, have some more wine." He reached for the bottle, a very sharp Retsina-like wine. Not very good.

She was going to object but didn't. At least there was the baked potato and plenty of sour cream and chives. She tasted a coarse, but surprisingly good caviar, raised her eyebrows, looked over at her husband.

Bob Detwiler was young—twenty-seven—round faced, with hazel eyes, and average height and build. He was a staff Central Intelligence agent on his first assignment in Russia.

Ostensibly, he was a salesman—his card read "European Marketing Representative, Com Pro Systems." He had spent the past several days since their arrival picking his way through the bureaucratic ladder at Amtorg, the Soviet Trade Agency. He had done well. Com Pro's product was called Newspeak, an inexpensive language translator, with micro cable components, interface boards, data transfer switches, a 48k memory, all contained in a $4'' \times 6'' \times 2''$ unit that looked like a cassette recorder with a small screen in place of the usual window. It had three learning levels, accepted tapes with a dictionary of 15,000 English, and in this case, Soviet words.

Amtorg had been impressed. This afternoon they told him they were very interested, wondered if he could arrange an immediate delivery for a test market in Moscow and some of the oblast, six gross, say. . . .

So this evening was something of a celebration for Bob Detwiler. On two counts. He had also successfully serviced an information drop today. In fact, just before his profitable meeting with Yuri Benevich Scolia, the last of the series of officials at Amtorg.

* * * * *

The meeting had been at four. Louise and he had had lunch at the Rossia Hotel at noon, and taken the number 14 bus to Gorky Park in the early afternoon. It was a lovely day, still very cold, but bright and sunny. Little triangular yellow flags fluttered overhead, men and women strolled the tiled promenade, there was music on the air from an amusement park behind them. Bob Detwiler pointed up at the ferris wheel, said something to his wife. She took his arm and pressed near him, as if she were cold. They walked to a metal-slatted park bench, unoccupied, in front of a large square planter filled with blue and yellow flowers. They sat, and Louise took out her cigarettes, offered one to Bob. He leaned forward toward her, holding a lighter, cupping his hands around the end of her cigarette and the flame. He leaned back and lit one for himself, pocketed the lighter, sat back tilting his head up to catch the sun, and exhaled.

Neither of them spoke. After several moments of silence, Louise leaned forward and said, "Let me take your picture."

Bob smiled, removed the Minolta from around his neck, handed it to her. She rose, unsnapping the camera from its case, removed the lens cap, and crossed in front of her husband, looking down at the camera. She aimed it at him, adjusted the focus, paused, frowned, called across to him, "Put out the cigarette, Bob," and resumed her scrutiny.

Detwiler leaned forward stubbing tobacco into a small chalked "X" on the concrete immediately under his seat. As he straightened, his right hand slipped across the underside of the bench, behind his knees. He felt it immediately, a sealed magnetic packet smaller than a postage stamp he knew contained the microdot the Agency had sent him for.

He sat back again, smiled a genuine, happy grin, and Louise snapped the picture.

"Stand up," she directed.

He did, slipping one hand in his coat pocket, tossing his scarf over his shoulder, striking a jaunty pose. She had laughed and snapped another.

* * * * *

When the waiter returned to the table he couldn't help but note the two slabs of meat, one untouched, the other cut once, but obviously not tried. He did not inquire how they had enjoyed their meal, but asked them in English if they would like coffee.

Detwiler met the man's eyes. He had bronze colored skin and a full mustache—probably Detwiler's own age, but wiry, smaller, high cheekbones, almost Indian looking, he thought. Probably Uzbek—maybe Moslem.

"How's the coffee?" Detwiler asked.

Vladimir Zolfin kept a straight face. "No serious casualties today, sir."

Detwiler grinned. "Two coffees."

* * * * *

He would leave Moscow for Com Pro's Luxemburg plant on Tuesday to fill Amtorg's order. With the weekend ahead the couple decided to join an Intourist group traveling north to Leningrad.

The next morning, early, they met downstairs in the quiet lobby with forty or so other travelers. It was just beginning to lighten outside. Louise commented how subdued the tourists were here.

"It's six o'clock in the morning, El," Detwiler had said.

Louise shook her head. "It's the atmosphere."

They had confirmed at the desk as members of the tour, their baggage had been removed to the railway station ahead of them; now they waited for the guide to appear. Louise was lighting a cigarette when Bob saw their waiter of the week past approaching at a fast clicking pace toward their knot of tourists.

Detwiler was about to say a friendly word, but Vladimir Zolfin moved past him without a glimmer of recognition, proceeded into the dead center of the crowd, and said snappily, "Ladies and Gentlemen, I am Vladimir Zolfin. I am your guide on this tour to the great city of Leningrad, home of the fabled Winter Palace and Palace Square, and the famed Hermitage collection." This information was rattled off with no particular expression or enthusiasm.

"We will proceed from here to the Leningrad Railway Station on Pereyaslavaskaya Boulevard, and board the Aurora Express. . . ."

There was a murmur of approval from the crowd. Zolfin did not pause. ". . . The train leaves *promptly* at 7:30 AM," he looked at his watch. ". . . travels an average of 85 miles per hour, and arrives in Leningrad *promptly* at 12:29 PM."

He finally paused, his expression was stern. "I will expect you to keep close together at all times. There is no signal from the train that she is leaving—we cannot wait for latecomers."

* * * * *

Bob Detwiler had felt the slightest twinge of concern. It seemed an odd coincidence that their waiter was also their tour guide on the occasion of their leaving Moscow. The information he was carrying was safe, he felt confident, but what was the man doing here?

They were in the "soft seat" section of the Express—first class accommodations down to the richly crocheted antimacassars that bibbed each red plush seat. Zolfin was sitting alone toward the back of their car, having delivered a litany on the train, and the towns they would be passing: Kalinin, Vyshniy Volocheck, Bologoye, Malaya Vistera.

"Can I buy you a drink, Mr. Zolfin?"

Zolfin turned away from the window and considered Bob Detwiler. He hesitated. "I will have tea. Thank you."

Detwiler put out his hand. "Bob Detwiler. We met at the hotel." He turned and looked down the aisle, called a steward and when the boy approached Detwiler pulled his translator out of his jacket pocket. He typed out, "Please give us tea," pressed a key to translate, and "dai'te, pazhah'lsta chai" lit up on the small screen. As Detwiler stumbled out the words, the steward's eyes widened.

He looked from the odd machine to Detwiler's round face, and he grinned and ran off to fill the order.

Vladimir Zolfin's interest was also piqued. Detwiler sat down next to him, and Zolfin nodded at the little computer. "I have never seen such a thing," he said.

"It's a real help when you're traveling." Detwiler handed it to him. "My pronunciation is pretty bad, but if you use one of these you can usually get what you need without embarrassing yourself too badly.

"I sell them for a company in the States," he said, leaning forward. "I've just negotiated a deal with Amtorg—here, you hit this key for the language you're entering in the machine, then type it out. . . ."

Zolfin posted, "Ya o'chen rat s vah'mee paznako'meetsa," and the translator obliged with "I am pleased to meet you."

Detwiler grinned one of his open all American grins. "Thanks," he said. "But you speak English very well."

Zolfin acknowledged the compliment with a nod. "I was fortunate—I am from Tashkent"—he looked up—the name of his home city instilled some light in his dark eyes.

"There is excellent schooling there—the largest number of foreign students—I had a . . ." He looked for the English word, then looked down at the translator, typed "dar," and smiled when "knack" came up. He held it up for Detwiler to see. "A 'knack' for languages. Have you been to Central Asia, Mr. Detwiler?"

Bob Detwiler shook his head. He noted that Zolfin did not refer to Tashkent as part of Russia. A little thing.

"Your family is there?" Detwiler asked.

Zolfin looked to the window again before he answered. "Yes. My family." He said it quietly, lovingly.

Detwiler was almost embarrassed.

The tea arrived. Detwiler looked up at the white jacketed steward and said, "Spasee'ba." The boy looked a little disappointed, and pointed to the translator. Detwiler grinned, took the computer from Zolfin, typed in "Thank you," hit the translator key, and the message, "Spasee'ba," appeared neatly in the center of the screen.

The tea was sweet and lemon scented. Detwiler looked over at Zolfin. "Tell me something about your country."

The darker man sipped his tea, then sat back. "Tashkent," he said. His face seemed to soften, then he said, almost harshly, "It was the first large settlement in Central Asia to be conquered by the Russians—in 1865." He looked over at Detwiler. "But they did not conquer our spirit, or our strength."

Immediately Zolfin's voice altered and he began the sing-song cadence of the tour guide. "Tashkent lies in a great fault-line area. There is an Uzbek story that in the early days the city fathers would plant their swords in the ground to know when the new year was begun. When an earthquake shook the blade loose a new calendar was started."

Detwiler nodded. "I remember reading about the quakes in the sixties. . . ."

"A lot has changed since then. Instead of restoring the city for the people—the Uzbeks, especially the Moslems—our conquerers have built new expensive museums—the Lenin Museum is there, the Opera House, a modern airport, all very beautiful, but these things are not for wheat and melon farmers."

"So you moved up here for work?" Detwiler asked. He didn't want Zolfin to compromise himself by saying too much.

"Yes." Zolfin sipped his tea. "Because of my English I work for Intourist on weekends and some holidays doing tours. During the week I am part-time at one of Intourist's hotels—the Rossia this week—" he shrugged, "next week at the National."

He paused, then looked at Detwiler as if wondering if this foreigner could understand. "My family in Tashkent is large. My obligations. . . ." He shook his head, a muscle clenched in his jaw. "Until things improve, I have to work a little more for them."

Detwiler was silent. He thought he did understand.

* * * * *

Bob Detwiler left his translator with Zolfin for the day and invited him to join Louise and himself for dinner that night. In Leningrad their party checked into the aging Astoria Hotel, lunched in the hotel's restaurant, and in a tight file, bunched down Khalturina Street toward the Palace Square. As they walked, Zolfin kept up a patter of information.

"Leningrad is in the Neva River Delta which has formed 110 islands linked by 700 bridges. It has been called 'Venice of the

North.' Until 1914 the city was named St. Petersburg, when it was changed to Petrograd, and in 1924 was renamed the City of Lenin. . . ."

Louise held Bob's arm as they walked. It was very cold. She looked up when they stopped in front of the Winter Palace. The huge building faced the square on one side and the Niva River on the other. A blue and white kazzoo-shaped tour boat chugged out of sight behind the Palace as Zolfin described its baroque architecture and bloody history. . . .

They spent two hours inside the Hermitage Museum, marveling at halls ornamented with delicately carved Ural stone, the intricate inlay work of the floors, the splendid chandeliers that carried the coats of arms of all the regions of Russia. They walked, hushed through the Hall of Twenty Columns, and a white marble Roman courtyard.

Of the more than a thousand rooms and two million items the spectacular museum holds, Zolfin used his perogative to designate which of the seven main sections and forty smaller ones his charges would visit. He stuck to antique culture and art from Greece, the Greek colonies on the Black Sea, Rome and ancient Italy; and the history, culture and art of peoples now living on Soviet Territory, namely in Central Asia and the Caucasus.

* * * * *

By the end of the weekend Bob and Vladimir and Louise had become friends, and although none of them spoke of it, they were all three cautious about its visibility, particularly in the company of the others. It was not encouraged, socializing—particularly with Americans.

Zolfin had breakfast this next day with a middle-aged French couple who spoke passable English. He had adopted the little translator for the duration of their stay in Leningrad, and found it a useful distraction for his tourists between museums. At dinner Saturday night, on his way to yet another table, he passed the Detwilers. Stopping casually, he said with a smile, "I should receive a commission. I think I have sold a dozen of your computers today."

Detwiler grinned. At the end of their tour Bob gave his new friend the translator as a gift. Zolfin was very quiet receiving it, but Detwiler knew he had sealed their friendship.

"I'll be in town next week," Bob Detwiler said, shaking Zolfin's hand in the Rossia Hotel Lobby back in Moscow. "Maybe we can get together then."

Zolfin nodded certainly. "I will find some expression of my gratitude."

"Not necessary, man," Detwiler said quietly. Then, as if remembering, "How can I get in touch with you?"

"I board in quarters wherever Intourist sends me. I will be two weeks at the National Hotel."

* * * * *

In Luxemburg Detwiler did more than personally supervise the shipment of Com Pro's Newspeak mini computers to Moscow. He met with the CIA auxiliary there to turn over his information and to tell them he thought he had found an ally in Vladimir Zolfin. He described what several hours of seemingly harmless questions over the weekend had produced.

Detwiler was a good agent. His profile was the perfect recruit. Vladimir Zolfin was a Moslem with something of a patriarchal complex. His "family" was not a mother and sisters, but Tashkent—all his people.

He needed money for his cause. He was educated but street-wise. He fit anywhere, and his job allowed him movement.

Armed with a specially outfitted translator, no different in appearance than the one he had given Zolfin, Bob Detwiler returned to Moscow.

* * * * *

Louise didn't accompany him on this trip. Bob got to the National Hotel at the lunch hour, paused in the doorway until he could determine which section of the room Zolfin-as-waiter was serving, moved into that area and found a vacant table.

Detwiler examined the menu. A bus boy filled his water glass. When Zolfin finally came to his table, Detwiler was delighted the man made little sign of recognition. His smile was in his eyes, his face remained impassive.

Detwiler ordered a roast beef platter and coffee, and added at the end of his order, "Can you meet me at the Old Moscow Arts Theatre tonight at 7:30? And bring your translator?"

Zolfin looked hard at Detwiler, drew a line under roast beef on his pad, nodded, and retreated toward the kitchen. Detwiler pulled a rolled *Computer Digest* magazine out of his overcoat pocket on the chair next to him, and opened it to an article he had been reading on the way over.

* * * * *

The play was "He Who Gets Slapped" by Leonid Andreyev, which had premiered in this same theater in 1915, according to Zolfin, and starred one of Russia's most admired young actresses, Olga Karpovna, a girl of great beauty who, it was rumored, had a lover in a very high place, and who played Consuelo the bareback rider in this classic Soviet allegory. She was saucy and sweet in the role.

If Zolfin was confused by the invitation, so surreptitiously agreed on, he made no sign, and both men seemed to enjoy the show.

During intermission they walked together toward the brightly lit lobby so Detwiler could have a cigarette. They chatted about the performances, Olga Karpovna, the very stylized circus set, the theatre's history, about which Zolfin knew a great deal.

It was after the play they walked and talked. Without preamble Detwiler told Zolfin what he had in mind, and what they were willing to pay. The translator Detwiler would exchange with him worked exactly the same way the first one had, but this one had an additional capability to transmit information, in code, when programmed to do so.

Detwiler admitted Zolfin might never, or rarely have occasion to stumble into a situation that would be helpful to them, but if he ever did, Detwiler assured him, he would be helping both Bob

Detwiler personally, and indirectly, his own peoples. The Agency provided generous compensation for valuable information.

They had reached Soviet Square, a small cobbled park with benches and statuary and tall yellow lamps, in front of the Institute of Marxism-Leninism. They sat and Detwiler talked some more, steam clouding his words in the cold night.

At first Zolfin just listened, watching Detwiler with his dark eyes. Then, hesitantly, he began asking questions. How generous, precisely? What kind of information? What kind of risks was he expected to take? How would he make contact, and how often?

Both men took out their translators, and Detwiler showed Zolfin the new function key he would use for transmissions. They discussed the fairly sophisticated code that had been built in to the equipment for this assignment, which Zolfin grasped quickly and with obvious delight.

It was nearing midnight. Only a few couples, all tourists it seemed, strolled the square. An officer passed them by, but did not stop.

When they stood over an hour later to walk back toward the National Hotel, they had exchanged computers. And Vladimir Zolfin had a third job.

CHAPTER SEVEN
Washington, March 12

The Secretary of State's office looked as much like the library in an English men's club as it could without a fireplace and a butler serving drinks. George Heath's wife had a thriving interior design business, and she considered their personal expense in providing an unusual, yet practical working environment for her husband well worth the advertisement it provided. For himself, his wife's talent was a source of pride; and although he would never compromise himself by trying to promote her business, Heath's obvious comfort in his surroundings was promotion enough.

A dark Persian rug in patterns of maroon and blue covered the floor; leather bound books filled three walls from floor to ceiling interrupted occasionally by a brass vase or ironwood sculpture. The fourth wall was a long window whose dark blue drapes were drawn open today, against snow falling in a darkening sky.

At one end of Heath's semicircular desk, an inlaid English hunter's desk, stood a small computer terminal and screen on which, it was rumored, he practiced tournament level chess with several distinguished partners in several different cities throughout the States. Comfortable seats were clustered in twos and threes in front of the curved desk, and brass floor lamps illuminated each seating group in a pool of soft yellow light.

Jefferson had met Al Schweman on his way to the Secretary's office, and the two walked in together; though neither of them spoke, there was an urgency to their pace that communicated concern and curiosity. Henry Clay, the President's Assistant for National Security, was already inside, walking stiffly back and forth in front of Heath's desk. James Booth, Counsellor to the President, was seated quietly watching Clay trace a path on the rich carpet.

43

Jefferson and Schweman quickly took seats. Clay acknowledged their arrival with a grim nod, but did not stop pacing and Booth looked up from the carpet at them, almost blankly. Even Schweman, who normally could not resist making a joke out of whatever situation presented itself, remained silent.

From behind his desk, George Heath looked annoyed. "Henry, would you sit down, you're making me nervous."

Clay stopped in mid-stride, looked a little offended, but sat down in a chair to Jefferson's left.

"Thanks, Henry," Heath said more kindly, and then he turned to the new arrivals. "You both know everyone here?"

Peter rose and extended his hand toward James Booth. "I don't believe we've met, Mr. Booth."

The President's Counsellor stood and stared at the younger man as if taking a photograph. Booth had two expressions, one which was about as empty as Little Orphan Annie's, the other so intense, the object of his attention often felt set upon in some strange way.

Jefferson felt as if he had just been recorded, or processed, or filed somehow; and then Booth grinned and shook his hand. It was as if he were admitting that something had happened.

Heath made introductions, then came directly to the subject at hand, summarizing for Clay and Booth the Ambassador's visit to Jefferson's office earlier in the day.

"On my advice, Mr. Jefferson went over to the Pentagon to talk to Bob Van Vleck about this Bering Strait incident. That was an hour ago—about the same time *this* arrived by courier," he indicated a manila file on his desk.

"After Peter left the Secretary's office, Van Vleck called me to relate a meeting he had just concluded with the Director of NSA. They've been picking up heavy Soviet propaganda targetted at Alaska; and new signals—burst transmissions—from the Soviets to ships at sea. A lot of unusual activity—none of it decoded, unfortunately—since December. Ten days ago they monitored a signal they were able to identify as coming from the Alaska side of the Bering Strait. . . ."

Henry Clay's arms seemed to propel his body out of the chair without any direction from him. "Why the hell doesn't the NSA report 'unusual activity since December' until March?" His face was flushed with anger. "And why aren't 'unusual' transmissions decoded? Do you know how much money that agency receives? Why don't they have people who can do the job. . . ."

"Henry, I appreciate your anger. We all feel—impotent because we don't know what's going on." Heath was trying to be patient, but with Henry he sometimes felt the way he used to when he was speaking to one of his grandchildren. "But you're not asking the right questions, and we don't have the time to discuss tangents. Please sit down."

Clay sat down. He didn't take criticism personally, which was fortunate, because his rather abrasive manner was often subject to censure. Of all the men closest to the President, he was the dissident. He shared with Harry Smyth the distinction of being the most outspoken; but where Smyth was blunt, Clay was sharp as a stiletto. Even physically, with thinning hair and a tall straight posture, he gave the impression of sharpness.

He had taught at the Harvard School of Russian Studies, and was consultant to the London-based Institute of Strategic Studies and the Shiloah Institute in Israel before accepting the position of Assistant to the President for National Security. Clay's ability to marshall facts in support of a position made him a hard man to argue with, and Heath had no intention of allowing this discussion to become a one man debate on internal affairs.

The Secretary of State continued. "All right. From what information we have thus far, we can conclude that this abrogation is no whim; that Kolkin, or Argunov—more likely Argunov—has been designing this play since December."

Al Schweman sat forward. "How was notification made?"

"Two hours ago, in Moscow, the Soviet Minister of Foreign Affairs called on our Ambassador," Heath said. "An unusual time for an appointment—7:00 in the evening there. He delivered a long note—it's in final translation now—but we've got a summary here." Heath tapped the file on his desk.

"What I want to know," Clay blurted, "is how they unilaterally abrogate a treaty concluded over a hundred years ago."

"There is some precedent," Schweman offered quietly. "That is as far as the Soviet's are concerned, there's a precedent."

Clay seemed surprised that there might be an answer to what he had considered a rhetorical question. He sat back frowning, arms crossed in front of him.

Schweman continued. "In 1921 the Russian Socialist Federal

Republic signed a treaty with Persia which, in precise language, nullified all treaties and conventions between Iran and the Tsarist government to that point. Just like that." He demonstrated with a snap of his fingers.

"The new government didn't want to be bound by old policy. They used the abrogation as a renunciation of Tsarist economic imperialism and sphere of influence strategies."

Clay started to raise his arm, but Schweman didn't pause. He had been at other meetings with Henry Clay. "Then in 1979, Iran announced its own abrogation of the 1921 treaty because it granted the Soviet Union a discretionary right of military intervention if its interests were threatened. To my knowledge, the Russians haven't ever recognized, or even commented on Iran's 1979 abrogation."

Heath hastened to take the floor again. "Whatever their reasons," the Secretary said, "the problem is compounded by the fact that the Soviets, claiming Alaska is theirs, regard the territory as being occupied by—and this is a quote—'hostile' forces. Namely American military forces.

"They're demanding immediate withdrawal of the United States from Alaska, to its pre-1867 boundaries, starting with the Elmendorf Air Force Base in Anchorage; and Shemya, a radar installation on the western tip of the Aleutians—both personnel and equipment. Then they require emigration of all civilians in Alaska— except for those who choose to remain with full local autonomy, and adopt Soviet citizenship."

The room was silent. It was too much for Henry Clay. "You know what this is, don't you?" he blurted. His right leg was crossed and his narrow ankle was flapping fitfully in the air. "Global adventurism!" He looked at the other men, a piercing grey look, and pointed his finger at James Booth.

"We might consider it a little reminder. Perhaps we're losing sight of some basics of Marxism; you might want to mention that to the President."

Booth, staring blank-eyed at Clay's finger, said in his very Southwestern twang, "Well, sir, we sure do have to make some kind of statement—soon—before the media grabs hold and things really get out of hand."

Peter glanced quickly over at Schweman who was obviously holding back laughter, staring hard at the floor.

Booth went on blandly. "Actually, the President is meetin' with Mr. Apple and the Senior Senator from Alaska." He paused and appeared to ponder that. Then he said, "Does anyone know the Senior Senator's name? I'm afraid it's slipped my mind."

Al Schweman looked up and would have provided the answer, but Booth, it seemed, had already forgotten the question. "The problem is," he was saying, "there's no gentle way of breakin' this kind of news. Best we can do is assure folks that bombs aren't gonna be fallin' in their back yards—try to keep things calm."

Henry Clay looked straight ahead and spoke slowly and coldly. "Oh, we can assure them of a lot more than that. We can assure 'folks' that the full power of the United States will be deployed to meet this Russian threat."

For just a moment Booth's eyes flashed.

Heath was sitting back in his chair watching this exchange, which wasn't really an exchange, with some interest. He thought perhaps it was time to put in a word.

But Peter Jefferson leaned forward. He held his glasses in one hand and was slowly polishing the lenses with a handkerchief. "What do you think this is *really* about?" he asked.

Clay turned sharply toward him.

Jefferson held his glasses up to the light and slipped them back on. "I mean, I can't believe this is serious—I can't believe its *Alaska* they want. And if it were, that they'd go about trying to take it like this. They've got to know we won't stand for it, no matter how new this administration is. And they've got to know how outrageous it will look to the rest of the world." Jefferson shook his head. "I think we should be looking elsewhere."

"You're quite right, Peter," George Heath agreed. "We should be looking at the whole board. But of course we've got to protect ourselves, and that's the position one is forced to defend when one is played on first. Tomorrow, I promise you, we'll consider the possibilities. Why don't you join us with your ideas—the Cabinet Room, at 2:00."

Jefferson nodded and made a note on his yellow pad, although he was not likely to forget a meeting in the Cabinet Room.

The Secretary continued speaking as he rose from behind his desk and drew the heavy drapes behind him. "Meanwhile, Al, I'd like you to prepare a request for an urgent meeting of the United Nations Security Council . . ."

The light seemed brighter inside, a certain intimacy warmed the room. They remained another ten minutes in Heath's office, concluding business.

All five men left together, Peter Jefferson and Al Schweman to their respective offices; and George Heath, James Booth and Henry Clay down the wide public staircase to a meeting at the White House. It was approaching 5:00 in the afternoon, the sky was clotted with dark clouds, and snow swirled in parallel lines through the glare of headlights on 21st and Virginia Streets outside the State Department.

* * * * *

Turning down the corridor toward his office, Jefferson leaned into his secretary's corner. Grace was replacing files in a large standing cabinet behind her desk. He looked at his watch and grinned. "Why don't you leave early today, Grace. You can get a fresh start in the morning."

Grace looked at him with amazement. Then she looked at her own watch, and burst out laughing. It was five minutes till 5:00. "You know why I really like working for you, Mr. Jefferson? It's your generosity. It's just so *moving.*"

Peter Jefferson nodded with a serious expression bordering on a frown. "Yes, generous to a fault, they say."

"Well, I'll take you up on it, and see you bright and early." Grace Sherwood shut the file cabinet firmly, locked it, and opened a small closet out of which she pulled a green plaid wool coat, boots, and an umbrella.

"Good night, Grace."

"Good night, Mr. Jefferson," Grace said, smiling as he left her alcove.

In his office, Peter Jefferson sank into a leather armchair on the visitor's side of his desk. It felt much later than 5:00. He loosened his tie and sat back for a moment, lifting his glasses off his nose and rubbing his eyes. Sighing, he reached across his desk to pick up the several messages that Grace had stacked neatly by his phone.

Leaning back again, he glanced down at the "While You Were Out" notations: Stu Boyington—he'd have to cancel their Thursday morning raquet ball; Al Schweman—from earlier in the day; the Thai Ambassador—for an appointment that would be tedious at best; and a last message, from Miriam.

Damn it! He had been anticipating this for a month, ever since news of his ex-wife's latest tragedy filtered down to him. Miriam's problem was that she simply couldn't take care of herself. Mama and Papa and starched white nannies took care of Miriam, and her husband had been expected to join that succession of caretakers: she had been raised to be somebody's baby. In the seventies, when the women's movement blossomed, Miriam felt alienated, and too uncertain to step off a pedestal that had supported her for as long as she could remember.

Her need for attention and reassurance had been attractive to him at first—some primal strain of man-as-protector that appealed to him at the age of thirty-three—and Miriam was ten years younger, after all. But her insecurity grew, even as his career did—something he couldn't understand. By the time he was in his late thirties, and involved in his work, and his attention was turned to the future, and other people took more and more of his time, Miriam's neurosis became impossible for them to live with.

She had gone back to live with her parents, remarried, for less than a year, finally moved out on her own and Peter had heard lately of her father's death, not unexpected. Miriam had stayed in touch. The first few years almost constantly; lately it had been better, but there had been three calls last month, and now it looked like it was starting again.

He sighed. He cared for Miriam, but she always triggered feelings of guilt in him.

His mind turned to Peggy Montague. If he thought about it, he could feel guilty about her too. Maybe he'd call her tonight. No, maybe that would look overly anxious. Was he anxious about her?

Abruptly, Jefferson rose from his chair. If he wanted to suggest any intelligent possibilities to the Secretary tomorrow, he'd better shift his thinking. In fact, maybe he'd run out, get a sandwich and come back here for a couple of hours. He could take a look at the Russian files, try to get some perspective. . . .

He turned toward the door just as Al Schweman's shaggy head appeared from behind it.

"Al!"

"Hey, Peter—I was hoping you'd still be here. How about we grab a bite and toss this thing around. Two heads? . . ."

Peter Jefferson grinned. "Great. I was thinking of doing just that, and I could use the company. Dinner's on me."

"Does that mean McDonald's again, Peter?"

"Generous to a fault—that's what Grace tells me."

* * * * *

It was a long evening, discussing legalities of treaty abrogation, poring over maps and through files of international events. It was after 10:00 when they said goodnight. Schweman declined a ride and Jefferson decided to leave his Porsche in the Department's underground garage as he often did, and walked home.

It was a dark night. The snow creaked under his feet as each step packed a print into the sidewalk. As he approached the Lincoln Memorial within whose Doric columns the great President sits, he paused and turned to look to his left at the Washington Monument piercing the sky like an illuminated arrow. Between the Lincoln Memorial and the towering monument half a mile away, lies a long narrow pool in which the tower points back in a shimmering reflection at the huge statue of Lincoln. Peter was moved, as always, at the grandness of this capitol city: its starkness, especially at night, its larger than life representation of invisible things, ideals. For no reason that he could fathom, he experienced a quick, unsettling flash of isolation. Even the quiet was quieter tonight, insulated, as the snow fell in big ragged flakes against the night.

CHAPTER EIGHT

Washington, March 13

The next morning at 9:00 AM, national and international wire services interrupted their normal reportage, and information terminals began stammering the news in continuous sheets of copy that began, "Urgent: Statement from the President of the United States and full text of Soviet threat to follow. . . ."

In one newsroom a copyboy stood transfixed in front of the telex, a styrofoam cup of coffee cooling in one hand, the other pinching his lower lip. Not until the page was licking the boy's shoe did he remember to move, tearing the story out of the printer and running toward his editor in the same motion, the jagged tail of paper flying behind him, coffee splattering on the linoleum floor.

It had been a routine morning at the New York Stock Exchange until their broad tape inched out a summary of the President's statement and that of the Russian note. Within seconds the air was aflutter with paper and the jangle of phones. Sell orders flooded the exchange and Dow Jones dropped forty points on huge volume within the next three hours. Trading was suspended at 12:20 PM.

In London the news was received at 2:00 PM, just before the second fixing of the day on the London Metals Exchange. Brokers there looked at one another and back down at their tapes. "What the bloody hell does *this* mean," said Lord Titterton to his colleague Mr. Edward Darbyshire at the Whittington Avenue Exchange. "I think it means the price of gold sets $100 higher by tea time," Mr. Darbyshire replied, checking his watch and then raising his eyebrows at the board.

National and local television and radio programming was interrupted for special news broadcasts. One new network technician at NBC was alone in the booth when a computer voice began prattling in his headset. The young man's eyes widened and his hands started tembling as he triggered the switch that asked affiliated stations to stand by. He remembered almost everything he was supposed to do given an emergency interruption, but neglected to key for station breaks or commercials in the subsequent newsroom briefing. As a result, the New York anchor, watching worriedly for a signal that never came, filled his air space by reading the complete text of the Soviet denunciation and demands to the American public.

The anchor man was steamed when he finally got off the air, after over an hour of reading and reviewing to three unblinking and unresponsive cameras; and so were the NBC Board of Directors and a glut of sponsors. But their coverage won great public acclaim for completeness and intelligence, and ultimately they were all satisfied: the anchor with a bonus and an improved contract, NBC with a special award later that year from the FCC. Even the sponsors took it like sports, once they had been talked to, and certain arrangements had been made. Unfortunately, the NBC technician who started this chain of events was fired the day after his blunder, and advised to consider a complete change of career.

A special late edition *New York Times* told the whole story with headlines that read:

USSR ABROGATES ALASKA PURCHASE TREATY OF 1867, CALLS FOR WITHDRAWAL OF UNITED STATES TO PRE-1867 BOUNDARIES IMMEDIATELY, STARTING WITH AIR FORCE UNITS.

SOVIET FOREIGN MINISTER ANDREI GROMYKO CLAIMS ALASKA IS TERRITORY OCCUPIED BY THE UNITED STATES

PRESIDENT BAKER ASSURES FULL PROTECTION OF ALASKA TERRITORY

URGENT MEETING OF UNITED NATIONS SECURITY COUNCIL TO DEAL WITH SOVIET THREAT TO PEACE

NATIONAL SECURITY COUNCIL TO MEET ON LOOMING CRISIS

CANADIAN PRIME MINISTER CALLS ON PROVINCIAL GOVERNORS TO PRESENT UNITED FRONT AGAINST SOVIET THREAT

DOLLAR EXPECTED TO DROP AGAINST ALL MAJOR CURRENCIES

* * * * *

The National Security Council was established by the National Security Act of 1947. Its principal function is to advise the President with respect to the integration of domestic, foreign and military policies relating to the national security. The Council's Policy Review Committee includes in its membership the Vice President, the Secretary of State, the Secretary of the Treasury, the Secretary of Defense, the Assistant to the President for National Security Affairs, the Chairman of the Joint Chiefs of Staff, and the Director of the Central Intelligence Agency who was presiding over this meeting of the Committee.

With the exception of James Pell who was meeting with the Prime Minister in Israel, and Simon Bell, attending a conference of Finance Ministers in France, and the addition of Peter Jefferson, all of the Policy Committee were present. The men were gathered around the end of the large oval table nearest the fireplace of the Cabinet Room. All of them had worked late into the night before, and most of them looked strained and tired. Harry Smyth was more rumpled than usual, Henry Clay and Larry Apple had a tightness around the eyes. Even George Heath seemed a little pale.

Heath and Jefferson sat with their backs to the French windows facing onto the Rose Garden. Last night's storm had left a thick quilting on the grounds; today it was too cold to snow, and the Rose Garden was stiff and sparkling. The room had been refurbished in the early '80s. It had been a cheerful blue and white, and now was a more decorous beige. Tom Jefferson's portrait had been exchanged for busts of Washington and Franklin who offered no opinion from separate niches on opposite walls.

The pale window drapery was drawn back against the white roll of the garden, antique candelabra adorned walls and ceiling. Leather chairs still slipped back and forth against a velvety-blue oval carpet over polished wood.

It was with his back to the low fire, at the head of the table, that Larry Apple sat now, directing a penetrating gaze toward Henry Clay.

Clay projected the intensity of a storm barely contained as he slapped the afternoon *Washington Post* on the table. "Have you seen this—this distortion?" he said. " 'Occupied Alaska,' they're calling it. *Our* papers. Practically *boasting,* 'Occupied Alaska.' "

"Oh, come on, Henry—it's jargon—they've been using 'Occupied West Bank' for years," said Harry Smyth, reaching for a pack of cigarettes on the table in front of him.

"That's exactly what I mean," Clay snapped. "Do you have to smoke, Harry?"

Smyth grumbled something that no one could quite understand, but he returned the cigarette to its pack.

"Occupied West Bank, Gaza Strip, Golan Heights—and now Alaska," Clay continued. "With no basis in fact or law. If we allow expressions like 'occupied territory' to be bandied about by hacks whom eighty percent of America believes, what chance is there for intelligent understanding of any goddamn situation. It's just damned incendiary."

Larry Apple inclined his head toward Clay from the head of the table. Apple was a master of dead-pan, and Peter Jefferson was reminded of some talk-show host. "I think the word incendiary is less than appropriate, Henry."

George Heath turned toward Peter and winked. Apple could always be counted on to hold Henry Clay down. There was likely twenty years difference between them, but Apple was too sure of himself to suffer feelings of intimidation based on something as negligible as age. He seemed very personable, but actually gave nothing of himself to any conversation. Certainly there were records on Larry Apple's private life, but he was in the position to say 'who wants to know?' and not many people asked. He was young, forty-two probably, good looking in a blonde, all-American way; he wasn't married—or maybe he was, to the Agency, some of his colleagues said.

He gave Clay a boyish smile. "But your objections are certainly sound. I'd write a letter to the *Post* if I were you."

Clay actually liked this boy. Principled. Disciplined. He nodded his head.

Apple stood to pass around a file folder to each seated man. On his left an easel supported a map, three feet by five feet, that included the eastern coast of the Soviet Union as far south as Vladivostok; the Sea of Okhotsk; the Bering Strait; and Alaska to the Canadian border.

"Gentlemen," Apple said, "I'm circulating two reports for your information. One is a summary analysis of satellite reconnaisance photographs taken over the last ninety days."

He moved closer to the map. "Briefly, they show no significant Russian activity on Sakhalin—over here." He pointed to the slender island in the Sea of Okhotsk. "But over here in Petropávlovsk—" Apple pointed to a city in the southern tip of the Kamchatka Peninsula bordering on the Bering Strait, "our people have detected extensive barracks-type construction near the air base, as well as construction extending existing runways in Magadan—here. No effort has been made to camouflage this renovation."

Harry Smyth was reaching for a bulge in his vest pocket which proved to be a roll of peppermint Lifesavers. He offered the package to Admiral Smilie next to him, who looked disquieted, and declined. Smyth popped a candy into his mouth with a little smile.

Larry Apple was concluding his remarks, turning toward Smyth and Smilie. "We can see clearly that in Petropavlovsk, the barracks stand out with very high definition. Admiral, would you like to comment?"

Smilie leaned forward with a straight back, pointing at the two cities across the table from him. "Both Magadan and Petropavlovsk could be staging areas for an airborne assault against critical defense facilities in Alaska. . . ." He sat back and lifted one of Apple's summary folders off the table. "If I'm not mistaken, you've gone into those facilities in some detail here."

Apple nodded.

The Admiral placed the file squarely in front of him and directed the rest of his comments to its cover. "We know the Russians have troop transport aircraft with a range capable of making the round trip from either city to Anchorage. They would not, however, have fighter cover unless they brought carriers into the vicinity—I have a report that the Novorossiisk, their newest Kiev-class carrier, has just come back into port after a six month tour of the North Pacific. Although it's available, it's not moving. *Nothing* is happening."

He looked up. "With the exceptions of the renovations Mr. Apple described, there's no military movement on land or sea."

"Nothing *seems* to be happening," corrected Larry Apple, "but as I've enumerated, about a third of our early missile warning capacity is centered in Alaska. The state represents a vital strategic position for us. For that reason the President has called for a meeting of the Joint Chiefs this afternoon to report on armed forces readiness."

This news was received with no comment from those present. Apple turned to George Heath. "Mr. Secretary, do you have anything?"

Heath nodded at Apple, lifted a one page summary clipped to a sheaf of support material. "According to Article. . ." he paused, adjusted the page a few inches farther from him, shook his head, and continued, "In Article 62 of the Vienna Convention on the Law of Treaties, there is a provision that a 'fundamental change of circumstance' must have occurred since 1867 when the Alaska Purchase Treaty was signed, in order to nullify the treaty. But this 'fundamental change' can only be used to denounce the treaty if two factors can be demonstrated: one is that the abrogating party prove that the new circumstances negate the essential basis for consent of the treaty, and the other is that they prove that the new circumstances will radically transform those obligations still to be performed by the parties under the terms of the treaty."

Heath looked up from this document. "*Legally,* this abrogation is not a possibility. We've already submitted a request for a meeting with the United Nations Security Council, and I feel strongly they'll support us."

He laid his papers down in front of him, then said, "That's item one. Item two is a suggestion made by Mr. Jefferson yesterday, that we try looking at this situation from a different angle. I'd like you to give him your attention for a moment, and then perhaps we can get everyone's point of view."

Harry Smyth raised his hand. "For a different point of view, I'm going to move around the table over to the State Department over there; I'm going to crack a window, if that's convenient to all present, and have a smoke. You don't mind if I smoke while you speak, young man?"

"Not at all, Mr. Secretary," Jefferson smiled.

"That's good, Mr. Jefferson," Smyth rumbled.

George Heath laughed. Harry was being particularly convivial today, but Henry Clay looked less than amused. As Smyth settled himself in his new chair, Peter Jefferson looked around the table. He chose his words carefully, and spoke slowly.

"Mr. Apple's report on the construction and reconstruction of barracks and airlifts in Petropavlovsk and Magadan supports my growing conviction that this whole event is a mask for some other operation."

Jefferson raised a hand almost defensively. "But you see, that's the way they operate. Dead-end research is traditional. Its function is to turn our heads in a direction away from the object of their own attention—to keep us busy while they proceed without interference."

Puffing on his cigarette, Henry Smyth had a paternal glint in his eye as he listened to Jefferson. On his other side George Heath's head was tilted, considering. It was hard to tell if Clay was listening.

Peter continued. "This morning the Department of State received an emissary from Deputy Chairman Deng Xiaopeng. He wanted us to know his thinking—that the Russians might be trying to arrange a situation which would allow them to mobilize troops, ostensibly for use in Alaska, but which in truth, could be used for an attack on the People's Republic through Mongolia.

"Now, I'm not convinced that's the plan. Magadan and Petropavlovsk are both too far from the People's Republic for that to make sense. If they wanted to invade China, they'd most likely attack from bases in Vladivostok or Kholmsk. But the *point* is," he said firmly, "Deng's first thought was, 'this is a ruse.' "

Peter looked up and across the table. For a moment he was startled by the brightness of the men facing him. Admiral Smilie, Henry Clay and Larry Apple were bathed in the cold pale reflection of the Rose Garden behind him. The Admiral's eyes, especially, seemed icy. Peter wondered if he was a silhouette to them.

Henry Clay, sharp in the light, sighed. "You may be right, Jefferson. It's that very thing that irritates me so. They insist on dealing with *serious* international relationships like so many nasty children playing children's games."

Peter had his mouth open to disagree when George Heath leaned forward next to him. "It's interesting you should use that analogy, Henry. But these aren't children, by any means. They're sly, powerful, and intelligent men, not to be taken lightly. But the *game*—that *is* interesting. They do play games. . . ."

Admiral Smilie addressed Peter Jefferson: "Still, you understand that we have to prepare to defend ourselves—not only against this threat, if it is real, but also against this kind of extortionist politics. . . ."

"I do understand. But while we're doing that, I'd like to figure out what Kolkin is trying to keep us from seeing while he asks us to look at Alaska and their eastern seaboard," Jefferson said, pointing at the map they had referred to earlier. "I'd like each of you to assume with me that this is a deception, and to entertain any suspicions you may have in other areas."

He was speaking a little more quickly now, not wanting to lose their attention. "For instance, what keeps suggesting itself to me is the Middle East. . . ."

Jefferson paused for a moment, then said, "I have no real foundation—just a feeling—but a scan of our Soviet files shows a lot of probing over there the past couple of years. . . ."

"Mr. Jefferson," Clay interjected, "the Soviets are interested in anything that. . . ."

"Well, of *course,* Henry," Larry Apple said, annoyed. "But this is a valid point, and the Mideast is certainly worthy of consideration." A slight smile, more in his eyes than on his lips, flickered. "The whole area is a tinder box right now. Incendiary, you might say."

Henry Clay shifted in his seat. Heath smiled openly across the table at Admiral Smilie, while Smyth lit another cigarette.

Apple did not pause. "We've every evidence that the coup that drove King Hussein out of Amman last year was engineered by the Kremlin through Syria; Mubarak has renewed civilities with the Soviets. . . ."

"Civilities, but no more, Mr. Apple," Harry Smyth corrected. "The man is an upholder of the peace—perhaps the only one in all the Mid East. . . ."

"No question, Harry," Apple hastened. "I'm just pointing out that things are changing rapidly over there: Arafat has said 'a plague on *all* your houses'—the PLO is by no means dead even though he is, at least politically; the Sinai is back to Egypt; the Saudis have refused us bases for Rapid Deployment . . . We could go on all day."

"There are other serious areas as well, of course—" George Heath added, "the Caribbean, Central America . . ."

"What I'd like to suggest," Jefferson spoke up, "is that we all try thinking in terms of Alaska as a diversion. And if anyone has any brainstorms, that you get back to me."

"That's fair, Mr. Jefferson. I think we're agreed." Apple looked around the table, and then down at his watch. "Is there any other business?" He looked up again, nodded, and said, "Then this meeting is adjourned. Mr. Jefferson . . ."

Peter raised his head.

"Thank you for joining us."

CHAPTER NINE

Washington, March 13

Grace Sherwood signalled with a frantic wave as Jefferson approached his office. She was on the phone, and he could see that there were three other calls waiting.

"Am I glad to see *you*," she said when she had taken everyone's name and number. "The phones have been crazy—and there are reporters and TV cameras lurking around all the entrances to the building—you can't even go out—they just fly at *any*body going out or in. We'll have to sneak out through the garage—it's scary."

Grace was really upset. "When you explained what was going on, I knew I could expect phone calls." She held up a handfull of pink slips. "But, Mr. Jefferson," her voice lowered, "people are saying really *frightening* things. . . . Do you think there's going to be a war?" This last was almost whispered.

"Look, why don't you ask the switchboard to pick up the calls and come in and sit down for a minute. We can talk about it. There's *not* going to be a war."

Grace looked at him seriously for a moment and nodded.

There was *not* going to be a war.

She called the switchboard, and followed Peter Jefferson into his office.

* * * * *

Grace had gone home, through the garage, at quarter till five. About an hour later Peter Jefferson leaned back in his chair. His back felt stiff. The walk home would do him good.

He left the building from the Diplomat's entrance on C Street, the same entrance that had offended the Russian Ambassador yesterday. It was cold and quite dark, and he didn't see any reporters. He put his collar up and shoved both hands deep in his pockets, turning south on 23rd Street. He thought he would build a fire when he got home.

Jefferson had moved to the Watergate during the year of his divorce. When he and Miriam separated she had gone back to live with her parents. Peter found their condominium apartment on Upper Connecticut Avenue lonely and uncomfortable. It had become a setting for her, no longer a home. He had moved to as anonymous an apartment building as he could find, and spent a year there as a resident. The place had hardly been a refuge, but the same year he was assigned to the Embassy in Rome. That move had brought him back to life.

For one thing, it returned him to a home he had known as a child. Jefferson's maternal family was Italian, his father's were third generation New Englanders, and Peter often felt himself torn between a searing romanticism and a damnable reserve.

Italy represented all that resounded in him and that was so difficult to express. They had moved to a small town outside Naples after the war to help his mother's family rebuild their home. Peter was an only child, but his mother's brother had four young boys and three daughters, all bright and funny and best of all, *family*.

They stayed five years, till Peter was ten, and by then he had learned about love and community and sharing. He had loved those years. Loved the green hills that rolled up and away from twisted cobbled streets, loved the colored banners that fluttered from balconies in town, but mostly he loved his family—all twelve of them—Mother and Dad, Aunt Sunny for Sonia, and Uncle Lino, Maria, Stefano, Giorgio, Peaches, Berto, Nina and Bo. And himself, of course, twelve.

When just the three of them moved back to Pennsylvania—and it was lovely there too, they lived out of Philadelphia, there were forests and long leaps of meadows and a big house *with his own room*—Peter felt as if he had left part of himself someplace else.

He found it on that visit, thirty years later. And then at the end of his tenure in Rome he returned to the sterile rooms he rented in Washington and thought they could have belonged to anybody but they didn't belong to him. He found what felt right at the Watergate Apartments, a spacious place for himself less than a mile from the blocky State Department Building across West Potomac Park. He had been back in Washington for nine months and the Watergate had become home.

Following the circular drive around the Lincoln Memorial, away from the glowing capitol dome, Jefferson cut under the Parkway Drive overpass and into the Watergate's sprawling outer entrance.

Inside the marble lobby he nodded to a party of three fashionably dressed middle aged couples on their way out for the evening. He recognized an ex-Ambassador to some remote country, couldn't remember his name or the country's, and a senior judge of the United States Court of Appeals. An empty elevator delivered him to the twenty-first floor.

Peter's apartment occupied a portion of two floors; one entered into a large living room with brick fireplace, white walls and a huge window looking west over the Potomac. A long grey sofa faced two low-slung easy chairs with a glass and chrome table between them, and the view of the river. Peter had installed a track of small hooded spotlights above one wall on the ceiling, each separate light directed toward a separate area of the room so that shafts of light fell at soft angles over the shoulder of a chair, a pale woven throw rug on the dark wood floor, a round Turkish ottoman, the potted ficus in the corner. A huge print of Chagall's "The Blue Circus" hung framed in glass behind the couch like a surprise.

What had sold him on this apartment was the semicircular staircase that wound up from the living room to two good sized bedrooms, one of which Peter used as a study. Intended to use as a study. Weeks ago he had installed a wall-sized book case which now yawned out on piles and files of folders overflowing the easy chair, a low table rounded with magazines that spilled onto the floor, the floor stumped with books in stacks of varying heights. This room also had a fireplace, and Peter's favorite piece of furniture, a large rolltop desk that had been his great-grandfather's a hundred years ago, and was today shut firmly, almost accusingly, against the confusion.

He turned a knob on a panel of light dials near the door, hung his coat in the downstairs closet and crossed over to the fireplace, blowing into cupped hands. He started a fire, and then went into the kitchen to fix himself a scotch.

It was approaching 7:00, and Peter realized he was hungry. He checked the refrigerator: not much there—a head of lettuce, a couple of tomatoes in the vegetable bin; but there were two smallish steaks in the freezer, and pretty fresh bread. Peter pulled the steaks out and went directly to the telephone. He punched Stu Boyington's number, and was unwrapping one of the steaks, balancing the phone on his shoulder, when Stu answered.

" 'Lo."

"Is that your state of mind, or a salutation?"

"Hey, Pete, I'm glad you called. How's it going?"

"Good, Stu, pretty good. How was your game this morning?"

"Oh, man, awful. I ended up playing with Marv Gold. He's an angry man, Marvin Gold. Never let an angry man onto a racquet ball court."

Peter laughed. "Marv Gold? An angry man? Are we talking about the same Marv Gold—the Gentle Philosopher?—*that* Marv Gold?"

"A diabolical disguise, Pete."

"I take it you lost."

"That would be a kind way of putting it."

"Is Di still gone?" Peter asked.

"Yeah, I just spoke to her. She's having a great time. Do you know it's sixty degrees today in San Francisco?"

He didn't know.

"She'll be back tomorrow, late afternoon. Ten days—I've really missed her."

"Have you eaten?"

"You mean since she's been gone—or tonight?" Stu laughed.

"I've got two steaks over here that won't take long to defrost—and I could use the company. . . ."

"Really? Thing's pretty slow over at State?"

Peter chuckled. "Not exactly."

"Sure, I'd love to come over. *I* could definitely use the company—not to mention the fact that I haven't had anything to eat since Di left."

"No wonder Marv whipped you—you've probably lost your strength. I'll see you soon?"

"Twenty minutes."

Peter hung up smiling, put the two steaks on a plate to thaw, picked up his drink and went upstairs to exchange his dark blue jacket for a soft pullover sweater.

In the white tile bathroom off the larger bedroom, he removed his glasses and splashed his face with cool water. Behind his eyes, the image of Peggy startled him. He leaned forward toward the mirror. He wondered what Peggy saw when she looked at him. It wasn't a bad face, certainly—perhaps a bit too angular. His eyes, he thought privately, were his best feature.

It seemed incredible to him to have run into her like that. Four years later—and she hadn't changed at all. If anything, she was more beautiful. Four years. Suddenly Peter stood up straight. Four years. She had to be married. Surely she had not remained single all this time—not someone like her. She'd probably kept her last name—a lot of women did that, especially professional women.

Peter felt as if the air had been knocked out of him. He walked back into his bedroom, finished the scotch in his glass, and decided to call her. Sitting down on his bed he reached for the city phone book on the bottom shelf of a bedside table, flipped to the "M"s and saw two listings for "P. Montague," one with an address on N.W. O Street, and one on Carroll Street. He dialed the first number.

"Hello?" she said.

"Peggy? This is Peter."

"Hi, Peter."

Pause. This was not going to be easy. "Am I interrupting?"

"No, not at all."

Another pause. "It really knocked me out to run into. . . ." he started, at the same moment she said, "I wondered if you'd call. . ." and they both laughed.

Peter relaxed just slightly. "You first."

"I said I wondered if you'd call. . . . I hoped you would."

He felt himself flush and was grateful she couldn't see him. "Can we have dinner together, Peg? Tomorrow?"

"I can't tomorrow. But Saturday I'm free—and I'd love to."

"Saturday—Saturday is fine. Shall I pick you up around 7:00?"

"Yes—you know where I live?"

Peter looked at the address in the book. "On O Street—where the Czarist Embassy used to be?"

"That's it—I'm right across the street. I look forward to it, Peter."

She wasn't married.

Of course, accepting a simple invitation to dinner didn't have anything to do with being married or not being married. They were friends—had been—even if one of them was otherwise committed now. Besides, what did it matter if she was married? It *was* only dinner. She had said she was looking forward to it, though, and that she had hoped he would call.

Peter shook his head. He picked up his empty glass and was coming back downstairs when the phone rang. He took it in the kitchen, told the doorman to send Stu up, then refilled his own glass and poured one for his friend.

Stu Boyington was a few years older than Peter. They had met years ago at a party neither of them could remember now, and had developed a quick, close friendship. Stu worked in an obscure agency of the Defense Department called the Office of Net Assessment. Peter recalled clearly searching for an explanation of the term Net Assessment in an old copy of the Joint Chief's *Dictionary of Military and Associated Terms,* with no success.

Stu had laughed. "Pete, if I tried to explain what Net Assessment was all about, I'd sound too much like a professor at the War College." He had grinned. "And I don't want to ruin my reputation."

He had commented that the newer dictionary probably did have a description of the Office, but as for a *definition*—that would be difficult since his job dealt intimately with the undefinable.

As their friendship grew into occasional shared evenings, Jefferson learned more about Stu's work. Net Assessment was, he concluded, a military analysis to determine which side in a competition between the United States and the Soviet Union, alone or with partners, would come out the winner. This calculation required data collection, confirmation of data combining the strengths and weaknesses of each side in areas like aircraft performance and defense suppression measures, fire support procedures, communications, and a bewildering array of other weapons systems, as well as consideration of the experience of personnel operating and maintaining those systems. All this so that opposing capabilities could be compared within various invented military scenarios.

The bottom line was sum total power and a possible "outcome" for either side in a projected conflict. Boyington candidly conceded that the whole process, based on a geometric progression of what-ifs, was imprecise. A net assessment was, Boyington had said, really a way of identifying security problems and opportunities, not an end in itself. There were too many variables for that sort of crystal ball gazing.

Despite the weightiness of his job, Boyington was naturally a good humored fellow. He was a burly man with thinning reddish hair and a healthy complexion. Tonight he was particularly ruddy.

"Man, it's bitter out there. You got a fire started? Oh, great."

Boyington dropped his coat over a chair as he angled toward the fireplace. He stood with his back to it, hands clasped behind him, looking around the room. "Place looks real nice, Pete," he said, accepting the scotch and soda. "How are things going with the study?"

Peter looked at his friend. "Let's talk about something else."

"Right."

He was on his way back to the kitchen when he tossed over his shoulder, "Say, do you know Peggy Montague over at Defense?"

Stu was looking at one of Peter's stereo speakers. "You got some kind of a buzz in this speaker, Pete."

"I was going to ask you to take a look at it. . . ." Shouted from the kitchen over the louder volume of a local jazz station.

Later, while they were eating, still in the livingroom, Stu said, totally out of context, "Peggy Montague—you mean that dynamite blonde?"

Peter looked up. Nodded.

"I thought she was with the CIA."

"National Security Agency."

"No kidding?" Stu shook his head, then picked up his napkin and wiped his mouth. "I heard she goes out with the Director."

Peter stared at his friend, remembering in a flash Newman's hand on her arm as they left Van Vleck's office. "Jerry Newman?" he said, hardly concealing his shock.

Boyington sat back looking confused. "Who's Jerry Newman?" he said. "I mean Larry Apple."

Peter stopped eating entirely. He picked up the flat remains of his drink.

"You, uh, know her?" Stu said, obviously curious.

"I met her in Europe, a few years ago—briefly—I just ran into her again."

"Mmm." There was a long pause.

Peter got up, still holding the unfinished drink. "How about a brandy—or a whiskey and coffee?"

"Good. I think I can fix that speaker."

Stu stayed for another hour, on the floor in front of Peter's stereo, sipping noisily from a mug of coffee laced generously with Irish whiskey. And they talked.

Boyington was concentrating on the back of Peter's tuner. "I just finished an analysis of our defense in the Western Pacific, and even with our Europe-first policy, I think we're okay."

He examined the two speaker jacks. "We've got a security treaty with Japan, although they aren't obliged to come to our aid; but we do have a Marine Air wing at Iwakuni, Japan, and just last year we added two more squadrons."

He evidently approved the terminal connection. "In addition," he picked up a Phillips-head screwdriver and addressed the offending speaker, "we've got a few B-1s and B-52s out of Guam. CINPAC wouldn't really help in the case of Alaska, of course, but there's cover out of Misawa. In a crunch we could move the Marine wing from Iwakuni to Misawa where Vladivostok would be within better range. . . ."

"How about the Soviet position in that area?" Peter was sitting forward in one of the low chairs, both hands cupped arond the steaming mug. "Could they launch an airborne assault against Alaska?"

"They could," Stu nodded. "But the loss of troop carrier aircraft would be very heavy. First there's the Alaska Air Defense Command. Second," he lifted the back off the speaker, "the Russians have some real limitations on movement of surface vessels in the Sea of Japan and the Sea of Okhotsk. They have the carrier Minsk, at least three cruisers and several frigates—look at this. . . ."

Peter got up.

"This wire's loose."

Peter took Stu's mug to refill it, while his friend continued as if there had been no interruption.

"But we could probably blockade most of the Soviet Pacific Fleet's access to the northern Pacific, and even if it got through the blockade, a long deployment to provide air cover for an Alaskan invasion is a high risk situation."

He leaned back against the couch. "No replacement aircraft would be available because there's no real logistic support except from Vladivostok, and that's too far. Petropavlovsk is a possibility, but again, the range for replacement aircraft is too great."

"Submarines, though. . . ." Peter began.

"Ah, yes," Stu said. "Close to half of all Russia's submarines are in the Pacific. Most, if not all of them carry nuclear missiles."

He started to replace the back of the speaker. "But they wouldn't be of much use in an airborne assault. In a situation like this, troop carriers simply have to have air cover, and only a carrier task force can provide that.

"They do have plenty of troops—the last time I looked they had two divisions in Sakhalin and one in Petropavlovsk and there's one airborne division in Khabarovsk. But almost all Soviet ground troops there are for use against any attack by the People's Republic. It wouldn't be easy to move those divisions around for an assault on Alaska."

Stu stood and lifted the speaker back to its corner, then sat down opposite Peter. "And I think you can forget any serious possibility of an amphibious attack. All the landing ships they have out there could barely carry five regiments. Hit and run strikes, maybe, but I just don't see a serious Alaska invasion threat, unless they want to go nuclear with a preemptive first strike. Their intermediate range ballistic missiles are mobile, though I suppose they could be moved to the Far East Military District and within range of Alaskan targets. But even there, they know we'd pick up that sort of redeployment with photo reconnaissance satellites."

"So what do you think, Stu?" Jefferson said, leaning back in his chair.

"I think this Alaska caper is strictly for the birds."

CHAPTER TEN

Washington, March 15

Every weekday morning there is a ritual observed by almost all of the hundreds of working men and women leaving the Watergate Apartments. They form a moving line that winds out of twelve elevators, slips by one of six too-small newstands, hesitates, then loops out any of a dozen rovolving doors down forty semicircular granite steps, toward the center of Washington and all its domes and towers and geometric malls. The tide is normally subdued, more so toward the beginning of the week. This Friday Peter Jefferson could distinguish a definite murmur.

He picked up a *Washington Post* and glanced across the front page. The banner was, "Alaskans Outraged by Soviet Abrogation." While he waited in a line of people similarly occupied, he unfolded the paper and saw a four column-inch map of the area Larry Apple had referred to yesterday, including the coast of Russia to the Canadian border, with arrows and flight patterns traced over it, and a rather lengthy caption.

Jefferson refolded the paper, came up with the correct change and followed the stream into a cloudless sunny day. Looking up at the sad, familiar shape of Lincoln as he rounded the monument, he thought he could feel something of Spring in the air. Snow still covered the wide lawns he passed, but it looked brittle today, deflated. The morning was cold but forgiving and Peter thought that by afternoon it would be warmer.

His office on the seventh floor was at the end of a stark too-bright corridor that halted abruptly at a square of carpet marking Grace's office. This carpet, the same natty brown as Jefferson's, was a considerable status symbol, and almost made up for the fact that Grace sat at a dead-end job—physically anyway—which, she had once remarked to a friend, would very likely, after some time, take some sort of psychic toll, and possibly, ultimately, affect her work.

She had not yet brought this matter to Jefferson's attention. She would wait till he was more comfortable in his own position before she mentioned hers. She had served in the State Department during the last administration, and had a certain amount of finesse in dealing with new bosses. "Besides," she had told her friend, "I think he might just be the kind of man who would notice something like that."

He didn't notice yet, evidently, because he gave her a smile and said only good morning and something like how's it going?— referring, she thought, to yesterday's mild hysteria.

She admitted it was going much better this morning, and offered to bring him a cup of coffee.

* * * * *

In their second or third meeting, George Heath had told Jefferson to consider his job that of an understudy. Not only should he be prepared to stand in for the Secretary, fulfilling obligations to various foreign and domestic ambassadors and other dignitaries, he also often would have to provide an opening act. He was a student under Heath too, in the art of consultation, foreign diplomacy and foreign affairs. In this latter effort Heath encouraged Jefferson to look at their work as a game in which it behooves a political player to process and fit together information quickly and accurately, to form a true representation of a whole international picture.

"We all play with our own concept of what the picture is," Heath had said, "and the better players are sensitive to how others affect the board and thereby change the picture. It becomes part of the way you see things; it alters your perceptions, changes your life really, that sensitivity."

It was true to a certain degree for Peter, who found himself listening for news and making mental calculations, trying to anticipate a next move. As he read the newspaper, for example, he tried thinking of each separate story, at least internationally, as a composite in a larger story. This, he realized, was dangerous. He agreed with Clay that the media offered an often distorted, if not downright inaccurate view of what was going on.

The paper was flat open on his desk to the second page. Peter sat slightly forward in his chair, left elbow on the edge of his desk, his hand supporting his chin. He read, "IRANIAN OIL PRODUC-TION AT 4.5 MILLION BARRELS PER DAY: Teheran demands OPEC cut Saudi Production." His eye slid over the article, stopped at the observation, "While the spot market price of oil hovers near $28 per barrel and Saudi revenue declines, there is little doubt that tensions within OPEC are mounting."

Jefferson sat back and took up his cup. At the bottom of page three the new President of Iraq formally approved an agreement for his country's reparation to Iran—the details were not disclosed in this article.

The five year war between Iran and Iraq had ended abruptly after Saddam Hussein's sudden and mysterious resignation. The cease fire agreement had been worked out with Soviet assistance, and not too long ago Moscow had openly agreed to replace all military equipment both Iran and Iraq had lost. As a gesture of their good will, Iraq was exchanging oil revenue for additional Soviet tanks. This was good, because the Soviets required considerable revenue to balance the cost of replacing all of Syria's aircraft lost in their fumbled efforts over Lebanon in 1982 even though Saudi Arabia had paid most of the cost of rearming Syria in 1983.

Jefferson thought it was funny the papers didn't disclose the amount Iraq had agreed to pay. He took another sip of coffee and without raising his eyes replaced the cup to a spot above and to the right of the paper. Then he turned the page. He scanned pages four and five. Unemployment was down slightly on page five, another nuclear plant shutting down on seven.

Grace walked in with fresh coffee. Personally, she disapproved of coffee. At least he didn't use sugar. She set the cup down. "Mr. Heath's secretary called to say he'd be in meetings today, and would you save 10:00 Monday for him to go over this week's reports."

She was referring to intelligence deemed necessary for the State Department by the CIA. These very secret files were deliv-ered daily by a young thuggy-looking messenger with bad skin, a secure briefcase, brown suit and several less obvious provisions required in his job. Grace was simply aghast the first day he showed up.

Jefferson was responsible for extracting the heart from these sometimes copious files. In the process he learned the whole body.

Knowing Heath would consider each piece of data an addition to his expanding, changing picture of the world, he prepared his reports as a series of bulletins, thinking his little boxed explanations worked as either jig-saw puzzle pieces or gamesmen. He emphasized powers or locations to facilitate positioning. He had been pleased with himself when the idea came to him.

Last week's summary had been submitted, in part, as follows:

Syrian military presence
in *Bekaa Valley* still seen
as growing threat
to *Lebanese* stability

PLO seen as less of a
threat without Arafat
Egypt wavering on Camp
David negotiations

United Nations:
Soviets support *Jordan's*
argument: self-determination
for Palestinian Arabs of
West Bank and Gaza
Moscow promises economic and
military aid program

Gulf Oil revenue declining
as major buyers move to
Rotterdam spot market below
Saudi market.
Iran increases production
over OPEC fixed levels.
Gulf Oil States not amused.

Long range *Soviet* objectives
in *Turkey* to weaken NATO:
Plan to destabilize military
government and reunite
Turkish Armenia with USSR

Kurdish leader
(anti-communits/Moslems)
proclaims free republic.
Khomeini threatens retaliation

"Don't I have something with what's his name from St. Thomas Monday?"

Grace walked around behind Peter's desk to adjust the blinds. "He cancelled. He has to have a root canal on Monday."

Peter winced. He wished she would spare him the details.

After she had left and he had readjusted the blinds, he closed his paper and walked over to a small safe tucked in the bookcase. Removing a rosy accordian file, he automatically assessed its weight. Not too bad today.

Cables were categorized geographically. Peter removed the Mideast from its envelope, and sat down, loosening his tie. The first transmission originated out of Jiddah and consisted of a complete bound-copy of what was described in the attached summary as a slick-paper book, or scandal sheet, assumed to be of Soviet manufacture. Circulated discreetly throughout Saudi Arabia and other Gulf states, the book claimed no publisher (Intelligence had placed its origins in Moscow), and it had generated shock waves possibly fatal to the House of Saud.

The Agency also had provided background to account for the damaging effect of this purloined text in a twenty page treatise indexed for Opposition Ideology, Economic Indices, Corruption, Repression, Precipitating Events (with an asterisk and "see attached publication"), Super Power Policies and Conduct, and Origin of House of Saud. "Corruption" had been underlined: the Royal Family in Saudi Arabia relied on piety for legitimacy— Islamic piety, which does not tolerate transgression.

Last month, Peter remembered, one of the Saudi princes had had his hands slapped for selling royalty oil on the spot market above OPEC prices, and just about the time the King had recovered from that embarrassment it was discovered the young prince had received a ten percent kickback from the buyer. Now with this book widespread enough to have ended up in Agency hands, the CIA considered the Royal Family in serious trouble.

Jefferson turned to the bound copy, page after page recounting violations by the Royal Family: repression of opposition, disappearances of well known leaders without explanation, economic extravagances. . . . He made a note:

Saudi Royal Family
could be out soon,
result of (presumed)
Soviet propaganda,

and moved the intelligence into an empty two-tiered basket on his desk.

The next report boiled down to:

Arms smuggling rampant
in *South Yemen*

Peter reached for the next cable, from Riyadh, a thick text describing a high-level maximum security conference of Gulf oil producing states, including Bahrain, Iraq, Kuwait, Oman, Qatar, Saudi Arabia, and the United Arab Emirates. He sat up straighter, adjusted his glasses.

He should have seen it before. A Gulf Oil Authority. According to the report, the suggestion was Saudi Arabia's—trying to ingratiate themselves back to favor, Jefferson thought.

By pooling the oil of its member states, the Authority could manipulate daily production levels and prices to consuming states, and effectively undersell Iran. In a very short time a Gulf Oil Authority could probably set Iran back five years economically.

It was tempting, especially to Saudi Arabia, whose own shaky position was threatened further by Tehran's demand that OPEC require a Saudi oil cutback.

The Authority would be consistent with Islamic jurisprudence: Islamic law provides that a contract may not be cancelled except by mutual consent of all parties. Their coalition would be cemented in permanence, and their lessees would be similarly bound—a contract for the sale of oil or the lease of existing facilities to produce and sell to a consumer state would override threats, or embargo.

Jefferson leaned back in his chair with the text still in his hand. The implications of such a union were staggering on many levels. Its effect on oil companies was of least concern to him. He turned in his chair to face the window. The sky was blue and tufted with tight little cumuli. His eyes dropped back down to the cable and he read it again.

CHAPTER ELEVEN

Washington, March 15

At the few decent places to eat in Washington, the best maitres d'hotel have developed a style beyond senatorial. They maintain their own portfolios of who's who, complete with photographs and sometimes very personal intelligence. In his own territory the maitre d' enjoys power equivalent to that of any of his clientele. These notables are his constituents, and he has laid out the restaurant in subtle precincts to accommodate them by rank.

Peter Jefferson and Peggy Montague were waiting for their table in Lion D'Or's amber-lit bar. She had asked for a dust dry martini; he found that a lovely description; she had been flattered, then flustered. The amber light made her hair seem like dusty gold.

He had dressed carefully in a soft grey Ralph Laurens suit, had spent a couple of minutes, at least, considering the cage of ties that hung inside his closet door, and had settled on a dark silk paisley. Frowning, with his chin raised and his eyes aimed at the mirror, he fumbled with the knot until he thought he had it right. He stepped back, tilted his head at himself, then moved in to the mirror again and loosened the knot a bit.

Peter hadn't known how he felt about this evening anymore, having spent the whole day anticipating it. He had gotten up early to take his car out to be washed and waxed till it glowed like a pearl. He joined Stu Boyington and Diane for lunch, spent an hour with Stu afterward asking questions about an idea that was forming—and it was really only then, while they were talking, that images of this evening didn't interrupt Peter's thoughts.

The thing about Larry Apple and Peggy. He really couldn't see competing with the Director of the CIA for the affections of a woman.

Of course, he realized she might not be involved with Apple at all—it was a rumor—and anyway what difference did it make—and why was it making him feel angry? Because he did feel angry. And although it was irrational, and unjustified, he felt angry with Peggy.

He had softened considerably at the sight of her. She came to the door in a fitted white wool dress—angora, he thought, perfectly simple and sophisticated. She wore gold earrings and no other jewelry. Her smile had been genuine.

Besides, he had directed himself not to make judgments. He was merely dining out tonight with someone he used to know. It need be nothing more than interesting. It needn't even be that.

Peggy put her hand on his arm. Leaning toward him, she said, "Isn't that someone we should know?" She inclined her head toward a tallish fair-haired man in rimless glasses exchanging pleasantries with the beaming maitre d'.

"Robert McNamara. He used to be President of the World Bank."

There was no wait for Mr. McNamara, and when the maitre d' had made that gentleman comfortable, he returned to Peter Jefferson.

They were escorted to a rather inconspicuous alcove near the entrance to the large warm dining room, guarded by an oil of a benign King of the Jungle. The room was panelled in dark oak, small gilt-framed paintings hung between tables. They ordered one more martini and tried to decide what status their seating assignment might signify. Their corner allowed them a view of most of the rom, but they themselves were fairly hidden.

"I'm going to consider it a compliment. 'Far from the Madding Crowd.'"

Peggy tilted her head to one side. "You sound like George Heath."

"How do you mean?"

"Sometimes he uses a quotation that seems appropriate to a situation. Surely you've noticed it." She smiled at him.

He looked at her seriously. "You're right. I wonder if I do that a lot. No, probably not—I'm not nearly as well read." He considered it a moment. "I hadn't realized."

She reached her hand across the table. "It wasn't a criticism, Peter."

He nodded and smiled at her, returned the pressure of her touch.

They decided on lobster a la Bordelaise and a Marquis de la Guiche 1979.

When their waiter had gone, Peter touched his glass to hers. "What happened after Rome?"

They had met at a ball at the Embassy during Jefferson's first year there. Peggy was attending an international conference for military scientists, and the gala was in their honor. Afterward, that weekend was a dream, or a fairy tale. She had been an apparition in white and gold, they had danced until dawn that night; and the next and the next, and then she had disappeared, back to the States. He had memories as perfect as a glass slipper.

She smiled. "After Rome I turned into a pumpkin."

He looked at her. "You can still do that."

"What?"

"Read minds."

She laughed. "As a matter of fact, that's part of what's been happening since Rome."

"Reading minds?"

"Well, not exactly. I've been doing some work in the area of parapsychology."

He lifted his glass. "That's right. I remember you talked about that. Remote viewing—wasn't that it?"

She nodded. "Mmm hmm."

"Is that with the," he hesitated just a fraction, then said, "Agency?"

She smiled and nodded again.

"So you're doing work for National Security *and* the Agency?"

"And an occasional little something for Defense."

"What do you do in your spare time?"

She laughed.

"No, really," Peter leaned forward. "How do you handle three jobs at once?"

She answered immediately, "I think of my work as one job."

He sat back, looked at her quizzically.

"All three fit together rather nicely." She had laced her fingers, now she let both hands fall apart. "The military and the CIA have both been doing research in parapsychology—remote viewing and psychokinesis, especially—for twenty-five years." She lowered her hands. "You can see the implications for state of the art espionage when you understand the subject, and then it becomes a strange kind of 'signals intelligence' itself."

Peggy shrugged slightly. "My work at Langley, right now at any rate, is just trying to establish a ratio of success."

"And you actually travel—mentally—to another place?"
She nodded yes.

"Is there any danger that a person might not come back?"

"I know just what you're thinking of," she said, and laughed.

"What?" he challenged, smiling at her.

"That Vincent Price movie, *The Fly*."

"How do you *do* that?" he said.

She shook her head, and he held up a hand. "No, never mind. I'm not sure I want to know how far that talent goes. Tell me what it feels like when you do come out of it."

She looked at him with serious eyes and an almost shy smile on her face. "It feels like being wildly in love," she said.

There was a pause like a heart-beat, and then with an awful clatter, an ebullient waiter appeared to set up a serving table and ice bucket. The man performed an extraordinary choreography over the wine, and served the plates like pallets pink and red with lobster, steamy with rice, and festooned with parsley.

The wine was perfect. The food was delicious. The conversation remained comfortably impersonal. They ordered raspberry soufflé with framboise for dessert, and agreed it was possibly the most delicious confection either of them had tasted.

While he waited for her to return from the lounge, and took care of the check which the waiter had presented like a valentine, Peter thought that all in all it had been a pleasant evening.

* * * * *

Peggy was staring at herself in the gilt-framed mirror in the ladies lounge. As far as she was concerned, the evening was a disaster.

It was because she had expected more—she had spent all day practically jangling with anticipation. There had been work to do, and she hadn't been able to concentrate. She had left a document entitled, "Statement of General Robert Hughes, Commander, United States Army Training and Doctrine Command to the U.S. Senate Subcommittee on Tactical Warfare, Committee on Armed Services" which began after a salutation, with the titillating statement, "I appreciate this opportunity to discuss the M2 Abrams Tank," to try on the new white dress.

She had turned in front of her mirror, looking back over her shoulder. She wasn't sure if it wasn't too obvious. It was a very sexy dress, she thought, but it was also an innocent white, and soft as smoke. She had sat down on her bed, then lay back. Her right arm rested over her eyes.

She had fallen in love with Peter Jefferson. Wildly in love, to be precise, for about sixty hours four years ago. That wasn't quite accurate—the feeling had lasted until she realized she wasn't going to hear from him; and still it persisted, like a lump in her throat. She didn't understand, never understood. After a long time, she put it away with other inexplicable phenomena.

But seeing him had brought it all back. Peter was a part of her life that needed resolution.

Peggy leaned toward the mirror to apply a light lipstick, she brushed her hair back with her fingers, left a dollar for the uniformed matron who sat bored in a padded straight back chair, and returned to their table.

Peter rose as she approached, helped her into her coat, and they left through the plush lobby into a clear cold night. He took her arm as they crossed the street and kept it while they walked the short distance to his Porsche.

"Feel like stopping for a drink someplace else?" he said, not looking at her, bending to open the low door.

"Why don't we go back to my place? I have some very fancy port."

He was clearly surprised.

Her house looked like an English 19th century dollhouse from the outside, pinched between two slightly larger townhouses. Immediately inside an intricately carved door they stepped down two steps to a rosy vestibule under a cut glass chandelier and into an elegant little livingroom. The walls were panelled in a dark grained wood; an unexpected pink sofa with rolled arms faced the small fireplace, along with matching chairs and twin glass tables.

There was a tall old corner cabinet of polished wood and glass lit from inside and containing a collection of cloisonne bud vases, bottles and boxes. And there was a flurry of wild baby's breath in a tall rose-colored vase on the bar. The south wall of the room opened through french doors to a small back yard with a swimming pool tiny enough to be funny, a sentry of cherry trees, and one dogwood pressed close to the house.

As she poured the rare, forty year old Sandeman and settled into a corner of the couch near Peter's chair, she said, "I've done all the talking tonight, you know."

Peter grinned at her. "Something I picked up at the State Department."

She nodded, smiling. "How are you liking the work?"

"Very much."

"And you like working with George Heath?" she asked, lifting her glass by its narrow stem.

His eyes definitely brightened. "He's great. Do you know him very well?"

"No, not really. I've been at two or three parties with the Heaths. At one deadly boring reception at somebody's home—I don't even remember whose—we both had sort of wandered off and quite independently found ourselves in this astounding library."

"Sounds like a scene from *Gone with the Wind*."

"Exactly." She smiled and leaned over the arm of the couch to place her glass on the table she was sharing with Peter. "The really extraordinary thing about this room, though, was a deeply bowed stained glass window, about eight feet tall. It looked like one of those glass elevators that ride the outside of buildings, or a slice of church."

She shook her head. "It was beautiful."

Peter was feeling very good. He was perfectly content to sit here just looking at this stunning woman and listening to her talk and sipping a liquid that tasted like mead.

Peggy smiled at him. "And set inside the semi-circle of this window was a chess table and two chairs."

"You're kidding," he said. "You've played chess with Heath?"

Peggy laughed. "I certainly have." She reached for her glass again. "I had no idea of his reputation. In fact, I thought I was a pretty good player." She tasted her wine, then said, still smiling, "It was a humbling experience—though I must say, he was a most gracious winner."

His glass was empty and he poured another slim amber inch of it. "I imagine he has a lot of practice."

She nodded. "Do you play?"

He looked up. "No—not since high school. But in Heath's department we use the kind of thinking you need to play—I've been thinking of relearning the game."

"What kind of thinking do you mean?" She held her glass out for him to refill, and he answered as he poured.

"We look at international events as moves on a board. I'm always thinking, if this country moves there, and then this other power moves here, then what should the next appropriate move be—or how is that move going to influence another player's choice, and how will it affect a fourth player down the road."

He replaced the bottle on a slip of a coaster, handed her the glass, and continued talking. "Like this Alaska episode. The abrogation of the Alaska Purchase Treaty is a surprise Soviet move, but it didn't just come out of nothing. It's a calculated maneuver in a much bigger game, or equation, or whatever you want to call it." Peter looked into the circle of liquid in his glass. "I'm sure of it."

Peggy looked at him. So serious. She remembered she used to love to hear him laugh.

For several moments neither of them spoke. Peter looked up then, as if just aware of the silence. He reached over and touched her hand on the arm of the sofa.

Peggy started, then laughed. "I guess I drifted off."

"I thought *I* had."

She smiled at him, and started to get up. "How about a cup of coffee and a game of chess?"

Peter's eyebrows drew together. "Are you sure? I doubt I'd be much of a challenge."

Peggy was moving toward the kitchen. She stopped and turned back to look at him. Then she grinned and pointed to a cabinet in the corner of the room.

"Chess set's in there."

CHAPTER TWELVE

Anchorage, Alaska, March 16

The Nushagak Inlet hooks into Dillingham, Alaska from Bristol Bay like a finger. The community is 914 strong, the one bit of industry a largish fish cannery hunched on the waterfront. About a half mile inland from the cannery is the city's downtown: a new hotel, an old-fashioned pharmacy with ice cream fountain, a five and ten cent store.

On Sunday at seven o'clock in the morning, still hours from sunrise, a vein of fire pumped itself from the heart of an explosion and tore through the Dillingham cannery. The force of the explosion awakened the proprietor of the hotel and one of his two guests—the other man had not been sleeping.

Earthquake! thought the proprietor, staring at his windows trembling in the walls. And then, Russians!

Within minutes, a dozen people had gathered in the cold night, flapping down the street in bathrobes, pulling on coats. The sky above the cannery was a bank of orange cloud. It was deadly quiet—as if all sound had been sucked out of the night.

The little band of neighbors moved slowly down the center of the street toward the cannery.

Toward the place where the cannery had been—for there was nothing here now but a scorched and smoking lot. The force of the explosion had rocketed flaming chunks of building into the bay, away from residential Dillingham. Debris bobbed and hissed in the narrow inlet competing for access to the wider Bristol Bay. Pieces that finally released into the bay sailed off under separate sheets of fire, westward toward the Bering Strait.

* * * * *

British Airways 747 Flight 58 out of London was in final approach to Anchorage International's 6R primary landing runway and was just crossing the DME mark ten miles from touchdown. Landing gear was down, the First Officer had just achieved 30 degree flaps, indicated airspeed was 152 knots. Everything was quiet in the flight compartment: the Captain was observing the First Officer's procedure, the Flight Engineer was watching his instruments. It was 7:00 AM. They had received clearance to land several minutes ago, and the radio was silent. The Captain could hear the Anchorage tower talking to another plane on the communication channel set at 118.31 Hz, and he planned to wait until touchdown to switch over to ground control 121.9 Hz.

Suddenly, over half way down the primary landing strip, a ball of flame erupted where 6L intersects with runway 14L. Flight 58 was too far away to hear anything, but its Captain could see the asphalt crack up like a jigsaw puzzle and fly apart in the air. He reached for his throttle quadrant, saying, "Full take-off thrust, gear up—let's *go*. . . ."

Just then, the radio crackled and a staticky voice said quickly, "Take a wave off. Take a wave off, 58 Heavy. You're cleared for a missed approach procedure. Acknowledge."

As the surge of his take-off thrust pressed him back in his seat, the Captain said, "This is 58 Heavy. I read you. Am executing MAP. What the hell is happening?"

But the voice did not respond.

"How's our airspeed?" the Captain asked the First Officer as he started a climbing right turn headed for 2,500 feet on a heading of 200 degrees.

"165 knots and increasing," said the First Officer. And then, "Man, these Americans sure know how to welcome visitors."

* * * * *

At exactly 0700, Honolulu time, the Navy watch officer looked up from his newspaper.

For a moment he didn't know what was wrong. Then he realized that the continuous chatter of the high speed printer behind him had ceased. And the monitor was blank. He stared dully at the empty screen, then around the room. The lights were on. Coffee perking in the corner. He picked up the phone. The phone was working. He dialed his Command Duty Officer and told him what had happened.

"Probably equipment failure over on Diomede Island," the watch officer concluded. "We've got a routine recon flight out of Elmendorf at 0900—I'll have him check it out."

* * * * *

At 7:30 AM the *Anchorage Gazette's* night editor was staring at the big clock on the far wall of the room. The day shift would be in at 8:00. The night shift in the news room consisted of himself and one gung-ho young reporter who persisted in referring to the night editor as Pops; something the old man despised. The boy had gone out to the airport—looking for a story, he said. The editor thought it more likely he was looking for that perky little girl at the Pan American counter.

The phone rang.

"City Desk."

"Hello. I am calling on behalf of the Free Alaska Committee. We have just performed a demonstration of our strength. We will resist *any* government that attempts to interfere with Alaska's solidarity."

"Who *is* this?" the editor asked, leaning over the phone.

"The Free Alaska Committee," the man said, and hung up.

The editor slammed down the phone. Ever since this damned treaty abrogation there had been crank calls—mixed in with legitimate ones from frightened citizens. . . .

The phone rang again. He snatched it up. "City. . . ."

"Hey, Pops, this is Bill over at the airport. Listen, there's just been a huge explosion—just missed a British Airways jet— destroyed most of runway 30R—get me a photographer out here right away. . . ."

As the editor began to call for a camera, the phone rang again. Jesus Christ, the editor thought. "Yeah, City Desk."

"Hello, sir, this is Hal Roberts over at the Dillingham Hotel. We've had a terrible thing here. . . . The cannery is gone. . . . Fire. . . ."

"Hold on, Mr. Roberts. When did it happen?"

"Just a half hour ago—forty minutes. . . . It looked like an atom bomb. I want to know what's going on. Have we been attacked?"

"No, no, Mr. Roberts—I'm sure it's nothing like that. Give me your number and I'll have a reporter get back to you. . . ."

* * * * *

At 0910, the Command Duty Officer in Honolulu received a signal on CINCPAC frequency. He switched to audio.

"Major Wright here. We're right over the site, sir, and your building just isn't there any more. I'm at one thousand feet—right on top of it according to my map. You want a chopper?"

"Yeah, we'd better take a closer look. . . ."

* * * * *

The disappearance of an entire electronic inelligence facility on Diomede Island was never made public. But reports on the incidents in Dillingham and Anchorage were enough to scare hell out of just about everyone, as Harry Smyth would say—and they did.

ALASKA UNDER FIRE was a favorite headline to accompany the earliest-breaking stories:

> In two locations in Occupied Alaska, bombs seriously damaged main runways at Anchorage International Airport this morning. At the same time in Dillingham, a city important to the salmon industry, a large cannery was leveled by a blast of heavy explosives. Casualties are not yet known. A group calling themselves the Free Alaska Committee is claiming responsibility. The FBI is investigating both incidents.

In twenty-four hours the bones of information printed above had been fleshed out. An army of cameras and reporters invaded the state. And when they arrived, fearless, armed with lights and lenses and pads and pens, they faced families, frightened people, there at the airport terminal, waiting to fill the empty plane back up and get *out* of here.

Reporters were refused access to the area of runway where the explosion had occurred until the FBI concluded their own investigation and the airport itself could make the area safe. Information was provided, however on the extent of damage, which was estimated at 2.2 million dollars. The crew of the witness 747 was interviewed, along with tower personnel. The explosion, which had been big enough, got bigger.

In fact there had been a casualty in Dillingham. The cannery's night security guard, an old-timer, was incinerated in that orange cloud Hal Roberts described to the CBS News correspondent. Hal Roberts had a boy in the Navy. He had a boy in the Navy and a hotel in a town where there wasn't anything left, to speak of. That's all Hal Roberts had in the world, and he didn't mind so much about the hotel, but if he lost his boy in a war. . . . Well, he just didn't know.

Many people, a little further removed, thought they did know. In San Francisco where a good demonstration is serious business, the Green Street office of the Consul General of the Soviet Union was the object of an outraged delegation of every kind of citizen. Two rock and paint throwers were restrained by the crowd before the police could get to them. Thousands of men and women packed the narrow street calling for the Consul General, who was not in town, to come out. Residents of the normally quiet neighborhood watched from upstairs windows. A television crew set up on two roofs.

In Washington protestors numbered over fifteen thousand. Wisconsin Avenue was finally closed to traffic. And the ornate Russian Embassy, normally so anxious for visitors, was surrounded by a phalanx of police keeping people back from the building.

There were similar scenes—mobbed streets, little violence, lots of anger—all through America. There were shared feelings: the effrontery of the Russian statement—the abrogation—had come home. The indignity of the gesture offended American pride. So there was a distinct climate of camaraderie, of sharing a larger common cause.

And still, no one knew what the Free Alaska Committee was or what they stood for, or why two bombs were planted where they were planted, or whether the Soviet Union had made any comment on the incident, or for that matter, on the abrogation of the Alaska Purchase Treaty which it was assumed, must have *something* to do with what the FBI was calling sabotage in Alaska.

Over the next several days the Oil Industry would call for defense of the Alaska pipeline. The Sierra Club warned of Russia as an ecological threat. Save the Whales picketed with Vietnam Vets who said *this* was something to fight for. And that was the general feeling.

CHAPTER THIRTEEN

Washington, March 17

Alan Baker's eyes were flinty, narrowed at a portrait of George Washington over the marble mantle across the room. He was holding the phone in his right hand, his left hand was clenched in a fist.

"I'll tell you this, Harry," he said in clipped syllables. "I don't give a damn if they're Russian Secret Service, or Eskimos, or boy scouts gone amok—I'm going to tell Smilie to get a carrier task force out there right away—and I'm not interested in how it's going to thin out the Seventh Fleet, or what the *Washington Post* is going to think."

Baker listened for a moment, and his hand relaxed. More calmly, he said, "I've been on the phone since 6:30 this morning with oil barons sure that the North Slope is under seige. Does that give you some idea of where I'm coming from?"

Another pause. "No, I'll have a statement in an hour. . . . Right." Without removing the phone from his ear Baker keyed his press secretary's extension, and moments later a wiry, wary young man stood at the door of the Oval Office, attempting to project the right combination of concern and confidence. He always lost it, though, crossing toward the President's desk.

Set in low relief, white in the white Oval Office ceiling, is a large reproduction of the Presidential seal, perhaps eight feet in diameter. Directly below the colorless replica is the same seal, but bright gold on a royal blue rug, the imperious eagle flat on his back with his wings and legs splayed clutching a branch of wheat and a quiver of arrows and flying from his beak the motto, "E Pluribus Unum."

The secretary's eyes were drawn directly to the floor whenever he stepped into the room, and when he crossed into a slice of the circle of gold stars that made the circumference of the woven seal, and under the ghost emblem on the ceiling, he felt something between transportation and claustrophobia.

When the press secretary left the President's office on this occasion, he was not feeling at all well, and he knew it was going to be a particularly bad day.

Alan Baker sighed as the young man skidded out of the office, then picked up the phone again. He would call Heath next.

* * * * *

George Heath agreed with Baker's decision whole heartedly. His particular interest in defense policy was the United States' commitment to its allies. He was concerned about Canada.

They had entertained a houseguest over the weekend, a long-time friend and prominent businessman. Martha had left them after pronouncing the morning warm enough, comfortably removed to a screened sunporch. The room was large, running the length of the south wall of the house, and Martha had created a forest of potted ficus and spathiphyllum, and boxes of bright red geraniums in the westernmost quarter. It was as much of country charm as she could stand. Big white wicker chairs and a wicker sofa with fat pillows as cushions, and several small tables occupied the remaining space. It was airy and green and white.

Heath's friend was rolling a fat unlit cigar between two fingers. "It's this way, George," the man had said settling back in the couch. "If the Russian bear crouches on the Canadian border, he becomes our new neighbor."

He frowned slightly, bit off the tip end of the cigar and delicately removed the nub of tobacco from his tongue. "Now we may not love our neighbor," the man deposited the bit of cigar into an ashtray, "but it's important to try to get along." He reached into his jacket for a lighter.

Heath had risen and walked away from the couch where his friend sat.

The man sucked rhythmically on the cigar until the end glowed, and then said to Heath's profile, "Suppose this new neighbor wants to make a deal with us—free access through Alaska for our logging industry, for instance. . . ."

Heath was looking out into a garden squared by high hedges of forsythia. The ground was wet, the sun bright and slanting in warm rectangles across the slate floor, bending over one wicker chair and part of the sofa. He turned abruptly to face the businessman.

"That's a fantasy absolutely without foundation, Charles. The bear isn't crouching on your border. And if he were, I doubt he'd be handing across cups of sugar, or that you'd be organizing a welcome wagon." His voice was tight.

His guest looked at him, surprised. "I'm sorry, George. I'm not trying to pick a fight. I'm just telling it like it is."

* * * * *

Heath had checked his computer screen, as he did every morning, to see if any of his correspondent chess partners had replied. In fact, his daughter had responded: N-QB6 to his P-KB4. And there was a note at the bottom of the screen: " 'Stake your counter as boldly every whit,/Venture as warily, use the same skill,/Do your best, whether winning or losing it,/If you choose to play!' (R. Browning). Do you love it? Your grandson just got his driver's license. God help us all. Love to Mother, Anne."

He had been smiling at that when the call from Baker came through. Alan had sounded stiff, and angry. At 9:45 a messenger delivered a copy of the President's statement, which would be released immediately:

> The President has ordered deployment of Pacific Fleet units to the area between Japan and Alaska. The Carrier Force does not anticipate a combat situation; deployment is for protection of Alaska only. However, should the need arise, the ships carry weapons more than sufficient to meet any offensive military action.

At 9:55 Peter Jefferson and Larry Apple met in the hall outside Heath's offices.

"Jefferson," Apple put out his hand.

They had met several times before, but Peter saw Larry Apple a little differently now. "Mr. Apple," he said, shaking the other's hand.

"Larry."

Peter motioned Apple ahead of him and they moved through a small reception office and into Heath's own. Inside, the heavy drapes were open and the light was bright, an intricate pattern of twined flowers bold on the floor.

The two younger men took seats close to Heath's desk. Peter placed a yellow pad filled with his black slanted writing on the edge, laid a manila file over that and sat back.

Heath read them the President's terse statement.

Larry Apple shook his head. "It's one for their side. I don't think there's much question but that Free Alaska is a Special Service team. I think I might even be able to tell you a couple of their names. But we've got nothing certain yet." He shrugged. "Maybe the explosives they used will tell us something—they're real pros, whoever they are."

There was a pause.

Peter thought this was as good a time as any to begin. He leaned forward and pulled two copies of his traffic report out of the manila file. He handed one copy to Larry Apple, and one across the desk to Heath. He referred to the bulletin he had listed first:

> *Bahrain, Iraq, Kuwait, UAE,*
> *Oman, Qatar, Saudi Arabia*
> create Gulf Oil Authority:
> price war with *Iran* pretty
> sure thing.

Heath read it and looked up inquisitively. Apple nodded his acquaintance with the facts.

"I've been thinking," Jefferson said after having described the workings of the proposed coalition, "that we could make the Gulf Oil Authority a very attractive offer." He sat back, touched the bridge of his glasses. "This union is a brainchild of the House of Saud. . . ."

He leaned to his left and looked down at the sheet Larry Apple was studying. "They've got some serious problems at the moment. . . . Look at item three on that report." He identified for them his notation on the alleged Soviet propaganda book against the King and his family.

"More than this," Peter went on, "Iran is sticking it to the Saudis—their production is threatened, which is a threat to their

economy, and ultimately their survival—and their personal reputa-
tions are about worth shit."

Heath recalled his friend's comment, "telling it like it is." His
expression was pained.

Larry Apple was watching Peter carefully.

"This Authority is going to be set up as a leasing cooperative.
There'll be an international membership, and it seems to me that
the one thing missing from the plan is security."

He reached for his yellow pad. "The Authority is sure to be seen
as ruinous by Iran, possibly by all the OPEC members. And Iran is
armed and itching for a fight." Peter paused. Both men were just
staring at him.

"Now wouldn't a lessee in the Authority require assurances
against any kind of messy interruption of their facilities?" Peter
crossed his legs. "And which of these states," he pointed at the page
still in Apple's hand, "is capable of providing that kind of assur-
ance?"

"Not to our satisfaction, anyway," Apple said.

"Let's assume," said Peter, "that Iran decides to object to this
Authority—or, also likely, that the Soviet Union considers it an
offense and decides to use their discretionary rights in Iran according to their 1921 Treaty. . . ."

Heath leaned forward. "But Iran abrogated that right of discre-
tion in the 70s."

"That's exactly why I know Alaska is a coverup." Peter rose
from his chair. "Russia hasn't acknowledged Iran's 1979 abrogation
of their 1921 Treaty, just as we'll never allow this year's abrogation
of our Alaska Purchase Treaty with Russia." He paused. "They're
using Alaska to create a precedent for an incident in the Mideast."
Again Peter pointed at his summary. "And this Gulf Authority could
easily be that incident."

There was a feeling of suspension in the room. Peter realized he
was standing and wondered when he had gotten up. He sat back
down.

"In any case, I doubt the Iranians would object to a little help
from their friends on this one," Apple said.

"What are you suggesting, Peter?" Heath asked.

Peter leaned forward. "That we get in touch with King Fahd,
and recommend that the United States provide him, the entire
Authority, and coincidentally ourselves as lessees, with some first

class security—specifically a rapid deployment force to keep an eye on things."

Larry Apple whistled under his breath. "Written into the lease."

Peter nodded.

Then Apple leaned forward. "By God, Jefferson, that's great. And Sultan and Fahd, the greedy Mothers, are going to eat it up."

"I'm afraid you're right," Heath said. "That's what rankles—the Saudis' highest priority in foreign affairs is to take whatever they can get from the United States with no conditions attached." Heath looked less than pleased. "Your idea, Peter, allows them the benefits of an American alliance, costs them nothing, and lessens their burden in inter-Arab politics."

"Exactly right," Peter said. "It's an offer they can't refuse." He smiled at the Secretary. "Think of it as a trade. They get some insurance against Tehran exporting too much fundamentalism, and we gain a position in the Gulf. Hell, the Saudis—none of them—will want to alienate the United States."

Apple nodded in agreement. "It's worth a lot more than lessee-provided security. With the RDF, our forces can effectively control the uninterrupted flow of oil." He seemed to muse, then said slowly, "It could even, under certain circumstances, be selective as to where that oil goes."

Heath looked puzzled. "Let's have a bit more on that, Larry."

"Okay, look at it this way. The Western European industrial economy relies heavily on Persian Gulf oil. If that's cut off, what kind of a prize is Western Europe to the Soviet Union?"

Peter had turned in his seat, Heath's brow was furrowed. Larry Apple went on. "The Siberian pipeline has been held up by sloppy work—let's face it, they're waiting for a source of industrial energy. . . ."

Heath held up his hand. "If that's the case, and we join the Gulf Authority we'll need to involve NATO. . . ."

"Absolutely," Apple agreed. "We'll need at least tacit approval from West Germany, France and the rest. But they'd see it as a way of reducing the threat of Soviet attack through Central Europe."

Larry leaned forward. "I'm sure Jim Booth, with his powers of friendly persuasion could make just that point. And I'd recommend he be the one to negotiate the lease in Riyadh. He's politically powerful enough, and he speaks for the President."

Heath had begun making notes. He looked up as Larry finished speaking. "He can go right from Riyadh to Rome, Bonn, Brussels and London." He replaced the slim gold pen over the single page in front of him. "I'll put a call in to Alan right away," he said, and reached for his phone.

CHAPTER FOURTEEN

Moscow, March 18

Vladimir Zolfin had met Josef Anatolovich Kirov during the Christmas season last year. On occasion they had shared quarters in service at an Intourist hotel. You couldn't call them friends exactly—Zolfin thought Kirov was something of a cry-baby, Josef thought Zolfin was a snob. But they helped each other out. The night Detwiler took Zolfin to the theatre Josef had covered a private dinner Zolfin was to have worked. Josef's bossy Ukranian mother was often requiring a change in his own schedule, so it was not surprising when the sad-eyed man asked Zolfin for a favor.

"You busy this weekend, Zolfin?"

They were in the National's big restaurant, empty of diners. It was six o'clock in the morning. The sound was the quiet conversation of a few busboys and waiters in the room, the small clattery chime of silverware being laid, and the clink of glassware. Zolfin liked this time, dawn, and quiet.

He looked over at Josef who was flapping a new white cloth over their round table. Josef looked pinched and unhappy.

"This is sort of a special favor," he said. "I'd give anything to do it myself—but my Mama says she needs me this weekend." He simpered.

Zolfin offered no opinion. "What is it?"

Josef lowered his voice further and leaned across the table. "Olga Karpovna—a party."

"The actress?"

"Shhh!" Josef looked around, then leaned again toward Zolfin. "*Please.* This is very quiet." He hesitated, then said, "A *private* party, you understand? At her dacha on the Black Sea. For the weekend."

His eyes squinted. "Oooh, I wish I did not have to ask you. But Mama's. . . ."

Zolfin didn't want to hear Mama's problem. "What transportation?" he asked.

"The caterer is flying Aeroflot from the hotel tonight. You'll be with his crew. There is a servant at her home, but they needed extra waiters. I want to know *everything*, Zolfin. Everything that happens. How she looks, who is there, what they say . . . ooh, I wish Mama didn't. . . ."

"How many guests?"

"Thirty, or less." Josef was pouting, laying silverware on the smooth cloth. Zolfin was silent.

"Well, will you do it?"

Zolfin hesitated a moment longer, then chuckled. "For Mama," he said, looking into Josef's worried face, "anything."

* * * * *

Olga Karpovna was twenty-eight years old. Her father had been a respected scientist, her mother an active Party member; their deaths in a plane crash had offered her her first wave of public sympathy and attention. She had been sixteen then. Her parents had never made much time for her, and she found the solicitations of their friends, well-placed upper class administrators and the like, quite pleasant. She had been frightened at what her prospects might be. She made sure not to lose their attention.

She graduated the University of Moscow with many of her parents' friends attending the ceremony. Interestingly, by now they were only the men. Alexi Kolkin had been one of them.

Olga Karpovna was a "smart cookie" as her Nyanya, housekeeper-nurse, was fond of saying. It was a description that irritated the girl.

* * * * *

Her "little mansion" sat like a piece of topaz on the Black Sea coast. Unlike the other impressive estates where many government officials kept a second home, and some fortunate writers and composers lived year round, Olga Karpovna's villa, higher up the hillside, had no tall fence to hide its exterior. It sat there shining in the sun, reflecting sky in big bayed gold-tinted windows. At night, lit from inside, it was a star.

The show would be closing next month. It made her nervous. So the party.

"Invite that tall skinny friend of yours," she had said to Kolkin. "The serious one." She was brushing her hair, seated in front of a mirrored dressing table. Alexi Kolkin sat in his underwear on the bed.

"Leonid Nikarin," he said, watching her.

"Natasha Marnovna finds him very attractive." She smiled at herself in the mirror, replaced the silver handled brush, and turned to him.

"And Anton Andrenovich Karche. He seems like fun." She crossed to the canopied bed. It had been his gift to her just after they had become lovers five years ago.

He took her hand, smiled up at her. He still could not believe his good fortune. She was so very beautiful. Rich chestnut hair, blackest eyes, and skin the color of cream. And she was good to him. He was an old man, but she had never complained.

If her nature was perhaps a little selfish, a little manipulative, it was understandable—artists were that way. If she was a little "wild," it was the times. If sometimes she frightened Alexi Kolkin, invoking feelings he could not quite understand, he told himself it was part of being in love. For so he was.

* * * * *

The house glittered that night. Three rooms connected by glass doors had been opened to the party. The women were all much younger than the men. And all much more colorful. They were dressed in bright taffetas and pale silks. They shimmered and shivered in the light. Every glass in the room reflected them. The parqueted floors gleamed and the girls danced.

The men (they were scientists, a very minor spattering of bureaucrats, artists, and the military) were more somber, dressed in dark suits or uniforms. They kept near the walls or gathered in groups of four or five next to pieces of furniture, as if to assure themselves of something solid as the girls twirled across their vision, candles flickered and the whiskey and vodka came around and around.

Near midnight Kolkin left a small group near the fireplace in the gallery off the livingroom. Here were two walls hung with tall theatrical publicity posters, theirs the only color in the small room tossed with white sheepskins and very modern Italian furniture— stark, slightly distorted thick chairs and armless sofas.

Kolkin was feeling congenial and quite high. He bumped and then leaned for a moment against the doorway into the middle room, sparsely furnished, polished floors, where the light was dimmer and more golden. It was a good party. A jolly crowd. He watched Anton Androvich Karche, the brass gleaming on his uniform, gesticulating in wide circles in some story for the amusement of two young women and several humorless looking men. Beyond them, someone was playing an old love ballad on the piano. A delicate looking girl was lifted to a seat on top of the piano, her petticoats settling around her.

At the buffet he saw Olga Karpovna bending toward a sad looking little man with narrow eyes and a stringy moustache. A moment later she looked up and around, saw Kolkin, pointed toward him, and took the little man by the arm. Kolkin straightened as they approached.

"Alexi Izmanovich," she said, "this is Issam Gayem. He is nominated to the Provincial Executive Committee. He is Ivan Lvovich Lubov's brother-in-law's cousin." Her eyes shone.

Kolkin nodded, saying, "Comrade," thinking how pretty his girl looked. Her dress was the red of ripe cherries. He felt himself flushing.

Alim Gayem immediately began to speak, rapidly, and in a dialect which Kolkin could not understand. He turned questioningly to Olga Karpovna.

She laughed. "He told me he is concerned about something. That was all I could understand." She moved close, rose up on tiptoes and whispered something in his ear. Before he could react, she had flown away, back into the party.

He felt slightly dizzy, looked over at Lubov's brother-in-law's cousin. The man took it as a signal to go on. The Minister touched Kolkin's shoulder, nodded to a settee in the corner near them.

The big man looked around, irritated, saw a waiter with a platter of canapes, signalled for him and said rather loudly, waving one hand at the roomful of guests, "Is there someone here who understands this language?"

In the din of conversation and music, no one even turned in their direction. Kolkin saw the girl on the piano lean forward to plant a kiss on Leonid Nikarin's forehead. The waiter spoke. With his blankest expression, Vladimir Zolfin said, "It is Uzbek dialect, General Secretary, sir."

Kolkin stared at him. "You speak this?"

Zolfin nodded and kept his eyes on the curled fish on the platter.

"Well, what does he want?" Kolkin said, impatiently.

Zolfin looked up at Kolkin, then over at Gayem who had been squinting at their exchange. He spoke in a low voice to the Minister, then listened to a minute long barrage.

Zolfin's heart was beating fast. He held up his hand finally, and the Minister ceased. Turning to Kolkin the young man said with an even voice, "General Secretary, sir, the Minister says he is honored to meet you, that he is honored to have been invited here. That Olga Karpovna is a gracious hostess, and he offers his respects to . . ."

"Yes, yes," Kolkin said irritably, lifting a shrimp from the plate Zolfin still held. "What else?"

Zolfin said something to the other man, while Kolkin looked around for another waiter. He raised his hand, snapped his fingers, and while the Minister gesticulated at Zolfin and the younger man nodded, his head bowed in concentration, a white coated man with drinks approached.

Kolkin accepted a half litre of syrupy vodka, poured a thimble-full into a little glass, and downed it. The second waiter refilled the glass for him, left the vodka, removed Zolfin's tray, and retreated.

Olga Karpovna and Natasha Marnovna walked across Kolkin's line of vision, arms about each other's waist. Young women, Kolkin thought. How lovely they are. Like flowers. There was loud laughter from a group of five people near the buffet.

He looked back at the moustached diplomat.

Zolfin almost sighed. "The Minister is proud to serve the Motherland from the Uzbek Republic, sir. His home is Samarkand." He paused.

Kolkin crossed his legs. He nodded very slightly at the young man. Gayem leaned toward Zolfin, touched his sleeve and spoke again.

"You know, General Secretary, that this is the home of our most beloved warrior, Tamerlane, whom the people believe is invested with great power."

Kolkin nodded, sipped his vodka. Tamerlane, Timur the Lame. He did know something of the story. Timur had come to power in 1369, defeating what remained of Genghis Khan's hordes. He had marched south then, taking Afghanistan and all of Persia, Baghdad and Damascus. While the Gulf and Middle East were darkened by his shadow, his home city Samarkand grew radiant, "the precious pearl of the world," according to Alexander the Great.

"Timur's tomb, General Secretary, is a holy place to many of our people. A mecca," Zolfin was saying.

Both Zolfin and Gayem's eyes seemed to be burning, fastened on Kolkin's face. He was struck by the compassion in the translator's voice. He leaned forward.

"I know of Tamerlane, Comrade. He was indeed a great General."

Gayem hastily engaged Zolfin again. The younger man cleared his throat. "Sir, the great General's tomb is in shameful disrepair— the earthquakes—"

Gayem had interrupted, then allowed Zolfin to continue. "There have been funds designated for its restoration, but the Minister says much of that money has been reallocated for new building, to encourage tourism, he expects. . ."

Zolfin hesitated saying more. Politically, if he were Gayem, he would have stopped right there. Still, he was asked to interpret. "The Minister believes you, sir, who are a brave and intelligent man, will surely see how humiliating this is to the people of the region."

Kolkin leaned back against the round, red plush back of the little sofa. He took another drink, then closed his eyes for a moment. The little man was incredibly naive. Did he really think Kolkin could do something for him and his shrine? And to bring this up at a party!

Gayem was probably the descendant of a sheepherder, Kolkin thought. That was happening more frequently now. He smiled broadly, suddenly feeling quite paternal. He put his arm around Gayem's shoulder, and said to Zolfin, "Tell the Minister I will be pleased to visit him in Samarkand and discuss his ideas. I appreciate his bringing the situation to my attention."

Again the other man spoke. Kolkin felt a flash of irritation, and then saw the tears in Gayem's eyes.

Zolfin said, "The Minister thanks you from his heart, General Secretary."

Kolkin squeezed Gayem's shoulder. "I assure you, Comrade, we have not forgotten you." He nodded his head somberly. "In fact, there are very confidential negotiations in the works."

Kolkin's head ended a nod with his chin down. He saw the glass empty between his two fingers, and raised his hand.

Zolfin lifted the decanter from the sideboard behind their sofa and refilled.

Gayem looked up at Zolfin and said something. Kolkin was noticing that the man's moustache seemed to move independently of his mouth. As if both the man's mouth and his moustache were speaking.

Kolkin released Issam Gayem and leaned back again.

Zolfin spoke carefully. "The Minister asks, sir, are these negotiations regarding the great General's shrine?"

Kolkin laughed, and hiccoughed. He put his finger vertically against his lips. "Shh," he said. "It is a secret, Gayem—" He leaned forward very suddenly looking hard into the Minister's eyes. "Tell the Minister that I will share this much with him, because I see how heartfelt is his love for his country—our plans focus on his part of the world, and if all goes well, we will do what Tamerlane did, and more, and Arabian oil will replace the fine Persian tile that has fallen from the tomb in Samarkand with King Tut's gold."

CHAPTER FIFTEEN

Washington, March 21

Stu Boyington slammed the winning ball off the back wall into Peter Jefferson's court. Peter was crouched slightly, calf muscles taut, about ten feet from the wall. When the ball made contact, he moved forward. The ball cracked against the hardwood floor with such force it rebounded high over Peter's head and out of reach. He couldn't get back fast enough.

Stu whooped, then crossed over to Peter and clapped him on the shoulder, grinning, out of breath.

Peter's expression was wry. "Man, you don't know anything about diplomacy," he said. "I'm going to contribute a plaque to the door of this court: 'Boyington's Court—Abandon Hope All Ye Who Enter Here. . . .' "

Stu laughed. "There's a place for diplomacy, my friend, but it's not on a racquet ball court!"

Peter raised an eyebrow. "*Very* good. I'll remember that."

Their glass booth was the first of six in a row facing an opposite wall of long polished wood bleachers on the mezzanine level of the club. As they walked down the carpeted corridor in front of the courts toward the showers, hollow pops resounded from other cubicles, a stacatto punctuation to their conversation.

"You ever notice, you get a whole different type in here in the morning than in the afternoon or evening?" Stu asked. "Di and I came down about a month ago. It was like a singles' club."

"Afternoons and evenings are reserved for the hopeful. They're also younger. And they're not here to play racquet ball." Peter gestured at the last court in the column: two of the President's Secret Service were hammering out a game. "Mornings are for the already committed."

* * * * *

105

It was the second day of spring—a cheerful sunny blue morning. In just the last day or so the trees had begun to bud: tiny green nubs on crooked limbs.

Peter took the steps to the State Department two at a time, feeling good. It really had been a good game. It was going to be an excellent day. And tonight he was seeing Peggy and he was looking forward to it.

When he entered his office, the phone was ringing. Grace was apparently not in yet.

"Oh, Peter, *there* you are!"

It was Miriam.

"Miriam—I didn't return your call. I'm awfully sorry. I heard about your Dad. . . ."

"Oh, I understand, Peter. I know how busy you are—your work. . . ."

"I'm really sorry. I am busy, but I should have called. I—I guess I didn't really know what to say. How's Mother doing?"

"She's wonderful, Peter. She's been so strong through all of this. But I sometimes miss him so much. . . ."

Her voice cracked. Oh God, was she going to cry? "Miriam. . . ."

"I'm sorry, Peter. . . ." Another pause. "We're always saying we're sorry to one another."

There was a silence. "Is there anything I can do?"

"Could we have lunch? Just someone to talk to would—I've grown up a lot this past year, Peter. I'd just like to talk."

He hesitated a little too long. He didn't particularly like the way he felt—put upon—it was selfish and unkind. "How about the end of the week?" he said. "Friday. . . ."

"Thanks," she said. There was a dry sound in the way she spoke it. Then it was gone. "Friday will be wonderful. Shall I meet you?"

"Sure. At the restaurant at the Madison?"

A pause. Quietly she said, "Thank you for remembering, Peter. The Madison. At noon?"

"Fine." Oh, damn. He hadn't remembered at all.

He hung up feeling deflated.

* * * * *

Just before two o'clock, Peter Jefferson and George Heath gained admittance to the White House through a private entrance, and turned down the second hallway to their left. Recently the long neutral walls had been hung with the portraits of eighteen presidents. Vanderlyn's painting of James Madison gazed intelligently across the middle of the walkway, James Monroe by Samuel F. B. Morse looked hopefully toward the President's quarters.

The two men proceeded through a large sitting room, and entered the Oval Office. Baker sat in a tall carved-back chair on the visitor's side of his desk near the unlit fireplace, leaning forward, hands clasped between his knees. He was listening to Larry Apple, on his left. Harry Smyth was tipped back in a large 1860 Shaker style rocking chair to the President's right.

Baker looked up as they came in. "Larry is just telling us about a report they received this morning from one of their contacts out of Moscow. Listen to this George." He rose and extended his hand across the desk. "Peter, good seeing you again. Have a seat over there." He indicated an armchair next to Larry Apple's. Heath moved to the sofa near Harry Smyth's chair.

"Go ahead, Larry."

Apple shifted in his seat to direct his comments to the newcomers. "We got some interesting information from a new recruit out of Moscow. He was called on to act as an interpreter for Kolkin at a party this past weekend, during which he confided to some minor Governor in the Uzbek Republic a plan which sounds like an invasion of Egypt."

Peter leaned forward, frowning. "He told a *minor* official in front of one of your agents?"

Apple sounded a little testy. He had already been asked that question by Harry Smyth. "The circumstances are such that it's unlikely there's any deception. Our man was there on a fluke, the Governor was trying to get a favor out of Kolkin—to repair some shrine in one of his districts." Apple held out a hand. "Kolkin was a little high . . ." he shrugged.

George Heath shook his head. "You have to admit, Larry, it sounds almost too good to be true. What exactly did he say about Egypt?"

"He said they have plans to do more than what Tamerlane did and when they've accomplished that the Governor would be able to replace his Persian title with King Tut's gold and Arabian oil."

"What the hell does that mean?" Harry Smyth said, dropping a match in a large amber ashtray on the President's desk.

Baker looked equally confused.

Peter Jefferson provided part of the answer before Larry could speak. "Tamerlane is a folk hero to the Moslems. The 'spirit of war,' they call him. In fact it was the day after Soviet scientists opened his tomb that the Germans invaded Russia—June 22, 1941. The Germans broadcast through the Middle East that the Russians had incurred the wrath of Timur and set loose the spirit of war on the people."

Peter turned toward Baker. "Tamerlane's career included the capture of Afghanistan and all of Persia." He stopped, looked at Larry Apple. "It does sound like a major assault."

Smyth tapped an ash off his cigarette. "Sounds like a damn riddle to me. 'Arabian oil, Persian tile, King Tut's gold.' "

"Tamerlane's tomb is made of jade and Persian tile," Larry Apple said, and then interrupted himself. "Look, I can only guess along with you what it means. To me it sounds like Kolkin has some deal with the Arabs to attack Egypt. I just wanted to put it out there. You can consider it questionable—just consider it."

"All right, Larry," Alan Baker said. "But I don't see that we can do much more than that."

George Heath nodded at Peter. "There may be something, Alan."

While the younger man described the Gulf Oil Authority, Baker lifted a small chunk of polished obsidion off a stack of papers near his phone. Listening, he fingered the smooth planes of the paperweight.

". . . Simply," Peter was saying, "the intention is to stabilize prices. . . ."

"Stabilize prices, like hell," Baker said. "OPEC will never stand for it. Stability in any sense in the Mideast is about as likely as—"

"A snowball in hell," Harry Smyth offered, considering another cigarette.

"OPEC will have to stand for it," Heath said. "Not only stand for it, but conform to the same prices, or lose their market."

Baker shook his head. "It'll never happen."

"It *is* happening," Heath said quietly.

Smyth's chair creaked softly back and forth.

"All right," Baker said, replacing the black stone on his correspondence. "So the—Authority—builds into its contracts bi-annual price and production reviews for its lessees. Is that it?"

Peter nodded.

"Great. And they think the Soviets are going to sit by and watch Iran go down the tubes? Or that OPEC won't retaliate?"

Actually, we were thinking the Authority might welcome some protection," Lary Apple said.

Baker stared at him. "Protection," he said, flatly.

"A security force," Larry replied easily. "To defend our interests in the Authority, as a lessee."

Harry Smyth stopped rocking. After a pause he turned to the President. "Alan, there's a Soviet base at Aden and Lehaj and one in Asmara. From those positions alone they could close the Red Sea. How many tankers do you suppose would enter the Red Sea with the threat of a Russian air offensive?"

"Wait a minute," Baker interrupted. "If we're talking about an air strike on the oil fields, Aden is out of range. And by the time the Russians were able to fly to an operational area—say southern Iran—you know they'd be looking at cratered runways. Even if they did land a division, they'd have only enough ammunition and supplies for about a week, right? Meanwhile, air cover would be minimal."

"Say they took the Saudi bases," Heath inserted.

"No—the Gulf States would destroy their own installations before that happened," Baker said.

Larry Apple held out a hand. "But Alan, if there's a Soviet build-up in the Gulf, which I'm inclined to believe is the case, there is very distinctly a threat to Oman, Kuwait, Saudi Arabia, and the others—they're in the direct line of fire, figuratively, anyway."

He replaced his hand on the narrow arm of the chair. "Economically, politically, we'd have to support a Gulf Oil Authority—you see that—and we have a head start on air support.

"What air support?" Baker said, leaning forward, staring at Apple.

"In the early '80s, after Saudi Arabia refused us operational airbase rights there, the National Security Council funnelled enough money through a dummy Liechtenstein Anstalt to buy 90 fighters—the new Lavie, from Israel. They're sitting at an airbase in the Negev."

Baker looked over at Harry Smyth who nodded his head in confirmation. The President sat back in his seat and Apple continued.

"We just send a 747 over with pilots and maintenance and off they go to Kuwait, Oman, or wherever they're needed."

Baker felt up against a wall. "You really think the Gulf States are going to go for it?" he said. "Reverse a twenty-year old policy, and let us set up shop in their oil fields?"

Harry Smyth watched a ribbon of smoke unravel in the air. "I think they would."

Alan turned toward him.

"The Saudi National Guard is strong," Smyth explained, "but spread way too thin; their government is in such bad shape, they couldn't survive a conflict now, and King Fahd knows that." Harry began rocking again. "Iraq is still refurbishing—they've got arms, but I wouldn't want to have to depend on their protection if there were a strike. Kuwait and the others haven't got much of anything in the way of troops. The thing is, our presence would discourage factionalism, not the other way around. They would have a common enemy, the Iranian kamikazes. They'd have to be crazy to say no. The Kuwaitis are just as worried by the Islamic Holy War group now as they were earlier. The car-bombs can just as easily be used against them as they were against us in 1983."

Alan Baker's head went back and for the first time that afternoon his face relaxed into a grin.

Harry Smyth looked confused, then he said rather gruffly, "Maybe they are a little crazy, but that's not what we're talking about defending."

Alan Baker shook his head, the smile disappearing from his face. "What about the implications for Western Europe. . . ."

"*Look* at the implications, Alan," Heath said.

"All right—okay. Let me talk to Clay and Smilie. I'll get back to you."

"Soon, Alan," Larry Apple said. "The whole feasibility of a move like this depends on our doing business with Saudi Arabia. And I'm not sure how much longer they're going to *be* in business."

CHAPTER SIXTEEN

Washington, March 21

Peggy placed two crystal wine goblets on the table and stepped back.

The dining area faced the backyard through arched doors where the sun had left a hushed last light. The room seemed very still. On either side of the glass doors were potted papyrus, already becoming delicate silhouettes against white wainscoting. A slender brass chandelier with six small lamps hung over a sturdy Victorian slate-topped table and four chairs.

She adjusted the light to a glow, went into the livingroom to put on a record. Soon the bittersweet sound of Mahler's Tenth filled the room. She stood there, closed her eyes for a moment, then went back to the kitchen, a simple room, too narrow perhaps, but with redeeming features: lots of cabinet space and tall cupboards, deep wooden countertops, a warming plate for the Wedgewood dinner set, and blue and white tile running in a band around the middle of the high white walls.

Peggy was dressed in slim dark slacks and a peach-color cowl necked sweater. She had taken time dressing; upstairs smelled sweet with bathsalts.

It had been a strange day. She had met with Dr. Springer at Langley in connection with a series of experiments he would be conducting over the next several months, and he had asked her out. Robert Springer was something of a celebrity in the scientific community. For some reason the dinner invitation had depressed her. And then Larry Apple had called to cancel a meeting with her and Jerry and had been particularly remote.

She was thinking about that, tearing lettuce into a glass salad bowl when the doorbell rang.

Peter had his arms full. "Tulips!" She smiled and lifted the huge cone out of his arms. "They're wonderful."

In the kitchen he half-filled a wide-mouthed vase with water, and brought it over to the counter where she had unwrapped the flowers.

"Are you okay?"

She lifted her eyes from the tall yellow blossoms, surprised. "Do I seem not okay?"

Peter looked at her seriously. "You seemed a little sad."

She smiled, arranging the flowers. "Thoughtful. Maybe a little sad, but for no particular reason. Just one of those days."

Peggy lifted the vase in both hands. "They're like huge buttercups—thank you, Peter. I'm going to put them in the entranceway." She turned toward the door. "Why don't you fix us a drink? There's ice on the bar in the livingroom."

The bar was a marble-topped Venetian cabinet with glass breakfront and a tall mirrored back. Peter looked at his reflection— he was wearing a black turtleneck sweater under a light-colored corduroy jacket, and khaki slacks. He unbuttoned his jacket, and set about making two drinks, as near to perfect as he could.

She met him as he was coming back through the living room, and took one of the large crystal glasses out of his hand. "Let's sit down. Everything is either cooking, chilling or breathing—we can just enjoy these." She touched her glass to his. They sat on the couch. "How was *your* day?"

"Real interesting. I met with the President this afternoon, with George, Harry Smyth and Larry. The CIA had gotten a very peculiar piece of intelligence out of Russia. . . ."

Peter described what the Secretary of Defense had referred to as a riddle. He told her about Tamerlane's tomb.

"Tamerlane." Peggy's eyes narrowed at her drink. "I know who he was." She turned and looked at Peter. "Tamerlane is the man who originated the veiling of Moslem women."

"What?"

"You didn't know that?" She looked at him with raised eyebrows. "Tamerlane's favorite wife was a beautiful Chinese girl who succumbed to the kiss of another man while her husband was off on some campaign." She paused, remembering the story.

"The lover was a famous architect, hired to build a monument to Tamerlane. The story goes that he kissed her with such ardor that it marked the girl, and when Tamerlane returned early from his war. . . ."

Peter was listening with obvious pleasure. He considered for a fraction of a second if perhaps this was a fable being invented on the spot, and decided not.

"He had the lover killed, and concluding that a woman's beauty was a threat to mankind, he ordered all the women in the land to cover themselves."

That's a great story," Peter said.

"Depends on your point of view." She grinned as she stood up. "I'm going to get things together for dinner. It'll be just a few minutes."

* * * * *

"You know, I meant to ask you last Saturday, about your family," Peggy said, as he helped her to salad. "Wasn't it a cousin I met—Nina?"

"Nina—that's right. They're great." He was thoughtful, serving himself salad. He looked up. "You know, I don't remember us talking about your family."

"I don't think we ever got around to them," she said smiling. She unfolded her napkin and smoothed it across her lap. "I have a wonderful family. Mother and Dad live in California." Peter was pouring wine. "In fact, this wine is from his vineyards—a birthday gift from last year."

Peter looked at the bottle. It was a 1976 Mondavi Cabernet Sauvignon. "He grows for Mondavi?"

"It's more a hobby," she said, lifting her glass. "Here's to families."

She took a sip, as he did, then went on, "Dad used to work in Silicon Valley—he still does some consulting there—but since he retired he and Mother have moved to Napa Valley. They'd bought some acreage back in the fifties."

"How large an operation?" Peter asked, slicing into a tender seasoned filet mignon.

"Very small. He's got about a hundred acres, but just a few small presses, vats, and so forth. He averages a hundred cases a year—keeps some himself, sells a small amount to Robert Mondavi, and gives the rest to friends and family."

"Do you have brothers or sisters?"

Peggy had two sisters, whom she described as the smart one, a physicist living in Tucson, Arizona, and the pretty one, a not particularly successful actress in Los Angeles.

"What's your title," Peter asked.

"The middle one."

He laughed. "That's not terribly distinguished, is it."

She smiled. "No, but it was comfortable. My parents weren't ready for the three of us—we were special kids from the beginning." She sipped some of her wine. "I was the least scarey of the three of us—the most 'normal.' They had less trouble with me, and always seemed grateful for my being in the middle, like a fulcrum. Do you know what I mean?"

He nodded. "I can understand that. I felt sort of like an anchor, myself—when we left Italy."

The conversation lightened. The dinner was simple: steaks, french beans, a large salad, hot bread and the ruby colored wine.

In the living room afterward, there was an awkward silence.

Peggy slipped off her shoes and sat using the arm and corner of the couch as a back rest. Raising her eyes to his, she said, "Do you feel as if you're sixteen years old and on your first date?"

He grinned. "I feel sillier than that. I feel as if I'm forty-four and on my first date."

They smiled at one another. "Would you like a brandy?" she said.

"Sure—I'll get them," he said, and rose from the easy chair across from her.

"Peter," she said when he was at the bar. "Can I ask you a personal question?"

He looked back over his shoulder at her. She wasn't facing him, her head was lowered. "Of course."

He walked back and sat down next to her, handed her the brandy.

She raised her eyes. "Why didn't you ever get in touch with me, after Rome?"

Peter looked at her, not knowing what to say.

She tok a breath, managed a reasonable facsimile of a smile. "Personally, our brief time together changed my whole way of looking at things. I count the days before I met you as Before Rome, and the time since as After Rome."

She took a quick gulp of her drink.

He looked down. Slowly, he leaned his head back against the couch and focused on a point across the ceiling, in his memory. "I don't know, Peg. Because I'm a fool, I suppose. At the time I was really messed up over my divorce—we talked about that. . . ."

He looked over at her, and she nodded. "To me, *that* was real life, and you—you were a dream."

He turned toward her. "Of course it was special. I thought it was too good to be true. That if I pursued it, it would dissolve in a cloud of smoke, or turn out not to be real." He reached over and took her hand. "So I let it stay a dream."

A tear rolled down Peggy's cheek. She didn't say anything, didn't seem even to realize she was crying. Peter leaned over and took the snifter out of her other hand, placed it on the table to his left. Turning back, he touched her cheek, then put his arms around her and hugged her close to him.

"I'm sorry for that, Peg. I know I blew it."

He held her for a long time, neither of them speaking. When they separated there was a closeness that hadn't been there before.

When he left she walked with him to his car and they kissed goodnight with great tenderness. He waited till she had closed the door behind her before he turned on his lights, and turned the car toward home.

CHAPTER SEVENTEEN

Washington, March 26

Five days later, Alan Baker placed a call to the Director of the CIA.

"Alright, Larry," he said. "Is this soon enough for you?"

"Only if you're convinced," Apple had answered.

* * * * *

The deployment of United States military into the Gulf States was called Operation Seward, for oddly sentimental reasons. It was negotiated during the next two weeks with no hitches. It was completed two days after King Fahd announced the formation of a Gulf Oil Authority.

Admiral Smilie, meeting with the Joint Chiefs, had determined that American ground forces would require light to medium size arms. Net Assessment had been concerned about safe overseas passage for supplies in one direction and tankers in the other. There were Soviet submarines in the Indian Ocean; the Red Sea-Suez Canal route might be even more dangerous. It was their conclusion that Soviet bases in Aden, Ethiopia and Socotra might have to be neutralized. They also insisted the six Soviet airbases in Afghanistan required cover. It was agreed Operation Seward would include two additional squadrons of air superiority fighters which with inflight refueling would reach Bahrain three days after the main elements of the Rapid Deployment Force.

Smilie suggested restaging a 1981 operation called Bright Star, a tactical exercise that had involved an airlift from the United States to Egypt in conjunction with the U.N. Peace Keeping Force in the Sinai at that time. It took twelve hours in 1981, for 2,500-plus soldiers, supplies, and planes to complete their mission to Egypt. This time there would be 18,000 soldiers, and they would stay.

The Army's VIII Airborne Corps, including the 82nd Airborne Division and the 101st Airmobile Division, was assigned to the RDF. With blessings of the Gulf Oil Authority, transport aircraft was assured of friendly airfields and overflight rights, along with use of Egyptian refueling facilities along the way.

President Mubarak's thinking was that it would do no harm to make this gesture to the United States: he was having problems with Libya's Qaddafi; at some point it was possible Egypt herself might require a reciprocal favor. Further, assistance to the United States now would ingratiate Mubarak to the Saudis. For similar reasons, President Numeiry of Sudan promised airspace and refueling facilities. Additionally, Israeli bases in the Negev were available. Forward staging areas were firm.

The final destinations were Muscat, Oman, Dhahran and Bahrain. Muscat was right around the corner from the Strait of Hormuz and access to the Persian Gulf. Oman had a beach-front view of Socotra; moreover, Omani armed forces were a bonus, having received a sophisticated British education: the Sultan was a Sandhurst graduate who in 1981 had invited his British chums to reorganize his service. Several years later, the Omani army had been expanded to 25,000 troops, trained and equipped by Britain. They supported 250 Chieftain tanks, a new version of the Saladin armored personnel carrier, and not generally known, 100 surface-to-surface missile batteries with conventional warheads capable of causing serious damage to Aden and the Soviet base at Asmara in Ethiopia. If that weren't enough, the French base in Djibouti, across the Gulf from Aden, was bristling with missiles: the French were there coincidentally, working out details of a new reactor for Iraq.

The former Air Force base at Dhahran would handle C-141 and C-5A cargo aircraft and fighters. Newly extended asphalt runways and facilities at Ras Tanura North made that base as strong as Dhahran. With the Bahrain Island, the rapid deployment force could effectively cover the Saudi core area of wells, refineries, storage tanks, pumping stations, pipeline and off-shore platforms, and keep an eye on the Soviets.

The men who designed Operation Seward were the Admiral Robert Smilie, swift and precise in his thinking; and Harry Smyth, cautious, methodical. They worked it out with maps and charts, they used equations to calculate their unknowns, their risks, their possible gains. They worked for four days alone. Then they began calling in colleagues for specific questions, or for more information. They cast the principals in the play: James Booth, Counselor to the President, would meet with Youssef Ibrahim, the head of the Saudi Foreign Liaison Office, as soon as arrangements had been made.

To accompany Booth, Larry Apple provided an agent who had spent two years at Oxford in Arab Studies. The man, a lawyer himself, took one whole day to brief the Counselor in the complexities of Middle East politics. He summed it up by pointing out that Mideast differences are inevitably religious. "Each and every sect is based on infallible truth, you see. But there can be only one Truth: a rival claim to represent true orthodoxy is a mortal challenge. Unfortunately," the agent shrugged, "the Koran is so vague and ambiguous. . . . Have you read it?" . . ."

" 'Fraid not," James Booth said, without expression.

"No, well, you know it *means* The Question."

The agent was disconserted by Booth's empty stare. He wasn't sure he was getting through. He thought maybe he should put it differently for the Counsellor. "Khomeini sees it one way, you know, as a fundamentalist; Muburak reads it like a populist."

Booth nodded blankly, and the agent took it as encouragement. "You see, there's a lot of tension there—anger—and somewhere under it all, a religious fervor that's uncommon."

General Thomas Becker, a tough Marine with combat experience near the Yalu River in North Korea was in charge of the Mideast side of the operation. Gene Jeffries, oil company executive, was drafted to brief General Becker on oil field operations, a nerve racking experience, as far as Jeffries was concerned. And Jeffries was concerned. He was envisioning the loss of 12,000 barrels of oil per day if just one active well were sabotaged.

Becker was impatient with the details and with this guy's whiny attitude, and his 400 dollar suit. He looked down his nose at Gene Jeffries (down a punched-in version of a nose, Jeffries noted), and said, "Look, I'll have five-man fire teams wherever you want. They can take care of your wells and your fields and your damn Arabs and Soviets, and stand at attention while they do it. Got it?"

Becker had other things on his mind—mainly airlift and resupply logistics. Thank God fuel wasn't going to be a problem. In fact, Becker had to admit, they were in better shape than they might have been. Congress had finally gotten generous with troop carrier aircraft, they had the right to military charter of commercial airline 747Bs on twenty-four hours notice, and there was also the Civil Reserve Air Fleet.

So Becker was feeling his oats. As late as last year it would have required twenty-six days to airlift a light Army division to the Mideast. Today, because of the sheer size of their airforce, it would take forty-eight hours.

Bob Van Vleck, Tom Becker and Admiral Smilie worked out further possibilities: without the Suez Canal, what would they need to carry out eight million barrels of oil a day through the Persian Gulf? They agreed that 400 tankers of 85,000 deadweight tons each could sustain such transport. Five convoys consisting of eighty tankers, traveling at 1,440 nautical miles at fifteen knots, could be outbound from the Gulf at any given time along the 5,000 mile route between loading points and drop-off positions in or near the South Atlantic; while five escort groups, inbound, shepherded empty tankers picked up near Capetown.

How to protect such maneuvers was the next question. The Navy would provide nine carriers and eighty-six cruiser/destroyer escorts on station. Additional ASW and attack carriers would be pulled in, given the long-term life of this mission, to cover overhaul and in-transit wear on instruments. Modified P-3ASWs would operate out of Diego Garcia—by 1986 their combat radius had been increased to 1,800 miles; they had achieved three hours skimming-the-sea on station at 1,500 feet.

Van Vleck winced when Becker said that with the Navy capability, neutralizing Socotra and Maritus would be "a piece of cake." Becker was a brute. The Secretary of the Navy repeated wearily that this operation was a peaceable, nonthreatening maneuver, being carried out with permisison, in the open. No one expected trouble. The Soviets would not risk their Indian Ocean submarines without available replacements.

"Certainly, we'll keep an eye on the Soviet fleet, General," Van Vleck said. "We have digital image processing and satellite surveillance for that." Van Vleck had been doing a lot of reading.

"As for Mauritius and Socotra, there won't be hostile action. "Try to think of yourself as a security guard, Becker."

* * * * *

The actual operation began on April 7 when General Becker departed the continental United States, touching down eleven hours later on Runway 01 at Riyadh. For two days after, the skies would be dense with monstrous birds. At Riyadh International they parked in the area set aside for military student flight training; at Bahrain International they were taxied to the Western Apron and Gulfair maintenance areas. C-5s and 141s swooped to rest in Abu Dhabi, Dhahran, Ras Tanura and Muscat; outside of Muscat, the planes split off to land at Seeb International, Sirab, Tarvi and Mesna. All superiority fighters and attack aircraft could be refueled and in ready status within an hour-fifteen minutes of landing.

In Abu Dhabi, the F-19s landed without incident, and the Commanding Officer, Major Pettit, turned to his wingman, watching khaki uniforms disappearing into a fenced compound.

"What say we grab a beer before checking out the accommodations?" He nodded at the corrugated houses blazing in the dusty compound.

The young man looked uncertain.

"Becker's gonna sit tight till we're all in . . . And believe me, you're gonna want a drink." He nodded again in the direction of their housing. "It gets real dry out here."

The younger man looked out over the shimmering runway, then back at the hot metal barracks.

The other man pointed over the runway to a hazy image of skyscrapers in the distance. "There's a place called Wimpy's on the edge of the city."

"Wimpy's," the wingman said, and grinned. "How'd you hear about it? . . ."

The two men walked toward the compound to check in and pick up a jeep for the short drive into town.

On the ground at Riyadh, General Becker snapped on a pair of dark glasses, and looked up and around. He knew the desert. The air was heavy. Heavy with heat, or sand too fine to see. One had to breathe carefully in this place.

Becker was met by the United States Ambassador to Saudi Arabia, the CIA Station Chief in Jidda, and Youssef Ibrahim himself—the man in all of Saudi Arabia closest to the King. In fact, it had been this ugly little man, whose face looked as if it had collapsed under the pressures of nose and chin, whose counsel had persuaded the King to accept the United States' plan.

They were a strange foursome: the General big and khaki; Ibrahim a flutter of white skirts and kaffiyeh; the Ambassador in black; Mr. Black of the CIA in white. They walked to a small pre-fab office thirty yards off the field.

Inside, the air was even heavier. An electric fan flew a tongue of blue ribbon into the air, but even the slip of cloth moved sluggishly. Becker did not remove his glsses.

With introductions and formalities done with, CIA Agent Black turned to General Becker and said, "I'm afraid the King has a problem . . ."

A wave of nausea hit the General. He stiffened.

Youssef Ibrahim raised a hand. His fingers were skeletal, long and almost impossibly slender. "Not *your* problem, General," the old man said softly. "But there have been threats against the King. In the event he deems it necessary to remove some of his staff and family to Khartoum we will need your help in transport. Several of your 747s will do nicely."

Becker let a little bit of air escape his lips. He had been prepared for this; Larry Apple had briefed him on the propaganda campaign against Fahd. "You understand, sir, that the President is my commander-in-chief. I'll have to have his word first."

Again the hand danced in the air. "Yes, yes, of course. Contact your commander-in-chief, then. If it is required, the King can be ready in thirty-six hours."

"With the President's approval, thirty-six hours is all I'll need."

Ibrahim's eyes bored against the dark lenses of General Becker's glasses. Then he turned and walked toward the door of the little room. He stood with his hand still holding the doorknob, a slice of vast empty sky framed in the door, the low roar of engines vibrating like heat waves in the air. He turned back for one moment. "It is good you are here, United States." And he was gone.

The Ambassador was sweating. His shirt stuck to his back. He wondered what might happen now. He still couldn't believe a lousy smear campaign could crack the foundations of a family who had been in power for well over fifty years. But damned if it hadn't. He looked up at Becker, wondering if this big fellow could handle whatever bizarre new cult might be in power tomorrow.

Becker was moving toward the door when the Ambassador stopped him. "General, there's a press conference I'm afraid you'll have to address tomorrow—4:00 PM. I'll pick you up at 3:00."

The Ambassador stopped at Becker's scowl. "All questions will be in English," he assured him.

"There'll be *no* questions," Becker said. I've got a statement—short and to the point. I'll be ready."

* * * * *

At 4:00 PM on April 8, General Becker faced some sixty members of the press and twelve television cameras. The reporter from *Pravda,* a handsome young Muskovite, took a seat nearest the door. The lights in the otherwise comfortable conference room and the heat outside that seemed to press against the walls overwhelmed the air conditioning.

Becker stood at a lectern in front of the room, his short speech typed on a sheet of paper. There was a glass of tepid water on the flat back of the podium. As he approached the center of the stage, he noticed a fly depart the rim of the glass.

He silenced the rustling of paper with a glare. When the room was completely quiet he began reading.

"Ladies and Gentlemen: A United States Rapid Deployment Force has been landed in Muscat, Oman, Dhahran, Abu Dhabi and Bahrain, with full agreement of the European Economic Council and the Gulf Oil Authority. Our mission is to provide long term security for the oil producing, refining and shipping facilities of Authority members."

There was a murmur in the room. Becker paused, looking up from his paper. The murmurs died. He had everyone's attention. That was good.

"Our presence here is our guarantee that the United States, our NATO allies and our new partners in the Gulf will brook no interference in the performance of their trade agreements."

He felt perspiration beading his upper lip. His mouth was dry, the air oppressive. He looked at the water glass and squared his shoulders. In the back of the room the *Pravda* reporter was squinting at Becker. There was an irritating buzz of cameras in the air.

Becker had paused, knowing that his next statement was pushing the line of diplomacy. He said with no expression on his face or in his voice, "Western Europe agrees that without Gulf Oil, they make a far less appealing target."

There were audible exclamations from the press corps. Becker continued, without raising his voice. "There should be no question of our commitment, or our capabilities to defend those commitments."

Without pausing further, Becker ended the press conference by turning the page he had been reading, face down, and saying tersely, "No questions. Copies of this statement at the door."

Before he had finished his last sentence, the reporters had risen. All but one. The handsome Russian was already out of the room, running toward the bank of phones gaping far down the hall.

CHAPTER EIGHTEEN

Moscow, April 18

It was raining—an unrelenting, diagonal rain that slanted one way and then another, directed by the wind to beat upon windows, to stripe the air, to puddle up so that even the surest step was undermined.

Alexi Kolkin stared morosely out his window. He had problems. He had deep problems.

He turned from the window, reaching inside his coat pocket for a small hinged tin. He saw his hands were shaking. Quickly, he snapped open the lid, fumbled two small white tablets into the palm of his right hand, brought the hand up against his face, tossed back his head.

He sank into a commodious straight-back padded chair behind his desk, took a sip of mineral water from a big crystal glass, and held his hand out in front of him. Shaking.

He would absolutely have to get control of himself. Absolutely.

His eye fell on the memo which had been waiting for him on his arrival:

MEMORANDUM
TOP SECRET

FROM: *Minister of Power & Electrification, Pyotr Neporozhny*
VIA: *General Nikolai Altunin*
TO: *Alexi Kolkin*
SUBJECT: *Nuclear power plant disaster*
REQUEST: *Need for Soviet Army Forces*

On April 14 the 1000 MW power reactor at Novovoronezh sustained an unexpected loss-of-load due to the rupture of a 4 cm pipe. The plant cannot be approached to ascertain how damage occurred to the pressure vessel.

Control room personnel were unable to activate the plant's Emergency Cooling System, which precipitated the meltdown, breaching the containment building. Immediate release of high radioactivity bathing Unit #1, 210 MW; Unit #2, 365 MW; caused plant abandonment by personnel of all units. Units #3 and #4, 440 MW, without personnel, went into meltdown about two hours later: result was a cluster meltdown.

Meteorological conditions at the time included winds from the north and east with velocity of over 65 Km/hr. Lethal downwind area is over 100 miles, over an arc of 60 degrees. The River Don is badly contaminated, and its water will be unuseable for years. Recommend immediate evacuation of Rostov and all cities on the route of River Don.

Release of radioactive gasses and particulates is estimated at over 19 billion curies of radioactivity, a catastrophe.

It appeared the Soviet warranty on their nuclear power program had just expired. Since 1974 fifteen pressure water reactors had been raised near principal cities of southwest Russia. A similar accident had visited the older model reactor in 1982 at Nizhni Tagil in the Urals. That was difficult and costly enough, but five shutdowns at one time was a disaster. A catastrophe, as Pyotr Illyavich Neporozhny had so graciously pointed out.

Foodstocks in the contaminated area could not now be distributed, let alone consumed. Industrial production would grind to a halt as the population was evacuated. To be honest, Kolkin could not even be sure that the eighteen airborne divisions General Altunin had requested would obey orders to move into a radioactive area. That's how bad things had gotten. The Soviet Union had lost the Donetz Basin, perhaps forever.

The situation was, as Pyotr Niporozhny had repeated to Kolkin in his first frantic phone call, out of control. Civil Defense was not capable of handling such widespread disaster, but repositioning airborne divisions from Armenia, Georgia and Azerbaijan to impose a military quarantine on the contaminated areas meant diverting at least half the divisions already in place in Southern Russia between the Caspian and Black Seas. All their planning for a move into the Gulf was effectively up in smoke—or in nuclear waste. They had no choice but to reposition those planes to augment Civil Defense for evacuating cities.

Kolkin dropped his head into his hands. He felt sick. He did not consider himself a superstitious man, but it was difficult to believe a natural course of events should have conspired to create failure of so much on so many levels.

Financially, things had never been worse—the arms race was draining the treasury, already depleted by having collateralized Polish loans with gold of 99.5% purity: it had been that, or risk political excommunication in Western Europe by invading Poland. Then there were the grain shortages of the early eighties from which they were still recovering.

Russian resources were diminishing daily: monetary resources, now military as well, when those eighteen divisions were pulled to control the contaminated areas in the southwest. And Russia had become a victim—of bad times, bad timing, and stupid accidents. For a very brief moment Kolkin wondered if as favorite son of the motherland, he might be made a victim too.

No. Absolutely not. What was he thinking! He was still President of all the Soviet Socialist Republics. No. Kolkin knew them all too well. They were too much divided, or too frightened, to dare challenge him.

And the blame. Was *he* to blame? Certainly not. Not for this damnable catastrophe, not for the disastrous turn of events in the Mideast. That ambitious ass Argunov, with no sense of timing. . . . So damnedly, stubbornly convinced of his own rightness. The ass! The fool!

He must stop this. . . . Get control.

He reached toward a left-hand drawer in his desk and lifted out a hard-bound copy of *The Brothers Karamazov* lying flat in the bottom of the drawer. The spine of the book had been separated, and Kolkin pulled an accordian-pleated sheet of pink paper from between the leather cover and the sewn pages.

He unfolded the note and read it. Then he took the sheet and pressed it to his face, inhaling deeply. He was an old fool, he knew.

He rose from his chair and walked back to the window, the slip of paper still in his hand. The rain was quieter now. The wind had died. Maybe it wasn't as bad as he thought.

He knew in less than a second it was exactly as bad as he thought. He leaned his forehead against the cool window glass.

* * * * *

Kolkin looked down the U-shaped table. They were all so much alike, he thought. Too short, too heavy—stumpy. Black-suited mushrooms, they were.

He would have to keep a tight rein on the meeting, that was all. He would direct his questions to that weasel Sorokin, to start. He would allow Argunov to wait. And then when the man was bursting, he would let the fool hang himself. The man had no control. . . .

"What happened in Libya, Comrade Sorokin?" Kolkin asked as if he were inquiring about the weather.

Two lines of heads turned toward Sorokin at the curve of the table. Argunov sighed.

Sorokin's eyes seemed to shift to his left, toward Bukov, but it was hard to tell. His head turned toward Kolkin, to his right. They stared at one another.

"Well, Comrade?" Kolkin prodded, his voice still light; the eyebrows, though, drawing together.

Sorokin's mind was racing. What the devil is he doing? Why is he asking *me*?

Argunov glanced quickly over at Bukov. Bukov was staring impassively at his hands.

Rather peevishly, Sorokin answered, "Nothing happened. Tripoli has perfectly adequate ground based radar facilities, but they did not notify any units of the Soviet Fleet. . . ."

"Nothing happened?" Kolkin interrupted. "There were over two hundred planes flying over their heads during one three hour period. . . ."

Sorokin's mouth was dry. "My reports indicate that they thought it was a tactical exercise. The United States had announced. . . ."

Kolkin shouted, slamming the table with his fist. "Are they such fools, they thought that two hundred transport and attack aircraft represented a tactical exercise?"

Sorokin's eyes narrowed. Several heads in the room bowed. "I have a report here," Sorokin said without blinking, "that many of the aircraft may have managed to bypass our radar equipment. . . ."

"Come now, Comrade," Kolkin said, smiling stiffly. "Do we have reason to believe the Americans have developed a military ability to become invisible to our equipment—without your having heard of it? Or perhaps your crew in Tripoli are double agents. Is that a possibility?"

Sorokin's lips tightened. He was being baited. This oversized hump was baiting him. In a fraction of a second his mind reviewed the Libyan situation, looking for something to put Kolkin off, while he figured out what was going on here. They all knew that Qaddafi was in trouble—losing his grip. His people had become disenchanted with long military duties, and a puritan way of life harsher than their neighbors. Qaddafi's extravagant development plans had been suspended with the reduction of oil income. And the lush Jefara plain around Tripoli, Libya's richest agricultural resource, was unproductive; Qaddafi had begged for Moscow to assist in irrigating the land—Moscow could not. Maybe this was some kind of payback. Perhaps he could shift the blame to the Minister of Agriculture. . . .

"I've heard that the Moslem Turks in Libya are very friendly with the French. . ." Kolkin said more mildly when Sorokin's answer was not forthcoming.

Sorokin flushed. How the hell did Kolkin know about *that*. Someone in his department? . . . "There is no foundation to those lies." Sorokin said stiffly, his neck starting to push out and forward, his voice becoming metallic. "I have kept a monitor on Turkish workgroups for over a year—they have no political ambition. . . ."

Sorokin was dead wrong. French Intelligence had been working with the Turks for two years or more. They had honeycombed the work force of over 50,000 Turkish nationals living and working in Libya, with cells of men and women who had been taught sabotage—literally on the job—and a variety of communications intelligence skills including wire tapping and code breaking.

Sorokin had become suspicious last year when a bomb exploded prematurely at the apartment of one of these Turkish workers, killing him and several members of his family. The Libyans had persuaded Sorokin's man in Tripoli that the lone Turk was a dissident with a grudge against his landlord. Sorokin was no fool, though—he had ordered infiltration of four factories and two refineries. His men made their ways into the work force—and discovered nothing. Turkish intelligence used the six clumsy KGB agents as an exercise in evasion for their own proteges.

Kolkin picked up a pencil, looked with apparent interest at the eraser end. "I haven't heard you mention equipment breakdown, Comrade."

"There was no equipment failure."

"But you would agree there *was* a failure?"

As the two men spoke, the other members of the Politburo were profoundly silent. Even the sound of rain had ceased.

"Yes, Comrade," Sorokin nearly hissed.

"Then whose failure would you say it is?"

Damn him, Sorokin thought.

The suggestion of a smile passed across Bukov's face.

Argunov felt blood rushing to his head. They were going to try to put it on *him*, he could feel it.

Without waiting for an answer, Kolkin leaned forward and stared pointedly at Argunov. "Perhaps we should *all* ask ourselves that question," he said.

Silence.

Sorokin realized round one was over. His neck slowly retracted.

* * * * *

Kolkin broke the stare and glanced slowly down the parallel arms of the table. He was feeling a strange detachment, as if he were watching himself carry out the charade of Chairman. The fact that no one was looking at him—or anyone else, for that matter, made the scene even more surreal. No witnesses, shot through Kolkin's brain. He snapped his head back to Argunov, more to make a connection, than continue. . . .

"Comrade Argunov," he said, lifting his hand. He noticed, without any feeling, that his hand was perfectly steady.

Argunov stared back from under heavy white brows.

"Comrade Argunov," Kolkin repeated pleasantly, "have you read a copy of this General Becker's statement regarding the American forces in the Gulf?"

Argunov nodded once, sharply.

Kolkin let the silence permeate the moment. Then he said, "Perhaps I misunderstood your Alaska program. I was under the impression that it was going to provide the time we needed to establish our own position in the Mideast."

Argunov's eyes were aching with the pressure in his head. The crescent scar, usually silvery pale, was shot with blood. "The program *did* work. It was . . ."

Kolkin was still sporting an almost pleasant smile, but he spat the words, "The program *worked*, Comrade? Are you joking?" The smile was dissolving, voice becoming louder. "The program was a disaster." No smile. Voice resonant, accusing.

Bukov leaned forward slightly, head tilted, as if measuring the weight of Kolkin's words.

"The program was a disaster for the motherland," the General Secretary went on. "It was you and General Vasilov of the Strategic Rocket Forces that called President Baker's inaugural announcement a provocation which would put him out of business. Now the European pacifists are supporting a greater use of conventional weapons for defense. Your premature release of information slandering the Saudi king was more than ill-timed, it was ill-conceived. Now, despite all the expense of our Alaska program, and the Saudi scandal, the Americans have weapons in place which can destroy bases on our own soil."

Kolkin rose from his chair. "And as if that were not enough," he continued, "what you called Baker's provocation has persuaded Holland and Denmark to accept Pershing II and Cruise missiles with conventional warheads, thereby uniting most of NATO."

His voice lowered abruptly. "You have set back foreign policy in this country 60 years."

Every man was now staring openly toward the head of the table. This was a scene which occurred perhaps only every twenty or thirty years—a Comrade's immolation—it was something to learn from: no member would ever forget it, and all knew they would never speak of it.

Argunov's face was darkening, his mind was rushing, words stumbled out of his mouth. "You dare accuse *me*. None of this would have . . . Blaming me for what Holland and Denmark did . . ."

He could hear himself not making sense. He took a ragged breath. "To say that I am responsible—it is to cover up the real failure. My plan was only a part of the maneuver—a small part—but it was successful. You see that . . ."

His outstretched arm beseeched his comrades but not one man met his eyes. Only Kolkin stared at him.

Argunov scraped back his chair and stood up facing Kolkin. His voice shaking, he said, "It was an intelligence failure. Failure to protect State secrets. There is no other way they might have anticipated the Mideast as part of our plan. My program worked exactly as we hoped. You wanted time—look! You had a full month. No," he said, suddenly running out of steam, "it is not my failure."

The room felt like a vacuum. Argunov took a deep breath. His hand fell to his side. He dared not look at Sorokin whose arms were crossed in front of him, head at an angle.

He was feeling a little dizzy, wanted to reach for the water, was afraid to make that large a move. The veins in his temples were pounding, painful.

He should not have put it on intelligence. Sorokin was too dangerous. Perhaps he could soften his last words by going in another direction. He took another breath while the table watched. He spoke slowly and too loud, to hear himself over the throbbing of his head. "There are other mistakes, Comrade," he said. "Mistakes far more significant than what you call mine."

Staring at Kolkin, as if for dear life, he continued, "They are mistakes that we have lived with for years: setting precedents, establishing failures as the norm. Who refused to authorize the invasion of Poland in order to pursue some misguided idea about détente? Now this same revisionism is rampant in Czechoslovakia, in East Germany. Marx says . . ."

Kolkin pierced Argunov with his look. The other man fell silent. "You are making another mistake right now, Comrade."

Argunov tried to see if Sorokin was looking at him. He couldn't tell.

"I will not defend myself to you," Kolkin said quietly. "*None of us* in this room will defend ourselves to you, Comrade Argunov."

Sorokin was not looking at Argunov. As far as he was concerned, Argunov was a dead man. He was staring at Kolkin, President of Russia and all the Soviet Republics, trying to unite them at the end, against someone who no longer existed.

CHAPTER NINETEEN

Moscow, April 18

When Boris Argunov left the disastrous meeting, he knew with sickening certainty, that his career was finished. He had to figure out what to do.

He went to his office, told his secretary he wasn't in for calls. He had no idea how long he sat there.

His stomach felt weak, and rage seemed to have accelerated his heart beat and the course of blood through his veins. And his mind—his mind was frantic, speeding with unconnected thoughts and pictures that crowded his head. He couldn't think. He couldn't think!

. . . . He remembered a woman he had known in Leningrad, a dancer she was. And he was newly appointed to the Politburo, and had felt so young. It was twenty years ago. The time had raced by. He remembered his stinging defeat last year, to Kolkin. . . . For no reason he thought of his dacha in Murom. He kept his greatest treasure there, a forest green Austin Healey—spent whole days fast-driving through the narrow wooded back road stretches, birch trees blurring like a white wall on either side, the top down, his hair flying. His friends said he should have been a racer. His friends!

How proud he had been when he got that car. That was seven years ago, the same year he had been awarded the little house in Murom. He pictured his study there which occupied a western wall of the house. He enjoyed the twilight in that room—watching trees become silhouettes outside his window, lighting the lamps, pouring a vodka. . . .

Out of this particular impression rose one of the records he kept in his study, and it served to focus him. The papers. He'd best destroy those papers.

Outside, as he climbed into the long black Zil and his young chauffeur walked around the car and got into the driver's seat, he

133

saw the weather had become quite fair. It was late afternoon. Where had the time gone? It would be dark by the time he got to the house.

Moving swiftly through Red Square and then through Moscow traffic to the city limits, Argunov thought fleetingly that it had been a long time since he had seen a blue sky. The thought turned into an omen and he was suddenly terribly frightened.

He leaned forward in his seat and said, "Faster," to the driver.

* * * * *

Alexi Kolkin left the meeting, feeling slightly nauseated. He had no stomach for this sort of thing. He had no doubt Argunov would not survive the night. If Sorokin didn't take care of it himself, Argunov would probably suffer a stroke anyway—his face by the end of the meeting had been practically purple.

He sighed and sat at his desk, absently fingering Neporozhny's memorandum. Argunov might already be dying of radiation poisoning. So might they all.

Kolkin quickly stood. Enough. He was meeting his Olga tonight. He would forget everything in her embrace. He would bury his face in her thick, sweet smelling hair, she would rock him like a baby and he would forget. . . . He took his coat from a tall hatrack that stood near the door.

Driving out of Red Square, Kolkin tried to clear his mind. He noticed how the leafy trees that lined quiet Ryazan Avenue seemed shiny, as if they were still wet with this morning's rain, and how newly green it all looked. He rolled down his window and took a deep breath of spring air.

* * * * *

Argunov's driver was pushing the Zil at 120 kilometers per hour. The old man was always in a hurry. Argunov had insisted he leave the main road, to avoid the Kostroma detour.

It was six o'clock by the time they reached the vast sweep of valley near Kovrov and 6:40 PM when the driver turned the car southwest to follow the railroad tracks into Murom.

Argunov had been leaning forward in the back seat. "Can't you go faster?" he said, and heard the high pitched whine of his voice.

The road had taken a sharp ascent, and the driver had the accelerator to the floor. He turned, for a fraction of a second, to Argunov's strained face. It was the last thing he saw.

For Argunov, it happened in slow motion as his car achieved the crest of the hill. It was a truck, full of peat, as it turned out, with a monstrous cartoon outline of Fidel Castro's face painted on the side, stopped squarely across the road.

Before his driver could turn back, before Argunov could form the words, it was over. The last thing he saw was Castro's leering smile, and the last sound the scream of steel against steel.

* * * * *

It was two in the morning when the phone rang in Dimitri Bukov's bedroom. His wife Adya had raised up for a moment, squinted at the clock, then pulled the covers close around her again.

Bukov sat on his side of the bed, listening, bare feet on the cold floor, his back to his wife who was silent, staring at his familiar shape in the darkness.

"What is it, Dimitri?" she said when he hung up.

He turned to her, held her shoulders and kissed her on the forehead. "An accident—I'm not sure how serious. That was Sorokin. He asked that I meet him at Kolkin's office." Bukov was already slipping on his trousers. "You go back to sleep."

* * * * *

Bukov was at staring Sorokin, unbelieving. They were alone in Kolkin's office. He had just heard about Argunov, who had never made it home where two soldiers waited for him. It was just as well, perhaps, and now Sorokin was telling him the rest.

The smaller man was speaking. "She was young enough to be his granddaughter. Disgusting." Sorokin's eyes were glittering. "Evidently one of her other lovers caught them together. He had a gun."

His speech was staccato, like an ill-learned script. "Imagine the scandal if it were known. Fortunately, I have cleaned it up. A very messy business."

Sorokin looked past Bukov's head. Bukov cleared his throat. "Is the girl . . ."

Sorokin glanced at the black window. "By now she is on her way to Mordovia. I thought it was for the best. She agreed. She will have a new name and a new life. She understands. If she disappoints us . . ." Sorokin shrugged. "She knows."

His eyes were terribly bright, Bukov found it difficult to look directly at the man. "Fortunately," he said, "she was between performances." His mouth thinned in a pinched smile.

"And the other man?" Bukov said, keeping his face devoid of any expression, his voice steady.

"And the other man." Sorokin walked over to the window and stared at his own reflection. "He tried to resist arrest." He turned back to Bukov's pale face.

They stared at one another. "Comrade, have a little vodka," Sorokin said, and pointed to a bottle, uncapped on the desk.

Bukov thought that was a good idea. He was glad he was seated, and that the bottle and two small shot glasses were within his reach. He filled both glasses to the brim, replaced the bottle, lifted the drink to his lips and drank half of it in one swallow.

Sorokin walked over from the window and picked up the other glass. "Nostrovya."

"Nostrovya," Bukov repeated, and finished his drink.

Sorokin sat down next to Bukov and crossed his legs. Kolkin's empty chair yawned at them. "I have drafted a statement, Comrade, I think is appropriate. Tell me what you think."

He nodded at a typed page lying flat next to the vodka on Kolkin's desk. Bukov picked up the sheet, hesitated before he sat back with it, and poured himself another vodka. With the glass between two fingers, and Sorokin's paper on his knees, he read,

Press Release for all International Wire Services:

In what all of Russia is calling a tragedy, President Alexi Izmano-vich Kolkin and Chairman of the Central Committee Boris Pyotrovich Argunov were killed Wednesday evening, April 16, when their driver apparently lost control of his vehicle and smashed into the guardrail at

Vladimirovich Bridge. The driver, Grigory Ivanovich Lyubimov was also killed.

The two men were on their way to a reception at Noya Yar when the accident occurred. Andrei Kolkin's wife is being treated by a physician for shock. Argunov is survived by a son Vladimir, in Minsk.

By unanimous decision, senior member of the Politburo, Dimitry Bukov, was appointed to fill Comrade Kolkin's position in an emergency meeting of the Politburo on Friday afternoon. A military funeral with full honors for both men will be held Wednesday, April 23 with burial beneath the Kremlin wall.

Bukov did not look at Sorokin. He drank the vodka. He had to be very cautious. Very cautious. He nodded slowly. "Yes, Comrade, I think this is fine."

Sorokin's eyes held his own. "Yes, I thought you would," he said.

CHAPTER TWENTY

Moscow, April 25

Dimitry Bukov was alone in the conference room, a large room, two hundred feet square, oak panelled, with a large square oak table and huge straight-back chairs. Alone, that is, but for Karl Marx staring impassive from one wall, and Lenin looking cynical and sure from another. The portraits were hung high on the walls, and angled down so the two appeared to oversee what transpired under their sight.

Standing against the walls, about five feet high, and proceeding all around the room, were narrow polished book cases each one of which supported from one to several clocks. These were timepieces from all over the world, some of them hundreds of years old. There were electric clocks, pneumatic clocks, pendulum clocks (one whose pendulum was a porcelain girl on a little enamel swing), program clocks, telechrons, sidereals, a watchman's clock, a mariner's clock, fan clocks unfolding their numbered pleats one at a time, a clepsydra from Sweden measuring time in mercury, its geared plunger sluicing silver drops up through a clear glass funnel and every drop moving the clock's jeweled hand one notch further around its face. There were hour glasses, half-hour glasses, egg glasses and half-minute glasses, a sundial, a telltale, a cuckoo clock from Austria, a French Empire clock, and metronomes, chronometers, and repeaters.

It was a priceless collection, and had been secured in this room when Kolkin succeeded to his position. In order to assure that Breshnev's grandchildren did not sell them off for more money than was good for them, he had ordered they remain in this room.

Bukov was walking slowly around the table, his hands clasped behind his back. The clocks drove him crazy, ticks and drips and chimes and gongs, and that damn cuckoo. There was some superstition about counting the chirps of the cuckoo to know the number of minutes or months or years one had left to live. He tried to remember how it went . . . He stopped and stared into the concave crystal of a brass-fitted pendulum clock. His reflection was warped in the glass, his nose grossly exaggerated, his forehead running like a road into his hairline. He stepped back and ran a hand over his dark slicked back hair, and sighed.

* * * * *

Adya was worried. Overnight her husband, her best friend, had turned into himself, excluding her. He had been gone the last several nights to meetings that lasted forever. The house was too quiet, her dinners were solitary. She wanted him to talk to her and was afraid to know what he might say. When he came home late at night she pretended to be asleep. Now everything was different.

Things were different, but Bukov was beginning to see a path through the muddle. He was still a pawn, he knew, but as a pawn he had the potential to become the most powerful piece on the board. All he had to do was move forward very carefully and avoid direct attack.

He thought of Nikita Khruschev who had played a similar game during his rise in the Party under Stalin. He had kept his mouth shut, and acted as Stalin's proxy in the Ukraine, had established Stalin's reign in Poland, had played along until the timing was right. Three years after Stalin's death he made his move—an act of extraordinary political daring—charging the dead leader with acts of cruelty, betrayal and oppression, accusing him of personal ambitions contrary to Marxist doctrine.

Where Khruschev had gone wrong, Bukov thought, was in his own extravagance. He had made promises he couldn't deliver. He was mostly bluster. Bukov, on the other hand, had style; his game had taught him discipline—and truly, he was smarter than Khruschev.

But he would have to deal with Sorokin. This was a very delicate matter. Sorokin was clearly in charge, waving his narrow vision of policy like a scythe. His comrades understood Bukov's position, and seemed to look at him (when they looked at him at all) with some embarrassment. Bukov was quiet, biding his time.

Sorokin was moving too fast. One week after the deaths of Kolkin and Argunov, and he was already dragging out military policy, dusting off doctrine that in Bukov's mind (and it would stay in Bukov's mind) would best be left moldering with times past.

For three nights they met in Kolkin's cold office, and Bukov listened to a babble of Manifesto and fantasies about a Soviet blitzkrieg on Western Europe. Sorokin had taken the United States General's warning as a personal challenge.

The night before Bukov had elicited Minister of Defense Marshall Svetlov to join them. Nervous, the pale faced Minister admitted their nuclear targeting was not sophisticated enough for him to say that the areas they could destroy would not turn out to be the ones the Soviet Union might need. A conventional war could not succeed now. Not yet. Pershing II missiles could not be immobilized before launching, and American Copperhead antitank missiles now available to NATO forces in quantity were deadly at ranges over thirty miles—tanks could no longer make a closely massed strike.

Bukov had watched Svetlov grow paler as Sorokin darkened, pummeling him with questions. A move on Western Europe would end in a stalemate at best. Bukov had sipped his vodka and thought about his options.

Sorokin wanted an offensive attack. To disagree or take any definitive action to divert Sorokin's lust for expansion and his desire to reassert Soviet power—and Bukov believed it *was* Soviet power Sorokin desired, not self-aggrandizement—would be foolish.

There were other ways, though, and he suggested a safer one—using proxy forces for revolution—Ethiopia, South Yemen, Cubans in Angola, even the Syrians had become arms of the great Communist body. It had worked before. The PLO had been their major, if temporary failure in Lebanon several years ago. Even that setback had worked to their advantage as late as last year with many PLO and the radical spine of Al Fatah's umbrella reorganizing and designing terrorist operations in the United States. Even the international denunciations following the destruction of the Korean Airlines plane in 1983 had died down. This act, Bukov knew, had been a duty of the Soviet military forces.

Bukov knew he had given Sorokin something to think about, without putting himself in peril. Marshall Svetlov had looked directly into his eyes and shaken his hand at the conclusion of their meeting. It was the first time any of the members of the Politburo had met his eyes since before his quiet accession to this post.

* * * * *

Bukov looked at his watch. It was after two o'clock. He wondered if Sorokin made him wait just to make it clear whose time was most valuable. For a fleeting moment he thought about leaving. Of course he would never do such a thing, but he entertained the thought for just a second.

Four separate clocks marked the moment: 2:15. Bukov sighed, and the door opened.

"Comrade Sorokin. . ." Bukov began.

Sorokin raised his hand as he approached the large table. "I have arranged an interview for you," he said, slapping his briefcase down on the table, unsnapping the clasps. "I think it is time this administration makes some statements for the record."

"Statements, Comrade?" Bukov said quietly.

"There are a lot of questions being asked, accusations."

"Accusations?" Bukov's eyebrows danced.

"Regarding interests in the Mideast, nuclear policy, and of course we must speak out about the United States in the Gulf."

Sorokin pulled a stack of papers from his case and turned toward Bukov. The man looked worried, but not frightened. Rightly so. *He* had nothing to fear. He was a perfect puppet, cool and well spoken, but not ambitious. Sorokin had never seen Bukov go after anything, or disagree with anyone. Yet the man was smart, he had put himself in the right place at the right time, and he had made himself a reputation for decency. By sharing with him the details of last week's unfortunate accident, Sorokin believed he had bound his puppet to him.

"Jean Aubusson has agreed to meet with you—he is considered impartial. . . ."

Bukov wondered if that were a joke. Aubusson?

". . . You will see that I have given you a dramatic announcement, Comrade." Sorokin's mouth twitched. "Comrade Kolkin had looked forward to this moment. He had planned to make a clear gesture of world peace on behalf of all Russia." His eyes drilled Bukov. "Now it is your privilege."

Sorokin handed over the papers. Bukov looked down at them. "I've provided both questions and answers. Review the materials—I think you will agree the presentation is properly discreet. We'll discuss it Monday before your interview at ten o'clock in the studio. Is there anything else?. . ."

Bukov looked up. His expression was calm. "Yes, Comrade. Pyotr Neporozhny has been calling regarding the evacuation in the south. . . ."

Sorokin shook his head, annoyed. "I will take care of it, Comrade—just learn that material," he said, poking his finger at the papers. Without another word, he grabbed his briefcase and started moving toward the door.

When he had gone, Bukov took the top sheet off the stack, pulled a chair back from the table, and slowly began to be seated. The chime of a pendulum jarred him. He hastily gathered up the pile of material, and left the room.

* * * * *

Jean Aubusson, a tall, thin, polished European, sat across from Bukov, pin-striped, with white shirt and grey silk tie, in the Kremlin studio.

Bukov looked quite relaxed: there was no evidence of the weekend's long nights, the hours he had spent sitting in front of his mirror rehearsing the play to be performed here, practicing the crossing of a leg with the same attention he gave the stress of a syllable in a particularly crucial answer. Nuance. Very important to Dimitry Bukov—always had been.

The studio was enormous, but Aubusson and Bukov were set up in a small partitioned area which included no more than two deep chairs facing each other at an angle, and a small table with water pitcher and glasses. The backdrop was a heavy paper drapery.

In front of them had grown a city of umbrella lights, video tape and sound equipment; and a crew which hustled around much faster than was necessary—moving, adjusting, and rechecking everything.

One man finally distinguished himself as director of the taping, said a few words to Aubusson and Bukov, then shouting for quiet, disappeared into the geometry of equipment.

Aubusson began. "Chairman Bukov, allow me to express my sadness at the untimely passing of your comrades Kolkin and Argunov."

Bukov inclined his head solemnly.

"There have been some rumors about the accident," Aubusson added.

Bukov looked hurt and then angry. "We have lost two great men," he said stiffly. "Two great statesmen. Obviously I will not respond to tasteless and insulting rumor." He paused, as if searching for a way to communicate his personal hurt. He began again, more softly. "Their loss is painful for the families of the two men, and painful for all of Russia, because in a way we are all family of Comrade Kolkin and Comrade Argunov."

Aubusson nodded understandingly, looked down his page of questions for a less delicate subject. "Do you have any comment, sir, on the newly proclaimed Free Republic of Kurdistan?"

"Yes." Bukov relaxed and crossed his leg, noting that the crease in his pant leg fell precisely down the center of his knee.

"The Soviet Union welcomes this new state. We are already in the process of executing a treaty of friendship."

"Will that treaty extend Soviet influence further into Iran or Iraq?"

Bukov looked coolly at Aubusson. "We hope it will extend Soviet *friendship* further into the Middle East."

Aubusson half smiled and nodded, as if in approval. Bukov didn't like this man. He was too much a dandy. Too cocky.

"What are your diplomatic relations with Saudi Arabia?"

"Diplomatic relations are very good," Bukov said smoothly. "There has been some concern about Shia fundamentalists from Iran taking advantage of government vulnerability, but we have been able to assure King Fahd's ministers in Riyahd there is nothing to fear from our Iranian brothers. Indeed we all share the wish for peace in the Middle East." Smiling, Bukov added, "And in all the world."

"And what do you consider a threat to peace in the Middle East?"

Bukov gazed steadily into camera three. "I think it is historically obvious who threatens peace there."

"Are you speaking of Israel?"

"Of course."

"Israel has said it will no longer tolerate missiles in Syria. Do you have any comment?"

Bukov was aware of a camera moving in on his left. For a split second he felt set upon. He shifted in his seat.

"Naturally, we must support our fraternal allies in Syria. Israel and the United States are naive to think otherwise. After 1982 we provided new and more powerful tanks and aircraft. We have also provided missiles and will continue to do so. Weapons are necessary to preserve the peace in Lebanon. We will, of course, continue to add to the Syrian military potential. Units of the Popular Front for the Liberation of Palestine now receive the same support we once gave Yasser Arafat's PLO. He became a liability, and Syria needed more Palestinians dedicated to the destruction of Israel. Anything less than an independent state in all of Palestine is unacceptable."

Aubusson showed no reaction. Instead, he asked, "What are your interests in Gulf oil, outside of Saudi Arabia?"

Bukov leaned forward. He found his camera and spoke slowly and evenly. "We do not now, and never have had any interest in oil there. What the Arab states have always wanted is non-interference by outside powers in their internal affairs."

Aubusson nodded. "So you do not sanction the United States intervention there."

Bukov smiled, but did not answer.

"What *is* your reaction to the United States having moved into the Middle East?"

"Reaction?" Bukov said with aplomb. "Amusement, perhaps. They have over two divisions in Saudi Arabia, and fighters and anti-submarine warfare planes. Who do they expect to be fighting? And for what?" He leaned back. "We have never had aspirations—as we now see the United States obviously does—in the Persian Gulf, or even the Indian Ocean."

"But the United States has called the Yemeni base at Aden a destabilizing influence on the area."

Bukov shook his head, reaching for his water glass. "That is absurd, as well. South Yemen required simple back-up units for what it considers a threat from Saudi Arabia and Oman." He sipped and replaced the glass, fine cut crystal, he noticed, on the arm-side table.

"How do you respond, Chairman Bukov," Aubusson asked, "to the accusation by NATO that over five hundred SS-20 missiles with three nuclear warheads each, which the Soviets have deployed in Eastern Europe, is excessive and a real threat to world peace?"

Bukov tried on his hurt expression again. "Those missiles are in place to support our brave Warsaw Pact troops and to contain the expansionist imperialists of the North Atlantic Treaty Organization. The excess is in the zeal with which NATO makes these hysterical pronouncements. There is no doubt that *they* wish to destabilize Eastern Europe—they are persistent in encouraging anti-Soviet activities in Poland, Romania, and other peace-loving socialist countries . . ."

"But can you reconcile the possible use of nuclear weapons against targets in Western Europe with defense of your country?" Aubusson asked, staring directly into Bukov's eyes.

"NATO claims their use would destroy large areas of Western Europe that the Warsaw Pact forces would have to occupy in order to frustrate such obviously imperialistic ambitions."

Bukov's face did not betray the irritation he felt at the interruption. "Our conventional forces are far more than sufficient to defend Soviet interest, Mr. Aubusson. And we have no need to destroy or occupy any areas in Western Europe." Yes, he thought he had spoken that well.

Again, Aubusson referred to his notes. "The reorganized Palestinian Liberation Organization now dominated by the Popular Front for the Liberation of Palestine, as you have said, enjoys Soviet support and has since 1983. What do you see as its real objective?"

"We have always supported the Palestinian cause. Now, with Syrian support, they can regain their legitimate homeland," Bukov said easily. "We have encouraged Syria to allow Palestinian units to advance their joint objectives in Lebanon and elsewhere."

"Yes," Aubusson said, looking up from his notes. "Syria would seem to owe a favor to her benefactors. I understand you have completely rearmed that country, and Iran as well."

"One cannot keep the peace without arms, Mr. Aubusson. One simply cannot," Bukov said, and again he felt he had saved himself. It was an interesting choreography, he thought. Damn the man, though.

"Do you have any thoughts on resolving the continued unrest in Lebanon, Iraq and Iran?"

Bukov straightened. He began seriously. "As you know, we have worked closely with Syria in making significant strides towards peace. But more than that, to demonstrate our commitment to restoring peace, the Soviet Union will call for an international conference in Geneva, to further a climate of communication and understanding. Several peace-loving Arab countries: Iran, Syria and Libya, as well as the Popular Front for the Liberation of Palestine, have expressed an interest in attending such a conference. Palestinians everywhere will see that we are their real friends, not some of the Arab states who abandoned Yasser Arafat in 1982 and again in 1983."

"Have you extended an invitation to the United States?"

"An invitation is being delivered as we speak."

"And you think they will accept?" the reporter asked.

Bukov couldn't quite tell whether the question was a ridicule, or in earnest. "Eventually, Mr. Aubusson, the United States must see that our motives are peaceful. Americans are a suspicious nation, but if they meet us as equals, across a table, they can know that our intentions are as benign as their own. It is the only way. We are making this first gesture—it is now up to President Baker to meet us halfway."

"Will Israel be included in this meeting?"

"Israel will be invited, although they have so far shown no interest in working out problems at the conference table."

"And if the Popular Front for the Liberation of Palestine refuses to attend a conference at which Israel is represented?" Aubusson prompted.

"The PLO need not attend. We have its proxy." Bukov looked for his camera. "You see, we will go to great lengths to accommodate all those who would wish to cooperate for the common peace."

Aubusson cleared his throat. "Some of President Baker's advisors have said that the real threat to the Middle East is the Soviet Union."

Bukov's eyebrows furrowed. With the slightest edge of irritation in his voice he said, "The Soviet Union has a tradition of assisting countries in *promoting* peace. I have just proposed a *convention* for peace in the Middle East. Historically, we have made sacrifices on behalf of peace in equipment, monies, even lives—look at our 20,000 fine young soldiers who were martyred in Afghanistan trying to maintain peace there . . . "

"Regarding Afghanistan, Chairman Bukov," Aubusson interrupted, "the United States has charged the Soviet Union with calculated duplicity in concealing its prolonged use of toxic weapons there and in Laos. They claim that yellow rain has killed over 75,000 defenseless people in those countries. How do you respond?"

Bukov didn't blink, but he was furious. There were to have been no questions on that subject. He uncrossed his legs. "The matter is under investigation by the Standing Consultative Commission; however the evidence that the United States presented to the U.N. Security Council is so clearly anti-Soviet, so clearly a form of mendacious propaganda, that I think no one can seriously consider it."

He paused. "You may recall not too long ago the Secretary of State agreed with Mr. Gromyko that such fabricated evidence should not be allowed to complicate Salt III negotiations. Similarly, I prefer it not to be a subject here, nor would I expect it to be a subject at our Geneva peace conference."

There was a nod from a crew man to the director, whose hand raised to catch Aubusson's eye.

With a charming smile that did not extend to his eyes, Aubusson sat back and said, "Chairman Bukov, thank you for spending time with us today, and for your honest and penetrating answers to the questions we have discussed."

Bukov nodded gravely, and said, "It was my pleasure, Mr. Aubusson."

Beautiful, thought the director. He signalled for a close-up of Bukov's face and called it a wrap.

CHAPTER
TWENTY-ONE

Washington, April 27

"Do you ever . . . eavesdrop?" he said to her one late Saturday afternoon. They were walking along the bank of the Potomac behind the Watergate. The walkway was bordered by a march of trees ruffled with green; an occasional weeping willow bowed near the river.

She looked at him curiously. "Eavesdrop?" They were holding hands.

"Parapsychologically speaking."

She looked down, smiling. Their shadows were long and overlapping. "Not for quite a long time."

They continued walking for a while, not speaking. Then she started laughing.

"What are you laughing about?"

"I can't help it—it's just funny. . . ." She shook her head, and then suddenly her eyes becomes serious, and she stopped walking. "Peter, I'd never do that."

He looked at her, at the late afternoon sunlight in her hair. Without thinking, he drew her to him, and as she looked up into his eyes, he kissed her.

It was a long, very tender kiss. They walked some more.

At a black wrought-iron park bench, they sat.

"Tell me a story about your childhood," she said.

Peter nodded, then looked out over the river which seemed bronzed by the sun. He turned toward her, smiling. "I've got a good one," he said, and lifted her hand to his lips.

"I was eleven, I think . . . yes, a year after we'd come back to the States—and my mother was afraid I was going to grow up antisocial—fifth grade had been very lonely . . ."

Peggy leaned back against the bench, tucked one arm through his.

"So she started encouraging me to join things—and she enrolled me in a ballroom dancing class after school."

Peggy laughed. "I went to one of those too. White gloves?"

He grimmaced and nodded. "And fat little girls. On my third lesson I smuggled about two pounds of shot into class. About the middle of class I excused myself, waited for Miss Beale—she was the piano player—to get into the next lesson, and then I came back and let them go."

Peggy smiled.

He chuckled. "Needless to say, dancing classes stopped."

"What did your parents do?"

"My father didn't see the humor in it, nor, I might add, did Miss Beale or any of the pink little girls. But I did make a couple of friends among the boys. And secretly, I think my mother appreciated the gesture."

They talked some more, and started back when the sky was pink behind them and becoming orange over the river. It was almost dark when they got back to Peter's apartment.

* * * * *

He had spent the morning reading about the development of the Saturn Missile program—a program Peggy had been instrumental in building, which fact made the subject more important to him. About a week ago Harry Smyth had asked him to work with the Under Secretary for Research and Development, in connection with the Salt III negotiations in Geneva—a rare honor, George Heath confided, for Harry to recommend anyone for anything. If Jefferson thought he could handle it, and still keep up with his other work, Heath encouraged him to do so. Saturn, Heath had said, was going to make some difference in the world.

As it had been in the 1982 SALT II talks, this year's SALT III agenda included a review of the Soviet/United States Anti-ballistic Missile Treaty, and Peter was trying to become familiar with the spectrum of systems the treaty covered.

Peggy was spending the morning at Langley, had gone shopping in the afternoon; she would meet him at his place toward the end of the day, they'd have dinner, then do some homework. That was the plan.

She arrived at his door at 5:30 behind a tumble of packages. Peter relieved her of an armful of boxes while she pulled a bottle of Montrachet 1979 out of a shopping bag.

"For dinner," she said, and kissed him lightly on the cheek. "It's so beautiful out, Peter. . ." she was on her way to the refrigerator with the bottle. "I ran into Diane Boyington at Saks, and wait till you see. . . ." She stopped in the doorway on her way back, looking at him critically. Frowning, she said, "Have you been working all day?"

He smiled at her. "You're very beautiful," he said. "And yes, I've been working, but it's been a good. . . ."

"Oh, Peter, you *must* share some of this day with me. Let's just take a walk by the river—it's a perfect afternoon."

* * * * *

Neither of them seemed in much of a hurry to get to work. They were sitting facing one another on the couch, the last of the wine in two glasses on the coffee table.

"What are you thinking?"

He hesitated, then said, "I'm thinking how crazy I was to have let you disappear for four years." He paused. "I had had all these old-fashioned ideas and *ideals* about marriage, and they had just crumbled around me. I was afraid to get near anyone for a long time after that. I needed to figure out what had gone wrong."

"Did you?"

"I think so."

She leaned over and kissed him. "Are you still afraid?"

He looked at her. "No. Not any more."

"Then, Peter," she said very gently, looking at their hands touching on the couch between them, "can I stay with you tonight?"

* * * * *

Much later, as she lay on the very edge of sleep, he kissed the top of her head and said, "Peg?"

"Mmm."

"Remember this afternoon when we went walking?"

"M-hmm."

"And I asked you about eavesdropping?"

She nestled closer to him. "Yes."

"What did you mean, 'not for quite a long time?' "

A pause. He felt her soft laughter against him.

"Peter?"

"Yes?"

"I love you."

CHAPTER
TWENTY-TWO

Washington, April 30

Grace Sherwood pushed against Jefferson's door with shoulder and hip, carrying two mugs of steamy coffee in either hand.

"Ah, Gracie," said Stu Boyington. "You make the best coffee in the world. When are you going to give all this up and come work for us?"

Grace handed him one mug and put the other on Peter's desk.

"We already feel as if we are," Peter answered for her, lifting the two inch stack of file folders Stue had brought over from the Defense Department.

Grace smiled, though she was not amused. Where did he get off, calling her Gracie?

When she had gone, Stu placed his cup on the edge of Peter's desk and leaned back. "I really like your girl, Pete," he said. Diane and I both enjoyed Friday night."

Peter's eyes raised from the rim of his cup.

"It looks pretty serious."

Peter smiled. "Yeah, it feels pretty serious."

His friend reached over and lifted his cup in a silent toast, sipping and setting it down again. "And now for something entirely new," he said. "Did you watch that interview last night?"

Peter snorted. "Yegorov was upstairs at 9:30 this morning with a transcript, and a formal invitation to Bukov's Geneva conference."

"Did you catch the part about 20,000 soldiers martyred in Afghanistan—'defending the peace'?"

Jefferson reached into a wooden basket on the right corner of his desk and shuffled through the top several sheets of paper, withdrawing a copy of the transcript Heath had sent down earlier. He glanced across a page toward the end of the interview.

"How about Iran and Libya as peace-loving nations." Peter looked up. "Do you know that last week 20,000 Cubans were airlifted into Tripoli? And that Qaddafi has enough Soviet hardware to arm as many more as Moscow can relocate . . ."

Stu shook his head.

Peter sighed, and tossed the transcript back on the desk. "What really interested me was his admission that Syria and the PFLP had joint objectives in Lebanon and elsewhere. Why do you suppose he'd say that? It's almost as though he had a concrete plan."

"I was hoping there'd be some question about Alaska—" Stu said.

* * * * *

April slipped into May and seemed to hold on with an overcast sky and intermittent rain. Peter Jefferson's week had been a crush of meetings, conferences, consultations and interviews. He had started looking forward to the weekend on Wednesday.

Friday morning Peggy had called him at work. "Peter, I've got a meeting at the White House. Can I stop in and visit after—around two or three this afternoon?"

"Sure," he said. "I'll take you home from here. What's it about?"

"I'll let you know this afternoon. And I've got my car—I'll take myself home, I want to change before I come over anyway."

"Peggy?"

"Yes?"

"Will you stay over? We could have the whole weekend." He felt a little awkward asking, but damn it, he couldn't just assume. . . .

He heard her smile in her voice. "I'll bring my toothbrush."

At 4:00 Peggy was sitting opposite Peter's desk. "I've never been to Geneva," she was saying. She was dressed in a light suit the color of sage. Her eyes seemed very green. "George Heath said you're going too."

"I just found out this afternoon. Heath was there too?"

She nodded.

He looked a little distracted.

"Aren't you looking forward to it, Peter?"

"Oh, sure." He smiled. "I'll show you the town." There was a pause. "So what was the meeting about?"

She laughed. "I'm not really sure. I was invited in for just a part of the meeting, and when I was ushered out, it was still going on. They were discussing whether mutual vulnerability is a nuclear deterrent."

She smoothed her skirt, then looked up and smiled at him. "It reminded me of late night rap sessions in college. In fact," she laughed, "I kept being interrupted by images of my roommates and myself with our hair in rollers passionately arguing the same issue."

"Who was there?" He felt uncomfortable asking.

Peggy's light recitation became more serious. "The President, George Heath, Henry Clay and Harry Smyth. Larry Apple was going in as I was leaving." She paused. "They wanted to know if there might be a problem if the Soviets knew they were vulnerable—without a credible antiballistic system—and that we were in a favorable position, having that credibility in Saturn."

Peter was leaning forward, both arms resting on his desk. "I don't understand. Saturn is still top secret. Are they planning to announce it in Geneva? Are we even sure Saturn *gives* us military superiority?"

She hesitated before she replied. "I don't have an answer to your first question. As far as I could tell, it was a pretty theoretical conversation."

She paused again, then said seriously, "But I was there to tell them that Saturn *is* a breakthrough for the United States, and that based on what we know and what we can assume, it gives us a distinct advantage in the arms race." She stopped, tilting her head at the frown worrying his face.

"The Red Army is composed of a bunch of young Turks, Peggy, who don't remember Leningrad, and who have a lot of dangerous toys—lots of them—SS 18s and 20s, seventy antiballistic missile launchers with ranges of from three to five thousand miles. . . ."

Peggy stopped. "And we have Saturn."

Peggy shook her head. "They don't stand a chance against us."

Neither of them spoke. Then Peggy glanced at her wristwatch. "It's almost 5:00, Friday afternoon, Peter." She looked up, smiling. "I don't know about you, but I've got an important date tonight. Will you walk me to my car?"

* * * * *

Saturday morning was pouring rain. Dressed in jeans and a loose pink sweater, Peggy was standing in the door of Peter's study with her hands on her hips.

Peter came around behind her, kissed her on the neck, and said, looking in, "What do you think?"

"I think if we don't just jump in there, that mess is going to root to the floor and pretty soon it'll start spawning small cartons and pocket books." She turned to face him, put her arms around his neck. "What do you think?"

"I don't think I'm ready for the patter of pocket books. Not yet."

Inside, he turned on the overhead light, and Peggy walked to the tall windows opening onto one of Watergate's strange concrete balconies which made the building look like a fortress, or an armadillo. Although it was fairly protected by the overhang of the balcony above, rain was pelting the floor and puddling outside the window.

"I love days like this," she said, turning.

He had knelt next to a large carton of books, and he looked up at her.

"What can I do?" she said, smiling, and moving across the cluttered room.

"It's not really as bad as it looks." He stood up. "They're all sorted by subject, sort of—if you want to start putting them on the shelves, in groups—you know, Russian studies in one section," he pointed to a stack on the floor, "books on government in another, reference books over there, nearer the desk. . . ."

She nodded, looking at the empty shelves. "How about if I dust these off first. When was the last time you were in here?"

"Before I met you—I don't remember. I'll go get a cloth."

When Peter returned, she had cleared off the arm of his big easy chair, and was sitting, turning a page in a book called *The Origins of World War III.*

She looked up when he came in. "This is serious stuff," she said, nodding at the open book.

He looked down over her shoulder. "Yeah." He bent and flipped through the first few pages, found the copyright date. "But it's old—1978—before talk of freezes or first use."

She accepted the dust cloth he handed her and got up, laying the book on an empty shelf. Looking around her, she spotted a footstool behind the big roll top desk. Stepping up on the stool she was able to reach the top of the bookcase.

As she ran the soft cloth over each broad, polished plank and rain tapped a quick rhythm on the window, she said, "How does Bukov see the nuclear age?"

Peter was sitting in front of a built-in double doored file cabinet in the wider wall of the room, with a lapful of green hanging folders. "It's not so much Bukov that we have to worry about—he's one of the few members of the Politburo who fought in World War II. He knows what it's all about, and I think he's pretty moderate, actually. It's Sorokin, the head of the KGB, who's really in charge—and Sorokin is a hard core Marxist, a revolutionist." He delivered a file to its track in the cabinet. "And you've got the Commander of Soviet Strategic Rocket Forces, Yuri Varikov. . . ."

"Vasilov," she said at one of the middle shelves.

He looked over at her, then turned back to his cabinet, smiling. "Vasilov—who's promoting the idea that the Soviets could 'win' a nuclear war—and who thinks a nuclear freeze is a way of keeping missiles in cold storage."

Peggy stepped off the footstool, and stood with her hands at her sides. "If that's their attitude going into a peace conference, then what's the point?"

Peter fed a last file into the cabinet and stood up to recover another armful from the chair. "Oh, there are a lot of good reasons. . . . Are you warm? I'm going to open the window a little."

He stepped around the desk while Peggy looked after him, and then she turned to a box of Italian books. "Tell me some good reasons," she said, beginning to place the fine, leather-bound volumes in a row on a middle shelf.

He came back to where she was working, stood against the wall with his arms crossed. "Well, for one thing, it's an opportunity to reaffirm our commitment to Israel's security. For another, Baker wants it known that we'll sit down with any nation in an effort to further peace."

Peter paused and bent to pull another box of books up to the case, then continued talking while he lifted an armful at a time onto the ledge in front of him and began placing them in the shelves. "This is the first time many of us will have met Bukov. Even as a figurehead, he's at the pulse of Soviet power. Then, we'll have a first hand view of Arab alignments, disalignments, and realignments. Possibly we'll be able to learn something new."

Peter stepped back to look at the shelves, then turned to maneuver a large carton nearer. He went on. "I'm interested in the status of the Israeli-Egyptian relationship. In why Qaddafi requires the troops he's gathering." He straightened, started emptying the box. "You know he's been raving about a 'Greater Libya" to include Chad and the Sudan . . ."

Peggy had stopped to listen to him. "You don't seriously think you're going to find out anything resembling the truth from Qaddafi—or any Arab delegate, for that matter . . ."

He smiled at her. "Maybe not from their prepared comments. But there are other ways of seeing what's going on."

She raised her eyebrows.

"You know," he said, holding out his hand to her. "Like how a person acts in a certain situation, how they respond." He drew her against him. "How you feel when you're with that person," he said into her sweet-smelling hair.

CHAPTER
TWENTY-THREE

Geneva, May 11

It is an eight hour plane ride on Air Force two from Washington to Geneva, and one crosses six time zones en route. The United States delegation had left Andrews Air Force at eight in the evening and would arrive at Cointrin at ten the next morning. Twilight didn't last long. Their plane seemed suspended—it was the obsidian night that moved under and around them. Martha Heath looked out the window to her right.

Peggy and Peter sat across from Martha Heath who was along to spend the opening days of the convention, do her wifely bit for the State, as she put it, and then on to a visit with their youngest, studying at the United Nations School for Simultaneous Translation in Geneva.

George Heath had been conferring with one of Admiral Smilie's men, segregated in a smoking section toward the rear of the plane. He made his way back, carrying a half-dozen file folders, stopping to speak with two members of the press corps, moving up, sitting on the arm of an empty aisle seat to exchange a few words with Harry Smyth's Under Secretary who sat with his briefcase on his lap.

When Heath arrived at their place, he handed Peter a file and sat down next to Martha. "Are you all right, my dear?"

"This drink is definitely helping," she said, then turned almost apologetically toward Peggy. "I'm a little nervous flying."

Heath patted her arm and turned to Peter, inclining his head. "Read that."

Peter opened the folder, and looked down the first page, hesitated, slowed his reading, then turned to page two. When he had finished he handed the file to Peggy.

159

Martha Heath, looking uncertainly at their serious faces, sighed and said, "I suppose you're going to discuss something grim. I think I'll excuse myself. I understand there's a movie upstairs."

Heath looked at her with a great deal of affection. "Do you want me to go with you, dear?"

"No, George, you take care of these nice people. I'm really fine." She smiled reassuringly, and unsnapped her seat belt. Her hand fell for a moment on his shoulder, and she walked from them toward the back of the plane, detouring across the aisle to make way for an approaching rolling bar.

Heath passed each of them a drink from the cart. When the attendant had gone he nodded at the file still in Peggy's hand. The document was a military assessment of forces in the Mediterranean, prepared by the Joint Chiefs, which concluded with the terse statement, "War potential positive."

"What do you think of that?" he said.

Peggy looked up. "We know the Soviets have been very active. I'd bet our reports on plane to plane communication between Asmara, Aden and Tripoli are responsible for this." She handed the papers back to Heath.

"I don't know how accurate their conclusions are," Peter said. "If I were Bukov, I'd want to be damn sure I could count on airpower to protect my submarines. Would *you* trust Libya?"

"Besides," Peggy added, "the RDF is a force to be reckoned with. They're in good position—and you've got the Sixth Fleet—" she handed the file back.

"They'd still be vulnerable to a Libyan saturation missile attack," Peter said.

Peggy looked over at Heath. "Don't you think any fighting would be localized? How likely is it that it turns confrontational?"

"Even if it didn't, Peg," Peter said, "a conflict of any sort out there would jeopardize our interests. Sea lanes of communication are vital to the flow of oil. Granted, we've got to watch the Aden Asmara axis, and Tripoli—but we know the position of every Soviet sub in the Indian Ocean, we've got AWACS in Saudi Arabia and Egypt, pre-positioned supplies in Bahrain and Oman, strategic bombers in Diego Garcia, Berbera. . . ."

Heath sipped his brandy, not commenting. He looked at his watch. Then he placed his glass on the shelf near Martha's empty seat, reached under his own chair and pulled his leather briefcase onto his lap. He hesitated a moment, and then, opening the case, said, "I'd like to show you something."

He replaced the file and removed a slightly larger than pocket-sized computer chess board, closed the briefcase, sat the small board on his knee, and started positioning pieces for both Black and White players. A horizontal screen below the board notated moves, and squares lit with the outline of appropriate pieces as Heath keyed them.

As he set up the board, he spoke. "We'll call the Soviets Black—" he looked up. "Black has a penchant for unorthodox moves, as we've seen, which leads to a great deal of portentious maneuvering." A slight smile, and Heath looked back at the board and went through a series of obviously rehearsed plays, in sequence. Peggy was leaning forward, watching the game take shape.

"Now," Heath said, warmly, "there's a distinct psychology involved in unorthodox play—the main one being an element of fear. White figures Black has some good reason—unknown to White—for these moves."

He had been directing this to Peggy, now he turned to Peter, and said, "However, unusual defenses *are* inferior lines of play. Always."

"Then why would a serious player make unusual moves?"

"There are three possible reasons," Heath answered, handing the board to Peggy and leaning back in his seat. "One is that Black is a poor player and doesn't know he's making inferior judgments. I don't think that's the case with our particular opponent. Two, Black is uncomfortable with orthodox rules of play, doesn't feel confident of winning that way—or three, he's doing it to confuse White."

He leaned forward, as Peter did, and Peggy turned the board around so that White's side faced Heath.

"You see, Black looks good here—his bishop is strong; let's call that the Libyan entity—but White actually controls the center."

He paused, pointed to the black pawns. "Now, Black's got a lot of pawns floating around out there—and those were weakening plays—Alaska was a weakening play. Rearming Syria and Iran, another bad move, is going to turn into a disaster for Black, as you'll see."

He sipped his brandy, glanced again at the over-all set up, then said, "Assume the White knight represents the RDF in the Mideast—the White pawn on Q4 is our Sixth Fleet."

Peggy nodded, and Peter looked up from the board to Heath's face. He was completely engrossed, with a distinct air of satisfaction about him.

"This conference we're going to seems to me to simulate a classic maneuver—I'm going to call it a castle on Black's part. . . ." He made the appropriate adjustment on the board, saying, "You see, the Soviets are creating a safe spot for themselves here, by moving themselves *behind* these pieces, which we'll say represent the Mideastern states." He indicated the major pieces, bishops, knights.

"However—" he took the board back, and as a ninth move, punched in White's Knight 1 to Bishop 3.

"How would you respond," he said to Peggy and returned the game to her.

"Pawn to Queen's Knight 3," she said after a minute.

He nodded, smiling, "Let me show you what happens." Heath worked the game like a calculator.

Peter cleared his throat. "Can you anticipate moves that literally, George?"

Heath looked up sharply. "Of course not." There was an edge to his voice. "I find it helpful in sorting things out." He handed Peggy the board again.

The horizontal screen had recorded these moves:

9. N/N1-B3	P-Qn3	12. P-B4	N-B3
10. B-Q3	B-N2	13. B-B4	QN-Q3
11. Castles	R-K1	14. Q-K2	P-B4

"White's next move is the surprise—and the clincher," he said. "Punch in Knight to Bishop 7."

The computer added an exclamation point to her notation.

"Now look what we've accomplished," Heath said, turning the board back.

"You haven't left Black much choice," Peggy said, smiling. She turned to Peter. "Do you see that?—White's Knight threatening Black's Queen?"

"So why doesn't the King just move here, and take the horse?"

Peggy looked at Heath and said, "That's exactly what he'll have to do. But the Knight's being used as bait."

Heath nodded. "Watch." He punched in Peter's suggested KxN as Black's 15th move, and then moved White's Queen to capture Black's weak Pawn: QxP. "That's a check."

Peter was leaning toward the small board, his brow wrinkled. "Then Black's King takes White's Queen," Peter said, straightening.

"And that's a checkmate," Heath said. "White's Knight moves N-N5."

Peter looked at that. "Okay, so Black refuses the Queen and moves back here, or here." He pointed to the two possible positions: K-B1, or K-N3.

"Either way," Peggy said; "if Black moves back, White plays the Knight to N-5, and then moves the same piece to R-2, and it's all over. If he comes out here. . . ." she pointed to N-3, "White moves this pawn to K-N4."

Heath punched that move in, then responded with B-K5 for Black, saying, "That's the only possible response. And White's next move, the Knight to R-4, is a mate."

Peggy read the board, and looked up with a grin. "You should send a copy of this to the Joint Chiefs—might make them feel better."

Heath laughed. Looking down the aisle, he said, "I think I should check on Martha. She doesn't enjoy flying." And he rose and left them.

Peggy still held the chess board. She looked over at Peter. They didn't speak.

* * * * *

The big plane slipped through the night into a suggestion of sunrise, and suddenly it was day. They were served a light breakfast, and at ten o'clock, Geneva time, Air Force Two touched down smoothly at Cointrin and taxied in a graceful circle to a loading area reserved for distinguished foreign visitors.

As the ranking member of the United States delegation to Geneva, the Secretary of State and his wife would be the first to disembark behind eight Secret Service men. The couple did not look tired and as they paused at the doorway of the plane, and waved, Martha's smile was of relief. Applause lifted toward them in spatters on the morning air. Peter Jefferson, Peggy Montague, forty-plus other members of the delegation, and six more Secret Servicemen, followed the Secretary of State down the stairway. Last out were eight members of the press pool and a television camera crew.

Their path was across a red carpet that stretched from the plane a hundred feet to a stand of microphones. Flanked by members of the Swiss government, President Maurice Fredl stood beside the American Ambassador to Switzerland, two rosy men beaming at the column of Americans as they approached. Behind the President reporters craned around a dotted line of uniformed soldiers.

Television cameras whirred as Fredl shook Heath's hand, and then his wife's. The older man said something not audible to the others, and Heath nodded and smiled and then stepped up to the microphones with the President.

"Secretary Heath, please accept a cordial welcome on behalf of myself and my government," President Fredl said, not to Heath, but to the small paper he held in his hand.

"We are honored to provide a place where a conference toward a better world can be discussed in a neutral climate." Fredl punctuated every several sentences by actually turning and smiling at Heath. Then he turned back to the microphone and lowered his head to his speech.

"My government wishes you every success in your negotiations, and as you know, we will wish Mr. Gromyko every success as well." He looked at Heath, smiled happily. To his paper, he said, "This is not the language of neutrality, however; it is a genuine wish based on the concept that 'success' goes beyond political lines. A true success will work for all people throughout the world."

Now he squinted over at the reporters—winging it. "So on behalf of *all* people, we are happy to have you here."

A few reporters, and most of the American delegation, applauded.

Heath stepped into the center spot and spoke clearly. He was a head taller than Fredl, and imposing in a handsome dark suit. He had no notes and he spoke crisply and did not smile. "Thank you for your hospitality, Mr. President. It is indeed our purpose to establish lines of communication and cooperation that will spell success for the world's people. And I think most of us are agreed that success means *peace* for the people of the world.

"Not only in the Middle East," Heath said, distinctly. "President Baker looks forward to hearing concrete proposals from the Soviet Union toward reducing the level of tension in North Africa and in the Straits of Bab al Mandeb—the entrance to the Red Sea. We also have plans to discuss justification for the existence of Warsaw Pact forces in numbers far beyond any realistic need for Soviet defense, which undermine an environment in which peace can be gained."

His voice softened. He looked at the small group of Swiss government officials, and said to them, "What we will work for in your beautiful country is 'un paix mondiale' which will last beyond our lifetimes. Thank you for your welcome."

* * * * *

The Intercontinental Hotel occupies an area of about six acres, and provides a retreat for business men, Presidents and vacationers alike. There are over a hundred rooms and suites, restaurants and bars, a swimming pool and sauna. And because there are rooms for banquets, receptions and conferences that will accommodate two to three hundred at a time, the hotel has been the site for many cooperative efforts—from weddings to OPEC meetings, and other international conferences.

As the lead car reached the Hotel's entrance drive off Chenin Du Petit-Saconnex, a guard of soldiers in full battle dress stiffened to attention. Automatic rifles gleamed on every shoulder.

In their car, Peggy leaned toward Peter and murmured, "Is that supposed to make us feel safe?"

* * * * *

His room overlooked a tiled veranda and further, an immense turquoise pool. Large sun umbrellas cast circles of shade on reclining lounges, and cut crescents over round white tables.

It was close to noon. Peter stood on his balcony looking out at a manic company of bathers—mostly silent at this distance, but animated and colorful, an occasionally a happy cry fought its way up on a slip of air.

Inside, a basket of fresh and dried fruits sat on a table near the windows, a vase of white roses had been arranged on another table near the bed. Peter had discovered a small refrigerator built into a low counter in a separate alcove, with four racks of one ounce bottles of every conceivable liquor, along with several splits of champagne, Perrier and tonic waters. On the countertop was an inventory of the refrigerator's contents and the prices in francs for each item. He had calculated he could have a two ounce whiskey for $12.50.

There was a quick rap on the door, where Peter met an elderly porter with his baggage.

"*La système, ça marche tres bien?*" Peter smiled, taking his bags.

"*Mais oui, monsieur,*" the porter replied. "*Vous êtes en Suisse. Bienvenue.*"

"*Merci bien,*" Peter said, and gave the man three ten franc notes.

He had just opened his suitcase when the phone rang.

"I want you to know I love you in Geneva too," she said.

"Perhaps we should discuss this over dinner."

"Good idea. Shall I bring the chess set, or will you?"

CHAPTER
TWENTY-FOUR

Geneva, May 13

Evening traffic was heavy, but their driver maneuvered the Mercedes limousine like a shark through water, and brought them within half an hour to a tree-lined drive that procedes the entrance of La Reserve. It is a sprawling hotel contained within its own vast park on Lake Geneva, and tonight the sky and water were equally calm, and in the fading light, a pale, pale purple.

They walked slowly through the large lobby, wandering really, around clusters of well dressed patrons meeting to dine or drink. The seven-to-eight o'clock crowd were primarily business people; visiting Arabs would arrive after nine to avoid the cocktail hour; and the Genevoises dine later than that. Peter could distinguish bits of conversation in at least five languages.

The plush dining room extended into a covered terrace with glass on three sides, overlooking the lake. They were given a corner table and Peggy was seated with the long terrace window to her right and Peter on her left with his back to the busy room. In front of him the lake made a watercolor of the sky in deepening shades of purple.

They had planned a totally romantic evening. Dinner here, a walk by the lake after, then dancing back at the International. Peggy had dressed in black chiffon, a tiered and scalloped dress that was almost a gown, and that made her feel as beautiful as the night.

They took some time with the menu, ordered a clear turtle soup with Amontillado, *à truite au bleu,* veal piccata and salad. Peggy recommended they try the Faina 1981.

When the sommelier returned with their wine and poured a taste into Peter's glass, he handed it across the table to her. She

169

smiled at him and tasted the clear dry wine, then turned and nodded at the steward to pour. Although he had seen such a breach of etiquette three times before, not counting some wealthy rock and roll stars from England who had stayed a week at the Hotel and who were so lacking in any sense of propriety one did not expect them to indulge in politesse, his expression gave none of his considerable astonishment away. He bowed over her glass, the heavy gold chain of his position separating from his vest until he straightened, and removed himself from their table.

"I don't think he approved. . ." Peggy began, and then her attention was captured by the lake, and she touched Peter's arm, and nodded to her right.

Outside, two sailboats glided through the water, now black and silver in the moonless night. As Peggy was speaking they had illuminated their sails, and caught by their reflections, fluttered and slipped like butterflies across a meadow.

Neither of them spoke for a moment, and then she said, almost to herself, "I *feel* like that with you."

Peter was about to answer when his focus shifted on the window and he saw in reflection three men being seated behind him. Peggy still watched the boat's gentle dance. Her hand still rested lightly on his arm.

He recognized two of the men immediately—one was Andrei Gromyko's aide, whose face was memorable for the thin line that was a mouth and eyebrows that raised in the middle giving him a perpetual expression of grim surprise. Vladimir Chorosky—that was his name. The other one, a hulk of a man in a dark well-tailored suit was almost certainly a Colonel in the KGB, one of Sorokin's.

Peter had not met either of these men personally, but during his assignment to Moscow he had attended at least one function at which Chorosky had been present, and it was during his time there—1983, he thought—that the Colonel had been appointed to Moscow's elite KGB. He remembered having seen a file on the man.

The third member of the party was unfamiliar. He was slender, with thinning hair and a short well-shaped beard.

It was the Colonel who ordered the first litre of vodka, loudly, and then turned to the bearded man and said, "To celebrate, Comrade?" His voice was thick. Peter wondered how much they had already had to drink.

The bearded man smiled. He had big teeth, a horsey face. He responded to the Colonel, inclining his head in Chorosky's direction. "Our Comrade does not look like celebrating."

Indeed, Chorosky looked uneasy and unnaturally pale. "It's not that, Mikhail Emilievich," he said quickly in a rather too high voice. "It is still so soon to celebrate. . . ."

"Always so tentative, Comrade," the Colonel said, scowling.

The man called Mikhail Emilievich just sat there, with his teeth.

"Then we will drink to a new world in the Middle East," said the Colonel. And then he said with a taunting voice, "You will not object to that, Comrade?"

Chorosky seemed to shrink in his chair.

"Hello? Anyone home?" said Peggy.

Peter was startled and turned away from the scene in the window. A waiter behind him ceremoniously placed the Russians' vodka on their table, with three crystal glasses, three small plates, and a platter of smoked fish and caviar, sliced cheeses and fruit, and a basket of bread.

Peter looked at Peggy, glanced briefly at the window and back again. He almost sighed. This was the sort of thing that made Miriam crazy. He leaned toward Peggy, took her hand in his, and brought his lips close to her ear.

"Look at the reflection—those three men are from the Soviet delegation—right behind me," he said as her eyes swept the window.

"It sounds to me as if there's something happening. . . ."

She was able to see only two of the three men in the glass. The bigger man was pouring for them all. The rather dapper looking fellow was lifting a slice of apple from the tray.

"I'd like to see if I can pick up what's going on," Peter continued in a low voice. "Would you mind—" He hesitated, then repeated, "Would you mind pretending to have a conversation with me, while I listen to them?"

"Is there any particular subject you're interested in?" she whispered back.

He smiled and said, "Anything but politics or religion."

She nodded and he brushed his lips across her cheek, and sat back. Lifting his wine glass, touching it to hers, he heard the bigger man say in a sneery tone, "Do you see that couple? Americans. They think nothing of making love in a public place," and he punctuated that judgment by tipping back his glass and replacing it, empty, on the table.

The bearded man poured again, and Peggy cleared her throat. "Did I ever tell you about my winter vacation last year?"

She knew she hadn't told him, but Peter smiled and nodded yes. Peggy sipped her wine, and took a breath. "Well, perhaps you'd like to hear about snorkling in Hanama Bay."

She sat back, looked out the window, for inspiration perhaps, and turning back, said, "I went in February. My friends Mitch and Jerry—I've mentioned them to you. . . ." Since he didn't respond, she nodded for him. "Anyway, they've got a penthouse apartment in Honolulu, and they gave it to me for three weeks last year. . . ."

"In three weeks, we will have military advisors in all participating states," the Colonel was saying to his companions.

Vladimir Chorosky glanced around them, nervous.

The Colonel interrupted himself to ask too loudly, "What is the matter now, Comrade?" Without waiting for an answer, he refilled Chorosky's glass.

"Drink up, drink up. You are what they call up-tight." The Colonel laughed at his use of the phrase, which he spoke in English.

The man called Mikhail Emilievich smiled and tapped the rim of his glass for the Colonel to pour.

Peter was reminded to refill their own wine glasses.

". . . rainbow fish that look like opals, and angel fish, and yellow fish with black stripes and red and purple fish—thousands of them—it was like peeking into another world. . . ."

Their soup was served, and when the waiter had left, Peggy laughed, and Peter tilted his head questioningly. "And turtles," she said.

"Turtles?"

"In Hanama Bay," she explained.

It didn't make any sense to him, but he smiled and nodded, and tasted his soup, returning his focus to the window.

Amazingly, more than a third of the decanter had been drunk on the table behind them. And Peggy said, "I tried scuba diving the next day, but I didn't really care for it. I felt like an intruder. Out of my element, so to speak." She liked that, and looked up to see if Peter had caught it.

Apparently not. He was watching Chorosky shakily spooning caviar onto a triangle of bread, while the Colonel handed a folded piece of paper across to the bearded man, and then downed two more shots in a row.

"Here is the formal reparations agreement between Iran and Iraq. Of course, this is quite confidential. . . ." The Colonel looked significantly at Chorosky who flushed, set his hors d'oeuvre down on the plate in front of him, and held his gaze there, on the piece of bread.

The bearded man had unfolded the paper and smoothed it open on the table. As a waiter approached their table, he removed the page to his lap and signalled for another litre. Their conversation stopped, the Colonel refilled all their glasses from the dwindling bottle, and Chorosky took the opportunity to have a bite of his bread and caviar.

Before he left, the waiter glanced over at Peter's corner table, raised a hand for a boy to clear their soup plates, and hustled off to pick up their next course.

"I've got a *great* story," Peggy said cheerfully. "In fact I must remember to repeat this one when you're listening." She took another drink.

"Don't you find this wine delicious?" She paused, looked at him with her head tilted slightly to one side as if she were listening to his opinion. "Yes, I agree. Now where was I?" Again she paused. "Oh, yes! New York city, 1968 or '69. My sister Rosemary and I were visiting our Uncle—my mother's brother—in New York during summer vacation from school. Summer, by the way, is *not* the time to be visiting New York."

She stopped again, looked out the window. Only one sailboat was left on the lake, and it had traveled some distance. It looked like a constellation. "We were coming home ridiculously late from a party, and walking toward the corner of 57th Street down Sixth Avenue, hoping to be able to find a cab. When we got to 57th Street, both of us stopped dead in our tracks." She tasted her wine again.

"You've got to sort of get the picture," she said. "It was probably three in the morning, totally empty of people—we had just been talking about how oddly quiet it was, like a dream, or the Twilight Zone—remember that? . . . And then we saw them—lumbering down 57th, all attached like in cartoon. . . ."

The paper was opened again on the table, and Mikhail Emilievich accepted another vodka. Chorosky's color had improved, and the Colonel had begun to list toward the bearded man, pointing to something on the paper.

"You see here, Comrade, Iraq will move these armored divisions through Jordan to near the Sea of Galilee, and then south toward Jerusalem."

Mikhail Emilievich nodded, reached for a slice of cheese, and said, "Of course there is the United Nations force in Lebanon."

The Colonel poured shots all around, and said, "Syria will demand their withdrawl. Two days later Jordan provides air cover with its American financed strike force, while Syria and Iraq strike through the Bekaa Valley."

Chorosky giggled.

Both other men turned to look at him, and he said, nervous again, "Well, you know Jordan's weapons are all made in the United States. What do you suppose this President Baker—" he whispered the name, "will say when all that is left of his precious Israel is a little strip from Tel Aviv to Gaza, and the Negev desert?"

The Colonel seemed pleased. "That is more like it, Comrade. You begin to appreciate the dimension of this plan."

Peter's brows had drawn together. He looked surprised and angry at the same time. Peggy stopped in the middle of a sentence and touched his arm.

He looked at her quickly.

"Are you all right, Peter?"

He just nodded, his eyes shifted back to the window. He looked pale, and seemed almost not to be there, and she wondered if that's what she looked like when she was "off" on one of her paranormal excursions. It was strangely disturbing. She noticed he had hardly touched his meal.

Chorosky had lost some caviar to his tie, but he didn't notice, and at this point he wouldn't have cared anyway. He sipped the good vodka and stared out toward the lake.

The Colonel was leaning heavily against Mikhail Emilievich's shoulder, and the smaller man who did not appear affected by the six small glasses of vodka he himself had consumed, pulled away with a shrug. Clearly, the Colonel's breath was terrible.

As he righted himself, Mikhail Emilievich said, "So then, Jordan takes the West Bank. And the area from Lebanon's border to the West Bank—Haifa and the Sea of Galilee?"

"To Syria," the Colonel said. And then he raised his glass and said loudly and thickly, "To Syria."

"To Syria."

"And you, Comrade?" Mikhail Emilievich said to Chorosky, whose eyes had narrowed at the window.

"Yes," Chorosky said, turning, "To Syria."

The three men drank.

"And to Libya, without whom none of this would be possible," said the Colonel expansively.

Peggy returned to their table from the lounge as espresso and a rare 1879 Armagnac were served. The waiter pulled back her chair, and kept a blank expression on his face as the Colonel called across to him for more vodka, and Vladimir Chorosky began fanning himself with his white cloth napkin.

Peter leaned back in his seat. He still looked troubled, but he managed a smile and lifted his snifter. "You are a jewel."

"So much for your concern about *my* eavesdropping," she smiled. "You've lost interest in the view?" She inclined her head toward the window.

Quietly he said, "That's the third litre of vodka they're calling for—and the conversation has turned to speculation on their Minister of Power and Electrification's love life."

"And that's not interesting?" She lifted her demi-tasse and tasted it. "It's just as well, I was running out of material."

"Peggy, I think we should get back to Heath right away." He took her hand. "Do you mind?"

"Of course not, Peter."

"But I want you to know this isn't the best Geneva and I can provide in the way of a romantic evening." He lifted her hand to his lips. "I'd like another chance to prove it."

She laughed. "I can't *tell* you how relieved I am."

They paid the bill and walked past the table behind their own. Chorosky was flushed and staring at a full glass in front of him. The Colonel was on his Comrade's shoulder again, and Peter overheard him say, with crass insinuation, "*Eto delovkus. . . .*"

There was a snicker behind them that chased them a foot or two, and was lost in the chatter of other diners.

* * * * *

Heath's suite had a comfortable sectional couch fitted neat and red into a corner of the sitting room. On either side two squat shaded lamps provided light. There was a large table with eight high-backed wooden chairs against the far wall, and a globe light over that illuminating what looked like a week of paperwork. Peggy noticed Heath's chess calculator amidst the stacks of reports and files.

Each of them had a cognac. Peggy held hers in both hands, as if warming them on the round glass. Peter was leaning forward. Heath seemed animated, pacing, head down, listening, occasionally nodding.

". . . then they toasted Libya," Peter was saying, " 'without whom none of this would be possible.' " He stopped, looked into his glass, then tipped it back and finished the last of the brandy. "That must have something to do with those Cubans in Tripoli. I couldn't help but think of that chess demonstration you gave us last night." He looked seriously at Heath. "I don't know precisely how they fit in—but it's obvious the attack is going to be supported on every side."

Peter got up to help himself to another ounce bottle at the bar. Heath was still pacing. They almost collided near the bar.

"I'm sorry. . . ." Peter too, was distracted.

"Sorry, Peter. . . . Please—help yourself. . . . Peggy?"

She shook her head watching them both carefully, a little concerned, and in some odd way, a little amused.

Heath considered the bottle Peter was opening, and reached for one himself. "If you knew two of the men at the table, is it possible they knew you?"

"No, I'm sure not. I know what you're thinking—it could have been a conversation they wanted me to hear. But I really don't think so." Peter poured his drink. "I've never been introduced to either of them. The big fellow I know just by reputation. When we left, they were more interested in Peggy than me, and. . . . I'm quite sure none of them knew me, or had any idea I speak their language."

"That kind of indiscretion, though, among men of their rank. . . ." Heath shook his head. They walked back toward the couch. Peter sat down, and Heath stood behind a dark flowered chair opposite them.

"I know," Peter agreed, "but they were drinking heavily—three of them had finished almost two litres during the time we were there—and the Colonel looked loaded when they first walked in."

"And this other man, the bearded one? . . ."

"Chorosky called him Mikhail Emilievich. Emilievich's first name was Emil. But it shouldn't be hard to find out who he is. Larry probably has a file on him. I'd guess a member of the Politburo. The Colonel sort of fawned over him, so the guy is probably a superior . . ."

Heath walked to the table, put his glass down. "No dates mentioned?"

"No. But if they're talking in terms of 'two days' after the UN is out of Lebanon, and we know there are Cubans in position in Libya, I think we can assume this thing is on a calendar, and this convention we're working so hard for—" he inclined his head toward Heath's table— "is another effort to divert us."

The Secretary was shaking his head, wonderingly. "It's remarkable that *you* were there, in that place at that time with a knowledge of Russian and—" Heath interrupted himself with a sigh. He lifted his glass, sipped the brandy, then looked at his watch.

"It's midnight here—6 AM in Washington. I'm going to put in a call to Larry. You'll excuse me?"

When he had left the room, Peggy touched Peter's hand. "I can't believe you," she said.

He grinned. "You too?"

"No, I believe *you*, I just don't *believe* you. That you could sit there hearing all that and contain it so well . . ."

"It was strange, all right." He leaned toward her and touched her hair. "I felt like a stereo recorder picking up a travelog on one channel, and Dr. Strangelove on the other—" He frowned and sat back, studying Peggy.

"What is it?" she said.

"That's what I was going to ask you. What was it you were talking about—something lumbering down 57th Street?"

She laughed. "Elephants."

"On 57th Street?"

"The circus—Barnum and Bailey—were arriving in town. You can imagine how we felt. We both just stopped on the corner and stared at each other. Six elephants. And then wagons, wonderful painted wagons. We held hands and followed them a mile down the dark streets. It was such a feeling of delight. I'll never forget it."

Peter took her hand.

"Larry is going to call you, Peter," Heath said, closing the bedroom door behind him. "I gave him your room number. He'll confirm it, but he thinks you should advise Mossad and Egyptian Intelligence immediately. If you leave tomorrow morning, spend a few hours in Jerusalem and then fly to Cairo, you can be back here in less than thirty-six hours."

"Is my phone all right?"

"The whole floor is fixed—every room has a safe phone."

"And he's going to get back to me—when?"

"Momentarily." Heath smiled kindly and said, "I don't mean to hurry you out, but in fact I have an assignment I had hoped to discuss with Miss Montague." He turned to her. "Will you stay a bit longer, my dear?"

Peggy said certainly she would stay. Peter looked at her, then at Heath, and stood.

"I'll walk you to the door, Peter," Peggy said.

It had not been the evening either of them had planned.

* * * * *

Peter figured it would be impossible to sleep. He wondered what Heath had to discuss with Peggy. The thought of her caused him an almost painful longing. He wandered across the room—his bed had been turned down—stepped to the window and pulled back the drapes to open it. The pool was still lit and lanterns hung like stars above the lawn.

He turned, found a fresh yellow pad in his briefcase and sat down to record with as much detail as he could remember, the conversation he had overheard.

The details—what food the men had ordered. . . . He interrupted himself to call room service for coffee—the color of their ties, which men had made which specific comment, helped him recreate the conversation with enormous precision. When he was finished, the dialogue read like a script, complete with director's notes.

The transcription had absorbed him completely. When the phone rang he was startled, and looked at his watch before he answered. 2:30 AM.

Larry Apple made no small talk. He provided terse, complete instructions, an itinerary, and told Peter the Geneva Station Chief would take him to the airport in the morning to brief him on procedure. "When you get there, just tell them what you told George," he finished. "Everything. And Peter? . . . You did fine."

His plane would depart at 7:30 AM. He'd have to leave the hotel by 6:00; he still had to change, pack an overnight case and his attaché. It was 3:30 now. There was no point in even trying to sleep.

CHAPTER TWENTY-FIVE

Geneva, May 14

Gary Moss was very young, Jefferson thought, to be the Station Chief for Central Intelligence in Geneva. He was a small, energetic man dressed in a dark suit and tie, with black unruly hair and dark eyes, which he chose to conceal behind opaque glasses. But he had signalled from the blue Peugeot, and when Peter walked over, had introduced himself by removing his glasses, and turning out his identification for Peter to read.

Jefferson got into the back seat on which there was a bulky manila envelope. As Gary Moss pulled out of the long drive and headed toward the airport, he said, "That's your James Bond traveling kit, Mr. Jefferson. It contains a first class ticket to Jerusalem, passport and identification for one Giorgio Garibaldi, Italian professor of political science at the University of Milan."

Moss depressed the lighter over his ashtray, held a cigarette pack up in an offer to Jefferson, then shook one out of the pack, and slipped it back onto the top of the dashboard. "As you can see from the immigration stamps on your passport, you've been in New York and London on different trips over the past four months. Most recently, you've completed a one month seminar in Geneva, and you're on your way to arrange another in Jerusalem."

Jefferson flipped through the book. "This passport seems different, somehow. . . ."

Moss nodded approvingly, lit his cigarette with his eyes still on the road. "About eight months ago the Italians issued a redesigned passport—too many of the old ones had fallen into the wrong hands."

Jefferson didn't say a word.

"Now, some other particulars: You have a small apartment in Milan—the address is on your driver's license; you are unmarried, considered something of a recluse, even by your colleagues at the University. While you're in transit, speak only Italian.

"You'll also find an Alitalia air travel card, some lira, about $200 in shekels, the same amount in Egyptian pounds and a few hundred dollars in travelers checks, cards and papers, mostly professional stuff, and a well-worn wallet." He paused. "Any questions so far?"

"These seminars," Jefferson said. "What's the subject?"

"Political and military history. I doubt you'll have to use any of this material to prove your identity. . . ." Moss executed a neat exit onto the freeway. "You'll be met at Ben Gurion International and at Cairo, and if everything goes smoothly, you won't have to speak to anyone other than those people you're going to see."

Moss glanced in the rearview mirror. "You've spent time in Europe, so you're familiar with customs and traits—on the plane, for instance, remember to hold your knife in your right hand, and your fork in the left."

Jefferson nodded. "If I'm supposed to be arranging a seminar in Jerusalem, why do I fly off to Cairo?"

"Your meetings are this afternoon and on Sunday. Saturday is the Sabbath in Israel—there's no work on that day—so you decide to fulfill a lifelong desire to visit the Egyptian Museum. As a professor of political science, I imagine the museum would hold a certain degree of fascination?"

"My next study program in Milan: Cleopatra Then and Now."

Moss grinned, flicked what was left of his cigarette out the window. "At Ben Gurion, try to be one of the last people off the plane. . . . You can pretend to be asleep after breakfast. . . ."

"That won't be difficult," Jefferson answered dryly.

"Just keep your seat belt fastened so the stewardess doesn't have to wake you for landing." Moss swung onto the Airport exit. "Our Agency man in Jerusalem will meet you at the airport—he looks a little like me, curly hair, about five foot ten. He's got photos of you, so he should be able to recognize you without any trouble. He'll address you as 'Professore' Garibaldi, and take you to your next communications point in Cairo."

Peter exchanged his own wallet and passport for Professore Garibaldi's. His own papers, Gary Moss explained, would be waiting back in Geneva for his return.

As they pulled to a stop under the departures canopy at *L'Aeroport de Genève*, Gary looked at his watch. "You've got twelve minutes. Check in at Air France, and look sleepy. Have a good trip, Professore. *Ciao.*"

In Italian, Jefferson answered, "*Grazie.* You guys have done a hell of a job on such short notice. Take care of yourself—*and* my passport and wallet. *Arriverderci.*"

* * * * *

He did sleep on and off during the three hour flight, and he was the last passenger off the plane. Exiting the canvas tunnel that fed from plane to terminal, he found himself in the arrivals area confronted by a convention of signs and arrows. The airport was crowded. He hesitated to walk too much further, worrying about his visibility. He stopped.

Immediately, from behind him, a soft voice said, "*Professore Garibaldi?*"

"*Si. Come sta?*" Jefferson turned smiling, and held out his hand.

The man did indeed look like Gary Moss. Must be "the" look this year in intelligence, he thought.

In Italian, the young man introduced himself as Lee Wilson, and asked the Doctor to follow him. As they walked toward Immigration, Lee spoke quietly. "I'm going to take you through Immigration, Professore Garibaldi. You have nothing to declare so customs should be a walk-through.

"Near the terminal exit our driver will get a signal from me and he'll bring the car around. I'm going to walk directly over to the exit, and I'd like you to pick up a magazine or cigarettes—anything—over at the concession shop for the few minutes it takes the car to arrive. You come join me at exit and we'll walk to the car together."

This seemed unnecessarily complicated, but Peter supposed Wilson knew what he was doing. And arrival formalities were accomplished easily enough. Wilson made a discreet show of some type of pass that waived a search of Peter's attache case. Once past Customs, they split up, and Jefferson browsed the newsstand where papers of almost every nationality were on sale.

He kept having to force the character Garibaldi into the front of his consciousness. He was tired, and it seemed more an effort than he had thought it would be to pretend to be someone else. Peter Jefferson kept slipping in, and he would have to grab for the professor.

He picked up a copy of *Il Tempo* and walked toward the exit where Wilson was waiting. A small grey Ford pulled up in front of both men, and Wilson tossed Jefferson's overnight bag into the front seat, then opened the back door for them both.

As the Ford shot forward, Wilson said, "Professor Garibaldi, this is David Haslawa, with Israeli Military Intelligence. . . ."

"Idiot!" Haslawa shouted, as an airport bus braked sharply in front of them. With a squeal of tires, he lurched around the offending vehicle, and said, "Pleasure Professor. I am your driver while you are here. We have a half hour to the King David Hotel." Another lurch around a cab. "You will check in, go up to your room, leave your suitcase there, and return to the car."

Jefferson just hoped they'd make it.

"From the King David, we go directly to Israeli Military Intelligence Headquarters," Haslawa continued. "You will meet with Yuval ben Dov, director of Military Intelligence, and the head of Mossad, Ariel Ne'man." He paused. "You must be someone pretty special, Professor, to rate that kind of audience."

Jefferson looked up into the driver's rearview mirror. Haslawa was staring directly at him. Instead of feeling gratified by the respect in the other man's voice, Peter wished he'd keep his eyes on the road.

* * * * *

The two men waited in the car while Peter went into the airy, polished lobby of the King David Hotel. As he stood waiting to register at the desk, a man walked up to him.

"Peter Jefferson! I *thought* it was you! What are you doing in Jerusalem?"

Jefferson turned and faced an elderly man, white-haired, frail looking. Peter recognized him immediately as one of his professors from Georgetown. But they hadn't seen each other in at least twenty years. . . . He responded in soft Italian, that the gentleman must be mistaken, he was Professore Garibaldi from Milan, not. . . Peter Jefferson.

The old man looked confused, and then apologetic. "I *beg* your pardon, sir. You look like a former student of mine. . . . It has been a long time though," the man shook his head sadly, "and my memory perhaps, isn't as sharp as it was." Still he stared at Peter.

Jefferson felt a sincere regret, but Garibaldi said, "*Scusi, signore, dovrei 'screver mi adesso,*" and turned back to the desk. The other man stood a moment longer, and then walked away.

When Peter returned to the car he told Lee Wilson and Haslawa about the incident.

"Sounds like you handled it fine," Wilson said.

"Yeah, but I don't know if Garibaldi can understand English, and I answered as if I had understood."

"I'm sure there's no harm done. But I'll check it out just to be on the safe side. Give me a description."

As Jefferson described the old man, and Wilson took notes, the name came to him. 'Hy—Hyram Novick," he said. "He was my economics professor. A great teacher. Damn, I hated to do that to him."

Wilson smiled slightly. "Not too large a price, I hope?"

"No. No, of course not."

* * * * *

At Headquarters, Lee Wilson brought Peter Jefferson into the building, showed his Agency identification and they were escorted to the first floor security office by two armed officers. Peter was issued a pass and they waited for a second escort to take them downstairs. This soldier was a dark, pretty woman who looked at Peter with undisguised curiosity, but said nothing more than, "This way, please," and preceded them to a small elevator down.

After another identity check they were ushered through a small, sparse reception area and into a conference room, not much larger. General ben Dov and Ariel Ne'man both pushed back from the table and walked around to shake hands. A redhaired woman, in uniform, sat with a small transcriber on a table in a corner of the room. She looked up when the two visitors walked in, brushed her hair back from her face.

The General was in full uniform, the insignia of his rank on the epaulets of his short sleeved shirt, pilots wings over his left breast pocket. "Shalom, Mr. Jefferson," he said. Then without further ceremony, he gestured to two grey metal chairs and said, "My friend Larry Apple tells me you have critical information for us."

They sat. Peter opened his attache case, and removed his transcript of the Russian conversation. Referring to his notes, he described exactly the circumstances of his having overheard what he was about to relate, and then he began.

His monologue lasted twenty minutes; there were no interruptions.

When he finally looked up, Wilson, Ne'man and ben Dov were staring at him. Ben Dov broke a lengthy silence by turning to the young woman behind him. "That's all Rachel. Will you see to that yourself?"

She nodded and rose immediately, a tall girl. In a few quick strides she was gone.

"What you are saying exceeds any intelligence we have from Syria, Iraq, Jordan or Libya," ben Dov said to Jefferson.

He looked over at Ne'man, who nodded, then said pointedly to Jefferson, "It is unfortunate for us the Jordanians are so well armed. And it is particularly fortunate for them. If they had to rely on the Soviet MIGS. . . ." He shrugged. Almost to himself he said, "Still, Grumman Hawkeyes were quite effective in sorting out Syrian planes over Lebanon in '82. They do just what the AWACs do but better. And if the Saudis use the AWACS in Jordanian airspace, well. . ." He seemed to catch himself, and stopped.

Ben Dov was looking with some concern at Ne'man. Quietly, he said to Peter, "We have developed an anti-tank missile which represents a truly significant advance over your own Copperhead. We have also developed a weapon something like your Cruise missile, but smaller, the Krait-2, named after a small venomous snake, designed to knock out the SA-5 missile sites in Syria. The one's the Soviets put in place in 1983. Actually, the Pentagon is aware of both of these," he smiled wryly, "so I am not giving you any classified information."

Ne'man nodded, and smiling slightly, added: "We also learned quite a bit about your Firefinder radar. It was used in Lebanon by the Marines along with the 155-millimeter howitzer in 1984. We now have artillery which, using our own version of the Firefinder with phased-array radar, can hit Syrian artillery or missile sites before their first incoming rounds hit the ground. The range is over 40 miles. We even think our new shoulder-fired anti-missile weapons can destroy Syrian SA-5s in the air as well as low-flying aircraft."

Abruptly, Ne'man stood. "Mr. Jefferson, you will have to forgive our lack of hospitality. Obviously, we have a lot of work to do now . . . I am interested to know if Cairo has picked up any of this. You will meet with Medhat Wahab, head of Egyptian Intelligence. He's a good man." Ne'man paused. Then he stuck out his hand. "Thank you."

* * * * *

It was after three o'clock. Friday afternoon traffic would be congested on the highways, the airport would be crowded. Jefferson noticed his overnight bag was not in the car.

"It'll be waiting for you at the check-in counter at the airport," Haslawa assured him, and made a sharp right turn at the corner which leaned Jefferson into his door.

Wilson, who seemed impervious to the car's careening progress toward the highway, turned on the seat and said, "That was quite a bomb you dropped back there."

Jefferson nodded, and for a while none of the men spoke.

As they neared the airport, joining a long line of slow-moving vehicles in the exit lane, Wilson said, "Don't forget who you are, Doctor. Check in at the Sinai Airways flight counter for your bag. Here's your ticket." He handed Jefferson an envelope. "When you land you'll be met by Ed Walker, Cairo Agency Chief—used to be in special service. He's about six feet, on the heavy side, dark brown close-cropped hair and a slight limp. Try to be one of the last out of the plane again."

Jefferson shook hands with both men and walked into Ben Gurion Airport with an hour to spare.

CHAPTER
TWENTY-SIX

Geneva, May 14

Tuesday evening the Hotel Intercontinental welcomed their guests with a formal reception. The room given over to the party was enormous. Two long covered tables were set up against either side of the room; in the back two bars did brisk business—one non-alcoholic in deference to some of the Mideastern delegates. Between the corner bars, twenty musicians sat stiffly on a raised platform playing a sort of up-tempo unidentifiable medley of tunes. There was frequent use of the triangle.

There were perhaps a thousand guests, and two hundred and fifty waiters, slipping discreetly through the room with trays of champagne or fancy hors d'oeuvres, pausing at clusters of men and women. Two photographers, retained by the Hotel, circulated too. They were old hands at this type of affair. Their cameras did not require flashes, they were unobtrusive, they did their job. And the music played.

George and Martha Heath and Peggy had stopped at one of the long laden tables where red and black and gold caviars sat in separate glass bowls on carved ice mountains. There were choices of chopped egg yolk, onion rings and lemon slices, and a spread of thin breads.

There were sherried shrimp, poached eggs in aspic, pates of every description, hot dishes: stuffed mushrooms, tureens of meatballs in spiced sauces, chunks of crab and lobster, melted butter, and pastries rolled, curled, pleated and pinched, strawberries dipped in white chocolate, finger cakes, nuts, dried and candied fruits, and cheeses.

Martha was dressed in a long, loose flowing gown the color of pewter, edged with beadwork. She sighed. "I hate eating at these affairs. There's bound to be a photographer catch you with a strawberry in your mouth."

Peggy wasn't hungry anyway. She was a little jittery. Their interpreter Ted Dancer, a tall young man, blonde, English looking, had just gone to deliver Heath's invitation to Bukov. Her eyes followed his progress across the room a way, until a waiter mistook her glance for him, and brought her champagne. When she looked up again, Ted had disappeared.

Martha decided to risk a strawberry. George had turned to listen to a member of the Israeli delegation, whose English was as hesitant as his selection of an appetizer. Peggy sipped her drink.

She saw him approach, and he made a thumbs-up signal as he maneuvered past a stand of draped Arabs, who frowned at the gesture and followed the young man with their eyes.

"You're on," Ted said quietly to George Heath. "Half an hour, in the lounge upstairs."

Heath looked at his watch. It was 7:50. Martha was watching Peggy. She took the younger woman's hand, smiling. "Don't worry, dear. It's only a game. Here. . . ." She nodded at a waiter who stopped smoothly in front of them, and carefully removed a glass for each of their company, returning Peggy's half-empty one to the tray.

"To the best man," said Martha Heath, lifting her glass to her husband. They drank, and the music played.

* * * * *

The Intercontinental Executive Lounge is furnished with oversized rounded furniture in Art Nouveau style. The ceiling is gilded, a three-dimensional houndstooth of diamond shapes from which four cylindrical white frosted lamps hang, matched by wall lamps of similar design around the room's circumference. Gilt framed still lifes hang between each soft light. A fancy platter had been diverted from the party downstairs and lay on a long buffet in the north end of the room.

The lounge had been arranged for clusters of occupants, six groups of eight or so could find comfortable accommodations here, but tonight the room was empty, save six.

Heath, Peggy and the interpreter Ted Dancer had arrived early. Heath was at a portable bar that had been stocked for their use and placed diagonally between the buffet and a long red plush couch. Across the dark carpeting from the couch, two tall armchairs faced a table on which Heath had set up the newest in American automated chess computers, flown in that afternoon for the occasion. Four other horseshoe chairs in the same red upholstery had been arranged to provide a view of the proceedings.

Bukov and his party were late. Peggy sat next to the board, Ted stood over her shoulder.

"Turn on the demo switch, Peggy. And the one that's marked 'auto play,' " Heath said, approaching them. He handed her a heavy round glass. They were both drinking sparkling water.

It was an amazing machine. A robot really, with a hinged arm and three fingers attached to Black's side of the board that could lift a piece and transfer it to the proper location. The arm simply moved over a piece, the fingers splayed, the arm lowered, and the fingers closed and lifted a piece and moved it. If Black captured one of White's men, it moved that man to a designated location on the side of the board.

Ted was staring at the thing. "What's this button—'emotions'?"

Heath chuckled, touched 'emotions,' and 'sound' and stood back, his hand on the back of Peggy's chair.

Immediately the machine seemed to come alive. It's moves were accompanied by a flash of light from any participating square. At a particularly good White move, the computer blinked and buzzed. Black's response took several silent seconds, and was followed by a cry and a wave of its arm.

Peggy was laughing when Bukov entered the room, followed by two men—an interpreter, bespectacled and bearded, who looked at Ted, recognized him and nodded, and one of the men who had been at La Reserve the night before.

Peggy stood; she made no sign she recognized him. But it was obvious he remembered her. It was Chorosky, the nervous one, Gromyko's aide. His brow furrowed. His eyes darted left and right.

Heath had moved forward to greet them, introducing Peggy and Theodore Dancer. Chorosky seemed reassured by the presence of their own interpreter. Bukov's eyes were on the table behind Heath. The machine was still playing out its game, chirping with glee over a particularly clever maneuver.

"Would you gentlemen like a drink?" Ted asked in Russian.

Bukov looked at the glass in Heath's hand. He wasn't sure why he was here—perhaps just a chess game after all. Sorokin would no doubt be furious when he found out, but there had been no time to clear this informal meeting with him. And Bukov felt confident enough—about his game, certainly; about his ability to handle whatever the situation—well, fairly confident. Certainly it would have been more than rude to refuse. It might have been taken as a slight, could have precipitated an unpleasant incident down the road. Who knew? Frankly, he was damned curious. Maybe it was just a chess game.

He decided he'd have a drink.

Chorosky thought not. Ted raised his eyebrows at their interpreter, who hesitated, then shook his head no.

Heath and Bukov touched their glasses and Heath said pleasantly, "*Nostrovya.*"

"*Nostrovya,*" Bukov replied, then extended his arm at the chess set, still blinking on the table, and moved toward it.

"I understand you're a master player, Mr. Secretary," Heath said. "I wondered if you had ever played our champion computer. It's called a Gladstone."

Bukov's interpreter, following, murmured a translation, and Bukov repeated "Gladstone," as he sat down in front of the board. He sipped his vodka watching the game for a moment. The robot deftly removed White's knight with a bishop, and hooted. Looking back up at Heath, Bukov's eyes were filled with laughter.

"Do your players train to expostulate so?" he said. "It has been a while since any of our champions played an American."

Ted translated.

"Is that right?" Heath said, sitting across from Bukov and turning off the set's sound and emotional response. The robot continued to move, decorously.

Heath's question was most polite. "I would have thought otherwise." He smiled. "Your interest in Alaska was playful enough."

Bukov listened with his head tilted, and smiled good naturedly, not responding to the barb. He turned his attention back to the game.

Peggy sat down in one of the round chairs near Heath. Both interpreters stood at the side of each man at the table.

Chorosky settled himself opposite Peggy, then rose and walked behind her to the buffet. As he passed, he said, "Excuse me," quietly and in Russian. Peggy looked up and smiled, saying, "I'm sorry? . . ." Chorosky shook his head, then pointed at the table, looked at her questioningly.

"Nothing for me, thank you. But please help yourself."
Chorosky nodded.

Peggy turned back to the game. Heath had shut off the computer, opened a panel on the front of the board, and was pointing to a series of buttons and light-emitting diodes, describing selections for levels of play and movement.

Bukov's interpreter was leaning toward the set, repeating the lesson, pointing, explaining. Bukov nodded.

"This switch," Heath pointed to one marked 'hint,' "allows the robot to help you out, if you're not sure what your next move should be."

Bukov laughed, said something to his interpreter which was not audible to the others and went untranslated. "It will play me?" he asked, looking up.

"Absolutely." Heath programmed the equipment, took Bukov's glass to freshen it, returned to the table.

Bukov had moved out his king's pawn to K4.

"Of course you do have an advantage over the computer."

Bukov looked up again.

"The machine can't receive messages from your staff of parapsychologists. Vladimir Zukhan may speak to you, but he can't speak to Gladstone."

Heath sat back down, crossed his leg, and reached for his own drink.

Peggy flushed. There had been rumors that Zukhan had won the 1979 World Championship for Anatoly Karpov. It was a suggestion that made Bukov's mouth tighten, and Chorosky turn stiffly from the table.

The robot had moved its pawn to K3. Bukov moved P-Q4, not looking up, but saying, "I am surprised you put any faith in those lies."

The machine duplicated P-Q4.

"Mr. Karpov has proved himself, before and since." He took Black's pawn. Bukov's voice was resonant. He had an actor's broad range, and its tone stayed in the air like an echo over Ted's quiet repetition.

Gladstone moved over Bukov's vulnerable pawn, lifted the piece and placed it on the side of the board.

Chorosky crossed back to the seat opposite Peggy. Her attention was trained on the board. There was no question. It was even the same black dress she wore the night before. Chorosky looked toward Bukov. Then he looked back at Peggy. Everyone here was dressed in black. Black and white. His eyes turned back to the four men. Black and white, like the tall cold chess pieces.

A shiver slipped down Chorosky's shoulders. He stood and walked to the bar.

Bukov looked up at him, annoyed. He had moved his knight KB3 and Gladstone played the same. They were playing rapidly. Bukov began to smile when his next move was duplicated as well. "Your Gladstone likes my moves," he said, raising his head to Heath.

Heath smiled. "It's a smart machine. It may be bluffing."

Bukov nodded and castled.

"Mr. Bukov, I asked you here for a different kind of game," Heath said.

Bukov's eyes raised from the board.

"It is a competition Mr. Baker wishes to extend."

Bukov sat back, looking evenly at George Heath. "And the terms, Mr. Heath?"

Heath listened to the translation, then said, "The terms are these; the Soviet Union has the opening move. We play with up to three of your intercontinental ballistic missiles, using dummy, non-explosive warheads."

He was speaking quietly, and slowly, for the interpreter. Bukov nodded at his young man, staring at Heath to go on.

"Our board is over the polar route, the target some point in the Western Pacific, away from shipping lanes."

Peggy glanced at Chorosky who had returned to stand next to his seat. He was staring at her. She looked back as Bukov spoke.

"Very interesting." He looked down at the board, then back up. "What reason does Mr. Baker have for this proposition?"

"Mr. Baker wants to demonstrate a defense system he thinks will encourage a consensus in our SALT III talks. We believe that the outcome of such a game will discourage your export of SS-20s into Eastern Europe."

Bukov cleared his throat. He looked again at the game, almost regretfully, and picked up Black's captured pawn. "Of course, Mr. Heath, there are certain requirements in our Anti-Ballistic Missile Treaty . . ."

Heath smiled. "I'm delighted at your concern. We will agree to suspend those provisions for the week of the contest."

"You have chosen a time?"

"Any time within a one week period beginning on Sunday, June 30, at 2400 Greenwich Mean Time."

Bukov nodded, replaced the pawn on the table.

"I realize this is something you cannot answer now," Heath said cordially. He stood, picked up Bukov's empty glass and his own. "May I pour you another?"

Bukov frowned, shook his head.

Heath moved between Peggy and Chorosky still standing stiffly by his chair. "Perhaps you can discuss this with your Comrades, and give me your answer tomorrow."

Bukov stared silently at Heath's back as his interpreter translated. This was very fast. Very surprising. He knew better than to make a hasty answer while he was unorganized, before he had spoken with Sorokin. He stood.

His interpreter moved like a shadow behind him, and Chorosky shifted on his feet. He, for one, would be happy to leave here.

"It has been a most educational evening," Bukov said, smiling. He nodded at the chess set. "Perhaps one day we will finish our game."

Heath held out his hand. "I would be pleased if you accepted the game, as a remembrance of our conversation."

Bukov showed his surprise by raising his eyebrows. He didn't speak for a moment, and his eyes were steady on Heath's, calculating. Then he smiled. He took Heath's outstretched hand and shook it. "It is very kind of you. Although I am not likely to forget our meeting, I accept."

Heath nodded. "Just do me this favor—if the machine breaks down, *don't* send it back to the States from Moscow."

Bukov's head fell back in a genuine laugh. "I understand," he said. "There is no warranty on this game."

CHAPTER
TWENTY-SEVEN

Cairo, May 14

Jefferson experienced a sense of déja vu as he walked slowly from the arrival gate into Cairo's airport terminal. He was gaining a serious appreciation for those men and women whose intelligence work required this bizarre lifestyle: meetings with strangers, alternating identities, little sleep, lots of travel, and the effort to hold it all together, and then look as if it was no effort at all.

Further, he thought, as a voice behind him said, "*Professore Garibaldi?*" this being walked up on from behind and addressed by someone he'd never seen before, was rather a jolt to the psyche—as well as confirmation of the very uncomfortable feeling that he was being watched.

"*Si. Come sta?*" Jefferson turned to shake Ed Walker's hand.

Everything seemed eerily the same: Walker took Jefferson through Immigration, produced a pass which substituted a nod for a search of his briefcase. Peter half expected David Haslawa to be waiting outside in his little grey Ford. But it was Walker who drove, a deep-cushioned grey Peugeot, and drove well.

The car was airconditioned and comfortable. Tinted windows did not disguise the shimmer of heat the road tossed up at them; Peter leaned back in his seat and listened to Walker.

". . . I've made arrangements for you to spend the night at Mena House. We can have dinner there. It's quite a lovely old place, elegant, really, in the shadow of the pyramids, and just a short drive from here."

"Our meeting is tomorrow morning?"

"Nine o'clock."

"Can you tell me anything about Medhat Wahab—the man I'll be meeting?"

Walker nodded. "Top man in Egyptian Intelligence. Very sharp, speaks excellent English, loyal and committed to Mubarak."

He turned off the dry highway, on to a newly macadamized road, heading west. "Wahab has immediate access to the President, but he'll probably have one of Mubarak's advisors with him; there'll be an interpreter, if that's the case." Walker hesitated, then said, "I speak Arabic myself—and Italian, by the way. In fact, I'm pleased to be able to use it again." He glanced over at Jefferson and smiled, almost sadly. "You can let me know how much I've forgotten."

Their conversation continued in Italian. Walker's manner was amiable and unassuming, and his accent was flawless. He seemed like a member of the family—but there was an air of melancholy about him.

Cars moved in a steady stream toward the city, and Jefferson asked if this was typical weekend traffic.

"Fairly typical," Walker replied. "But even during the week it's very heavy. And pedestrians have no rights here. The rule is, if you feel like crossing a main street, sit down until the feeling goes away."

At Al Ahran Street they bridged the Nile, another ribbon like the highways, and turned east a mile and then south. The sky seemed metallic, the day was beginning to cool, and Walker turned off the air conditioner and opened his window. He nodded toward the west. "There it is."

Mena House raised itself like an oasis, a great stone building set in green flowering gardens.

They took the drive in silence. By the time Walker pulled up to the white gravelled parking area the sun had angled close to the horizon and was back-lighting a huge pyramid in the west. Jefferson got out of the car and stared. Its solidity was like an anchor. He had never seen anything like it: photographs meant nothing.

Walker stood next to him for a minute. Finally he said, softly, "They're almost—spiritual, don't you think? That's Cheop's Pyramid." He pointed south. "You can just see the top of Chephren—it sits in the Valley—and just beyond, even lower, is Menkaura."

Jefferson shook his head. He could think of no appropriate response to this sight, in any language.

They stood a while longer, and then Walker said, "You'd probably like to wash up. Why don't you check in and meet me in the bar in half an hour. I'll reserve us a table meanwhile, and I've got a couple of calls to make."

Jefferson thanked Walker warmly, and they walked the hundred yards or so to the Hotel's entrance. The lobby was all marble, ornate with carvings etched into columns, over doorways, and around the huge windows. The "desk" which swept around one wall was made of white marble and dark polished wood. It was cool and dark inside, and quiet. A young man was walking the circumference of the lobby lighting gas jets in yellow glass lamps high on the walls.

Professore Garibaldi received his key and was taken to his room by a mute boy dressed in white. Upstairs the boy opened the windows which faced an incredible maze of garden below, and then he began backing out of the room, half bowing.

Peter gave him two Egyptian pound notes, and the boy bowed more deeply, and was gone.

Jefferson looked around. The room was carpeted in Persian tapestries, the walls panelled in dark rich wood. A great brass bed stood against one wall, and two chairs to flatter a throne room stood on either side of the balcony windows.

He paused at the open window, and looked over the darkening garden. The air was like perfume—a golden, musky scent, almost intoxicating. And the flavor of the place was opulent and exotic. Peter took a deep breath, and turned back to the room.

He opened his small bag and pulled out a fresh shirt and his toilet articles. Twenty minutes later recalling Professore Garibaldi, he shut the windows and left his room for dinner.

* * * * *

On his way through the lobby—it had the feel of a courtyard, Peter thought—he passed a man and woman who were stopped at the long curved reception desk. The woman was draped in silver and black silk, and she was veiled, hair covered and face hidden, except for her eyes—and they were luminous and kohl black.

Her husband, a man about Jefferson's own age, was speaking quietly with a hotel employee, and the woman looked up just as Jefferson walked by. It was for only the briefest moment. Her eyes dropped immediately. He didn't stop, of course, or even slow his pace. But her look had pierced him: the image of a dark woman, dark eyes, in rich silks, beautiful and unknown.

He found Ed Walker at a corner of the bar, and joined him for a drink before dinner. They spoke in Italian.

"I'd sure like to come back sometime, when there is some time. . ." Jefferson said.

"Yes, it's an astounding place. There's a feeling here—of history, I guess. And then, of course, the mystery of it all . . ."

They drank to that.

"What about this hotel?" Jefferson said.

Walker sat back. "It used to be the King's royal hunting lodge—built in the mid-1800s. It was converted in 1869 to accommodate guests who arrived in droves for the opening of the Suez Canal. King Khedive Ismail Pasha. He loved parties. By the turn of the century it had been enlarged again, and became a celebrated gathering place for crowned heads of state—and those folks who were the inspiration, God bless'em, for today's jet set."

Walker tossed down the end of his gin and tonic. "Since then other additions have been made—new annex just a few years ago—and now a group called the Oberoi manage and maintain it."

They took fresh drinks with them into the Rubaiyat, Mena House's main dining room. It was a lavish Moorish hall. The tables were covered in deep rose-colored linen; Waterford crystal and sterling flatware gleamed in soft lamplight on each table; and shadowed walls and ceiling, diaphanous hangings, the whisper of fans turning slowly from the ceiling, the whisper of conversation, created a compelling intimacy. A startlingly clear picture of the veiled woman slipped through Peter's mind.

Walker ordered for them both, in Arabic, a full dinner that came to their table on wafts of spice and steam over the next two and a half hours. It began with Red Sea prawns broiled in a tandoor, Indian mogul style, with a hot sauce, and a local dry white wine from the Village Granelis near Alexandria. They drank a cup of consomme flavored with sherry, and then the main course arrived: veal in a creamy morel sauce, saffron rice, carrots and zucchini. A bottle of Ptolemee, a light, dry red was served with the veal and chopped salad with tahini dressing; and fresh strawberries and ice cream, and rich Turkish coffee.

And that just about finished Peter Jefferson. Seeing him suppress a yawn, Walker smiled and said, "Why don't you turn in, Professore. I'll meet you at eight in the lobby. . . ."

"And I'll leave my bag in the room. . . ."

Walker chuckled, and signalled for the waiter.

* * * * *

Across Nozda Street from a treeless patchy park, sits a block of narrow little buildings all in a row. They are offices: two dentists practiced in one building, a small graphics business in another; there were several lawyers housed here, oil connected concerns, a fabric wholesaler. And in one building like all the rest, in rooms behind an accountant's office, Medhat Wahab and three other men rose to greet the two Americans.

Wahab introduced himself by name, and two of the others with him as "associates." One of his associates, and the interpreter, were in uniform. Wahab was a muscular man in his fifties, with curly, close-cropped hair, full lips and penetrating dark eyes. He spoke English carefully, and explained that the interpreter would intercede if he had any difficulty understanding, so Jefferson could speak freely.

Walker sat in a corner of the room, on a folding chair. Jefferson was given a position in a semicircle with the other men. The interpreter sat to his right, and to Wahab's left. For the next hour, Peter recounted the information he had brought. All the men listened so intently, it was as if his words were being sucked out of the still air. Occasionally one addressed the interpreter, or Jefferson directly.

At the end of his long description, one of the unnamed men asked the interpreter a question which he related to Peter: "Was there any reference to the country Chad?"

"No." Jefferson understood their concern. Qaddafi had strolled into that country in 1981. The French had been embarrassed, but non-resistant. The only reference he had heard regarding Qaddafi was the oblique toast to Libya.

There was a rather lengthy conversation in Arabic among the three men. Jefferson heard a couple of city names he recognized: Largeau, Abeché—both cities in Chad, south of Libya—and El Geneina just over the Sudanese border across from Abeché. Peter glanced over at Ed Walker who looked completely oblivious to the burst of rapid conversation.

In English, Wahab asked, "Any word of Asmara or Kassala, Mr. Jefferson?"

"No sir. But I have heard reports that there are Cubans and East Germans in both locations. I have no other details, I'm afraid."

Again the three ranking Egyptians conferred. Walker was examining a loose button on his jacket. Wahab looked silently at Jefferson. There were no more questions. All the men there looked unmoved. Peter wondered if they already had this intelligence. In Jerusalem, Ne'man had been angry, ben Dov had not hidden his worry. But these men just stared at him with their dark eyes.

Medhat Wahab rose and put out his hand. The meeting was over.

* * * * *

They drove directly to the airport. While Walker followed the fast-moving tide of traffic, he told Jefferson what the men had been saying. "They've evidently gotten intelligence that the Cubans have moved down into Chad from Libya, and they've got reports of unidentified convoys—trucks—moving in number from Largeau toward Abeché." Walker glanced at Peter. "Last count, the Libyans had at least three launchers for Russian SCUD missiles—and that was 1981. Those guys are thinking they've got at least twice that many now—and their range is sufficient to take out the Aswan Dam from Libya. If that's what's coming down by convoy . . ." Walker let the sentence dangle, and shook his head.

He turned the car east, and adjusted his sun visor. "You want the airconditioner?" he asked, looking over at Peter.

Peter shook his head.

"The French sent some military units into Chad when Qaddafi started to flex his muscles. They did have an interest in protecting the Habre government. But then the cost of keeping them there became a political problem for Mitterand. Now most of them have been withdrawn, and Libya has just about annexed all of the northern part of Chad including Largeau and Abeché."

Jefferson nodded. "That's what I've heard. Furthermore, if you were Qaddafi, would you mess with the Egyptians?. . . They've got alliances with members of the Arab League and the Organization of African Unity. When the Sudanese get mad they get serious—and they don't take prisoners." He paused. "What shape is their army in?"

"The Egyptian army?"

Peter nodded.

"Active—around 450,000; *plus* they've got the National Guard, the Frontier Forces and Security and Defense Forces. That's another 100,000. And they've got good equipment—$600 million a year's worth."

Walker shook his head. "It's sad really. Egypt has a terrible housing shortage. That money should have gone into development. Sadat had to make some tough choices: the army kept him in power and he had to keep the generals happy. There wasn't ever enough money for both the army, and the Nasserites, and so-called Islamic activists whose vision was to decentralize Cairo, build whole new towns outside the city . . ."

"There never is enough," said Jefferson, as the car swung surely toward the airport.

CHAPTER
TWENTY-EIGHT

Geneva, May 15

Once again Doctor Garibaldi was the last passenger off the plane, but this time there was no design and no deception: Peter was exhausted and had fallen asleep directly after lunch.

The stewardess "hadn't the heart" to wake him. For a second he wasn't sure where he was. Then he wasn't sure exactly who he was supposed to be. He looked at the pretty girl waiting for him in the empty aisle, and realized he must seem ridiculous sitting there, staring at her, alone in the plane.

Quickly, he said in Italian, "I'm so sorry, young lady. I seem to have overslept. . . ." and smiled what he hoped was a fairly innocent smile, gathered his bag, briefcase and jacket together, and nodded, "*Grazie e arriverderci—*" and left the plane.

He went through Immigration as Doctor Garibaldi with some slight nervousness. He had no Ed Walker here with a comfortable manner and a yellow pass. Imagine getting busted now.

But his bags were apparently not of interest, and he was beginning to anticipate being Peter Jefferson again—in just a few minutes. . . .

When the uniformed officer glancing through his passport looked up and said, "*E stato un viaggio breve, Professore. Per quanto tempo rimarra a Gineva?*"

Peter forced himself to play his part a little longer. "*Per un altra settinora, signore.*"

The man nodded, thumped his seal over the page, and handed the book over the counter. "*Si diverta allora, Professore.*"

* * * * *

It was 4:30, Geneva time. He wondered if Peggy would be at the Hotel. He couldn't remember Saturday's agenda. He decided to try, and walked toward a row of compartmentalized phones in the open airport lounge. He dialed information and got the number of the Intercontinental and waited while the phone rang four times . . . five . . . in Peggy's empty room.

He had better luck with a call to the Secretary of State who seemed glad to hear from him, and asked that he come up as soon as he arrived back at the hotel.

* * * * *

Martha met him at the door, with excessive solicitude.

"Peter, you poor dear, you look awful. . . ."

He hadn't realized it was quite so bad.

"Is everything all right?"

He smiled at her. "Just tired."

"Well, of course—you must be exhausted. Come in, come in." She turned, gesturing to her right, walking into the sitting room. "Just put those bags down right over there—George, darling—Peter Jefferson is here. . . ."

Peter followed her in, deposited his bag and briefcase against the wall, and sank into the deep patterned chair opposite the couch.

When Heath walked in Peter began to rise.

"Don't get up," Heath said, holding up one hand. He touched Martha on the shoulder as he moved behind her to the couch. Sitting, he looked at Peter critically. "You look terrible."

Martha laughed lightly. "I think this is where I came in," she said. "I'll leave you two to talk—perhaps Peter will join us for dinner this evening, George."

"No thanks, Mrs. Heath. I'm going to clean up—try to do something about how I look—and give Peggy a call. . . ."

"Oh my, I'm afraid you're going to be disappointed. If you do change your mind, you're welcome," Martha said, and left on that line.

Peter looked questioninly at George Heath, who said, "Tell me how it went."

"All right, I guess. I gave them the news. In Cairo it felt like they'd been expecting something. In Israel Ne'man and ben Dov were obviously upset. Ne'man, especially, seemed hard pressed to be civil. . . . I took some notes on the plane. . . ."

He started to get up again, looking toward his briefcase.

Heath gestured for him to stay seated. " 'Nobody likes the man who brings bad news.' We can go over it tomorrow—on the way home."

Peter looked at him. "On the way home?"

Heath smiled. "Let me explain what's been going on—"

Peter sat back and loosened his tie. He listened to Heath's account of his proposal to Bukov, with astonishment.

"How long has this been in the works?"

"Since the convention came up. You remember Larry suggesting we make an effort here to promote SALT III. . . . I brought Peggy in the night I asked her to stay—after you had left."

Peter looked disturbed. He rose and walked toward the bar. Quietly, he said, "Aren't we taking a hell of a risk?"

Heath nodded. "It is an enormous gamble—but here's the thinking behind it. . . ." He sat forward. "A nuclear exchange between the United States and the Soviet Union is simply not acceptable. Schell may have exaggerated in some ways, but his book, *The Fate of the World,* convinced people there had to be an alternative to mass suicide—if he'd had a Soviet counterpart with a free press, a lot of just plain folks from Minsk or wherever would be out getting signatures on nuclear freeze petitions—like they are here, and throughout Western Europe."

Heath turned to the window behind him, pulled back the drapes. It was early evening by now. Geneva's soft light dusted the room. The Secretary turned back. "A great many responsible thinkers support the idea that a partial defense against nuclear missiles is better than no defense at all. We can't afford to abandon our nuclear program while nuclear weapons exist."

Peter nodded. "I understand that, George. But we've got new countries joining the nuclear membership every year."

"And the Kremlin is as worried about that as we are," Heath inserted. "Believe me, they have no interest in the end result of a nuclear exchange that leaves them a remnant of what they are now, even if the United States ends up in the same condition."

He leaned back. "Alan is convinced—and I've got to agree— that if someone is crazy enough to order a missile launch, it will be one of the newly armed countries—not the Soviet Union, and not ourselves."

Peter was leaning with one arm on the polished bar. "Okay," he said. "Partial defense wins over the argument that anything less than full defense invites casualties."

"And that's the concept on which the Saturn program was formulated—partial defense. The technology was all there, and compared to the cost of city defense against saturation attacks, not to mention counterforce strategies, Saturn was the cost-effective answer."

"But we don't even know if it works."

Heath didn't respond at first, then he said quietly, "We're going to find out. If it does, we will have created the atmosphere for winding down the arms race."

"And if it fails? . . ."

"If it fails, we'll know exactly where we stand."

Neither man spoke for a moment, then Heath continued. "It may also put a wrench in the works building against Israel and Egypt. For the next month and a half, the Soviets are likely to be concentrating on infiltration defense, rather than attack. If the timing is as critical as your discovery makes it seem Saturn may alter the entire game."

Another silence. Peter tried to collect his thoughts. Finally, he said, "Have they responded?"

Heath leaned forward, smiling. "Don't look so worried." He sat back, saying, "They called this morning to accept, on the condition that the entire episode be strictly top secret. Absolutely no public knowledge either before or after, no matter what the outcome."

Peter unbuttoned his collar. "I believe I'll have a drink." He turned toward the shelf of glasses, then looked back over his shoulder. "You?"

Heath shook his head, smiling.

As he lifted several ice cubes into a glass, Peter said, "I would have loved to be able to tap into the phone lines last night. . . ."

"Oh, I'm sure there were several members of the Party who didn't sleep last night. . . ." Heath chuckled. "You'll be happy to know *I* slept like a baby."

Peter returned to his chair. "Where do we go from here?"

"We've already begun. Peggy left this morning for Washington. She'll be working with Major General Cooper at NORAD, as the Pentagon's liaison."

Peter looked at Heath, not sure he was hearing him right. His expression must have said as much, because Heath almost laughed.

"She's one of the few who's worked on Saturn from its conception. Alan asked for her specifically."

Peter took a drink. He didn't know how to respond. 'That's great' wasn't particularly appropriate. In fact, he felt more regret than anything else. Except maybe tired.

Heath was still speaking. Peter realized his shoulders had slumped. He sat up straighter.

". . . We'll be leaving after the opening speeches tomorrow—I'll be interested in hearing what Bukov has to say. I imagine our agreement will change the tone of whatever they had prepared."

"Can we just leave like that, on the first day of the conference?"

"Certainly. We were here to show our support—the rest of our delegation stays."

Peter nodded and was about to say something more when Martha walked back into the room.

"Good heavens, George, are you two still talking? Let the poor man get some sleep."

* * * * *

Bukov's speech had indeed been affected by his conversation with Heath. He had worked hard on the original, had worked harder getting it past Sorokin. At five this morning a hotel administrator had tapped on his door and delivered a coded teletype, six pages, a new opening speech. By six o'clock, Chorosky had prepared him a transcript.

Sorokin had been outraged by the game. Of course they would accept. The Americans were trying to manipulate them. The fools!

And Bukov had thought immediately of a fool's mate. In a rush of understanding he knew that there were second stakes. He let Sorokin go on.

In this game providence had maneuvered Bukov into a fool-proof situation. His solar plexus thrilled with the realization. Sorokin was going to ride them into this fray, and whoever won, Sorokin would lose. If the United States had some magic weapon, Sorokin's loss would be shared by all of Russia. Even if the United States were defeated in this missile test, Sorokin wouldn't wait, he'd have to press the advantage, he'd move on the Middle East—that absurd plan, to expect anything from Qaddafi—and Bukov could easily forecast the outcome.

"If they want to show us what they have for us, well, we will take a good close look." Sorokin's voice had been shrill, even at that distance. Bukov had moved the receiver back from his ear.

"Most accommodating, these Americans. *Most* accommodating."

But Bukov wondered. He would never have taken the gambit. Of course it wasn't his game yet. The rewritten script was a bristling, hardline attack on the United States, focusing on presumed anti-Soviet aggressions. The text got slightly hysterical on the presumed purpose of the conference—and blamed Israel and Egypt specifically for obstructing peace in the Middle East.

Bukov ran his hand over his head. He looked at the clock near his unslept-in bed. He wouldn't have time now to prepare. He hated playing the villain. And he didn't dare change a word of it.

* * * * *

The following day the *New York Times* described his monologue as "an impassioned panegyric delivered while standing in front of a looking glass—he almost walked through it into wonderland.

Heath spoke after Bukov, with great control. He presented an overview of the entire Middle East, and he did not leave out Russian interests, but defined them succinctly; he warned of indirection, and then the spread of Middle Eastern problems, like a scourge into other reaches. He gave as an example India's rebuilding its nuclear reactor with Libyan money, and receiving Soviet instruction on how to penetrate Pakistani radar . . .

In a statement that surprised everyone present, he strongly—almost sternly—suggested that West Germany take steps immediately to prohibit the export of Tornado aircraft, Roland II surface to air missiles, mobile missile systems with target tracking radar, and Marder armed personnel carriers to Saudi Arabia. In a thinly veiled reference to history, Heath then asked, "Does anyone want to see German weapons used in the volatile Middle East? In view of what my government is doing to move away from nuclear deterrence, are not these conventional weapons more appropriate for use where they are made? He paused and looked directly at the Soviet group.

While Heath spoke, Bukov sat stonily next to Chorosky, his hands over his ears, as if to hold out any intrusion on the simultaneous translation his headset provided.

". . . We have to ask, then, just whose interests are served without a comprehensive Middle East settlement?" Heath paused to allow his listeners to ask themselves that question. "The answer is clearly, and sadly, the Soviet Union." More strongly, "The United States calls on the Soviet Union to recognize that humanity is at stake here. More than oil concerns, military deals, trade or treaty— *humanity* is being pushed to the brink. We must agree to stop that pushing—at all costs, because humanity is priceless—and then there will be room for peace."

CHAPTER
TWENTY-NINE

Washington, May 17

Heath and Jefferson were met at the airport and driven directly to the White House.

It was not a long meeting. Detailed reports would come over the next few days. Peter was standing in front of his apartment door at 8:30, juggling his suitcase, briefcase and keys. The phone inside started to ring, and he knew it was Peggy, and he couldn't find the right key.

By the fourth ring he got the door open, dropped both bags on the sofa and picked up the receiver in the kitchen in the middle of the sixth ring.

"Oh, Peter, I was just going to hang up. . . ."

There was a silence.

"Peter?"

"I'm . . . sorry, Miriam, I just walked in."

She laughed a little nervously, then said, "How are you?"

"Well, I'm pretty beat, to tell you the truth. I just got back from Geneva."

"Oh. . . ." She sounded a little hurt. "Was it a good trip?"

"It was—interesting, that's for sure. Look, can you hold on a minute? I left my keys in the door. . . ."

He put the phone on the counter and went to close the front door. He'd cancelled the lunch they'd planned together over a month ago on three separate occasions; he wasn't going to be able to put her off again. Loosening his tie, he went back to the kitchen.

"I'm back."

Pause. Her voice seemed smaller: "I was wondering, Peter, if you were free for lunch sometime this week."

He hated having this effect on her. He could almost hear her shrinking. "Sure. . . . Listen, Miriam, I am sorry. I know it must seem like I've been avoiding you—really, it's been work. . . ." He also hated making excuses. He *had* been avoiding her.

"I know for sure I have no appointments tomorrow—can you make it then?"

"Yes—yes, that'll be fine. At the Madison?"

"Twelve-thirty."

"Okay. Thanks, Peter. I'm really looking forward to seeing you. . . ." She waited for him to say he was too.

"All right, I'll see you then. Night, Miriam."

Quietly, "Bye, Peter."

He hung up the phone feeling lousy. He walked over to the refrigerator and opened the door. He knew very well he had cleaned it out before he left, anticipating he'd be gone at least two weeks, but he stared into it anyway. There were two German beers on the bottom shelf, an apple, a small block of cheddar cheese. He took a beer, and then picked up his bag in the living room and went upstairs.

Sitting down on his bed, he dialed Peggy's number.

A man answered the phone. "Peggy Montague's residence," he said.

Peter was silent for a second, while he processed this information. "Is Peggy there?" he managed, finally.

"May I tell her who's calling?"

Who the hell *was* this guy with the proprietary air? "Yes—this is Peter Jefferson."

"Peter Jefferson. I've heard quite a bit about you, Mr. Jefferson. I'll get her."

What did that mean?

A moment later Peggy picked up the phone. "Peter! You're back. . . . How are you? How was the flight?"

"Who was that?" he said, as lightly as possible.

"My Dad. My parents are here for a couple of days. They hadn't been able to reach me—naturally—so it was a complete surprise when I got back. They arrived two days ago, and they'll be here till Wednesday."

Her Dad! "That's great! Am I going to get a chance to meet them?" he said.

"I'd love that. How about dinner Tuesday?"

"That'll be fine." He hesitated. "Is there a chance of seeing you before then?"

She laughed. "Before then is just one day, Peter. . . ."

"I know," he said.

"I don't think so. I've got two meetings tomorrow night."

Peter leaned back against the headboard, and closed his eyes. "You're going to be pretty busy for a while."

"Not so busy we won't have time together. . . ."

A short pause. "I'll let you go. . . ."

"Peter, are you okay?"

He opened his eyes. "Yeah. It's just—it hurts not to be with you."

He couldn't believe he'd said that. He sounded like *Miriam,* for God's sake.

"Peter. . . ."

"Listen, I'll see you Tuesday. Enjoy your visit with your folks. . . ."

* * * * *

The next morning, sitting at the library table, Peter tried to concentrate. He still felt as if he was in transit. He had to prepare a lengthy report on his visits to Jerusalem and Cairo, had all this traffic to deal with. He had had a call from the Under Secretary for Research and Development at the Defense Department to set up a meeting next week. He dropped a legal-sized pad on the stack of cables, and pushed back from the table.

He should never have agreed to see Miriam today. Not with all this work. He felt wound up and still exhausted. It wasn't a comfortable feeling.

His intercom buzzed. "Mr. Boyington is here. . . ."

Thank God, a sane friend. . . . Peter walked toward the door as Stu strode in. Peter smiled. "It's good to see you, old man. What are you doing here?"

"In the neighborhood, thought I'd check in. How was your trip?"

They shook hands. "Fine—just fine. . . ."

"What'd you guys pull over there?" Boyington asked, sitting down in one of Peter's leather chairs. "Net Assessment has been busy as hell the past two days."

Peter took a chair near him. "Sorry about that, pal. It was nothing personal."

"You all right, Peter? You look terrible."

Peter looked up at his friend. "I'm going to get a complex if one more person tells me that." He got up and walked over to the big table. Turning, he said, "Do you have a minute to talk?"

"Sure."

Peter half leaned, half sat on the edge of the table, facing him. "I'm getting together with Miriam for lunch, and I feel—I don't know—nervous. . . ." He paused. "She's so needy. I hate hurting her, and it seems I do everytime we see one another. But in a way I'm the one who ends up hurting: this kind of," he looked for the words, ". . . anxiety, and guilt. . . ."

"Not to mention what it's going to do to your digestive system."

Peter just looked at him.

"Peter, you're just going to have to be up front with her. Your marriage ended four years ago. If she doesn't know it yet, you're going to have to tell her."

"But I don't know how to do that without hurting her feelings. . . ."

"You're not responsible for her feelings. You're responsible for your feelings. A relationship where one person is anxious and guilty and the other is hurt. . . ." Stu shook his head. "It's not the kind of relationship she should be pursuing, or you should be tolerating. Just say so."

For a moment Peter was silent. "You're exactly right," he said, finally.

"Thank you." Stu grinned. "Diane, you know, is into this sort of thing—I just pick it up from her."

* * * * *

He had been able to get back into his work after that. It was warm. He had hung his light, khaki colored jacket over a chair, and sat with an onionskin copy of a request for military support: Sudan was asking Oman to provide protection against Asmara and Aden.

TO: *Harold Smyth*
cc: *George Heath*
          Admiral Robert Smilie
FROM: *General Thomas Becker, Marine Corps for RDF Muscat,*
          Oman
DATE: *June 28*
RE: *Defense directive SR-467d23-85/Information copy*

Request for assistance from General Numiery, Sudanese Army Chief of Staff on June 27, to Colonel Alexander Page, British military advisor to Sultan, in view of new and potential threat to Khartoum from Asmara and proximity of base at Aden. On recommendation of Col Page, Omani Army moving west for positioning missiles near border with South Yemen.

Very low altitude helicopter resupply for these units nightly; surface to surface missiles en route by H.M.S. Nelson, British submarine. Missiles to be positioned near Habarut on undefined border of People's Democratic Republic of Yemen. (Exercise treated as routine patrol of Dhufar area.)

U.S. air cover from forward base at Thamarit will be made available if necessary, per your consideration.

Another country heard from, Jefferson thought. He flipped through an attached summary of political and diplomatic history going back to the formation of the People's Democratic Republic of Yemen in 1970: *"Marxist, violently opposed to the 'conservative' Arab states, excepting only Libya from abuse. Diplomatic relations with North Korea, North Vietnam, Cuba, Soviet Union. Trade relations with the People's Republic of China.*

"Hostilities in 1972 with North Yemen, who rejected the People's efforts to extend its political sovereignty north. Cease fire signed in 1976, the Sultan's army having driven the Marxist faction behind a border running from Hauf on the Arabian Sea to the northwest."

Jefferson turned to a similar survey on Oman. His eye ran down the page. *"Economic Development: Beginning 1975 through present, Omani oil revenue used for development and to secure tribal loyalty to the Sultan whose Armed Force is operated out of Seeb.*

"Military: British Jaguar strike aircraft: U.S. made F-5E; modern ground-based defense system."

The last page was a map of the areas described, with a dotted line indicating the Omani movement west.

Jefferson's intercom buzzed. He dropped the cable into a growing pile of memos on the Middle East, and answered the phone.

"It's noon, Mr. Jefferson."

"Thanks, Grace."

He returned to the table, put the cables still to be read in one large envelope, those he had gone through and which related to the Mideast and northern Africa in another, and the last pile, miscellaneous other notifications in a third. He locked them all back in his safe, picked up his jacket, took a deep breath, and left his office.

* * * * *

He saw her before she saw him. Her head was down, blonde hair pulled back in a severe bun. She would have looked like Mo Dean, except for a rather too extreme ensemble: very flouncy skirts and sleeves in a blue and white stripe.

As she neared the entrance to the Madison she looked up. Her mouth formed an 'O' of surprise and then stretched immediately to a determined grin. She really wasn't tall enough to wear a dress like that.

Without hesitating, she walked up to him and kissed him on the cheek. "Hi," she said brightly.

He drew back, not meaning to, and saw the measure of it in her eyes. He took her arm and said, "New hairdo?"

She glanced up at him quickly, but he wasn't looking at her. She decided not to answer.

They were taken directly to a table, and for a few awkward moments went through the ritual of choosing a drink and studying the menu. When the waiter arrived to ask if they would like a cocktail, Jefferson said, "Two Tom Collins, and I think we're ready to order. . . ." At which Miriam looked up with some surprise, and then back down to the menu in front of her. She asked for the Palace Court salad. Jefferson ordered broiled snapper.

When the waiter left, Miriam looked straight at him and said, "Score one for you, Peter."

"What's that mean?"

She waved her hand, as if to clear her words from the air between them. "I'm sorry—I just thought we'd take some time over lunch, to talk. . . . You seem to be in an awful hurry. . . ."

She was right. It was rude of him. She had changed, though—four years ago she never would have responded with annoyance or hurt. Maybe she had given up suffering in silence. Good for her.

"I'm sorry, I didn't mean to be rushing us," he said.

She didn't say anything, but took a sip of water.

"How's your mother?" he tried.

"I didn't come here to talk about Mother. . . ."

Another surprise.

Nervously, she picked up her napkin and unfolded it on her lap. With her head still lowered, she said, "I wanted to talk about you and me."

"Miriam. . . ."

She raised her head. "No, Peter—I have to say this."

The waiter appeared with their drinks. They sat silently until he left.

Miriam touched her glass. "In the beginning, we had a really magical relationship, Peter. I think what went wrong was that you were growing—as a person and in your career, and I felt as if I was being left behind. Your job especially intimidated me. . . ."

He remembered. Embassy receptions, important to his work, and exciting to him early in his career, had devastated her—all those people speaking all those foreign languages. . . .

"I was too shy, or something. . . ."

Frightened, he thought.

"But over the last couple of years, I've changed."

"Miriam. . . ."

"Let me finish. . . . this isn't easy for me." She was staring down at the table cloth.

Jefferson had a sudden rush of feeling for her.

She looked up, saw some compassion in his eyes, and went on. "I can't believe what we had that was so fine can have died. I'd like to . . . see you again, spend some time . . . to see if maybe. . . ."

The salad and fish platter arrived. The waiter seemed to realize he was intruding, and retreated quickly.

Jefferson picked up his fork.

"Peter? . . ."

He sighed and put down the fork. He tried to think how to respond.

"You've met someone else," she said.

He looked at her, surprised, then said, "Yes."

She picked up her cocktail, staring at him. "Well, good for you." She took a drink. "Still, I don't think your tortured reaction to this meeting is really appropriate."

He shook his head. "You're being unfair," he said quietly.

"Maybe so." She put down her glass, picked up her napkin and placed it on the table. "I don't think I'm hungry, Peter. Would you get me a cab?"

He stared at her a moment, then raised his hand for the waiter.

Minutes later they walked through the hotel lobby and onto the sidewalk. Peter spoke to the doorman, who stepped smartly to the curb and flagged a Yellow cab.

As they walked over to the taxi, a familiar car pulled up behind it, and with some shock, Peter watched Peggy Montague step out, and after her a handsome older couple.

Peggy looked as surprised as he must have. Miriam, waiting for Peter to open the cab door, looked around at the two of them. There was a moment when no one spoke. Peggy's father took his wife's arm, and stood watching this rather awkward tableau.

"Peggy. . . ." Peter cleared his throat. "Peggy Montague, this is my ex-wife, Miriam Jefferson." He turned to Miriam. "Miriam, this is Peggy."

Peggy flashed a quick smile and held out her hand. But Miriam wasn't smiling. She said only, "Excuse me," walked around Peter, opened the door, and got into the cab. Her face was stiff.

He bent toward the window, but she was already speaking to the driver, and the car pulled away quickly. She didn't look back. He turned toward Peggy. "I'm sorry," he said. "She was upset."

Peggy took his arm. "I understand. . . . Come, meet mother and dad." Her eyes were smiling.

They turned to her parents, and Peter put out his hand. "I'm really happy to meet you."

Her father, a tall, tanned man with Peggy's warm smile and same green eyes, clasped his hand. "Good to meet you, Peter."

As he shook her mother's hand, she said, "We're looking forward to dinner tomorrow evening."

"Thank you, Mrs. Montague. So am I."

A moment of silence, everybody smiling at everybody else. Then Peggy said, "We're meeting an old friend of my dad's for lunch. Can you join us for a drink?"

He would have liked to, but thought he'd better not.

CHAPTER THIRTY

Cheyenne Mountain, Colorado, July 4

1200 Greenwich Mean Time: General Arthur Cooper watched the great white knuckled Cheyenne Mountain tap against a porcelain sky as he approached. He smiled to himself, liking the image.

Art Cooper, as anyone who knew him would attest, was a truly remarkable man. Women particularly, were enchanted by his poetry and alienated by his lack of warmth. That coldness, and steely nerves, were the source of rumors that he was not quite human. Behind his back they called him the Bionic Man.

He was in excellent physical shape, a handsome man with shaved head, well formed dark eyebrows, and ice blue eyes. He was fifty-six, had achieved the rank of four star General in the Air Force, wore five rows of ribbons over his pilot's wings, had a great deal of power, and liked it that way. He was also very sensitive to the line at which his power stopped. The President had the final word, even here.

North American Aerospace Defense Command sits inside the top of Cheyenne Mountain at 9,500 feet. The air was thin and cold at this hour. Cooper checked his watch as they entered the 1,416 foot-long tunnel.

They slipped through the 25-ton blast doors that could close in thirty seconds, effectively sealing Command Post into the heart of the mountain. He turned in his seat to watch the light recede.

Two minutes later the General stepped out of his car, and walked the short distance to the metal doors of the Post. A Lieutenant saluted. Cooper inserted a plastic card into a computer lock, and the doors slid open silently.

The large, cream-colored room was buzzing softly with equipment. Eighteen separate graphics display screens glowed in front of eighteen separate officers playing keyboards like virtuosos. Cooper walked down a well polished aisle and stopped behind a young

221

woman monitoring a display of the United States and Canada with lines of information rolling like credits across the screen.

Then he moved two machines down to a red neon-type outline of Europe and North and South America, over which undulated slow blue ribbons of light representing orbiting satellites.

What he received here was gathered via telescope and camera, satellites in synchronystic orbit, radar and radio receiving equipment with both land and seabed sensors in Korea, Alaska, New Zealand, Greenland and Italy. He had over one hundred main frame computers and related software, processing many millions of bits of information hooked into his Post from Space Communications Center nearby.

Some of his radar network included phased-array radar which scan large expanses of space in fractions of a second. Cooper also received information from the north central United States—the Perimeter Acquisition Radar Attack Characterization System, which could pick up an intercontinental ballistics missile in the terminal phase of flight. Another part of NORAD's space track mission were radars of the Ballistic Missile Early Warning System at Clear, Alaska; Thule, Greenland; and Fylingdale Moors, England.

Cooper had been instrumental in designing a system to replace radar vulnerable to electronic countermeasures the Soviets were installing on their newer missiles. Now Early Warning used immobile detection antennae pulsing power into space at 140 GHz. per second, in the shape of a large fan. Initial detection of a missile occurred when the offending object penetrated a reconnaissance radar beam. This interruption would be accomplished within seconds of a launch, and would alert tracking antennae to lock a narrow ray on the missile, establishing its trajectory and probable point of impact.

A large screen in a portion of the north wall was manned by four intense-looking officers monitoring reconnaissance satellites in synchronous orbit. They would receive almost instantaneous transmission of any Soviet missile launch. By late 1985, the Missile Tracking System used those satellites to observe infrared signatures of missiles, and compare these with previously observed infrared signatures from the booster burnout of missile rockets. In addition, these satellites, fed accurate trajectory computations, could continue to track up to twenty missiles *after* rocket booster burnout, and transmit data sufficient to show their tracks on a rolling-map of the area over which they were traveling.

While Alan Baker was taking his oath of office, NORAD was installing a defensive anti-satellite system to minimize Soviet use of space interceptors capable of disabling reconnaissance satellites.

The reconnaissance satellites were able to detect a Soviet Intercontinental Ballistic Missile launch by computer in less than a minute, matching any object moving through space with the orbits of all known satellites and space "junk." If the computer couldn't make a match, the object was labeled an unknown.

With an unknown on screen, Cooper would follow the book: he would alert all four Command Posts: NORAD, Strategic Air Command, the National Military Command Center at the Pentagon and the Alternate National Military Command Center in Fort Richie, Maryland, to begin formal evaluation procedures to asess data. This evaluation, conducted through a Missile Display Conference, was more often than not, routine.

However, if data could not identify the object, a second step would be taken: initiation of a Threat Assessment Conference. In summer of 1980, it had gone that far—all senior personnel, including the President, were called. But it was determined that the "threat" was based on erroneous data, and the third step, a Missile Attack Conference, was never convened.

They would have less than twenty-eight minutes, from point of launch to point of impact to accomplish all that, and respond to an attack.

Cooper's deputy was pouring a mug of coffee for him as he entered his sparse glass office. The room was raised on the south wall, affording him a complete view of the floor. He took his seat, staring down at the precision movement below him. His deputy handed him his coffee and lifted a clipboard off the desk.

The relationship Cooper had with his deputy was about as intimate as any he had ever achieved—on any level that mattered. It boiled down to the younger man's total loyalty, even devotion, and Cooper's cool presumption that he deserved it.

In his well-modulated voice, Thomas ran down what had transpired in the General's absence. "We picked up two Yankee-class submarines ready to dock at Socotra, probably for resupply—and followed them, submerged, for four hours. The equipment is all functioning beautifully."

Cooper nodded, sipped his coffee.

"We've identified four Typhoon class subs in the Indian Ocean not far from Diego Garcia, and six more docked at Vladivostok. And at sea near Murmansk, 1402 GMT, two Kirov-class guided missile cruisers with four Sovremennyy-class guided missile destroyers.

"We're watching those to determine a fix. There's also a Kiev class carrier about eight hundred miles south of Shemya, Alaska. . . ." He paused and ran his eye down a printout attached to his board. "No unusual escorts. . . ." He looked up, "But you told us to keep an eye on them. . . . No unknowns, everything matched in orbit."

General Cooper nodded again and raised his cup, an acknowledgement and a signal for his deputy to pour.

The younger man left his clipboard with the General, and retreated to his own desk outside Cooper's door.

Cooper spent the rest of the morning, as he had every morning for the past two weeks, reviewing every piece of equipment and data under his tutelage. Cooper felt proprietory toward his computers. Having learned their language, he had found a clarity of mind much like his own. Finally, there was someone to talk to. When he had been assigned to Cheyenne Mountain, he felt as if he had come home.

At 1400 Greenwich Mean Time, Cooper rose silently from his console, a Multipulsing Optical Thermo-Echo Resolver which had been given the acronym MOTHER even before he came along, and stepped toward the door. His deputy, tall, blonde, silent too, followed at a respectful distance through the hall of screens, bypassing the elevator, down a flight of stairs to the lower level of Command Center.

They paused in the doorway. The shield of North American Aerospace Command, a sword crossed by lightning, hung like a talisman over one wall of the room. Facing each other over a diagonal spread of illuminated buttons were rows of two-man teams, each pair sharing a screen and telephone. At random intervals printouts chattered out of slots behind each diagonal array, were checked by one man while the other continued their monitor, and collected by an officer making rounds of the room.

The General nodded to these technicians as he toured the room. He was listening to the pulse of this nation's protection, he thought, the murmur of men and women responding to the hum of machinery.

Well, there was nothing yet.

He returned to his office, sat down in front of MOTHER. His console assimilated information from every other unit in the Center. It could review the orbit of known satellites, focus on any area of the world. He touched a key and the Mediterranean Sea shimmered on his screen. He watched a slow red line, then seven more, lengthening across the unit in front of him. These were the thermal tracks of eight Soviet submarines. Two of them, he could tell, were Hotel-class nuclear-powered attack subs; the others, Delta-class with suborbital missile capability. Nothing new here.

Communications lines were open to the Pentagon, Fort Richie, Strategic Air Command in Omaha, and the Canadian National Defense Headquarters in Ottawa.

Cooper's phone buzzed softly.

With no emotion, a clear voice reported, "1518 and 32 seconds, Sir, an unknown originating near Moscow."

Cooper looked out at the large wall-screen below him. His deputy entered the room, stood behind him and to the right. The zeroes on the missile warning display had disappeared and were showing the number three, indicating a launch of three missiles. Cooper asked for confirmation, waited six seconds to determine that all Centers were receiving the same data, and then pushed a button on his terminal. A split-image appeared: on the right side of the screen the area of the launch was illuminated; on the other side, programmed for satellite warning, nothing. It took less than ten seconds for infrared scans to locate the unknowns and start tracking. As soon as the trajectory was calculated, the figures appeared underneath the image on the screen, along with latitude and longitude of the launch site. The split-screen dissolved and was replaced by an outline map and three illuminated dots north of Moscow.

Cooper said, "Impact?"

The disembodied voice responded, "Preliminary trajectory shows point of impact south of the Aleutians."

From the moment the launch was spotted it had taken 20 seconds for a computer match to eliminate all known objects in space, and space junk. Within two minutes, the Early Warning System at Site One and Two in Shemya, Alaska would be able to give NORAD a confirmation on trajectory and impact points.

"I've got better input now, General: key #5."

Cooper touched #5, the screen faded, then produced a bright curved red line. The line crept in a slow, three-unit arc, but Cooper knew it was traveling at about 1500 miles per hour and would reach a speed of almost 15,000 miles per hour before it was spent.

At 1519 and 32 seconds GMT, his deputy handed Cooper a single earphone with a small microphone attached to the mouthpiece, and he was now in communication with the lower level of his Command Post. All incoming lines to NORAD were cleared of non-essential traffic.

At 1521 GMT, the voice resumed, crackled slightly, "Track divergence of almost eight degrees. Could be a gravitational and magnetic anomaly approaching the polar region—or a mid-course correction."

Cooper's arc was still intact. Shemya had not yet picked up the unknowns. "Check again," the General ordered.

"There it is." The voice was faster, more urgent. "You can see it now on Missile Tracking . . ."

Indeed, on the floor, and now on MOTHER'S screen, one thread of the neat red arc was slipping slightly off course.

"Give me preliminary track and probable point of impact on unknown three," said the General. There was nothing in his voice to indicate any urgency.

It was now 1521 and 52 seconds GMT. The voice came back at 1522 and 13. "Unknown three veering east, target area tentative as Denver, Colorado." A pause. "Pick up from Shemya, sir." Pause. "Target area one and two confirmed to impact 725 miles south-southwest of Shemya, in the Pacific."

1523 GMT. So far no word from the Pentagon, Fort Richie or Omaha, but Cooper knew they were receiving simultaneous information. He touched a button through to the Pentagon. "Cooper here. I'm assessing unknown three as a potential threat to the continental United States. Do you concur?"

An equally cool voice responded, "Affirmative. Advising the President and Admiral Smilie."

That was it. Now it was up to them. It was 1523 and 30 seconds Greenwich Mean Time, four minutes and 50 seconds since the launch. They had twenty-three minutes and ten seconds left to make their decision.

* * * * *

The National Military Command Center is a small complex—considerably smaller than NORAD in Cheyenne Mountain—located in the inner sanctum of the Pentagon. Twin steel doors and armed civilian and military guards, isolate the area from intrusion, and a wire-mesh screen surrounds it to defend against electronic eavesdropping.

The heart of the Center, or the brain, is the Data Processing room whose equipment receives directly from the same sources as NORAD, and shares MOTHER'S multi-operational talents. This is where Peggy had spent most of her twelve and fourteen hour days since July 1, preferring shared anticipation here to the stark silence in the private room she had been assigned on a sub-level floor. She had at her disposal four modified display screens, and three mainframe computers and software, which provided communication with all principal United States Military Commands, and with the three Saturn launch sites, hastily installed in utmost secrecy in the tradition of the project itself, named for the rings of secrecy which had guarded its development.

Installation on the heavily wooded island near Seattle in Puget sound was the last one in place, completed on June 27. The next forty-eight hours were spent testing equipment, communications networks to NORAD and the Pentagon, and back-up systems.

And since then all of them had been waiting. On the first day a pool had begun: at ten dollars each, the one who predicted the correct day and GMT of launch, stood to celebrate louder than the rest. On the second day everyone was still up. On the third day, nervous. On the fourth, strangely silent and communication checks were more frequent. As the week whittled down signs of tension built—voices were shriller, silences longer, chairs jerked backward; the staff seemed not able to keep still, or at least not able to sit still. Bets were eighty percent on July 7, and Peggy was praying it wouldn't last that long.

It bothered her that over the last couple of days the niggling thought had crept into her head that her career was—not on the line exactly—but bound to be affected by what happened here. It seemed pretty small-minded, when the stakes were really so much bigger.

She knew the Saturn program inside out, from concept to design. Each missile had been designed with eight targeting 'black boxes,' operating behind advanced laser eyes. Each black box was programmed to focus on any one or all of eight segments of a fan-shaped area that stretched from the easternmost tip of the Soviet land mass, to a line northeast of Calgary. There was a second Saturn launch site in North Dakota and one in Maine. The three locations had enough overlap to protect against blind spots.

After a launch, each Saturn laser beam would swing across a horizontal and vertical arc of ninety degrees at half-second intervals, so that no point in the arc was left uncovered for more than a split second, its energy source using the supercold of outer space to increase power to the laser beam. The high-intensity flashing lights on commercial aircraft operate similarly, covering a 360 degree arc at one second intervals for collision avoidance. Once targeted, Saturn had a two-tiered defense: one designed for destruction of incoming missiles above 500,000 feet, and a lower altitude system designed to intercept and destroy up to thirty attacking missiles once the high-altitude layer had been penetrated.

Using a newly developed solid fuel propellant, Saturn could achieve 500,000 feet, or 94.70 miles, in one minute and forty seconds. Because of its multi-directional capabilities, Saturn would not have to reach that height, the probable apogee of an intercontinental ballistic missile over the polar route, or take that much time. According to every test, analysis, projection and calculation the missile would not fail. But one faulty computer chip, one stress-ridden sheet of thin metal, one mechanic whose mind was on something else, one miscalculation. . . .

At 1518 and 32 seconds, when she heard the report of an unknown, Peggy felt a certain relief that now there was less than a half hour.

At 1521 Peggy got word of the track divergence. Saturn had a mid-course correction capability of its own—she knew every minute detail of its system. Still, she closed her eyes for a moment, took a breath, and turned to her Duty Officer at the computer next to hers.

"Joe, alert the President and the launch site on the Island. Is Mr. Smyth here?"

"He's with the President, ma'am."

Six other men were attending separate terminals with a concentration that seemed to warm the air in the cold bright room.

The duty officer was on-line with the Situation Room at the White House when Cooper confirmed his assessment of a possible threat. It was 1523.

Nine minutes to launch. "Get me an open line to the President." Her voice was perfectly even. She heard herself speak from a distance. She had expected to feel anything but this cool detached participation.

The officer picked up a white phone recessed in the console to her right, pressed two buttons. "You've got Baker on one, and Major General McDonald on the Island on two. Cooper is tapped in over here," he touched a small speaker under his screen. They were watching exactly what Cooper was seeing, the slender, stretching arc and an even more slender divergence already cutting a new path through space.

1524: "Peggy? This is Alan Baker."

"Yes, Mr. President."

"I want you to go ahead and launch whenever you're ready." His voice sounded tight.

She became aware of people gathering outside their glass room. Officers, technicans, scientists, and some Pentagon brass. Where had they come from? Peggy saw that her Duty Officer's hands were shaking slightly.

"Did you get that, General Cooper?" Peggy asked quietly into her microphone.

"Affirmative. Are you ready to go, Island?"

"Affirmative." It was 1526 and 28 seconds GMT. "We'll launch at exactly 1531."

There was a pause as every eye checked the wall clock and the horizontal row of red lights below it. Each light ticked off thirty seconds.

At 1530, after three minutes of silence, McDonald said, "Commence countdown."

Outside the Data center at least fifty men and women had gathered, staring into the cold white soundproof room, crowded against the glass and steel walls, silent. Peggy could feel them on the back of her neck.

She switched her phone to broadcast. At 1531 and eight seconds, McDonald said, "They're off and running. It's a perfect launch."

The tight group outside moved and shifted slightly. Still not one of them spoke.

It wasn't over yet. There was a minute still to go. Peggy's eyes were stinging. The light was very bright.

At 1532 and 27 seconds by the wall clock, Cooper's voice, as unemotional as ever, announced, "Contact. Check your screens."

Indeed, the arc and its delicate shoot had stopped their progression, and were dissolving.

His words, "Stand by for confirmation from PARCS," was lost in the cheer that rose and tore out of the throats of the people outside and in the glass room at the Pentagon, at the Island launch site, and at NORAD. Even Cooper, when it was done, turned to his Deputy and clapped him on the shoulder.

And Peggy Montague bent her head and wept.

CHAPTER
THIRTY-ONE

Moscow, July 8

Bukov stood staring out the window in the office that had been Kolkin's. From here he could see into the cobbled yard where the men would arrive. It was early still, the courtyard empty. He put his hand in his pocket, fingered a carved ebony pawn he had become accustomed to carrying.

* * * * *

Last night had been his weekly chess game with Uncle Vassily, his father's brother, a man with no sense of humor, Bukov thought privately; but he was a challenging chess partner. He refused to play with the American chess set. His eyes had narrowed as Bukov demonstrated its abilities. He probably would have spat, had they been some other place.

So they had sat in his small study, over his old wooden set, their fat wooden pawns advancing carefully across the board. Adya had served them honey cake and tea.

Adya. She had lost weight. There was worry in her eyes when she looked at him. Of course he had been distracted lately. And these past twenty hours since the outcome of the missile game there had been a fury near hysteria among his Comrades. Every one of the ten other members of the Politburo had been in touch with him, by phone or messenger. Today he had received a letter from the ailing Minister of Foreign Affairs. Gromyko called it a humiliation that would irreparably affect foreign relations for the next hundred years, if they were fortunate enough to survive another hundred years. . . .

Interestingly, no one blamed Bukov.

He had tried to assure his wife that it was nothing important, a minor political crisis. He was meeting with these men tonight. As soon as he had established his position things would be the way had been. But she didn't understand. He had a position already. What was there to establish?

He couldn't explain.

Last night the game turned at the sixteenth move, when his pawn took Vassily's white bishop off the board, en passant.

His uncle had blinked, raised his rheumy eyes to Bukov's, and hissed, "Son of a bitch. . . ."

En passant, Bukov thought, he had gained position.

* * * * *

A car pulled up to the Minister's Building and General Alexandr Altunin and the Minister of Defense Marshall Svetlov climbed out. From Bukov's vantage, they looked small and stubby crossing the short distance to the doors. Bukov tightened his hand around the pawn in his pocket, and turned from the window. He walked over to his desk and lifted a pad off the green felt top, looked at a photograph of Adya, laughing into the camera. He touched the edge of the frame, sighed, and left the room.

Sorokin was the last to arrive. He looked rather more frail than usual, his eyes darker. Everyone seemed to be shrinking around Bukov. No one spoke as Sorokin came toward them at the opposite end of the room, and took the empty seat to the left of Bukov's.

The chair to Bukov's right was empty; Svetlov sat next to it, and across from Generals Yuri Vasilov of the Strategic Rocket Forces, and Altunin. Bukov could feel an incredible tension in the room. He allowed a moment's more silence. He would have to handle this with extreme delicacy. He glanced at Sorokin, then stood and moved between his chair and the one to his right. He rested his left hand on the high back of his own chair, and looked at General Vasilov.

"What happened, Comrade General?" He made sure there was no accusation in his tone.

Vasilov was a short man, with a moon face. He flushed. He hated this. He had had nothing to do with their stupid game. He had been against it from the start. A game! They were playing games all of a sudden.

He stared up at Bukov. "We carried out the launch just as instructed." He stressed the word instructed. "Our equipment picked up their missile on radar within a minute of launch. The source was a point located near the city of Seattle in Washington state." There was a slight tremor to his voice. He cleared his throat. "Seven minutes later our missiles and theirs disappeared."

"Disappeared, Comrade?" Bukov repeated.

Still staring at Bukov, he said, "They were disintegrated."

Vasilov stopped speaking. There was a moment of silence. Bukov was staring at him, his head tilted. He nodded encouragingly.

"Our own launch was perfect." Vasilov's hands were clasped on the table. He turned his attention to his knuckles. "Since we had no accurate data on gravitational anomolies, one of our missiles was pulled slightly off target."

He looked up at Bukov. "The American weapon managed to eliminate this 'lost missile' at the same moment the other two were destroyed." His hands felt damp. He put them in his lap, and said, "We must conclude they have developed a midcourse correctional capability."

Marshall Svetlov rose from his chair on the other side of the table. It was as if he could no longer contain himself. "Why have we had no intelligence to suggest the United States had any such project in the works? . . . It is a disgrace. . . ."

He looked across at Bukov, almost defiantly. Then he turned and stared purposefully down at Sorokin. Sorokin did not look up. He seemed to collapse in on himself, catch himself, then straighten. It looked like a shudder in slow motion.

There was a silence during which Svetlov sat back down and Bukov turned away from the table and walked a few feet back and forth, pinching his lower lip with two fingers. Stopping behind the second empty chair, he looked carefully at Sorokin and said, "Comrade, how is it American research and development has come this far without our knowledge?"

Sorokin cast a beady eye at Bukov. It was too dark in the room. Shadows swept over the table. The weighty chandelliers glowed dully and with no appreciable influence on the light. Sorokin did not answer and the stillness was deadly.

Agitated by a feeling of oppression, the Minister of Defense Marshall Vetlov interrupted the uncomfortable silence. "If our intercontinental and medium range ballistic missiles can be disintegrated by a weapon about which we know nothing except that they are non-nuclear—" His voice was higher pitched than usual, "how long can we continue to persuade anyone that Soviet nuclear superiority is indispensible to defense of the Motherland?"

Well, well, Here was Svetlov making a play, Bukov thought, surprised. And turning the issue away from what was in fact an intelligence failure. What was he doing?

Svetlov's voice began to tremble. "Do we even *have* superiority? We have numbers—but one missile of theirs knocked three of ours out of the game."

Very interesting, Bukov thought. Sorokin was staring at the pale-faced Minister.

"What do we do against this mystery weapon? Given this weapon, are any of ours useful?" The Minister stopped suddenly.

Sorokin's jaw tightened. He seemed to inhale strength from the shadows. "All right, Comrade, that's enough. We know the Americans can retaliate against a first strike. . . ."

"Perhaps *prevent* a first strike. . . ."

Sorokin's hand slapped the table. The sound was like an electric crack in the room. Svetlov shut his mouth.

"But would they retaliate, if they knew we would launch a second strike, and a third. . ." Sorokin went on, his voice gaining its normal stridency.

There was no response from any of the men. Bukov considered that he wouldn't really want to hear the answer. He thought of the phrase "mutually assured destruction," which he had heard for the first time in Geneva. Bukov had been standing through this exchange, and he felt suddenly nauseated. He broke the silence by pulling back his chair. He sat.

"Comrades," he said, "when Heath proposed that we make this test, he said he hoped it would influence our decisions in SALT III. You know their President Baker is pushing a return to conventional weapons. Perhaps we should be discussing that. . . ."

Yuri Vasilov, Commander of the Strategic Rocket Forces, was sitting stiff as a bristle. He looked with ill-disguised contempt at

Bukov. "Are you considering making my entire command obsolete, Comrade?"

Bukov looked up at him, surprised.

"Quite the contrary, Comrade," Sorokin answered for Bukov. "The United States may have a superior detect and destroy device that works over an empty polar route against our ballistic missiles, but its potential is still untried."

Bukov lowered his head.

"And SALT III is not the question." Sorokin lifted a pencil from the table and looked at it as if it might have the question printed on its slim wooden shaft. "Nor is the question one of intelligence," his eyes pinned Bukov, "*Comrade*. The question is, how does this affect our plans in the Persian Gulf?"

No one spoke. Bukov looked up. His eyes locked with Sorokin's. He took a breath, and said, "Comrade, putting aside for a moment this recent consideration, there are some obvious risks in relying for anything on Iraq and Syria. . . ."

Marshall Svetlov interrupted. His voice was whiney, defensive, Bukov thought. "How can you say that, General Secretary? We replaced the MIG-27s the Syrians lost in the war with Lebanon in 1982, we've rearmed Iran after that insane war with Iraq. . ."

Bukov tried to hide his disgust. They couldn't see what Sorokin was doing. The man had nothing more to lose—pursuing this useless war in the Middle East was in fact his only means of surviving the blow he had just taken.

He turned away from Svetlov, and looked at Sorokin. This was really a conversation between the two of them anyway. These others were like those little animals that followed their leader over the edge of cliffs. And Sorokin, with his ferrety face and sunken eyes would carry them all down. Bukov's future was at stake here too.

He tried again. "King Fahd is no longer so insulated from the domestic turmoil in his country. There are thousands of Shiite Moslems and even more Palestinian Arabs a rock's throw from his oil fields, and the Palestinians are openly unfriendly after Fahd turned his back on them in Lebanon. All he did was claim credit for trying to get that fool Arafat out of Tripoli."

Sorokin's pencil tapped against the table. Without looking up, he said, "Fahd is in no position to do more than hang on, Comrade—" He sounded almost dreamy. "If it makes him feel better, he can look at this as an opportunity to remove those Palestinian dogs from his doorstep, and send them back to Jordan—permanently."

"Further, Comrade," Sorokin said, looking up at Bukov, his eyes glittering now, "the Shiites can work to our advantage. If Fahd has to call on the United States for protection because of some uprising, let us say, and they become embroiled in a situation there, their hands will be quite full." Sorokin looked around the table. "After all, they can't be everywhere at once."

He raised his chin. "We have already agreed to Iranian objecties, Comrades. I call for an immediate adoption of this offensive."

Silence. Bukov looked at the other men. They were going to go for it—give Sorokin this chance. He would make one last effort that kept reasonably within the bounds of dialectic. He turned to Marshall Svetlov. "Given the recent nuclear disaster in the southwest, and the diversion of eighteen of our divisions to assist Civil Defense, can the Minister of Defense give us an analysis of our current military status. . . ."

Svetlov looked down, then quickly over at Sorokin, who didn't appear to be listening any more. "Comrade Bukov," the Minister said with a poor effort at sarcasm, "The plan does not require the Red Army to participate personally. We have our friends and allies, well armed, in the front line."

Sorokin seemed to come back. He looked across at Bukov and spoke in a thin, tired voice. "We cannot wait any longer, Comrades." He stared only at the Secretary, but addressed them all. "This fiasco of 'the game' is an invocation by the United States. The power of the Party is challenged." His right hand went up to his temple for a moment. No one spoke.

When he was twelve years old, Sorokin had had the wind knocked out of him by a bully in school. He had felt that same explosive sickness when the word came of their defeat by an unknown missile, and it had lasted all day now.

Sorokin looked around the table. His voice sharpened. "Aside from what we can see is an obligation to the Soviet reputation, we have business to attend to. The Persian Gulf is not a gambit in some game. . . ."

Bukov had been watching the smaller man. Sorokin was being pulled into a vortex. He was right. The war they would direct was no gambit. That had already been taken and lost. Time now for the pawn's play. "Is the consensus to go ahead, then, Comrades?"

Sorokin nodded sharply.

Bukov turned to Yuri Vasilov and General Altunin next to Sorokin. They hesitated, nodded. Across the mahogany table, Marshall Svetlov inclined his head.

"I will call a full meeting of the Politburo, and we will proceed." Bukov paused, looked down at the pad in front of him. "Now," he said in a pleasant, let's-change-the-subject tone, "what are we going to do about that nuclear accident in the southwest?"

He pushed back from the table and rose while they considered his question. Hands clasped behind his back, he walked slowly to the window, then turned on the balls of his feet.

"Mr. Heath is already making a fuss, and Pyotr Neporozhny, our respected Minister of Power and Electrification, is slightly hysterical." He looked expectantly at the four men.

General Altunin sat up a little straighter. He was a listener, not a talker, but the cleanup was his affair, and he knew how they must respond. He had a deep, raspy voice. "You remind Secretary Heath of Three Mile Island. Go so far as to admit this was even a little worse. Then assure him that appropriate steps have been taken to safeguard contiguous areas. And prepare a limited damage assessment." He paused, looked at Bukov, glanced at Sorokin. "We cannot deny it, but we can deny it is serious." He shrugged.

Bukov watched for any sign from Sorokin, saw nothing. "All right, General, do what needs to be done—and please, talk to Neporozhny. . . ."

CHAPTER
THIRTY-TWO

Washington, August 1

Admiral Jerry Newman sat in shirt sleeves tipped back in his chair, looking critically at the walls in his office. He supposed it was time to migrate some of his collection. He gazed with particular admiration at Phasianus cochicus, the Ring-Necked pheasant, directly across from him.

Newman's avocation was bird watching. Unfortunately his windowless room, and his responsibilities as Director of the National Security Agency left him little opportunity to pursue the hobby. So he had done the next best thing: he had resurrected a twenty-one volume set of Rex Brasher prints on the *Birds of North America* from his attic, had framed them in chrome channeling and hung them, rotating lots of forty at a time once or twice a year, on three of the four walls. The fourth wall supported a large green blackboard on which a few complex equations were still printed in chalk from yesterday's late meeting. His office was affectionately known as the birdhouse.

The phone buzzed.

"Say, Jerry, I've got something on that radio traffic that Operations has been working on between Tripoli, Damascus and Asmara. You got a minute?"

"Sure, Al. Come on up."

Al Renshaw appeared minutes later with a thick bundle of computer printouts. They were an interesting team, Renshaw tall and angular, with slightly bulging eyes; Newman small and rounder. Emu and quail, Newman had decided years ago.

Renshaw was younger—in his early forties—a graduate of MIT, and Deputy Director of Operations for the National Security Agency overseeing the entire spectrum of electronic intelligence, from intercept to cryptanalysis, traffic and pattern analysis, high level diplomatic systems to low-level radio traffic. He sat down in an uncomfortable chair in front of the Director's desk, blocking Newman's view of a blackcapped chickadee.

"What is it?" Newman asked, glancing down at the top page of the printout.

"The Soviets, trying to throw us a Laffer Curve," Renshaw said. "It took a combination of our general and advanced Soviet systems, *and* a lucky break, to hit it out of the ball park." He sat back, proud of himself. "At first, we thought it was just a shift to a higher level code—until this stuff started showing up they'd been using a pretty primitive cryptography. But pattern analysis decided there was something more because of the increase in traffic. . . ."

Newman was focussed on the sheets in front of him. He flipped several pages, stopped, followed one line with his finger top to bottom down the page, turned it over, looked up. "Why don't you tell me what you've got here—then tell me how you got it."

Renshaw grinned. "Sorry . . . Okay, it's a new computer language—a combination of Fortran and Cobol—it's not even encoded, so their use may be only short term." He leaned forward. "It's a communications system that can direct commands all the way down the regimental level . . . Page 70, I think—you can see contact in Damascus, Amman, Asmara, Aden, Lahaj, Tripoli . . ."

Newman turned to page 70, looked at the sheet and then back at Renshaw. "In fact," Newman said, "wherever there are East German, Syrian and Cuban military units."

His deputy nodded. "All part of a Command, Control and Communications system, and all Soviet designed."

Renshaw paused. In the quiet, Newman rose. "Go on," he said, and turned to the blackboard behind his desk, picking up a dusty eraser.

"Libyan, Ethiopian and Syrian systems use radio transmission, and they've clearly got a synthesizer hook-up to the Soviet computer that allows them to printout whatever the command happens to be. They're using Arabic, Spanish and Coptic, depending on point of origin and destination. Every unit gets its own clear text, and knows just what it's supposed to be doing and when. They can keep mistakes way down."

Newman was cleaning the board with large circular swipes. He did not respond, and Renshaw continued talking to his back.

"Just to make sure, we ran it through the Platform computer. These printouts are translations of actual traffic over the past three weeks." He nodded at the material taking up most of Newman's desk.

"Its mostly simple stuff, to tank infantry and aircraft units, but there's a lot of positioning of various units and maneuvers on a grid map—which we don't have. I've given you the English translation under every command." He paused. "It's been quiet for the last twenty-four hours. . . ."

Newman turned from the board, the eraser still in his hand. The calm before the storm, he thought. If the system had been designed for short term use, and had already been working for about a month, they didn't have much time. . . . He replaced the eraser, sat down, tapped the desk in an irritated, nervous gesture.

Renshaw grinned. "I think we can jam the whole program, Jerry."

Newman's eyebrows raised.

Renshaw seemed to unfold out of his chair. He began to pace in long strides in front of the desk. "Not only that, but all we'll need to cut off their communications is already aboard the Sixth and Seventh Fleets. *And* I can tell the French in Chad and Djibouti just how they can do it, and the British in Oman. . . . We've all got the same capability—they just don't know it."

"How long will it take to confirm a jam?"

"Less than twenty-four hours—if they start traffic again on the same frequency." Renshaw stopped pacing. "If they switch frequencies, though—" his forehead creased, "it'll take some time. . . . I don't think they'd change the signal—not now."

Newman stood. "I think you're right. And I think this could be what Larry Apple had been waiting for. Newman held out his hand across his desk. "Good work, Al. Tell your people."

* * * * *

Admiral Robert Smilie looked down at a report from Larry Apple. Evidently the French had installed an optical transceiver with the Turks in Libya, with a receiver in Bandol, about forty miles east of Marseilles. For his personal illumination no doubt, someone had attached a short description of an optical transceiver.

His eyes narrowed. He wasn't an engineer, damnit. He felt a certain tightness in his chest whenever these technical reports passed across his desk. He had to force himself to absorb the information. Cooling diodes, indeed. To reassure himself, he rose and walked around his desk to a framed document on the opposite wall.

The President had sent him a copy of *Times* Military Affairs analyst Drew Middleton's column of April 15, and signed it with a note that read, "Just a few heads, anyway. . . ."

"Admiral Robert Smilie has done the impossible. Without knocking heads together, he, the Secretary of Denfense, and President Baker have shown that common sense pays off in dollars and cents. It is particularly appropriate to say so on this date when American taxpayers make a large contribution to the Defense budget.

"We can be grateful for Smilie's clear vision: he saw that as a battlefield weapons platform, the AH-64A helicopter was greatly overrated (as the Army must have known since Vietnam).

"It is widely believed in Washington that a change in battlefield doctrine by the Joint Chiefs of Staff influenced the President's decision to transfer A-10 ground support aircraft, no longer current for our defense, to Israel and Egypt.

"Smilie seems to have persuaded his colleagues to adopt advances in smart weaponry to the modern battlefield. At the same time, he has persuaded them to use the A-10 in areas where more sophisticated hardware cannot be maintained properly and tanks have become the principal offensive weapon on the ground."

There was a quick rap on the door, and Smilie turned hastily from the article and reached for the doorknob to his right.

"Afternoon, Admiral."

"Captain."

John Murdock, tall, slim, with fiery hair and a flushed complexion, had a standing four o'clock appointment with Smilie. He followed the older man to his desk and sat down in a smooth green leather chair studded with brass buttons.

Their appointment was a tutelage. John often felt like a school teacher coming to a lesson with a bright but obstinant student. Together they examined a global survey of the day's military events. Of special interest on this date, was a rundown on number and position of Soviet warships in the Mediterranean Sea and Indian

Ocean—up considerably from last week—and unusual troop movements in Ethiopia, Chad, Syria and Libya.

"What the hell is going on over there, Murdock?" The implication was that Murdock was somehow to blame.

But John Murdock had worked with Admiral Smilie for seven years: "I don't know, Admiral—but I understand the French are working on a translation of some voice transmissions from the Turks in Libya that should give us the answer."

Smilie looked up sharply. Wasn't that what he'd just been reading about?

Murdock's head raised too, from his reports. He looked at Smilie questioningly.

For a moment neither of them spoke. Murdock could fairly see the Admiral's brain calculating like a computer behind his pale eyes.

In fact, Smilie was figuring that military movement in the Mediterranean Sea and Indian Ocean was escalating too rapidly. Given Newman's earlier call, he was calculating how long it would take to get a French translation of a Turkish transmission out of Libya, and then an English translation of the French translation of the Turkish. . . .

"Cut an order, Captain," he said abruptly, and his eyes seemed to snap. "I want all Sixth fleet units, CINCLANT, CINCPAC, and Becker in Riyadh, on Def Con Two.

Murdock was writing furiously into a small notebook.

". . . ASW aircraft surveillance increased, particularly in the Mediterranean and between Diego Garcia and Aden, and an urgent request for an accurate fix on missile boats in Tripoli and Benghazi. I want positions on every Soviet and Libyan submarine."

Murdock looked up. *Every* submarine. He looked back down, made a note. He knew better than to bother Smilie with the fact that immobile subs were difficult to spot—they were small enough to look like coastal clutter to most radar equipment.

"Meanwhile," the Admiral was already reaching toward his phone, "I'll get to the President, and notify Smyth and Heath. Call me when you're ready to issue the order—oh, and prepare copies for Israeli and Egyptian Intelligence."

Murdock rose and turned to the door without a word. His orders, with the President's approval, went out to all Fleet units at 1602 Eastern Daylight Time.

* * * * *

Less than twenty-four hours later the Secretary General of the United Nations received a communique from Syria's puppet President of Lebanon, demanding immediate withdrawal of U.N. forces in Lebanon from the Bekaa Valley.

Thirty-six hours after Smilie's orders had gone out, Libyan and Cuban troops crossed Sudan's border with armored personnel carriers and air cover. From the east, more armored columns of East German and Cuban troops crossed over the Sudanese-Ethiopian border with aircraft from Asmara providing cover. Traveling swiftly through the western desert stretches of Sudan, Cubans and Libyans were now 600 miles from Khartoum.

Forty-eight hours had passed when reports of Syrian armor and troops began moving south through the Bekaa Valley in Lebanon, and Israeli Military Intelligence reported Iraqi armor moving into Jordan in great force.

* * * * *

Peter was standing behind his desk slipping on a lightweight jacket, getting ready to leave, when Grace walked in.

"Telex," she said. "Just in." She handed him a printout. Immediately the phone outside started ringing. She looked annoyed. "Are you gone for the day?"

He looked up from the sheet. "Unless you think it's important."

Grace nodded and left the room. A moment later the phone stopped ringing.

Peter sat back down and read the bulletin again.

"Khartoum subject to heavy attacks by unidentified aircraft from Asmara. Air raids concentrated on outskirts of city near Khartoum airport.

"Anti aircraft fire reported. Three unconfirmed hits on enemy planes in first assault."

Peter tipped his chair back and took off his glasses.

The Sudan was getting it from two sides. Qaddafi didn't have the strength to do it alone, even with his Cubans; but with the

Ethiopian Army and its Warsaw Pact mercenaries—well, that was a different matter.

He remembered the last toast the three Russians had made at La Reserve. To Libya, without whom none of this would be possible.

It was happening exactly as described, with Syria and Iraq moving from the north and east, and now Libya was attempting to seal the south and west. It was an enormous program.

He wondered if Egypt and Israel were prepared . . . They'd know soon enough . . . If not, he doubted there'd *be* an Israel; and Egypt—Egypt would be incorporated into a new Soviet-influenced power constellation. In which case the American position in the Mediterranean Sea would become gravely vulnerable.

His chair rocked forward. He slipped his glasses back on. That couldn't happen. Not without a fight. According to Heath, General Becker was champing at the bit. And Peter had been copied Smilie's orders for Sixth Fleet readiness. It looked like it was going to be a long hot summer, or maybe a very short one.

He laid the telex with the others that had accumulated over the past forty-eight hours, in the basket on his desk, and made a second effort to leave. Again, Grace stood inside his door. She nodded at the phone. "The Secretary of State."

Peter sat down again.

"Peter, the Israelis are voting on preemptive action against Syrian missile sites. The President is addressing Congress; we're to meet him at the White House in an hour."

Peter looked at his watch. It was five o'clock. They agreed to walk over together. Peter switched lines without hanging up and dialed Peggy's service. It was virtually impossible to know where she would be at any given time.

"Mr. Jefferson? She just phoned in a message for you. Just a moment . . ."

Peter waited.

"Here it is: 'Looks like dinner's off. But I'll see you at the White House tonight.'"

CHAPTER
THIRTY-THREE

Washington, August 2

The basement complex two floors below the White House looked to Peter like a city out of a science fiction movie. It was a labyrinth of white corridors and glass partitions, home to a slick computer system and a maintenance population of technicians wearing stylish uniform overalls in bright colors—purple, yellow, blue, green. A staff of Army and Navy personnel from a stock Warner Brothers movie moved among the polished set and crew.

Outside the door to the Situation Room, behind a microwave component to protect them from electronic surveillance, Harry Smyth stood over Peggy's shoulder, watching a screen she was prompting.

They looked up as Peter and George Heath approached. Peggy smiled.

Harry straightened. He looked tired, or sad; his face was softer than usual, his shirt rumpled. He was carrying his suit jacket. He nodded. "George. . . . Jefferson—you can go right in," indicating the doors behind him.

Peggy had turned her attention back to the keyboard. The computer was the ALLO-34, a sister to General Cooper's MOTHER, that coordinated "ALL Other" systems. The numerical prefix designated location—34 stood for the Middle East. Peggy looked over her shoulder. "Peter, would you ask Jerry Newman to come out. . . ."

He turned at the door to say he would, but her back was to him again. She was explaining something to Smyth, who shook his head, not understanding. She patted the chair next to hers. Smyth sat down.

A young Captain standing by a bank of phones opened the double doors to the Situation Room. It was large and white and circular. The center of the room supported a large round white table in which twelve phone consoles were recessed like the numerals on a clock. Each console contained a pair of color-coded receivers, a panel of lights and keyed buttons. At the head of the table, Alan Baker was leaned over, a white phone crooked between his chin and shoulder, scribbling notes onto a pad.

James Booth sat to Alan's right at one o'clock, listening to the same conversation on his own white phone. He was pushed back from the table, slipped down in his chair with his legs stretched straight out in front of him. He was the only one in the room who looked undisturbed. He even looked cool. Compared to the data center outside, regulated for temperature and humidity, this room was uncomfortably warm.

Behind the table, Admiral Smilie was standing stiffly next to the Secretary of the Navy Robert Van Vleck, indicating an area on a large map, with a circular motion of his hand. Henry Clay had been pacing between the map and the table. He stopped and sat down next to Booth. He looked unwell.

Jerry Newman stood with Smilie's deputy, John Murdock, at a wall-computer set into the north quadrant of the room.

Henry raised his eyes in their direction when Heath and Jefferson entered the room, but made no other expression. Smilie was pointing at a position on the map. Neither he nor Van Vleck turned around.

Peter walked over to the computer and in a low voice gave Newman Peggy's message. He nodded, distractedly, said a word to Murdock, and left quickly.

Alan Baker hung up. Booth pulled himself upright and replaced his own receiver. "George," Baker said. He put out his hand.

They shook. Heath took the seat to Baker's left. "Anything new on Khartoum?" he asked.

"Not since reports of the Asmaran air raid." Baker looked strained, but his voice was clear. "We're confirmed on East German and Cuban troops movement into Sudan from Ethiopia. . . ."

"We know they're moving," Clay interrupted, "but we don't have precise location. We know there's fighting, but can't say whether it's local resistance to guerilla raids or an actual military offensive, or a *pillow* fight, for God's sake." He pushed away from the table.

Baker looked at Clay as if he were going to respond, then decided against it. Instead he said to the others, "We do have some good information from Egyptian Intelligence. After Peter's meeting with Mehdat Wahab, they decided to make us privvy to a secret alliance between themselves, Sudan and Oman."

Henry Clay turned back to face Baker. Jim Booth slid several copies of the terms of their coalition across the table, and as Peter leaned forward to take one, Clay pulled back his chair and snapped up another.

"It's their answer to the Libyan, Ethiopian, South Yemeni agreement to resist conspiracies . . ." Baker turned to Booth. "How does that go, Jim?"

" 'Conspiracies of international imperialism, Zionism, racism and reactionary forces.' " Booth chuckled.

Peter looked up from the paper. "Qaddafi is going to get a lot more than he bargained for."

"Even with resistance though," Clay said, "the Ethiopian Army is a quarter-million strong."

"They have the bodies," Baker agreed, "but information has it they don't have the ability to operate and maintain their hardware . . . South Yemen, on the other hand, I see as more of a threat . . ."

The door slid open. The young Captain hesitated, spotted John Murdock, walked quickly toward him.

The President continued speaking, facing Heath and Jefferson. "We're also getting very cautious reports from the French Securité Exterièure. Their Turkish network in Libya is evidently ready to move . . ."

Henry Clay jerked toward Baker. "But they're not saying what the hell the move *is*." He turned to George Heath; his hand flew out from his side. "How the hell are we supposed to operate if we have to worry about tripping over our goddamn allies because we don't know what they're doing? Cooperation. Simple cooperation, that's all I . . ."

Alan Baker rose and faced the stiff, pinched face of his Assistant for National Security. Annoyance flashed in his eyes and was immediately controlled. Smilie and Van Vleck had turned at Clay's outburst and stood staring at the two of them.

Softly, almost soothingly, Baker said, "Henry. It's hot. We're under a lot of pressure here. There are problems, I give you that." He reached his arm out and put his hand on Clay's shoulder. "I don't want dissension at this meeting. We're making the best of a less than perfect situation. That's what a crisis is. Things don't always go well."

They stared at one another. Baker dropped his arm. Henry ran his hand over his head. "Sorry."

"Okay." Baker looked around, and sat.

Peter quickly raised his hand. "Is there anything further on what's happening in Israel? Did Shamir . . ."

He stopped speaking as John Murdock handed Baker the message the Captain had delivered.

Baker looked up. "Here it is." He read, "Syrian tanks spotted in force east of the Litani River. United Nations Forces will not respond."

In the quiet, Harry Smyth came through the doors and took a seat near Peter. There was a nasal hum from a black phone in front of George Heath. The President leaned over, listened, then picked up a blue receiver in front of him. Jim Booth did the same.

"Mr. Prime Minister."

There was complete silence in the room.

All Baker said was "I got a copy," and then, "I understand." He shook his head. Another pause. "We'll do everything we can." Gently he replaced the receiver and looked up.

"Shamir won't wait any longer." He glanced at the horizontal row of separate round clocks over the door opposite him. It was 6:30 PM, 3:30 AM in Israel.

Jim Booth stretched. "It might be sportsman-like right about now to have a little powwow with Chairman Bukov."

Baker nodded. "Admiral, can you give me what we've got on Soviet positions?"

Smilie turned to John Murdock. The Captain handed him a clipboard. He approached the table, laid the board down, and showed Baker the appropriate columns of reports from NORAD: eight Soviet submarines identified in the Mediterranean Sea, thermal tracks indicating three originating from Tripoli.

Harry Smyth was lighting a cigarette. He waved out a match, said, "What you may *not* want to mention is that we've got five Orions ready to go from the NATO base in Italy with ASW gear, and I understand National Security has devised a system to jam communications between Mideast centers." He blew a funnel of smoke away from the table and grumbled, "Damned smart group of young people."

"What about the Indian Ocean?" Baker asked.

I'm waiting for confirmation, sir," Murdock said. "One carrier task force, for certain. Over a half dozen subs, but we don't have origins; and there may be as many as another six out there."

"How long will it take you to put through a call to the Kremlin, Captain?"

"Not more than ten minutes—assuming the Chairman is there."

"I reckon he'll be there all right," Jim Booth said easily.

"Would you set it up then?"

"Yes sir." Murdock turned, and then turned back. "Is there anyone here who speaks Russian? We've got a translator, of course, but it helps for picking up nuance to have someone. . . ."

Baker looked over at Peter Jefferson. "Pete, you speak Russian. You want to sit in on this—give me your impressions?"

Peter nodded, as Murdock walked quickly to a door next to the computer installation.

* * * * *

The hotline had been installed by agreement between the United States and the Soviet Union in 1964, and had gone through sophisticated changes over the years. The primary system was still a teleprinter, one in the Roman alphabet and the other in Cyrillic. But quantum advances in computer and communications technology had added three new complementary systems.

One was a voice capability with a synthesizer for simultaneous translation at each end. In the early 1980s, the synthesizer could only provide a rough translation. By 1983 users received highly accurate and complete computerized translations in microseconds. In 1984 both countries agreed to a video display installation. With this newest addition, each speaker could see the other, watch facial expressions and match tones of voice. The hotline was the next best thing to being there.

The room was small with three chairs and one red telephone. Murdock picked up the phone and spoke a coded message into the receiver, waited, punched several buttons on a panel inset on the wall, waited a moment longer and touched a key which focused the twenty-six inch screen on part of a desk and an unoccupied chair halfway around the world.

Baker seated himself so that only he could be seen by the small camera tucked below the screen. Buttons glowed on a long console in front of the President, an oscilloscope to the right showing a steady green line. Peter sat next to Baker. Murdock handed them both a single earplug fitted with a tiny receiver.

A moment passed and Bukov sat down. The camera drew closer to his broad face and sleek dark hair.

Baker began speaking to Bukov's unsmiling face. "Good day, Chairman Bukov. I hope all goes well with you."

Bukov frowned, cleared his throat and said, "Good morning, Mr. President." He squinted his eyes slightly, as if assessing the President's condition. "I understand you were ill two days ago. Are you fully recovered?"

Smiling slightly, Baker said, "Your intelligence is a little off, Mr. Chairman. It was my annual eye examination. I'm feeling fine. I'd say, though, your agent is doing less than accurate work."

"His specialty is not medicine, Mr. President." Bukov smiled.

Abruptly, Baker came to the point. "Chairman Bukov, you are aware of recent developments in Sudan and Syria?"

Bukov looked confused. "Developments? Can you be more specific, Mr. President?"

There was the flash of anger across Baker's face, quickly gone. "I'm talking about Soviet weapons being used offensively, as we speak, by Libya, Syria, South Yemen and Ethiopia."

A moments silence. Bukov's gaze did not falter. He spoke smoothly. "You are calling concerning the use of Soviet manufacture by legitimate purchasers, Mr. Baker?"

The President's eyes showed annoyance. Then he smiled. "You are arms merchants, after all."

Bukov frowned.

"I'm calling to suggest that your 'customers' may ultimately cheat you out of a profit, Baker said. "Colonel Qaddafi has personal ambitions. President Assad of Syria, the new government of Iraq and Jordan, each have their own reasons for fighting this war. It should not be a Soviet war."

Baker paused. Bukov's face was expressionless.

"Do you understand what I'm saying?" the President asked softly.

A smile played at Bukov's mouth. "Oh, yes, Mr. President. You are quite clear." His voice hardened. "But I hardly think it is your place to make recommendations to me. We *may* decide we can no longer continue as a spectator. Colonel Qaddafi has a divinely revealed duty to impose Islam on the decadent secular system of Egypt. He has asked for our assistance."

"Chairman Bukov, do you feel *you* have a divinely revealed duty to impose Marxist theology on the people of a Moslem country?"

Bukov hesitated, pressed his index finger against his headset. "Mr. President, let us dispense with this banter. You initiated the conversation. Do you have some constructive proposition?"

"Yes I do, Chairman." Baker shifted in his seat, leaned forward. "I propose your government continue precisely as a spectator. In that way you will not have to spend the next several years working out a bothersome damage assessment." His voice was matter-of-fact. "We've already located all Soviet submarines and two guided missile cruisers in the Mediterranean. We've pin-pointed a Soviet carrier task force and ten submarines in the Indian Ocean. You're no doubt aware of the effectiveness of digital image processing, and of our ASW and Cruise missile capability. . . ."

"Are you threatening me, Mr. Baker?"

"Not at all, Mr. Chairman. I'm only reminding you of what we both know. The United States has no interest in reducing the size of the Soviet Navy. That's something we can negotiate in Geneva, when the Libyan *khamsen* has subsided.

Bukov's head turned slightly. He was listening to someone on his right, out of camera range. When he turned back, his face was bland. "Thank you for your call, Mr. President. Our Minister of Foreign Affairs will take another look at your position." The screen compressed to a dot of light, flickered, and was dark.

* * * * *

It was resolved that Libyan bases, their submarines and any smaller surface craft threatening or likely to threaten the Sixth Fleet would be ordered neutralized by cruise missile counter attack. That at first sign of offensive action, the Soviet Command, Control and Communication system feeding between Damascus, Asmara, Aden and Tripoli, would be jammed. Then they waited.

Smilie didn't take the waiting well. "Where the hell are those A-10s," he said through clenched teeth more than once over the next hour. At ten after eight o'clock, he found out.

Larry Apple walked in behind Peggy, tossed a telex onto the table. "Israel just hit and destroyed eighteen Syrian missile sites near Damascus. They are all Soviet-manned SA-5 sites. Israeli intelligence also located the Syrian C^3I installation and just blew it away with air to ground missiles."

There was unprompted applause. The air seemed lighter. They waited some more.

Sandwiches were brought in, ham and chicken salad, orange juice, coffee. Larry had drawn Peggy away from the table. They were standing not far from Murdock at the computer console, each holding a cup of coffee. She was dressed in a cool white suit.

She smiled at something Larry said, brushed her hair away from her face.

Behind them John Murdock turned. "I'm getting something from the Enterprise."

At the same moment a messenger appeared at the door. Henry Clay read that communique aloud: "Syrian units moving down from Lebanon—Iraqi and Syrian armor supported by military units and air cover—west between Irbid and Der'a in Jordan—anticipated to reach the Israeli border within twelve hours."

Admiral Smilie had joined Murdock at the computer. He looked up. "The Enterprise combat air patrol just reported a series of explosions on the ground at Wheelus Field, Tripoli." He glanced at Henry Clay, then went on. "There's fire and heavy smoke—they can't tell the extent of damage—maybe the jet fuel storage tanks." A sparse smile cut his face for a moment. "Those must've been the French Turks in Libya. Nice job."

Clay sat down.

"What we don't need now," Peter said quietly to Heath, "is to hear that the Libyans have hit the Sixth Fleet."

Close to ten o'clock reports began coming in from Egypt and Sudan. Sudanese army units with antitank weapons and Egyptian planes firing cannons had already claimed twenty-plus Ethiopian tanks in a pitched battle after three hours. One air battle between the Egyptian and Ethiopian Air Forces employing F-16 and MIG-25 fighters was broken off after thirty minutes.

Within minutes of that report, another was received: Word from Cairo that five Egyptian divisions had struck into Libya and were advanced as far as Tobruk. They had used one seaborne diversion; two or three regiments had come ashore from amphibious ships. From the air, the Egyptians had caught an excess of sixty planes on the ground at a base near Tobruk.

"Right *on!*" This from Jim Booth.

Then they heard that Libyan forces were moving east from Chad, and at the same time AWACS from Cairo were recording aircraft leaving Benghazi and moving south. "Maybe a paratroop operation set up for a refuel at Abeché and a drop near Khartoum," Clay volunteered.

"I don't know, Henry," Smyth said, shaking his head. "Sudan doesn't have much in the way of roads. But those Antonov 22 troop carriers are really sitting ducks if the Egyptian Air Force has enough fighters within range. . . ."

At midnight, Murdock stood away from his screen as Smilie leaned toward it.

He looked up, pale. "I can't believe this. Give me a printout, Murdock."

The Captain ran two hard copies, handed one to the Admiral and one to Baker who had joined them.

In a voice tight with anger, Smilie read, " 'Routine combat air patrol from Enterprise hit by six Foxbats with Libyan markings over Gulf of Sirte. Two Foxbats destroyed by CAP. CIC officer reports radio traffic between Libyan pilots *in English* during silence order to CAP. Two transmissions thus identified. End of Text.' "

He was silent. Then he said explosively, "Jesus Christ, Murdock—Qaddafi is using American contract pilots."

"Maybe not American, sir," Murdock said hopelessly. "Maybe they're British, or Libyans who know the language. . . ."

Henry Clay dropped his head into his hands.

"They don't say what damage to the Enterprise?" the President asked.

Smilie shook his head. "I can't believe it. *American* pilots— what the hell are we fighting for, anyway?" He looked up.

From behind him, Murdock said, "Sir, the New Jersey is reporting. . . ." He stopped. "She's been hit, sir." He looked up at the Admiral. "She took down eight missiles, though, point of origin Aden."

Smilie's hand slammed up against the wall.

"How much damage to the New Jersey, Captain?" asked Smyth from the table.

Murdock consulted the screen. "Minor, sir. To the superstructure only. She took some debris, is all."

Smilie looked at Baker. "I'd like to order a counterstrike on Aden."

There was a pause. Baker looked over at Harry Smyth. "Admiral," he said in a tired voice, "direct the Sixth Fleet and the New Jersey and its escort to take whatever non-nuclear action you think appropriate."

Smyth nodded, and added, "It's likely we'll see some air action. I'd notify Becker in Riyadh."

Admiral Smilie signalled affirmatively, then turned to Murdock. "Get me the C.O. of that Omani group so he knows what to expect."

Murdock punched out a code on a dark blue phone, listened for a moment, handed the receiver to Smilie.

"Colonel Page, are you in good position for a launch against Asmara?" He listened. . . . "Let me give you the tactical information, Page. . . ."

For the next few moments, in terse language, Smilie laid it out. There was another pause. "How long before approval in Muscat? . . . Okay. Now look, Page" his words slowed.

"We've got approval for a counterattack on Aden and Lahaj. I want to be able to say that a launch on Asmara was done on *local* initiative and with approval from Muscat. The United States has provided you with the tactical information, and the Omanis have decided their obligations under the agreement with Sudan and Egypt. Do you understand me? . . . Good man, Page . . . anticipatory strike. . . . You got it."

Smilie hung up. "He understands exactly what we need."

"He should," Larry Apple said. "It's going to make him a hero."

" 'Good show,' is how he put it," the Admiral said.

CHAPTER THIRTY-FOUR

Washington, August 4

Peter and Peggy had left the White House together in a soft grey rain. It was about five in the morning, quiet, even cool. After he had pulled out of the garage and into the street he reached over and put his hand on hers.

"Breakfast?" he asked.

"Not for me. There's food at the house, though, if you want something. All I want to do is sleep. For about a week."

They were quiet on the short drive to her house. Windshield wipers marked time. The streets were wet, their tires hissed at the rain. They drove under a canopy of trees drinking rain and Peter parked in front of the house. They held hands walking to the door.

After they had pulled the curtains and crawled into bed, he found he couldn't sleep. He stared up at the ceiling, his hands clasped under his head. He looked over at Peggy curled next to him. She had fallen asleep almost as her head touched the pillow.

Carefully, Peter climbed out of bed, slipped on his trousers, lifted his shirt off the chair near the bed and his glasses from the bedside table, and went downstairs into the livingroom. He stood for a moment in the doorway, then walked across the room to the french doors. It had stopped raining. The sky was already bluing. It was the end of summer, not yet fall. He turned and walked over to the couch and sat down.

He sat there for perhaps a half hour while the room brightened. He heard the paper thump against the front door, and he didn't move.

A minute later, Peggy was standing in the doorway behind him. She was wearing a blue silky kimono, her hair was tousled. She came into the room and he turned and looked up at her.

She tilted her head. "Is something wrong?" she asked.

"I couldn't sleep."

She came around and sat next to him, touching his hand. "Can I do something?"

He looked at her seriously. "You can marry me."

"What?"

"You know, like in love and marriage." He lifted her hand to his lips, then said, "What do you say?—it might be fun."

She laughed and threw her arms around him.

* * * * *

Sixty miles offshore, between Tripoli and Benghazi, forty fathoms deep, four Los Angeles Class attack submarines cruised the Mediterranean Sea, ready for war. Their weapons were the new British-made Marconi Mark II torpedo and an advanced sonar system. Their mission had been converted from "patrol" to "search and destroy."

On each of the four ships the scene in general quarters was much the same with personnel monitoring sonar and seabed sensor signals near both Libyan naval bases. Command Control Center in each was small and cramped. Every available space on the vertical bulkheads and the overhead was patched with screens and switching panels, both instrumentation and nuclear power. Overhead, four convex screens with audio systems as repeaters gave a picture and voice report from Ballast Control, Fire Control, Main Propulsion and Communications. All personnel were strapped into their seats at the waist and shoulder.

In the Los Angeles's Communications Control Center, a cool young Lieutenant, the Weapons Officer, placed a call to Command.

"Sir, we've picked up three contacts on the seabed monitor about three miles out of Tripoli, bearing 195 degrees, distance approximately 55 miles. The signature shows all three are Foxtrot class. . . . Yes, sir, they'll be in sonar range in about forty-five minutes."

When the Lieutenant Commander hung up he turned around with a grin. "Looks like we'll see a little action after all."

The Lieutenant and his three companion ships were spared the knowledge that Libyan aerial reconnaissance had picked up their thermal tracks, and an old Antonov 22 had been sent out like a bloodhound after its quarry. On the surface, however, the Enterprise lobbed a patrol of F-14A fighters at the old dog, and five minutes later one Sidewinder missile sliced it in two.

Thirty minutes later the Lieutenant dialed his Command Center again, his eyes trained blue and unblinking on the screen. "Sir, we have three Foxtrots on sonar now—bearing 192 degrees, distance, 11,000 yards . . ."

It took a few seconds, and on the bulkhead panel directly in front of him three of four lights turned from red to green—three torpedo bow tubes were ready to fire. Their new Cruise missiles used acoustic and infrared homing, and their own on-board mini computer was programmed to pick up Foxtrot noise signatures as well as those of other Soviet submarines. The Weapons Officer had heard they were good, but this was their first real test under combat conditions. The officer monitoring the extremely low frequency communications system for a signal from the Enterprise was hardly breathing.

Three minutes had elapsed from the moment the command was given to fire, and the moment their sonar screen went blank. "Contact lost," the Lieutenant said jubilantly. "I think we got all three."

Two minutes later the officer next to him received confirmation: "Alpha Tango confirms target destruction."

* * * * *

Alpha Tango described the digitally interconnected system which uses sensors, weapons delivery systems and computers to track and identify a hostile submarine, elect the appropriate weapon and photograph the results. First developed and deployed in 1980, it had become an incredibly sophisticated system in the second half of the decade. Confirmation had been slow in coming because the Enterprise was monitoring a battle on the surface as well.

A medium intensity attack had been launched from a point not far from Benghazi, and Libyan shore-based cruise missiles had managed to reach the carrier task force's outer zone. At the crucial moment of penetration an onboard phased array radar system called Aegis SAM, automatically triggered a response and task force destroyers launched a barrage of Tomahawk missiles obliterating all but three of the Libyan shore-launched antiship weapons. The three found their target square amidships on the guided missile cruiser U.S.S. Ticonderoga whose Phalanx inner zone defense system was not enough to stop the new Exocet missiles. The Ticonderoga was completely disabled and with a destroyer escort it hobbled out of the battle area, listing heavily to port.

Having computed the precise point of launch origin, the Enterprise's CIC officer issued the order to strike back with air to ground Harpoon II missiles. In less than two minutes, four F-14s were catapult-launched, and three minutes later flung their screaming rockets into the offending shore sites. What was left was a smoking rubble.

* * * * *

In the Indian Ocean, after a three hour flight, twelve aging B-52s launched a battery of cruise missiles 300 miles at the South Yemeni bases at Aden and Lahaj. Satellite reconnaissance photographs of Lahaj showed heavy damage. Four runways had been badly cratered, three were obviously useless; over 100 aircraft were counted as damaged beyond use, and four jet fuel tanks had exploded in a billow of fire that climbed 400 feet high. Most important, the South Yemeni air defense system at Aden was hit and destroyed. Now the laser-guided cruise missiles lobbed almost insolently from the New Jersey's deck took out most of the remaining targets.

Using Magic missiles to finish the job of neutralizing both Soviet built bases, twenty U.S. flown Lavies operating out of a renovated base at Thamarit in Oman destroyed sixty MIG-25s almost immediately after they had taken off. To complete the mission, a second pass of Lavies dropped cluster bombs on remaining targets of opportunity.

* * * * *

Air Force Major William Holloway, in an interview with a New York Times reporter two days later: "It was a combination of good luck and better timing: their radar had picked us up, so they scrambled their fighters—we were there at just the right moment."

The interviewer asked what had happened in Asmara. Holloway replied he didn't know—their was a debriefing at Thamarit later that day, however, and there should be some statement then.

What had happened in Asmara was a combination of the skill of British and Omani forces working together, and a certain element of surprise. The Omani had positioned themselves as a wall against the South Yemen border and on the afternoon of August 13 had received helicopter delivery of new, supersonic Cruise missiles with a range of almost 5,000 miles. They hadn't had to fire a single shot, having moved undetected right up to the border. Working all night, the Omani prepared their weapons, and at 1800 launched half their store. Only a handful of MIG-25s, hidden in a maintenance shed for repairs, survived.

Meanwhile, Ethiopian pilots who might have provided some air cover over Kassala, found Asmara's runways cratered by Cruise missiles. There was no place for these planes to land, the French in Djibouti discouraging use of their base. As a result, over sixty planes plunged into the Indian Ocean, though only five pilots went down with their ships, the others having ejected safely from the sky.

The entire assault on Asmara had lasted twelve minutes and served to effectively demolish it as an operational air base. Reconnaissance satellites detected no activity at the base after 1845.

* * * * *

Things were going badly in Kassala. Without the necessary air cover over that city, the advance of the Ethiopian army had slowed to a crawl and finally a halt. In the capital, Addis Ababa, Colonel Mengistu had called an emergency meeting of the Dirgue, his consultative committee. Also present was senior Soviet advisor General Vladimir Varenikov. The General was dropping his own bomb on the distressed gathering.

"Colonel," the General said softly, "I advise you to try to cut your losses—in short, withdraw from Kassala. My government cannot intervene with force, and I am afraid we all expected too much from Colonel Qaddafi."

Indeed as they spoke, thirty Libyan C-130 transporters were roaring off newly constructed runways at Dougia, Largeau, Biltine and Abeché in Chad toward Khartuom. Waiting for them on an intercept course were eighteen deadly Egyptian F-16s. Qaddafi would have his pride slapped back in his face.

Varenikov's orders had come directly from his Minister of Defense. "Of course you can do as you choose," the General shrugged. "Moscow is expecting better results in Israel than we have seen in the Sudan, and I have been asked to return home tonight."

He avoided their eyes as he left the room.

* * * * *

The Soviet Minister of Defense may have expected something better, but he was to be sorely disappointed. The Israelis had never subjugated their Armed Forces to their beliefs, as had many Arab states, particularly Syria, whose army had been trained by Soviet military advisers. As a result, officers in the field were allowed little initiative and had difficulty adapting to changes on the battlefield. In addition, President Assad trusted only his Alewite supporters, and they didn't always make the best use of their limited skills.

The Israeli Defense Forces were meticulous and devastating. From private to general, each man knew he had to do his best, because survival of the State depended on training and tactics on the battlefield and in the air. The IDF made the most of their resources, whether an Uzi machine gun or an F-16 fighter. Syria had learned this lesson in 1982, but because of religious and other differences, they hadn't profitted from their humiliating military experience. Their armor, pushing south down the Bekaa Valley while Iraqi and Jordanian armor was concentrated in two areas: Der'a, and a point forty miles north of Amman, Irbid.

On August 16, using Copperhead and antitank missiles with 155mm Howitzers, the Israelis destroyed over 600 T-72s near Der'a. Early the next morning at the first call of the *muezzin* when the devout Moslems had prostrated themselves toward the south and Mecca, Israeli Air Force A-10s carrying Masada antitank missiles, supported by air cover from Kfirs, rose out of the misty-morning west and destroyed another two hundred.

On August 18, Israel's Minister of Defense was interviewed by David Kaufman of the *New York Times*.

"Every one of our aircraft returned safely from the series of attacks into Jordan," the Minister said. "We were fortunate that the enemy armor was so heavily concentrated. In tank warfare, especially in this kind of terrain, dispersal is axiomatic. Our A-10s came in at such low altitudes that the Soviet SAM 8s and 9s could not be effective. Submunitions from the Massada were able to pick up the microwave emissions from Jordanian Mobile Air Defense. Masada simply zeroed in on the critical components of their defense, and we were able to knock them out.

"Jordanian F-15s did not perform well against our Kfirs. It is possible they had not been retrofitted with a rear compressor variable vane assembly. The Jordanians also made a mistake in using the F-15 for air to air missions instead of air to ground work. Air to air is much harder on the plane's frame and the engine itself.

"When American technicians were expelled by the new government in Amman after King Hussein was overthrown, Palestinian Arabs took over maintenance. Due to their inexperience, the F-15s simply could not perform well in an air to air defense environment. . . ."

The Minister of Defense could be so generous with his analysis because the Israelis had basically eliminated the Jordanian Air Force. It wouldn't help them to know what they'd done wrong with their F-15s because there weren't any left.

CHAPTER
THIRTY-FIVE

Moscow, September 1

Dimitri Bukov was alone in his office, standing over the chess computer that had been Heath's gift. Two fingers pinched his lower lip, his eyes were directed at the robot arm hanging over the White Bishop.

There was a hesitation, like a tremor in the slim mechanical arm, and then a clear fast swoop down, and the bishop was captured.

Bukov's hand fell to his side. He turned, and walked to the window behind the desk. He stared outside. It was going to rain again.

This was the tenth time the robot had responded in precisely the same way to the game he had constructed. He had tested the possibilities on four levels of play, and it was obvious an opponent would *have to* commit himself to the bishop's capture in order to preserve his own position.

Without realizing it, Bukov nodded affirmatively. He turned to his desk, pulled back his chair and sat down, reaching under the yellow glass shade of his desk lamp for the chain. In the soft light he added several notes to the project he was working on.

He was writing when the phone console to his left buzzed, and the newly appointed Minister of Defense was announced.

Mikhail Emilievich Browkaw was a slender man with thinning hair and a beard, which seemed to accentuate a somewhat horsey face.

Bukov rose and gestured for him to be seated. The Minister's eyes were on the chess game, silent on its own table against the wall, still awaiting Bukov's next move.

Mikhail Emilievich Browkaw was a man Bukov didn't particularly trust. He preferred men easier to see through. This man knew more than he said. He stored information. This could, of course, work to Bukov's advantage. Still, Bukov had decided to treat the man with caution.

"I have heard of your American chess game, General Secretary," said Mikhail Emilievich, nodding at the set.

Bukov watched the Minister. "Do you play, Comrade?"

Mikhail Emilievich met Bukov's eyes. "It is one of my greatest pleasures."

Bukov's face opened in a smile. With a little more warmth, he said, "Really? Let me show you, then. . . ." He rose and walked around the desk. Mikhail Emilievich stood and joined him at the table.

"Sit down there, Comrade." Bukov took the other chair, pushed himself a little closer to the set.

"I was in fact, playing a little game you might be interested in." Bukov hit a series of keys to return the computer to a beginning position. "I've designated the board to represent the Carribean." He was repositioning the players. He looked over quickly to see how Mikhail Emilievich was responding. The man appeared to be concentrating for all he was worth on the board.

Bukov pressed the starting series, and began pointing at various areas of the black and white board. "Here is Cuba; opposite, Panama; the Lesser Antilles here; Hondurus, Nicaragua—Central America, here."

Mikhail Emilievich looked up, surprised.

Bukov was watching him. He smiled. "Just a mental exercise, Comrade," he said lightly. "Are you interested?"

Mikhail Emilievich was struck by Bukov's smooth self-confidence. He nodded.

* * * * *

Peter Jefferson was standing with his back to the door, staring out into a gray morning. Two single raindrops hit the window one after another and broke up, then nothing.

Grace walked briskly into his office with coffee and a late morning edition of the *New York Times*. "I guess we can close the file on the Alaska Purchase abrogation today." She placed the coffee on the desk as he turned, and handed him the paper, pointing to a small story at the bottom of the front page.

Dateline: The Hague
INTERNATIONAL COURT OF JUSTICE RULES AGAINST
SOVIET CLAIM TO ALASKA: In a unanimous opinion, the judges
of the International Court of Justice held that the Alaska Purchase
Treaty cannot be unilaterally abrogated by a party to that treaty. . . .
We find unpersuasive the Soviet Union's evidence of changed circum-
stance, as required by the Vienna Convention. . . . We hold, therefore,
that the United States is sovereign with respect to what was conveyed,
and the claim by the Soviet Union that Alaska is 'occupied territory' is
completely without merit.

There was a related side-bar that reviewed the incident. It seemed a long time ago.

He looked up to see Larry Apple hesitate in the doorway. "Hey, Larry, come on in." Peter held his hand out over the desk.

"Morning, Pete." They shook hands. "I'm waiting to see George, thought I'd stop in."

"I'm glad you did. . . . Grace, would you get Mr. Apple a cup of coffee?"

Larry sat down. "Thanks." He had a huge stack of papers with him, and placed the whole pile on an empty chair.

"You've been keeping busy?"

"Real busy—that's what I wanted to see George about. Actually, I spoke to him last night—I'm getting some very strange signals from the Kremlin."

"What kind of signals?"

Larry crossed his leg. "Combination of things. For one, I've got an agent reporting out of Moscow that Sorokin hasn't been seen or heard from in two weeks. There are rumors that he's sick, or dead, or in a camp shoveling coal. . . ."

Grace knocked lightly on the edge of the open door, came in with coffee, and put the steamy cup on the edge of Peter's desk. When she left, she closed the door behind her.

Larry took a sip of coffee.

Peter shook his head. "Man, they play hard."

"Yeah. You win some, you lose some." He put his cup down, then looked at Peter. "Speaking of which, I understand you and Peggy are going to be married."

Peter nodded.

"Congratulations. You're a lucky man."

"Thanks, Larry. I know it."

Larry looked down at the stack of material next to him. He hesitated, then counted down several pages into the pile, pulled out an onion skin memo and looked back up. "That's one thing—a distinct change of venue in the Kremlin. Between Sorokin's presumed disappearance and Svetlov's retirement. . . . Another thing is this." It was dated the previous day, to George Heath, Admiral Smilie, Robert Van Vleck, Harry Smyth, Henry Clay.

"National Security Agency confirms Central Intelligence findings of heavy build-up of Soviet submarines and MIG-27 aircraft in Cuba. Substantial air activity picked up by radar and AWACS. Radio traffic in both Russian and Spanish reported, all routine so far. Submarines identified to date are Delta III class. SCALEBOARD missile sites photographed near base at Cienfuegos with advanced Soviet air defense system. Over fifty Mi-24 HIND D and E attack helicopters identified on ground, as well as Su-24 Fencer ground support aircraft in significant numbers."

Peter frowned.

Larry looked around, then rose and separated two files from the material with him. He gestured toward the library table against the wall and Peter nodded and walked over with him, switching on a low-slung ceiling lamp directly over the table.

"These are analyses of the last four SR-71 passes over Cuba," Larry said, dealing five glossy 8 × 10s side by side on the table. They were high-definition photographs of the Russian-built base at Cienfuegos.

"They were shot at 75,000 feet under good conditions at around 11:00 yesterday," he said. "Now, over here," he pointed to a scattering of dark shadows in the Caribbean Sea, "in addition to the four Delta III class subs we had last week," he indicated the second photo, then came back to the first, "we've got six Oscar class."

Peter leaned over the table.

"According to NET, they're fairly new models: they carry about twenty-four anti-ship cruise missiles with a range of over 300 miles, and they can be fired submerged." He touched a spot a short distance to the west.

"Perhaps more serious, is the appearance over here—" third photo— "of fifteen Regov-class amphibious assault ships. Each one can carry 500 naval infantry troops along with amphibious armored personnel carrier attack helicopters, and up to ten T-72 tanks."

Peter straightened and looked at Larry.

"As if that weren't enough," Apple said, moving to the fourth reconnaissance, "these two Kiev-class task forces which were on a 'show the flag' visit in Africa are now moving toward the Caribbean." He looked up. "It'll take them three days to get to Cuba."

"Doesn't that 1963 agreement Kennedy signed with Breshnev limit 'offensive weapons' in the Caribbean?"

Apple nodded. "But they also agreed, in 1970, to abandon plans to station a permanent Soviet force in Cienfuegos, and we can see in these photos," he picked up the last one and handed it to Peter, "they've continued expanding base and anchorage facilities. In fact, they've maintained the base at combat-ready status since 1965."

Peter stood staring at the print in his hand. "We can file a protest. Note the Delta IIIs and Kiev carriers carry nuclear missiles. . . ."

Larry nodded. "And they'll probably withdraw those ships, but that won't affect any of the others." He paused. "According to Smilie, we've got two Trident-class submarines just outside Jamaica; he's with Harry Smyth this morning working out a recommendation that the President put them on alert."

Peter looked up. There was a moment of quiet, and he walked back to his desk and sat down.

Larry Apple returned to his chair opposite. "There's even more." He picked up his cup, drank, and then replaced it. "This morning, I got a report from an Agency team in northeastern Afghanistan. They picked up an unexploded missile designed for use as a missile—full of nerve gas."

"My God," Peter said.

"At first they thought it was bomb, but it was dropped by parachute. It didn't explode because the barometric pressure trigger was set for a much lower altitude."

Apple stood up and paced back and forth. "To get it out—they took it through Pakistan—our technical people had to disassemble the whole thing. It's definitely of Russian origin—in fact there was no attempt to conceal that. It works on a binary system, and uses an electrical circuit to set off a small charge. The two major compounds then combine to produce nerve gas."

"So this one was a dud?" Peter asked.

"Oh, no," Apple said. "The barometric trigger didn't activate the electrical circuit at the altitude our team found it.

"But here's what's of particular interest: remember in 1982 when that Soviet sub went aground in Swedish territorial waters? Well, the Swedes measured everything they could reach . . . Now, we know the Soviets standardize their missile launch tubes, and this jewel we found in Afghanistan conforms to a Delta III-class launcher."

"Wait a minute," Peter said. "You're not thinking those Delta IIIs are carrying nerve gas in the Caribbean?"

"I'm thinking it's a possibility." Larry sat down again.

"We'd be pretty naive to think the last few months haven't put incredible pressure on the Kremlin hawks. Sorokin's missing, and we can't be sure Bukov is really in control."

"So you think all this is a move into the Caribbean Basin. Perhaps Grenada with its Marxist government and a big new airbase. Venezuelan or Mexican oil or even to establish a military presence in the area. After all, the Sandinistas have not done much in Nicaragua, and the guerrillas in El Salvador are not making much progress."

"Yes, that all crossed my mind." There was a moment of quiet. Larry considered his next words. "Do you know Bob Springer?"

Peter frowned. "Springer . . . doesn't he work in the parapsychology department out at your shop? I haven't met him, but Peggy has mentioned his name."

Larry nodded. "You know anything about psychokinesis?"

"A little. Peggy said some people can move objects from a distance."

"Well, that missile we found—the nerve gas—its electrical circuitry is about as simple as a toy train set's." Larry paused again.

Peter swivelled around in his chair. "You're saying we could detonate these missiles in Cuba kinetically?"

"I'm not saying we should. According to Springer, and I showed him a drawing of the circuitry, we might be able to. And he told me he had just the man who could do it if anyone could."

Apple leaned forward and spoke to Jefferson's profile. "If you had to choose between letting the Soviets spill 'yellow rain' over Central America or wherever—and detonating the damn things a hundred fathoms deep in a sealed sub, I think you'd pick the latter."

Peter turned and faced the Director squarely. "I wouldn't want to be the one to make that choice. We don't even know what parapsychology is. If it's a weapon, do we have any international agreements covering its use? I doubt it. There's that 1925 Convention, but are we violating it, if it's carried here by the Soviets for use in the Caribbean Basin?

"Has Heath seen all this stuff?"

"Not yet. But I gave him the gist of it over the phone." Larry Apple looked down at his watch. "He may be in now—do you want to give him a call?"

* * * * *

By the time they entered George Heath's large comfortable office, rain was tapping persistently on the window. Heath was just putting the phone back in its cradle.

"We have real problems. Larry, that was your Deputy Director of Operations. He knew you were on your way here. I'm calling Alan right now, and you can listen in."

In less than a minute, he had the President on the phone.

"Alan, Larry Apple and Peter Jefferson are on extensions here, because we all have to think pretty hard. There's not much time. I've just talked to Larry's DDO. He has hard evidence that six Antonov 400s left Moscow six hours ago. Each one can carry an SS-20 and launcher. They're just about ready to land in Libya, and this has been confirmed by Sixth Fleet radar.

"The DDO said these planes have the range to reach the Caribbean with a refueling stop. We think the destination for all six is either Cuba or Grenada.

"I have told our Ambassador to the Organization of American States to check with Venezuela. Admiral Smilie is on his way here, and so is Smyth. We may have to get consent to send aircraft to Maracaibo with instructions to divert the Antonovs to Maracaibo or shoot them down. If they're headed for Cuba we may have to divert them to Tyndall Air Force Base in Florida. That's going to be a little dicey, because of the Soviet aircraft in Havana now. And those 'show the flag' carriers can provide the air cover that was missing in the Alaska caper."

"George, I just want you to think about this and then join me in an hour."

Heath's voice was somber. "We'll be there, Alan. It's beginning to look as though the military may be running the show in Moscow, but they're risking a lot on this move. See you in an hour."

Heath turned back and stared at the display screen of his chess game, frowning.

"You heard all that, so try looking at it from the Soviet point of view. I've played this thing out a half dozen times since you called, Larry." Heath pointed to the upper right quadrant of the illuminated chess board on his screen.

"Based on what you told me, Larry, I've laid it out so this area represents Cuba." His hand moved down. "Now I'll have to change it a little to add Venezuela, probably as a pawn. We don't know what it can or will do yet.

"This is the Lesser Antilles," he pointed to four squares in the lower left of center. "Panama," he looked up at Peter, "Grenada here and Venezuela, here." He tapped the screen.

Larry Apple was sitting on the edge of the desk.

"And the pieces?" He asked.

"It's the bishop, Grenada, I'm troubled by. U.S. troops are all gone, and there's only a lightly armed police force on the entire island. The new airport is finished and can handle anything from an Antonov to MIGs . . ." Heath shook his head.

"I'll need to work it out now. My guess is that the lead plane has some troops plus light tanks. That's the way it was done in Budapest in 1956. Secure the base to beyond its perimeter, and then the others can land."

Heath looked up. "What have you got for me, Larry?"

They reviewed the series of photos that Peter had seen earlier. Heath looked at each one carefully but made no comment.

Peter was still looking at the computer screen. Pale rain was falling outside. "Who's black in this game?" he said finally.

"We are. I'm looking at it from their point of view." Heath sounded relieved to return to the subject obviously uppermost in his mind. "This bishop is sitting somewhere in the Caribbean, probably Grenada, and it's a sacrificial piece. Black is being maneuvred into a forced play."

"You think something like this is happening now, George?" Peter said as he moved from in front of the display screen next to the desk and sat down facing Heath.

George nodded. "I do, and Grenada is a key piece on the board."

Peter looked at the older man. "Does the game ever end?"

Heath looked down, and said nothing for a moment, then met Peter's eyes. "Truly, it does not." His tone was soft but matter-of-fact. "It's something you learn to live with."

"What's harder to live with," said Larry Apple, sliding photographs back into their proper order, "is that no one really wins, but there are lots of losers and occasionally some draws."

"Are you becoming a cynic at your age, Larry?" Heath said, smiling for the first time that morning.

Larry looked up, surprised. "Possibly."

Heath smiled and stood up. "Alright, now we can go over to the White House and see if this game will be better than just a draw."

As they all left the office of the Secretary of State, the rain continued to fall.

AUTHOR'S NOTE

The Alaska Deception has no final resolution at its end. And for a good reason. For over 2000 years, states have tried and failed to solve problems through violence, namely, military force. At this time, for example, Iraq and Iran are still at war after almost four years. The casualties on both sides have been very high. On a smaller but still lethal level, Angola is in a state of undeclared war with South Africa over a territory known as Namibia. In a different part of the globe, Vietnam is in a state of undeclared war with Cambodia, and the People's Republic of China, feeling threatened by Vietnam, not only supports Cambodia but, briefly, moved its troops into Vietnam. Peking called this a punitive warning to Hanoi, or some such phrase. There is also an undeclared war in El Salvador where its present government receives aid from the United States. The point to be made here is that without any historical exceptions, a tyranny is always governed by a minority with the support of the military, e.g., Syria, the Soviet Union and Vietnam.

The Middle East, however, is almost always at war, usually inter-Arab e.g., Iran and Iraq. For the last thirty-six years (1948–1984), Israel has been the target of attack in five wars: The War of Independence (1948–1949); 1956 when hostilities almost erupted into war with Egypt; the Six Day War (1967); the Yom Kippur War (1973), and in 1982, the war with the PLO and Syria in Lebanon. This last one is still going on, and no one can really say when it might end or what will be the likely outcome. Will Syria, for example, withdraw its troops? Will Lebanon enjoy peace so it can rebuild Beirut into the beautiful city it once was?

Some historians may remember June 14, 1982. On that date, Israel reluctantly agreed to a ceasefire in the area east of Beirut under pressure from the White House. The Soviet Union had warned the United States that it viewed the threat to Soviet-armed Syrian troops "with grave concern." Instead of replying to Moscow that Washington would try to persuade Israel to agree to a ceasefire, but *only* if Moscow persuaded Syria to withdraw from Lebanon, it yielded. Thus, it was Israel which first agreed to the cease-fire without any concession from either Moscow or Damascus.

When the reader finishes The Alaska Deception, he is intentionally left in doubt of what President Baker will do. Will he, for example, warn General Secretary Bukov that the United States views the Soviet presence in the Caribbean "with grave concern?" The answer is yes. Of course, he will. If the warning is ignored, will President Baker approve the use of military force against Soviet ships and troops at Cienfuegos or the Soviet carriers moving west into the Caribbean? We don't know the answer to this last question. However, the people around President Baker will almost certainly recommend the use of military force, because the threat or the threat potential is real, not imaginary. They would argue that the line of attack authorized in Moscow was weak and a poor move on the board. The point to be made here is that, in chess, the player who makes the last mistake always loses.

One other point needs to be made here. As long ago as 1946, John von Neumann, a distinguished mathematician, said that computers would turn out to be more important than nuclear weapons. Sophisticated computers have transformed defensive war into a contest of information rather than of firepower. Precision guided missiles with conventional, non-nuclear explosives favor the defense. Many of these can be described as deep strike weapons. For the most part, they are inexpensive and very accurate. A Copperhead anti-tank missile, for example, costs about $40,000 and is lethal at ranges up to about 30 miles. It can, however, destroy or disable one or more modern tanks which cost about $3 million each.

As this kind of deep strike technology becomes even more effective and less costly, nuclear weapons, both tactical and strategic, tend to become less attractive as weapons. Why, for example, would any rational government want to devastate an area it was attacking, using tactical nuclear weapons? Would this same government use such weapons knowing that part of its own territory would become a radioactive wasteland when the country attacked retaliated?

Even in space, the technology is not far from the point where ground-launched and inexpensive anti-ballistic missiles using lasers or particle energy can destroy strategic nuclear weapons in space, e.g., the Saturn. It is reasonable to assume that the computer revolution may eventually displace weapons of mass destruction and replace them with weapons of human scale. This revolution has produced computer-aided design, manufacturing and engineering. It has also produced sophisticated guidance systems as well as the information required for targetting. As a result, enormously expensive nuclear weapons such as the MX, the Pershing II and the Soviet SS-20 as well as other Soviet nuclear weapons, will tend to obsolesce and eventually become obsolete. They are all immoral, and no sane government can for a single moment entertain their actual use, whether first or retaliatory.

In the conflict described in The Alaska Deception, neither President Baker nor General Secretary Bukov entertained such use. Both of them knew the frightening consequences of doing so. Even fiction, however, can make a point, and I hope the reader senses what it is.

I have tried not to be a judge, only a narrator. The reader must be the judge.

William M. Brinton
May 1, 1984